"A nightmare vision of two unspeakable horrors: ancient supernatural evil and nuclear catastrophe."
—*Mystery News*

"Campbell has always shown a keen awareness of social tyranny, and in this . . . intense supernatural novel he evokes a peculiarly nasty hybrid form of it. . . . Despite the darkest borders, it's a brave book."

—Fritz Leiber

"Beautifully written . . . pervaded by an increasingly chilling atmosphere of dread and anxiety."
—*Publishers Weekly*

"*The Hungry Moon* will solidify Ramsey Campbell's position in the top rank of today's dark fantasists."
—Charles L. Grant, *American Fantasy*

Look for all these TOR books by Ramsey Campbell

DARK COMPANIONS
THE DOLL WHO ATE HIS MOTHER
THE FACE THAT MUST DIE
THE HUNGRY MOON
INCARNATE
THE NAMELESS
OBSESSION

RAMSEY CAMPBELL

THE HUNGRY MOON

A TOM DOHERTY ASSOCIATES BOOK

For Steve and Jo
Stalwarts of fantasy

THE HUNGRY MOON

Copyright © 1986 by Ramsey Campbell

Reprinted by arrangement with Macmillan Publishing Company

First Tor printing: June 1987

A TOR Book

Published by Tom Doherty Associates, Inc.
49 West 24 Street
New York, N.Y. 10010

Cover art by Jill Bauman
Cover design by Carol Russo

ISBN: 0-812-51662-1
CAN. ED.: 0-812-51663-X

Library of Congress Catalog Card Number: 86-8342

PRINTED IN THE UNITED STATES OF AMERICA

0 9 8 7 6 5 4 3 2 1

Acknowledgments

As usual, I owe most to my wife, Jenny, who helped the book take shape as I wrote it and kept an eye on the continuity. Jean Hill accompanied me to a Billy Graham rally in Liverpool, but I proved to be in no danger of succumbing; indeed, the unexpectedly low-key preaching was received with a good deal of Liverpudlian skepticism by the congregation. Stan Ambrose of BBC Radio Merseyside's *Folkscene* authenticated "Harry Moony," a song that appears to conflate several different Peak District folk traditions.

And I mustn't forget Phil Booth, who sent me a jigsaw to keep me occupied while I searched for words, and the inventor(s) of the compact disc, whose music helps me not to stray from my desk.

"The human race has a terminal disease called sin."
Billy Graham

"Go down Harry Moony, harry us no more,
We've flowers to please you, to leave at your door."
Old Derbyshire street song

". . . sustolere monstra, quibus hominem occidere
religiosissimum erat, mandi vero etiam saluberrimum . . ."
The elder Pliny, on the druids

". . . to fear the moon, to feed her as she must be fed,
and never to look upon her feeding . . ."
Druidic triad quoted by Posidonius

"There is no humor in heaven."
Mark Twain

Nick Reid stepped out of the newspaper building into the deserted Manchester street and wondered what the silence reminded him of. He took a cool breath of early morning air and stretched, wincing at the bruises he'd brought back with his report from the picketing. An unanswered phone rang in an office on Deansgate; a single car cruised past the department stores on Piccadilly, sending pigeons up from the roadway to wheel above the gable windows. Nick ran his fingers through his crinkly hair and tried to let the silence be itself. It couldn't be important to remember; he just wanted to wake up so as to drive home and sleep. He glanced up as sunlight snatched at the steep roofs through a gap in the clouds that were rushing a storm toward the Peaks. Memory seized him then, it felt as though by the scruff of his aching neck. "Diana," he gasped, and then he realized what else was wrong.

He limped into the building, across the lobby that turned his footsteps high-pitched, up the stairs to the library. The blank gray screens of microfilm readers gleamed dully under the tubular lighting of the small white room. He ought to call Diana—he couldn't even remember how long it had been— but surely there was no need to wake her up. He began to leaf through the file of the last few weeks' issues, looking for the article about the Peaks.

He found it in last Monday's issue, one of Charlie Nesbit's pleas to the readers not to take their holidays abroad when Britain had so much to offer. It read as Charlie sounded in the pub at lunchtime, poking the stem of his pipe at his listeners or puffing at it whenever he made a point he regarded as unanswerable: the Peak District is our oldest landscape, God's gift to walkers but still unspoiled by tourism. . . . Nick scanned the paragraphs that listed places to visit, then reread the article slowly, hoping he was wrong.

But he hadn't missed anything. There was no mention of Moonwell.

He made himself remember his first sight of the small town, the empty streets, the singing on the moors above. He was tired, that was why he was having trouble remembering, but had Charlie been tired too? Unless he came in unusually early, Nick wouldn't know for hours. He had to know. He limped back to the office next to the library, through the maze of glass cubicles, to wait at his desk.

An office boy dropped the morning edition on the desk and woke Nick from dozing. His report had been edited, even though he hadn't said that the police had seemed to resent his presence as much as the pickets had. Some of the feature writers were at their desks now, but there was still no sign of Charlie Nesbit. He was probably at breakfast, Nick thought, and grabbed the phone.

Charlie's wife answered. "Just a minute," she said curtly, and stifled the receiver with her hand. Beyond it Nick heard her complaining, "That's the sort of thing I mean," and then the receiver fell on wood. There was a muffled argument before Charlie demanded, "Well, what's so important that it can't wait until I've finished eating?"

"Charlie, it's Nick Reid. Sorry for interrupting."

"Glad you did, to tell you the truth. What can I do for you?"

For a moment Nick didn't know, and remembering felt like starting awake. "This may seem an odd question, but was the article you wrote about the Peaks subbed at all?"

"Not anywhere it mattered, no." He sounded amused. "Why, have they been toning you down again?"

"Not more than usual. No, I was asking because you didn't mention Moonwell."

"Where?"

"Moonwell. You know, the place where I ran into all that religious hysteria. Even you thought they were going a bit far when I told you about it."

"Good God, son, are you still riding that hobbyhorse? Can't you leave people's beliefs alone? There's few enough beliefs around these days, it isn't up to us to shatter them." He snorted and went on, "Anyway, we've got a bad line here. It sounds as if you keep saying Moonwell."

"That's right. It used to be the old Roman lead mine.

2

Where they decorate the cave every year, or they did until this year. Come on, Charlie, you must remember that."

"I'll tell you what, sonny, I've been at the paper a good few years longer than you, and it's been a bloody long time since anyone's accused me of not doing it properly or had reason to. Now, I don't know what bee you've got in your bonnet this time, but you've caught me in the middle of an argument and I'm not about to get into another. Just take it from me, there's never been a place called Moonwell in the Peaks."

There is, I've been there, Nick wanted to shout, but Charlie had cut him off. Nick replaced the receiver, trying to stay calm, and reached in his jacket for his address book. Had he called Charlie in order to postpone calling Diana? What was he afraid to hear? Perhaps only the sound that greeted him when he dialed her number—the dull, high-pitched tone that meant it was unobtainable.

The exchange could be busy, he told himself, and called the operator. "Moonwell," he said, and when she came back to check: "Moonwell in Derbyshire." Finally he spelled the name for her. "I'm sorry, sir," she said, "there's nowhere of that name."

Nick stared at the Moonwell number written in Diana's handwriting, saw the notebook tremble as his arm propped on its elbow wavered. "All right," he said, feeling oddly calm, as if now that his unstated fears were realized he would know what to do. It wasn't until he reached the stairs that he began to run.

Rain speckled the pavements and showered his face lightly as he ran to the car park. When he climbed into the Citroen he felt as if he'd gone past needing sleep, though his glimpse of himself as he adjusted the driving mirror didn't look entirely convinced, his large, dark, humorous eyes gazing out of his round face with its prominent cheekbones, broad nose and mouth, squarish chin that never seemed to have been shaved quite closely enough. He started the car and drove toward the edge of Manchester.

The Stockport road was full of lorries heading for the Peaks. Once a boy scout band held up the traffic for five minutes, and Nick lost count of the number of traffic lights that turned red just as he was approaching. Outside Stockport and the Manchester boundary the small towns began, narrow winding streets, terraces crammed with houses. Here and there one side of the street was occupied by a factory to let, the long blank limestone wall yellow as clay in the rain. Old folk in dusty cars pottered along the middle of the road, slowing for pedestrian crossings even when nobody was near, and Nick felt as if he would never reach the peaks that rose above the slate roofs. Then the road straightened and widened for a few yards at the edge of a town, and he trod hard on the pedal. Overtaking four slow cars, he raced toward the moors.

The gentle slopes glowed half a dozen shades of patchy green beneath the glum sky. Heather flared purple, limestone edges tore through the green; spiky drystone walls divided the rounded slopes like old diagrams of the human cranium. As the narrowing road wound higher, shrinking to a car's width wherever it crossed a river, the walls beside the verges fell away. A car had crashed through an arrowed barrier at a sharp bend and was rusting fifty feet below the road. Soon the barriers gave out, and only ditches separated the road from the steepening uplands, where sheep ripped up the tussocky grass and stared yellow-eyed at Nick's car. He hadn't seen a house or a signpost for miles when he realized that he no longer knew where he was going.

He stopped the car on a level stretch of road and switched off the engine. The side windows were printed with dots and dashes of rain, which smudged the peaks ahead. The windscreen wipers thumped and squeaked repetitively as he reached for the AA book and turned to the Peak District road map.

Eventually he closed the book on his forefinger and turned frowning to the index. Mooncoin, Moone, Moonzie, he read, and searched up and down the column in case the name was out of order. It was there, he told himself fiercely, opening the book again at the map. He could locate himself roughly on the page, where the main roads were fewest and farthest apart; the green blotch beside the Sheffield road must be the forested slopes ahead. He swiveled the book and moved his head as if he could rid himself of the blind spot that way. A sense that the name was there on the page if only he could see it made him want to cry out, lash out, anything to break the spell. He closed his eyes in case relaxing was the answer. Suddenly he didn't even know what he'd been looking for.

He lashed out blindly and punched the horn, which blared

4

thinly at the deserted road. "Diana," he shouted, his voice flat and trapped in the car, "Diana from Moonwell," and remembered her long black hair whipping in the wind across the moors, her pale tapering face, wide greenish eyes. The memory broadened for an instant, and he recalled the day he'd met her—remembered driving away from Moonwell through the old forest beyond the pines.

"Yes," he breathed. He started the car and drove into the rain that pelted the roof and blotted out the peaks. He had to trust his feeling that the forest ahead was the one he remembered, had to trust that his instincts had guided him right so far. The pines rose above him until the slope to which they clung in their thousands was almost vertical, and he thought of a green army, giant arrows in the quiver of the limestone, green missiles. He almost drove past the road that plunged into the forest through a stony gap, its steep mossy walls streaming.

The trees closed overhead and cut off the sound of rain, as if he'd driven into a tunnel. He switched off the wipers and was alone with the hum of the engine. Now and then a gobbet of rain slipped through the branches overhead and spattered the windscreen, though he couldn't see the sky. Relaxation and the green dimness must be lulling him, for he didn't notice when the pines gave way to oak and ash. The road, having sloped down into the woods, was rising as the trees crowded closer. Either clouds or branches were massing overhead; the road had grown so dim that he switched on his headlights. The ranks of trees beyond the beams made him think of cave walls, their trunks stone ridges, dripping. He kept his gaze ahead, watching for the sky; he'd be out of the forest any moment now, if it was the right forest—surely it was. Exhaustion must be stretching time for him. He trod harder on the accelerator, gripped the wheel, eyes burning as he kept his gaze from straying to the moist dark walls, trees really. Suddenly they fell away, and he was out beneath the tattered racing sky.

The unfenced road led up toward a skyline strewn with rocks, a backbone spiky as a dinosaur's. Beyond it, he remembered now, the land fell steeply on the left toward overgrown chunks of rock large as cars. Once he reached the crest he would be able to see Moonwell above the dry valley, the single road beyond the town leading up to the moor. Yet

5

he lifted his foot from the accelerator as the car surged forward, for he had an unsettling impression that the rushing clouds had come to a standstill overhead.

He ought to get to Moonwell before his exhaustion played any more tricks, if that was what was happening. Above all he wanted to see Diana, make sure she was safe. Fast but not too fast, he told himself, and pressed the pedal gently. There was no sound of traffic ahead. He'd switched off the headlights and was pressing the pedal more confidently at the moment when both car and landscape vanished into the blind dark.

Earlier That Year

As soon as Diana's class were together on the moor, they began to clamor to go to the cave. Now that they were out of sight of the school they obviously felt freer to be themselves, red-haired Thomas telling feeble jokes to make his cronies giggle, Sally pushing her taped spectacles higher on her nose and blinking like a grandmother, advising her friend Jane to keep hold of her hand. Ronnie even slipped a catapult out of the pocket of the baggy trousers he'd inherited from his brother until Diana gave him a warning glance. "We'll have to see if we've time for the cave," she told the forty-three of them. "Now remember, we want to see lots of work in your workbooks."

"So Mr. and Mrs. Scragg will know we've been working," Jane said.

"So they can see what a good class you are." Maybe they were as streetwise in their way as the kids she'd taught in New York—they'd need to be when they went up to Mrs. Scragg's class, quite a few of them after the summer vacation. Kids were tough, she told herself, but when she thought of putting any child into Mrs. Scragg's hands for three years, sometimes she wanted to weep.

The sky was clearing. The burst of May sunlight seemed to rearrange the landscape, opened out the moors and under-lined the drystone walls with shadow, tinged clouds on the horizon green to show that they were peaks threaded with glinting streams. The sounds of the town had already fallen behind, and the two main Manchester–Sheffield roads be-tween which Moonwell was the only town for miles were out of sight as well as hearing. Diana stood for a moment, her hands in the pockets of her zippered cardigan, the sun on her face. The silent brightening of the landscape felt like her first sight of Moonwell, her sense of having come home.

When clouds hid the sun her hands wanted to pull the overcast apart, but she held them out to the children instead. "Who remembers what I told you about sunshine?"

Dozens of hands went up with cries of "Miss, me, miss." She was hoping Andrew Bevan might respond, but he was hiding behind Sally's and Jane's mothers, who were helping supervise the outing. "Is that hand up or down, Sally?" Diana said.

"Up, miss," Sally protested, sounding hurt, and had to grab her precarious spectacles. "Miss, you said there's less sunshine here than anywhere else in England."

"Right, because of the clouds and the mists. And that's why you must never—come on, now, you all know this."

"Go on the moors without a grownup," they said in a ragged chorus.

"You said it. Remember, people have got lost on the moors for days. Now let's find somewhere you can sit and work and we'll see how the afternoon goes."

She led them up the grassy path to a bank where they could sit in groups in the midst of the heather. She chatted to the mothers and unobtrusively watched the children work. The landscape kept drawing her gaze, the miles of heather and bunched grass, the unearthly sameness broken only by an infrequent drystone wall or a dried-up stream bed the color and cracked texture of burnt cork, the lonely whisper of grass, the flight of a single bird. The path would lead you downward so imperceptibly that you mightn't notice when the peaks sank out of sight, leaving you only the horizon of the moor. The slopes brightened again, and Diana felt as if she'd made that happen by watching. Perhaps she felt so much at home because her family had originally come from the Peak District, though now she had no family at all.

Soon all the children had filled a page or more with writing and drawing. Andrew's picture of a bunch of heather was out of proportion but colorful. "That's good, Andrew," she said to stop him from scribbling it out, and praised the others wherever she could. She smiled then at all their eager faces. "Okay, now I want you all to stay behind me and hold your partner's hand."

As she led them to where the path forked, slopes raised themselves ahead like giants awakening. One branch of the path led up over the moors, the other followed the edge above Moonwell, past the cave that apparently had given the town its name. For hundreds of yards around the bowl of barren land that sloped down to the cave, the moors were threadbare, grass and heather giving way to bare gritstone. She went up to the edge of the bowl and held up one hand to stay the children. "This is as far as we go."

Two hundred yards away, at the center of the stony bowl, the cave gaped. Presumably someone had once thought it looked wide or deep enough to lose the moon in. It was really a pothole, fifty feet wide at the mouth and surrounded by a drystone wall. The first time she'd come here she had stepped over the wall, only to discover that even at high noon in summer you couldn't see bottom; walls that looked smooth and slippery as tallow plunged straight into darkness whose chill seemed to reach out of the bowl to where she stood now. Though she understood that eventually the shaft bent, as far as her emotions were concerned it might as well go straight down forever. Even though the children were safe beyond the edge of the bowl, she couldn't help wishing she hadn't brought them there. "Never go any farther than this, okay?" she said, and waited until they all promised.

They started shouting then, trying to make the cave echo. Some voices made a noise down there, not all—Diana assumed it had to do with pitch. She watched Ronnie wondering if he could get away with a shot from his catapult, and she was about to wag a finger at him when Sally's mother cried, "Andrew!"

Diana swung round, fearing the worst. But Andrew had only strayed back toward the path, and was stooping over something that had crawled away from the bowl. Children crowded round him. "Yuck, it's a lizard," Sally squeaked.

Jane stepped back with a cry of disgust. "It hasn't got any eyes."

As Diana hurried after the rest of her class to see, Andrew stepped forward and trod heavily on the creature, ground his heel into it and looked round as if he hoped the other children would be impressed, but they shuddered away from him. "It must have come out of the cave," Diana said, glancing at the mess of white skin and innards. "A pity you trod on it, Andrew. It's very unusual for anything like that to

11

come into the open. Never mind," she said quickly, for the boy's mouth was trembling. "While we're here you can tell us how you help to dress the cave."

His small, thin, pale face with its hint of eyebrows looked resentful. "I make a bit of a picture with flowers," he muttered as if he hoped nobody would hear.

"You use petals, don't you? And then your piece and all the others fit together like a jigsaw." Throughout the Peaks towns decorated wells with pictures made of flowers and vegetation, a Christian tradition which gave thanks for the water that had stayed fresh during the Plague and the Black Death, but which seemed to reach back to more ancient beliefs. Watching the townsfolk carrying floral panels big as doors up from Moonwell to fit together at the cave last Midsummer Eve, Diana had felt as if she'd stepped back in time, into a calm that the world was losing. But Thomas was whispering "Petals," nudging his friends and sniggering, and Diana found that she didn't feel calm so close to the gaping cave. "I think it's time we headed back," she said.

"Tents all round," Andrew muttered, and pretended he hadn't spoken. He was right, Diana saw: the tents on the slopes above and below Moonwell made a ring around the cave and the town. Campers and walkers kept Moonwell going now that the lead mines were exhausted, concrete lids covering the abandoned shafts on the moor.

The path led back to the edge of the moor, and suddenly there was the town between a chapel and a church, tiers of limestone terraces like one side of an amphitheater, the murmur of small-town traffic. Diana led her class down the nearest zigzag path and along the High Street, past townsfolk gossiping on street corners, greeting her and the children. Her class fell silent as they reached the stony schoolyard with a few minutes to spare before the final bell.

Mr. Scragg was in his office, caning a boy taller than he was. Some of Diana's class tittered nervously at the sight of the headmaster standing on a chair. Sally's and Jane's mothers stayed outside the gates and looked away. Diana herded the children to her classroom just as the bell rang. "Hush now until you're out of the building," she told them, and headed for the staffroom.

The air in the small dingy room was laden with stale smoke from Mrs. Scragg's cigarettes. Mrs. Scragg was sitting in her armchair, which looked too small for her large bones. She thrust her broad, red face, whose upper lip was even redder from plucking a mustache, at Diana in her pugilistic way that often reduced children to tears. "Found your way back safe, did you, Miss Kramer? Here's someone you ought to remember."

"I hope Miss Kramer's pupils aren't getting used to having everything their own way," said the woman in the other armchair, tipping a bottle into a baby's mouth, "now I'm not here to deal with them."

"I'm sure Miss Kramer knows what we expect by now, Mrs. Halliwell."

"You can bet on that," Diana said sweetly, and went to her locker. Childbirth hadn't improved Mrs. Halliwell's view of children, it seemed. Best to leave before she had to bite her tongue, Diana thought, and was closing her locker when Mr. Scragg came in.

His face looked flushed from the caning. He kicked the door shut with his heel and brandished a magazine at the women, glaring at it from beneath his bristling gray eyebrows. "Look at this muck I found in Cox's desk. He won't be holding anything before he goes to bed tonight, I promise you."

"From that bookshop, I suppose," Mrs. Scragg said without looking. "What else can you expect from people who'd sell books in a church? A pity the town didn't listen to me while they could. There's a good few regret letting them move in there now that it's too late."

"Too many strangers moving in, if you ask me," Mrs. Halliwell complained, and Diana felt her glare on the back of her neck. "No wonder there's so much vandalism and theft all of a sudden. And those hippies squatting in the holiday cottages, filthy creatures. God forgive me, but I wouldn't have minded if they'd poisoned themselves to death with their drugs."

I wouldn't have taken you for a native with that Irish accent of yours, Diana thought of saying to Mrs. Scragg. "Modern times get in everywhere," she said, meaning to joke.

"Not in this town they don't. They're far enough away that we can see them coming. Here, I'll show you what we think of them." Mrs. Scragg took the magazine from her husband as if she were holding a soiled diaper. It was a *Wonder Woman*, Diana saw, just like the comics she'd read in her childhood, metal bra and all. Mrs. Scragg ground her cigarette into the face of the woman on the cover, dragged the red-hot tip over the glossy paper until the scantily clad figure was crossed out. "Clear enough? You can tell your friends at the bookshop that's what we think of anyone who sells muck to innocents."

"I don't think the Booths even sell comics," Diana said, but she might as well not have spoken. "Excuse me now, would you?" She hurried out of the stale room, along the shiny bilious corridor past her empty classroom. All she could do was as much as she could, she told herself: not just educate the children but strengthen their resilience, prepare them for years alone with the Scraggs, except how could she prepare children like Andrew? She stepped out of the school and lifted her face to the sun. More and more since she'd come to Moonwell she felt there was something else she could do, if she could only think what it was.

3

Business was slack at Booths' Books, despite all the unfamiliar faces the summer had brought to the town, and so Geraldine strolled along to the Bevans' shop. June Bevan was vacuuming the display of rucksacks and Primus stoves and climbing gear, her long brownish hair with its hints of gray swinging lankly beside her face. She straightened up, round-shouldered still. "Gerry, tell me you've just come for a chat. You mustn't let Andrew take advantage of you."

"I'm going past the school anyway," Geraldine lied. "It's no trouble."

"Well, it's very kind of you to say so. We do appreciate you and your husband taking so much interest in him. I hope he says so if he ever speaks up for himself."

"He's quite chatty when you get to know him."

"Really? I mustn't know him very well, then." June's small crowded face with its prominent cheekbones went blank. "Anyway, I better hadn't keep you or we'll have him hanging round outside the school making people think nobody wants him."

Somebody does, Geraldine thought, and you should—but she shouldn't be so quick to judge. The Bevans had befriended her and Jeremy when Mrs. Scragg at the school was trying to turn people against them, circulating a petition against letting the deconsecrated chapel be used as a bookshop. Some of those who hadn't signed seemed to feel guilty now even if they didn't go to church, especially those who had children in Mrs. Scragg's class. Geraldine was tempted to have a showdown with the woman, but not now, not in front of Andrew. She made her way to the school along the High Street, past shops displaying clothes and wool and local artists' paintings and fossils gathered on the peaks.

Andrew was lurking behind the stone gatepost, chewing his nails to clean them. He stuffed his hands into the pockets of his long gray flannel shorts and looked away from Geraldine in order to smile at her. "You look good and grubby," she said.

He glanced down at his grimy legs and fallen socks, and seemed to shrink into himself. "Don't worry, you'll wash," she said, taking his hand. Any eight-year-old should be dirty and untidy and tired by the end of the day: Jonathan would have been—but it was wrong to think about him while she was with Andrew. "Aren't you talking to me today?" she said.

"Yes," he said with a shaky laugh, but that was all until they came in sight of his parents' shop. His thin, pale face kept glancing at her when he thought she wasn't looking, and he didn't notice the horse's turd at the edge of the pavement until he trod in it. "Fuck and bother," he muttered, and flinched automatically.

Geraldine managed to keep her face straight and look as if she'd heard nothing special. She held his elbow while he scraped his sole on the curb. As she let go he blurted, "I like being in Miss Kramer's class. I wish I could be forever."

"I'm sure she'd like you to be, Andrew," Geraldine said, and couldn't think what else to say. She opened the door of

15

Bevans' for him, to June's cry of "Just look at you, where on earth have you been?" She gave June a placatory look and went on to the bookshop.

The seventeenth-century Nonconformist chapel had fallen out of use twenty years ago, but had only recently been deconsecrated. It had seemed a perfect setting for the bookshop she and Jeremy had had to move from Sheffield when the mounting rates had forced them out, especially since living quarters were already built onto the chapel. But as if the undercurrent of righteousness among the townsfolk hadn't been enough, Geraldine thought wryly, they'd had to employ Benedict Eddings to help them convert the chapel.

Jeremy was failing to reach Benedict by phone as Geraldine went in. "You might tell him the alarm went off again at three o'clock this morning," he said, tugging at the black beard that covered his face from his cheekbones down. "I really would be grateful if he'd give us a call as soon as he gets in." He put down the receiver and beamed at Geraldine, crinkles spreading from his large blue eyes across his square face under his high, balding forehead. "No need for me to give his wife a hard time on his behalf."

He gave her a tame bear hug and said, almost too gently and casually, "How was Andrew?"

"Better than sometimes. I should have brought him to choose another book." She disengaged herself eventually, feeling somewhat overwhelmed by Jeremy's hidden concern for her: if she were going to break she would have done so years ago. Jonathan was somewhere, that was all that mattered—perhaps only in her imagination or somewhere like an endless dream. "Come on, let's fix that shelf," she said.

When they'd secured the bookcase that had begun to sag away from the wall the day after Eddings had built it, she replaced the books while Jeremy made dinner. Halfway through dinner in the small white dining room with its view of the heathery slopes, they heard the Bevans come home. June was still scolding Andrew. "Just you get upstairs and make sure the water's hot. What must Geraldine have thought of you looking like a little tramp? Have some thought for me if you've none for yourself."

"I won't be used like that," Geraldine said with an edge to

her voice, but telling June so might make it worse for Andrew. She put on a tape of Sibelius instead, music bleak as bare mountains, to blot out June's continued scolding. The tape hadn't been playing ten minutes when June rang the doorbell. "Could you turn the music down a little? Not that we don't appreciate good music, but the boy's just gone to bed. The sooner he's asleep the sooner we'll have some peace, God willing."

Presumably he'd been sent to bed with no dinner. "Send him over here if it's peace you want," Geraldine suggested, but June was already marching away to her house. Geraldine turned down the volume and finished her meal, though her stomach felt tight. She was helping Jeremy clear up when the bell rang again. It was June's husband, Brian.

"Is he in? Not interrupting anything, am I?" he said, and stepped over the threshold without waiting for Geraldine to invite him in. He had a soft round face with a jutting jaw that she thought he thrust forward deliberately, sallow skin tinged bluish under his eyes, curly sideburns that trailed down to the hinges of his jaw. He went into the kitchen and found Jeremy washing the dishes. "Got you doing her jobs, has she? Listen, I hope mine didn't offend you before."

"Your . . . ? Oh, you mean June. It was Geraldine she spoke to, actually."

"You know how she gets when she's on edge. Andrew was being stupid, contradicting her. Hadn't even the sense to keep his mouth shut. Anyway, listen, I wanted to ask if you were going out tonight."

"We weren't planning to. Why," Geraldine said, "would you like us to keep an eye on Andrew?"

"I should think you'd had enough of him for one day. No, if you're not going out, come round for a drink."

"We're hoping to have the alarm fixed," Jeremy said.

"You'll hear Eddings from our house if he ever turns up. Say you'll come or she'll think she offended you. Besides," Brian said as if this left them no option, "we want to talk to you about Andrew."

When he'd gone Jeremy called Eddings, only to learn that he was still out patching up his handiwork. "Let's brave the hospitality," Jeremy said with a grimace. A vacuum cleaner was bumbling about the Bevans' entrance hall. "You'd think he could have wiped his feet after coming round to see you," June said by way of explanation, and ushered them into the front room.

Porcelain was everywhere: shepherdesses on the mantel-piece above the gray brick hearth that surrounded the simulated coals of the gas fire, Chinese figures on shelves around the walls, a china tea set on the Welsh dresser. Geraldine couldn't see where there was room for Andrew to play, what with all that and the television and videorecorder and the pine bar at which Brian was waiting to serve. "What'll it be? Anything so long as it's Scotch, gin, or martini."

June handed out paper mats and slipped one beneath her tumbler of martini before she sat down, sighing. "Maybe now I can relax after worrying about Andrew all day."

"What's been the matter?" Geraldine said.

June stared as if Geraldine were being facetious. "Don't you know where that American woman took them? Not just up on the moors but right by the cave. If you even set foot on the moors you should take a map and compass and food in case you get lost."

"I think that's only on a long walk," Jeremy said.

"My father said if you even set foot on the moors. Still, I suppose you feel you've got to defend his teacher, seeing that she's a friend of yours."

"We got to know her from taking Andrew to school," Geraldine pointed out.

"She's all right as teachers go, except she thinks she knows all about kids," Brian said. "What she needs is a man to teach her a few things, if you take my meaning."

Geraldine looked away from his wink. "You were saying you wanted to talk about Andrew."

"We wanted your opinion, as long as you see so much of him." Brian took a swallow of his Scotch and looked hard at each of them in turn. "Maybe you know more about these things than we would. What I want to know is, do you think he's queer?"

"Odd, you mean?" Jeremy suggested.

"Not just odd, *queer*. I suppose you'd call it gay, though I'm buggered if I know what they've got to be gay about." Brian's face was reddening. "Do you think he's . . . not a man?"

18

"He isn't yet, is he?" Geraldine said. "He's only a little boy. Most of us aren't sure what sex we are until we're at least in our teens."

"People round here are, let me tell you, and he better had be if he knows what's good for him."

"I'm sure he's as normal as any of us," Geraldine said, wishing he were, hoping he would be.

"That's my feeling too. I didn't see how he could be queer. It isn't as if anyone could have got their hands on him." He turned grinning to Jeremy. "I'll tell you something now. I used to think you might be one of them, what with all the time you spend in the kitchen and that name of yours."

June broke the awkward silence. "If Andrew's normal that way, then what is wrong with him?"

"In what way?" Geraldine said.

"In just about every way you can think of, God help us. He's near the bottom of his year at school, though your teacher friend has brought him up a bit this year; I suppose we must give her that. And out of school he's even worse, under my feet from dawn to dusk and won't go out because nobody will play with him. Not that you can blame them when he never acts his age. Talks like a baby half the time."

"Perhaps if you encouraged him to talk a bit more . . ."

"Talk *more!* Dear Lord, when I've had a weekend of him sometimes I think my head will never stop aching. I dread the summer holidays, I don't mind telling you. If you had a day of him I don't think you'd be so anxious to encourage him."

"I wouldn't mind."

"Well, let's not let him spoil the evening," Brian said as June pursed her lips. "Who wants to watch a video? You two haven't got a machine, have you? I've something here you might like."

He reached behind the bar and produced an unmarked plastic box. His sudden eager good humor made Geraldine uneasy even before he said, "It isn't what you'd call hard core. More of a comedy."

"I don't mind pornography," June said with what looked like a brave smile, "as long as it doesn't involve children."

Geraldine sighed inwardly and took Jeremy's hand as the film's few credits faded. Brian began to chortle as the target for a game of marbles proved to be an anonymous vagina. Geraldine refused to look at him, though she was sure he was

19

gazing at her to see how she reacted, making her conscious of her long legs and large breasts, of the heat spreading up her heart-shaped face to her close-cropped silvery hair, to the tips of her slightly pointed ears. She hoped furiously that she wasn't blushing.

"That's what I call a game of marbles," Brian spluttered as the winner took the woman as a preamble to an orgy. At the first spurt of semen in the film Jeremy cleared his throat. "I really think we should make sure we don't miss Eddings."

"You've never got to go yet," Brian protested, and jumped up. "Come with me first anyway, I've got something else to show you."

Jeremy glanced back helplessly at Geraldine as he followed Brian upstairs. She would have suggested switching off the tape, but June was staring at the screen with a tight-lipped smile that didn't invite any kind of approach. Overhead Geraldine heard a buzzing that surely couldn't be what it sounded like. The tangle of flesh on the television screen looked almost abstract to her by the time the men came downstairs.

"Any time you want a rest from Andrew, bring him round to us," Jeremy said in a casual tone that was meant to deny the rest of the evening. He was clearly as anxious to leave as she was. She took his hand, and they hurried out into the velvety evening. As soon as they were beyond the Bevans' gate he muttered, "You'll never guess what he wanted to show me."

Geraldine's suppressed mirth threw her words about. "Not a vibrator!"

"Damn right, and how big their bed is. He was dropping hints about a game we could all play when I managed to edge my way out. I've a good idea who he had in mind for prizes."

"Just shows you what goes on behind net curtains."

"I could have done without knowing. Do you fancy a walk? Eddings won't be coming this late, or if he does he can be inconvenienced for a change. And then I've something to read to you."

They often read to each other in the evenings. She didn't realize how tense the Bevans had made her until she stepped onto the moor above the town. A cold wind snatched at her out of the dark as the higher slopes began to take shape against the black sky—take shape because something else was rising into view, an unstable white forehead above the edge beyond which the cave lay. She calmed herself down, even though the white rim was swelling too large, its outline trembling. Of course it was only the moon, magnified by mist. She held Jeremy's hand and stood where she was until the moon was clear in the sky. It showed how much the Bevans had worked on her nerves that the sight of the incomplete moon above the cave made her so inexplicably nervous.

4

"Just one more call," Hazel said to her parents, searching the phone directory that was open on her lap for a name that she hadn't yet marked. She dialed and put on her official voice. "Mr. Fletcher? My name is Hazel Eddings and I'm calling you on behalf of Peak Security. I wonder if you're confident that no burglar could ever break into your house . . ."

"Here's Benedict now," her mother Vera said sharply, too late to stop the call, as Hazel's husband poked his sharp-chinned face into the room. "Whenever you're ready," he called, jerking his arms to adjust his cuffs while he tried to fix his bow tie.

"You'll never manage that," Vera rebuked him. "Here, let me." She followed him into the hall, and so it was only Craig who saw Hazel duck her head away from the phone, looking hurt. "No need for that kind of language," she murmured, and dropped the receiver into its cradle as if she didn't want to hold it any more.

"What did he say, sweetheart?" Craig demanded. She looked so vulnerable that his heart seemed to twist, as it had fifteen years ago at the sight of her in her first evening dress. But she blinked her eyes bright and smiled at him as if nothing had happened. "I'm fine, Daddy," she said, and strode into the hall.

Dressed like that, she looked even more like her mother, black hair piled above her long white neck, emphasizing her dark eyes and delicate bones like Vera's. Craig took Vera's arm and sensed that she'd heard Hazel's last words to the phone but thought better of commenting now. Benedict opened the front door and waited for the others to precede him so that he could set the alarm. "I may have to dash off after dinner," he said. "If you like, Craig, you could come along."

The Eddingses lived on the moorland road just outside Moonwell, in a cottage with blue shutters and whitewashed walls. The first few hundred yards toward the town were unlit, and Craig held onto Vera's arm. Once he slipped on a leaf that rain had plastered to the road and felt himself skidding into the dark.

The lights began at the church, the outermost building. Lamps stretched the shadows of willows across the lumpy graveyard full of headstones, postering the church wall with the shadow of an oak. The small peaked porch was lit, Craig saw. "I'll just get the newsletter," Benedict said. "Come in if you like."

Small blurred gargoyles poked their heads out of the thick walls beneath the high sloping roof. Light streamed onto the sparkling grass through the tall, thin arched windows, each of which contained three figures in stained glass, crowded so closely that they looked almost like a single figure—indeed, as a child Craig had thought some of them were. The memory made him feel unexpectedly childlike as he followed Vera through the porch into the church.

Beneath the pointed arches of the vaulting the nave was calm and welcoming. Unbelievers welcome too, he thought as Vera leafed through the visitors' book. "A pity more people don't come in, it's a pretty church. Figures are up this year, anyway," she said, and then, "Oh, dear."

Hazel glanced over her mother's shoulder and gave a cry of disgust. Someone had scrawled "Piss off" across a page full of signatures. All the signatures were dated earlier that month. Before Craig could comment, Hazel cried, "That's what happens when people stop believing. They've no respect for anything, even God."

"I think God will forgive them, Mrs. Eddings," the priest said, emerging from behind the high oak pulpit. He was a squat, beer-bellied man with a cheerful red face and straggling gray hair. "I'm more worried that folk like yourself may be offended. I think *that's* a sin."

Hazel stared open-mouthed at him. "You don't think insulting God is a sin?"

"I'm not sure that whoever wrote that rather silly comment had God in mind at all. I rather think they hoped to shock whoever read it. After all, this church has been here for close to eight hundred years, and the foundations for much longer —you can feel that, can't you? Yet that isn't a split second in the eye of God. Think how much less important this bit of childishness must be."

"Are you sure you ought to speak for God like that?" Benedict said.

"Well, it rather comes with the job, you know. I do believe God forgives, and I think you can feel that here too." He turned to Craig and Vera. "You're Mrs. Eddings' parents, aren't you? Do I hear you're thinking of joining my parish?"

"Sorry," Hazel intervened. "Father O'Connell, Craig and Vera Wilde."

Craig shook the priest's hand, which was strong and warm. "If we retire we might come to Moonwell—we might even carry on doing legal work. But I ought to tell you," he said, taken aback by his own embarrassment, "we aren't what you'd call churchgoers."

"If you're pubgoers you'll find me there too. You're from Moonwell originally, aren't you? Did you ever help dress the cave? We still make up the panels in here, you know. My personal opinion is that it strengthens the church."

"I'd be happy if you got to know Father O'Connell." Hazel lowered her voice as if she didn't want Craig to hear. "You aren't getting any younger."

In the street Craig said, "I quite liked your priest. At least he doesn't believe in the hard sell."

"Maybe he ought to," Benedict said. "Nothing wrong with being aggressive for God. He lost quite a lot of his congregation when he preached against the missile bases, as if he didn't realize the fear of them is bringing people back to God. They want strong leadership now that there's a base so close to Moonwell; they don't go to church to hear that kind of thing. I really believe he had the chance to turn our whole town back to God if only he hadn't been so soft. That's why

23

we've so much crime here now, because people won't stand up for what's right, and no wonder when even their priest seems afraid to."

"Still, you're helping prevent crime, aren't you?" Craig said, rather than suggest that Benedict had something to thank crime for. "How's business since you changed the company name?"

"It wouldn't be half what it is without Hazel," Benedict said, patting her head. "Changing the name is standard business practice, of course."

So tell us the reason, Craig thought. There would be time enough to pursue it. Just now he was regaining his sense of the town, the way no terrace was quite in line with its neighbors, the stretches of the High Street that had no pavements, only grass verges from which the bellies of barrel-shaped drains protruded. Streets led down from the town square through the terraces toward the dry valley, and the sight of the crooked skeins of lamps descending into a gathering mist made him feel nostalgic and peaceful. He mustn't feel too settled, he reminded himself as they crossed the square to the Moonwell Hotel.

The hotel was four stories tall, the smallest rooms up under the steep roof. The restaurant had space enough to cope if all the rooms were occupied, but since they never were, Craig hadn't booked a table. Perhaps he should have, for every table in the high paneled room with its polished dance floor was taken.

"Well I never," Benedict said, strong words for him. Presumably the people, mostly middle-aged, were a coach party, since they all seemed to know each other. The Wildes and the Eddingses found seats at adjacent tables, but they had hardly sat down when the couples at the tables rose. A minute later the restaurant had emptied, leaving the four of them with echoes, crumpled napkins, used cups and plates.

"It's a good thing we'll be having wine," Craig said to the waiter who came to clear the table of their predecessors' leavings, "or you'd have sold none this evening." By the time a matronly waitress brought their meals, he and Vera had drunk most of the wine and were calling for another bottle, despite a surprised look from Benedict that stopped just short of reproof. As Craig cut into his chicken Kiev, he thought again of Hazel in her first evening dress. "Remember the first time we dined at Sheffield Town Hall? You had chicken Kiev then. You couldn't work out how they put the garlic butter in. You said it was like a ship in a bottle."

"Did I really?" Hazel said with a smile.

"Hazel remembers quite a lot about her childhood," Benedict said.

"I'm glad," Vera said, and blinked at him, though his pale voice had been neutral. "Or shouldn't I be?"

"Well now," Benedict said, and Hazel interrupted, "It's only that I happened to mention to Benedict how you and Daddy used to dress at home."

"How we didn't, you mean," Craig said, picking cork off his tongue.

"I know you were trying to be modern, ahead of your time really, but—you don't mind if I say this now, do you?—I never liked it when you went around like that. I'm glad it's going out of fashion. Mind you, just the other day Benedict had to knock on someone's door and ask them to put some clothes on their little boy while he was playing out in his garden."

"They didn't sound very Christian to me," Benedict added.

Vera put down the glass that she'd stopped short of her lips. "So what else didn't you like about your childhood, Hazel? Let's hear the rest of it."

"Mummy, I didn't mean to hurt you. I wouldn't have said anything if I'd known you would take it that way."

"No, please," Vera said, and withdrew her hand as Hazel reached for it. "I'd rather know."

"Just little things. I know you didn't keep me away from religious activities at school, but I always felt as if Daddy wanted to. And I wish you'd let me go to Sunday school but I thought if I asked you might feel I was trying to say you weren't enough for me. I wouldn't have been, I hope you know."

"You wouldn't have said it, just thought it, you mean."

"Oh, Mummy," Hazel cried, lowering her voice as the sound echoed through the empty restaurant and brought a waiter's face to the kitchen doors, "say you aren't offended. I was always afraid we'd end up talking like this."

"You're a surprise to me, that's all," Vera said, blinking back tears, and Benedict cleared his throat. "I'd better be getting back to work," he told Craig through a last mouthful of his main course.

"I'll come with you. Perhaps you could pick me up when you've been home for the van."

"Just as you like," Benedict said in a tone that implied they should leave the women to themselves. His footsteps faded, sounding thin and prim, and then Craig tried to intervene. "I know you didn't mean to hurt your mother, Hazel. We both realize you've got to be yourself, we've no right to try and keep you the way we'd have liked you to be, but at least you might leave us our illusions about ourselves."

Hazel grabbed his hand and Vera's. "You're the two people I most care about in the world. I only say these things because I worry about you."

"No need to," Craig said. "If there's a God he can hardly blame us for not being equipped to believe in him." Both women looked reproachfully at him, and he resented feeling glad when Benedict came back.

As soon as he was in the van, which was piled with tools and new timber, Craig said, "So what did you want to talk to me about?"

Benedict turned the key again as the engine sputtered. "I thought you might like to see how I look after my customers. I hope you'll agree we deserve to succeed."

"Meaning," Craig said as the van lurched forward, "you're not doing as well as you think you deserve to."

"We could be doing better. We would be if I hadn't been landed with those alarms in lieu of payment when the firm was going bankrupt. I just need to liven business up, get myself a new van, smarten up our advertising, maybe employ someone part-time to deal with the work I'm not perfect at. I've worked out the initial costs. They wouldn't be outrageous."

"I hope your bank manager agrees with you."

"To be honest, he wasn't very encouraging. We owe the bank some money, unfortunately."

He halted the van at the end of the village. "Then what do you propose to do?" Craig said.

"I was rather wondering if you and Vera might be able to help."

"Able, possibly. What had you in mind?"

"Three thousand would be ample to put the business back

26

on its feet, and twice that would pay off the bank as well. We're talking about a short-term loan, you understand. I'm sure we'd be able to pay most, if not all, of it back by the end of the year."

"I can't comment until I've talked to Vera. I shouldn't raise your hopes too high if I were you," Craig said as they climbed down from the van.

The booksellers looked as if they'd been ready for bed. "This is my father-in-law," Benedict said, which didn't seem to please them much. They led the way into the bookshop, and Benedict snapped open the microcomputer that controlled the alarm system. "Just as I thought, this is what you did wrong," he said, and demonstrated with exaggerated patience. On the way out he stopped in front of a bookcase. "Oh, have you fixed it? I would have done that for you," he said peevishly.

"Business is business," he said as he restarted the van, "but I do wish I could afford not to work for such people. Did you see what they'd put where the altar should be? A table full of books about superstition. Perhaps you don't think there's any difference."

Craig gave a noncommittal murmur as Benedict drove back to the hotel. The women had already left. "Do remember I'm not asking for the money purely for myself," Benedict said on the way to the cottage, mist drifting across the deserted main street into the headlights.

Vera had gone to bed, and was asleep. Craig found that he'd wanted to talk, and felt lonely. He lay beside her, feeling the aches start in his bones, trying to fall asleep before their nagging prevented him. A stab of pain in his left calf brought him lurching awake, gasping. The plunge into sleep had felt like his fall into the disused mineshaft, his boyhood fall that was always waiting in his dreams when he was nervous. He peered at the room as moonbeams probed the curtains. He closed his eyes and drifted until an impression startled him. In the hotel restaurant he'd thought fleetingly that the diners didn't just all know one another. The feeling lingered that they all knew something he didn't know, and were waiting.

27

5

"What's that we just backed into, Mr. Gloom?"

"Some silly fool standing on the pavement, Mr. Despondency."

"Must have missed him, he's still standing. Great balls of fire, what's he doing now?"

"Banging on the car boot as if we hadn't noticed him. Hey up, he's banged it open."

"Here, here, what's the game? Get your hands off my car or I'll have the law on you."

Too late Eustace realized that he shouldn't have started improvising, because now he couldn't think of a punch line. "That really happened to me here today in Sheffield, but don't tell anyone, will you?" he said, reverting to his normal voice. It didn't sound much like his in the headphones they'd given him; it was high-pitched and overeager and more regionally accented than he'd thought possible. He could see his face reflected in the studio window beside the patient face of the producer, his hair sticking up above his perspiring forehead, his mouth only a little wider than his broad nose. He made his mouth into an O, his features turning into an exclamation mark, and for the first time the producer laughed. But this wasn't television; Eustace was auditioning for radio. Above all, he had to keep talking.

He shouldn't have brought Gloom & Despondency on so soon. He should have told the incident with the car as it had happened—him slapping the boot and the driver accusing him of trying to steal from the car—because then he could have led into what had happened at the bank. The teller hadn't been convinced that the signature on the check he'd made out to cash was his, and when he'd signed it again for her it had looked even less like the signature on his check card. As for the photograph on his union membership card, she'd stared at it as if he must have bought it in a joke shop. So far it had been a pretty average day, but he'd missed his chance to use it now. All he could do was go into another routine, the one he'd meant to save until the end. "How do I love thee? Let me count the ways," he said solemnly, and couldn't bear the sound of his amputated voice any longer; he pulled off the headphones and let them dangle from the table. "One . . . Two . . . Two and a bit on Sundays . . . Four if you count the times when I have a touch of the old trouble . . . Five when you do . . . ."

He could still hear his other voice, squeaking mouselike beside his thigh. He felt parched for a laugh, even a smile from the producer. "Don't tell anyone, will you?" Eustace said, hoping that this time the man would realize it was his catch phrase, and wondered why the producer was holding up one finger, drawing circles in the air. When the producer sawed it across his throat, Eustace said "Thank you" and stumbled to his feet, knocking the earphones to the floor, tripped over a cable and wrenched at the door until he realized he was trying to open it the wrong way. He struggled past it in time to hear the producer say, "You'll agree that wasn't worth the tape, let alone my time."

"He needs a proper audience, Anthony," said his colleague, who'd invited Eustace.

"What do you want me to do, Steve, drag them in off the street?"

"No, I'd like you to see him on his own ground. You were the one who said we ought to be giving more local talent a chance." He turned to Eustace, who stopped mopping his forehead. "When are you next on at that pub I saw you in?"

"The One-Armed Soldier? Thursday week."

"We've got to go to Manchester that week anyway, Anthony. Come on, trust me. We'll stop off to watch Eustace on the way back, and if you still don't see what I saw in him I'll treat you to dinner."

"I'll let you know. By the time these auditions are over I may well be ready to punch the next clown I see on the nose."

"Hear that, Eustace? He made a joke, there's still hope for him." Steve guided Eustace out by one elbow. "I know you won't let me down," Steve said.

He wouldn't, Eustace vowed as the bus climbed out of Sheffield. Yellowish gouges of mines scarred the grassy slopes; a reservoir, a fallen slab of the cloudy sky, stretched to the horizon, sinking as the bus labored upward. Thursday week might change his life. No longer just the Moonwell postman and a treat for the customers at the pub, he'd be the man who was hiding inside him waiting to be noticed. He'd be worthy of Phoebe Wainwright's notice.

The bus let him off at the edge of the pine woods. He walked through the green calm, breaking into routines when he felt like it. "Tea in the pot, Mr. Gloom." "Best bloody place for it, Mr. Despondency." They summed up Northern dourness at its worst; their behavior wasn't even that much of a parody, to judge by the way his audiences at the pub recognized them.

A sharp wind met him as he emerged from the old forest. Above him the ridge overlooking the town looked charred against the lumpy, piebald sky. "Don't miss Eustace Gift at the One-Armed Soldier," he announced, blowing himself a fanfare as he gained the ridge, "but don't tell anyone, will you?" He swallowed his last word, for he'd been overheard. A man was resting on the ferny bank beside the road.

The man placed his long hands on his knees and stood up as Eustace faltered. He wore a denim suit, shoes with thick soles, a rucksack. His face was angular, cheekbones thrusting forward; his hair was clipped close to his head. His eyes were unnervingly blue. Shyness made Eustace speak before he was ready. "Heading for Moonwell?"

"Sure am."

Californian, Eustace thought, having been educated by television. Eustace made to hurry past, but the man fell into step with him. "I hope you weren't thinking I was crazy," Eustace said eventually, awkwardly, "because I was talking to myself."

"Not at all. I knew who you were talking to up here."

Eustace didn't like to ask who. "What brings you to Moonwell?"

"Good news."

"Oh, good. That's good news," Eustace babbled, unwilling to risk anything else.

"And the greatest challenge of my life."

"Really? That must be—" Eustace blundered, and gave up. Thank heaven they were entering Moonwell. Noticing how dusty the man's shoes and trousers were, he wondered how far he could have walked. He made to stride ahead, but the man took hold of his arm. "How do I get above the town?"

"Along here," Eustace said reluctantly, and led him off the High Street. At the end of the unpaved side road, a stepped path led up to the moors. "You'd be doing me a favor if you'd help me to the top," the man said.

Eustace took pity on him, since he seemed exhausted. Yet as soon as they reached the moor, wind hissing down the grassy slopes to set the heather scratching, the man revived. "I know my way now," he said, and when Eustace made to retreat, "Come with me. It isn't far. You won't want to miss this." He waited until Eustace stumbled after him along the path, wondering what he'd been talked into. The man's face pressed forward into the wind until the skin turned pale with stretching, and Eustace began to feel he'd rather hear at secondhand about whatever was coming. But he hadn't thought of an excuse for turning back when the crowd of people appeared above them on the slopes, cried out, and started singing.

6

Nick drove away from the missile base and wondered how best to contradict himself. There were fewer protesters at the base today than there had been last week. Most of them came from Sheffield or farther away, very few from the Peak District, and none at all from Moonwell. It looked as if the Defense Minister had been proved right after all.

The site of the base had been moved away from Sheffield into a dale at the edge of the Peaks. There had been protests that it was too close to the reservoirs, and a few that it was too close to Moonwell. When the couple who ran a bookshop in Moonwell had written to the Defense Minister, they'd received a letter that all but said Moonwell was small enough to be expendable. That had brought protesters out of the Peaks, but not for long. Today's demonstration had been entirely peaceful—too much so, Nick thought, for its own good. Whatever report he wrote, he could imagine its carrying some such headline as PEAKS ACCEPT MISSILE BASE. Looks like another job for the masked man of the airwaves, he thought, his wry grin fading as he wondered how hard a time Julia would give him.

He'd been broadcasting anonymously on her pirate wave-band in Manchester for almost a year. They'd met at a fund-raiser for Amnesty International, not long after she'd started broadcasting. When she'd learned he was a reporter she'd begun to probe his feelings, his frustration at seeing his reports toned down or distorted, how he'd resigned himself to being satisfied when the newspaper let a token left-wing observation of his slip through into print—the best you could expect when the newspapers were owned by fewer and fewer proprietors and were becoming mouthpieces for bigger and bigger mouths. But there was an alternative, she'd told him, her eyes sparkling. He wouldn't be the only reporter who was using her radio station to say what his paper refused to let him say.

He turned off the Manchester road and drove across the moors. There ought to be a town on the moorland road, if he wasn't mistaken, or at least a pub for a late lunch. He'd grown fond of Julia; over the months during which he'd visited her sagging Victorian house in Salford, with the radio equipment in the cellar, they'd made love several times. But recently her attitude toward him had changed: people must know who he was on the air, she kept saying. He ought to name himself and see what his editor did then—Nick's name would make the authorities think twice about closing her down. Nick doubted that his name carried much weight, and touched though he was by her promise that she would always have a job for him, he didn't think he would achieve anything by putting his career at risk. Lately, to placate Julia, he'd taken to attacking himself by name on the air.

He switched on the car radio in case he could hear her, but her waveband was swamped by an American evangelical station, a rock group singing "Have a nice day, Jesus, have a nice day." He turned the radio off and planned how to scathe Nick Reid. He thought of Julia's soft lips, long, cool arms, long legs wrapped around his. The car sped across the moors, miles from the main road now, and he wondered if he'd been mistaken about the pub. He'd stopped the car so as to consult the road map when he heard the singing.

He rolled the window down. Moors divided by infrequent drystone walls glowed sullenly under the packed sky. A bird caught by the wind plummeted and swooped, water trickled in the ditch beside the road. A shift of wind brought him another snatch of song from somewhere ahead. It sounded like a choir.

He put away the AA book without consulting it. There must be a town ahead that was conducting an outdoor service of thanksgiving, as the townsfolk often did in the Peaks. He drove up the next slope and saw the town, past a couple of farmhouses and a blue-and-white cottage. It looked typical, terraces built of limestone and gritstone, small gardens brimming with flowers, a narrow main street that cut off his view of the rest of the town as soon as he drove in. The shops were locked, the streets deserted.

He parked the car in the town square and got out, stretching. A telephone rang somewhere, a dog barked. The pub was locked too, he saw. It didn't seem worth driving in search of another so close to closing time. The choir was still singing, out of sight above the town. He locked the car and went up.

A path at the end of a terrace of cottages led him onto the moor. As he stepped over the edge, the singing surged toward him. There was a moment when it seemed to come from everywhere on the empty slopes, then from the churning sky. He went along the trampled grassy path through the heather toward a stretch of bare rock from beyond which he thought the sound was welling. He wasn't prepared for what he saw as he reached the top.

The barren land sloped down to a large pothole surrounded by a drystone wall. The stony bowl outside the wall was full of hundreds of people and the sound of a hymn.

Opposite Nick, by the wall where the lip of the pothole was highest, a man was kneeling by himself.

Dozens of people had turned to stare at Nick. He stepped down into the crowd so as to be less conspicuous. Not everyone was singing; some people looked bewildered, even suspicious. Nick had almost reached the front of the crowd when, with a shout that echoed from the slopes and startled birds out of the heather, the singing ended.

Nick halted between a plump woman with a cheerful, delicate face and a couple with a restless child. The kneeling man had closed his eyes and raised his face to the sky, lips moving silently. He gazed at the crowd then, his keen blue eyes searching out face after face. "I am Godwin Mann," he said in a light yet penetrating voice, "and that's why I'm here."

The plump woman snorted, whether derisively or not Nick couldn't tell. "He means he's here to win people for God, Andrew," the woman on his other side murmured to her son.

"Please don't kneel unless you want to," Godwin Mann said, "but I'd like you to be seated until I ask you to stand up for God." When people stared at him or at the bare rock they were being asked to sit on, he added, "If anyone would like a chair or a cushion, just raise your hand."

Many hands went up, rather tentatively. In response to that, a large wedge of the crowd behind Mann headed for a nearby line of tents, came back with armfuls of cushions or folding chairs. Some of the crowd spread coats to sit on, though they still looked dubious. Nick suspected that some of them were sitting down because they resented having to stand, perhaps resented having been brought here at all. He was beginning to wonder what precisely he'd stumbled onto, all the more so when the Californian said, "I guess some of you may think I was discourteous because I didn't tell you I was coming, but I didn't know how long it would take me to walk."

"From America?" a man wearing a butcher's apron muttered.

Mann gazed at him. "No, from Heathrow Airport. I wanted to be sure I was worthy to speak for God."

Nick sensed how those who'd grumbled about sitting on the ground felt ashamed of having complained. Score one for the evangelist, Nick thought as Mann went on. "Don't think

I'm saying I'm better than any one of you. Listen and I'll tell you how I was until I asked God into my life."

He took a deep breath and glanced at the sunless sky. "I was brought up in Hollywood. My father was a British movie actor, Gavin Mann." When a murmur of recognition went through the crowd he said a shade more loudly, "I'm not here to speak ill of my father, but I was brought up in the worst ways of Hollywood. At five years old I was drinking alcohol, at ten I was smoking marijuana, at twelve I was snorting cocaine. Fifteen years old and I visited a prostitute. And one year later a man came into my bedroom who used to swim naked with my father. I'm afraid my father only remarried after he divorced my mother because his fans would have expected him to. Well, I found out that night what my father did with his men friends, and the next morning I cut my wrists, as you can see."

He held up his arms, displaying the pinkish scars like stigmata, to the audible dismay of the crowd. "My father got me to the hospital, but I wouldn't tell anyone why I'd done that to myself. All I wanted was to be left alone to get well so I could go someplace by myself and finish myself off."

The woman beside Nick was dabbing at her eyes and jerking her son's hand when he asked her what was wrong. Nick felt uncomfortable, and suspicious of Mann's weepy technique, especially when Mann said, "The morning of the day before I would have left the hospital to kill myself, God saved me."

He gave a wide self-deprecating smile. "Maybe that sounds presumptuous, thinking God would take the trouble for someone like I was, but let me tell you He'd do the same for anyone just so long as they ask. See, every day a counselor from Mission America came to the hospital, and I'd turn my back on her not knowing I was turning my back on God. Only that last day I heard God telling me not to turn away, and I told that counselor everything and accepted God into my life."

The wedge of the crowd behind him whooped and waved their hands. They were the main choir, Nick realized. "Some of you may be thanking God you aren't like I was," Mann said to the townsfolk in front of him. "But are you really without sin? As God looks down on this unspoiled landscape, do you think He takes pride in everything He sees, or does

He grieve for his greatest creation, you and me? Can anyone here stand up and say that sin has passed your town of Moonwell by?"

He let the silence answer him. "You see how much you know but don't like to talk about. These days it isn't fashionable to talk about sin or even about God. Rock musicians turn hymns into sex songs, sacred music gets used in television commercials, churches are turned into markets as if man no longer needs God. But people still need to believe, and that's why they're turning to magic and drugs and worse stuff to fill the gaps in their lives, but all that does is widen the gaps to let in sin. How could they face God if the bomb dropped now? What sort of eternal life do you think they can expect? I'm not here to argue the rights and wrongs of nuclear war, but if that missile base on the other side of these moors were to be nuked right now, I know that I shall go to heaven, because Paul's gospel tells me so."

Some of the townsfolk nodded at that. "Maybe some of you are saying to yourselves that it's okay for me, because I have faith. But so have you. You had faith when you got up this morning that your house hadn't been burgled. You had faith when you went out into the street that you wouldn't be run down by a stolen car or a driver high on drugs. You have faith now that we won't see the nuclear cloud over these moors and there won't be an earthquake that will spill us all down this evil hole."

He stared down into the cave with what seemed to Nick unnecessary vehemence. "Let me put it another way," Mann said, raising his blue eyes again. "How many of you can say you have no faith at all? Are you really prepared to die alone in the dark, rejecting God? Christ died on the cross for you, He made that act of faith to show you how much God loves you and wants you to accept Him, and if you reject that, you're condemning Him to die alone without you, condemning Christ to die alone in the dark, crying out 'Why have you forsaken Me?' You may call yourself a Christian, you may believe you lead a good Christian life, but hear this: you can't take what you need from Christ and leave the rest, you can't say, 'Thank you, Jesus, I've got all I want from you now, just give the rest of that stuff to someone who needs it.' You can't think your way to God. Unless you let God into your life to show you how to live, unless you accept Him whole like a child does, you're turning your back on Him and your name is Judas."

He was hitting his stride now, Nick thought, not sure whether some of the crowd were restless with resentment or guilt. "But God wants you to know this," Mann said. "He wants you to understand that He sees your doubts, He sees if you're afraid to confess your sins, He sees if you aren't sure of your faith, and He wants you to know you needn't doubt any longer. One act of faith will bring God into your life. Remember, the thief on the cross had only to turn to Christ and all his sins were forgiven, he was that day with Christ in Paradise."

His voice was rising, echoing in the cave. "Can't you feel God looking at you now? He's looking at you and loving you as if you're the only person in the world, knowing all your problems and doubts and temptations and sins and wanting to help you if you'll only let Him, only turn to Him for help. He knows if you think you can't live up to Him, can't live by His Commandments. That's why the Commandments ask so much of you, to make you turn to God, because unless you let Him into your life you can't live up to them. Can you feel Him loving you now, praying that you'll turn to Him? That's right, *God* is praying for *you*. All He wants is a sign that you'll let Him into your life, and I'm going to ask you to give Him that sign now. I'm going to ask you to stand up for God."

He put his hands on his thighs and shoved himself painfully to his feet. As he stood up, his legs wavered, and he stumbled against the drystone wall, dislodging a fragment of stone. It skittered down the barren slope and over the edge of the cave.

It struck rock twice on the way down. Nick sensed that the crowd was holding its breath, as Mann appeared to be. They heard a faint chink far below, and a fainter sound that might have been the stone slithering further into the dark. Mann gripped the wall, staring down.

Someone coughed, and Mann looked up. "I'm asking you to stand up as a sign that you're ready to confess. Don't be afraid that your sins are too terrible to be confessed. There is no sin so vile that God will not forgive, and no sin so trivial that it did not help nail Christ to the cross. Will you stand up now as a sign that you are ready to confess if called upon, or am I the only sinner here?"

The choir stood up at once. For a few moments none of the townsfolk did; then people began to struggle to their feet, and suddenly there were hundreds. Nick wondered how many of them might be standing up so as not to be noticed. He remained squatting, and found he was unreasonably grateful that at least the plump woman was still sitting next to him.

"I was brought up in a Christian family," a woman in the choir said loudly, "but we never obeyed God's word without question. When my parents died I wanted to die too because they hadn't left me enough to believe in, I turned to heroin until God's word saved me . . ." As soon as she fell silent an ex-alcoholic spoke up, and then a man who used to beat up his wife and five children. Mann's eyes brightened as the parade of confessions went on, as if he were drawing energy from the public display of faith. He seemed almost to glow, a small intensely clear figure under the dull sky.

Suddenly a young woman standing close to Nick swung round, almost losing her balance. "Mrs. Bevan, I stole money from the till when I were helping in your shop."

"Oh, Katy, never mind," said the mother beside Nick, flapping a nervous hand at her. But Mann had noticed. "Don't be ashamed, whatever it is," he called. "No sooner confessed than forgiven."

Katy faced him and the crowd. "I betrayed someone's trust. She give me a job to help me make ends meet and I stole from her," she cried, and burst into tears.

"You mustn't make so much of it, Katy, it's nothing compared to some of the things I do," the shopkeeper protested, and winced out of her husband's reach as he tried to quiet her. "I give in to lust," she told Mann, her voice growing louder. "I do things you shouldn't do even when you're married. Me and my husband look at pornography to give us more ideas, as if the way God made wasn't enough."

"You never said you felt like that," her husband mumbled, reddening. "I never knew I was making you do things you didn't want to do. It should be me who's confessing."

"Your marriage will be whole once you ask God into it," Mann declared. The clouds were breaking overhead, and the urge to confess seemed to spread through the townsfolk as the sunlight spread. All at once people were confessing to pride, vindictiveness, lapses of faith, envy, drunkenness, selfishness . . . "Can you feel God loving you?" Mann cried. "Can you feel Him smiling?" Nick felt he was taking advantage of the sunlight, but around him people were nodding in agreement with Mann, smiling uncertainly, even beaming.

"Let us give thanks now," Mann said eventually. "We thank You, God, for giving us Your word to show us how to live our lives, to make everything clear to us . . ." The choir joined in, the townsfolk following raggedly. As the prayer came to an end, Mann glanced at the sun. "Soon it will be the longest day of the year," he said, "and I really think by then your town may be God's, a truly Christian community. But I believe God would ask one more thing first. A truly Christian community can't keep a pagan tradition alive."

The plump woman beside Nick peered sharply at Mann. "I know you may think it's just a charming old custom," the evangelist said, "but that's where Christianity went wrong, trying to swallow paganism instead of stamping it out once and for all. I want to ask you a favor on God's behalf. Will you think about leaving this cave as it is this year, not decorating it for once? No need to answer now, but can anyone here say that the picture you make out of flowers is worth offending God for?"

"I'll speak up if nobody else will." The plump woman supported herself on Nick's shoulder and heaved herself to her feet. "I'm Phoebe Wainwright and I organize the cave-dressing. I think you're making things too black and white. The tradition's part of what we are, and I'm sure I'm not the only person here who thinks so. Why, even some of the children I've delivered help me dress the cave."

Somewhere in the crowd Nick heard a murmur: "She doesn't even go to church on Sundays." Otherwise the townsfolk seemed embarrassed, resentful that she'd spoken up.

"I don't ask you to decide now," Mann said to them. "Next time we meet here you can let God know what you've decided. I only ask you to remember that paganism was always Christ's enemy. But a town where God has been invited into every home is a great defense against evil, and so

I'll ask you one more thing: next time we meet, I'd like those of you who stood up here for God to bring anyone who hasn't asked God into their lives."

Some of the choir had slipped away to their tents for handfuls of silver balloons. They let the balloons, which were printed with the words "God Loves You," flock into the sky, blotting out the sunlight for a few moments. The meeting was breaking up. Nick limped toward the front of the crowd, taking out his pocket tape recorder; there were several questions he wanted to ask Mann. But he wasn't out of the crowd, quite a few of whom were converging on the evangelist, when someone grabbed his arm.

===== 7 =====

The young woman who'd stopped Nick had a tapering face, wide greenish eyes, long black hair that the wind was tossing. He was rather pleased to have been halted by her, until she spoke. "Could you tell me what you're doing?"

She was a New Yorker—one of Mann's followers, obviously. "Just going for a word," Nick said, indicating Mann.

"About what? Exactly what have you been doing? I think we're entitled to know."

"So far I've just been watching." If Mann's followers were all as paranoid as this, what had they to hide? She was staring at his tape recorder. "I haven't been using this," he said, "if that's what you were thinking."

"Then why did you bring it at all?"

"I always carry it, it comes with the job. Now if you'll excuse me, I'd like a word with your leader. He may want to talk to me even if you don't think so."

She grabbed his arm again. "Aren't you with his congregation?"

"Only by accident. I happened to be passing. Take it easy

with the arm, would you mind? I'd like to be able to use it when you've finished with it."

"Sorry. Here, please, put it somewhere safe." She was peering at his tape recorder and stifling a giggle. "That's not a field telephone at all, is it? I thought you'd been using it to organize the response."

"I thought that was what you were doing to me on behalf of the god squad."

"Looks as if we're on the same side after all. Maybe we should start again. I'm Diana Kramer, and I take it you're a reporter."

"Nick Reid from Manchester. You're not from round here, surely."

"I came here last year. I teach school in Moonwell. Don't let my accent fool you into thinking I'm mixed up with these guys."

"You've got your doubts about them, have you? Can I quote you?" When she nodded he switched on the recorder. "Go ahead."

"It's just that the whole thing seems so organized to get the response this guy Mann wants. Nobody from Moonwell knew he was coming so far as I know, and if they did they certainly weren't telling. But the hotel's full of people he sent on ahead of him, and so are all the tents around the town. It doesn't feel like religion to me, it feels more like a bloodless invasion."

"I'll put that to him. Anything else? Would you like to tag along and hear what he says?"

"Sure, if you like. I might catch something you'd miss."

The crowd was dispersing around them. Mann's followers waited beside the path to speak to the townsfolk, making sure nobody slipped past without answering. A lone figure who'd been watching from a higher slope turned away across the moors. "Who's that?" Nick said.

"It must be Nathaniel Needham. He lives out there. I hear he's the oldest native of Moonwell."

They made their way across the barren slope to Mann. "Don't be ashamed to bear witness to your neighbors," he was saying. "That's one of evil's greatest triumphs in our time, that people are embarrassed to talk about God or say publicly that they believe in Him." Though his face was glowing, he looked exhausted, all the more so when he saw Nick's recorder. "You want to talk to me?"

"I'd like to if you've time. Nick Reid from Manchester, the *News*."

Mann frowned. "News travels fast."

"That you were here, you mean? I was just passing. Would you rather not have the publicity?"

"If the faithful want to come and join our congregation they know they'll be welcome. I can't think of any other reason why anyone would want to join us, can you? Unless to hinder God's work, and I hope you wouldn't want that any more than I do."

"Excuse me," Diana said, "but you seem pretty sure you know what people want. I mean, your people damn near occupied the town so you'd get a welcome."

"I don't think anyone would object if that means God occupying their hearts, do you? And I think He has already for many of the people of this town. I guess you aren't one of them."

"I wasn't born here, no. I still don't understand why you picked this town."

"Because I had faith I would be welcome here. If you can handle the idea, because God told me I was needed here."

"For what? To stop them practicing a ceremony that's hundreds of years old?"

"I'm afraid so." Mann's face seemed to thrust forward against a strong wind, eyes glittering. "It's the oldest of all the druid ceremonies in England, maybe you didn't know."

"I didn't, but I'd say that was all the more reason not to interfere. We don't have traditions that old ourselves; we shouldn't be jealous of people who have."

"God is a jealous God, or hadn't you heard?"

Nick intervened. "But how significant do you think this ceremony is? I mean, how much influence can it really have?"

Mann fixed his electric blue gaze on him. "While these druidic rites keep being practiced, evil gains ground in the world. Saying they don't matter any longer is like saying there was never anything to fear in the dark, it was only primitive man who thought so. Let me tell you something. The year after I dedicated my life to God, He led me to a cult of

42

Satanists in Hollywood, and some of the people I saved are here with me now. God gave me the power to seek out evil. That's why He sent me here."

He seemed suddenly to feel he'd said too much. "So what can I tell you that you'll print?" he said more quietly.

Nick asked him standard questions and received the answers he expected: Mann was against abortion, divorce, pornography, "permissiveness in all its forms," and on the side of marriage, obedience to authority, a return to order . . . Nick tried to draw him out on the subject of his presence in Moonwell, but Mann slumped all at once, his mouth drooping. "I'll go down now," he said to two of his followers, who helped him toward the town.

Two more of them buttonholed Nick and Diana on the path to ask if they'd been won over by Mann's preaching. "I'm just a reporter," Nick said, "and this lady's with me." Once out of earshot he murmured to her, "I hope you didn't think I was presuming, saying you were with me, since you asked so many of my questions."

"I didn't really, did I?" She made a comically apologetic face. "Breaking your arm and now elbowing you out of your interview. You should have told me to shut up."

"No hard feelings. You got him going where I mightn't have, made him say more than he'd have wanted to, I thought. Let me buy you a drink to show I don't bear grudges."

But the pub, the One-Armed Soldier, was still locked. Nick had meant to phone in his report about the missile base. "You're welcome to use my phone," Diana said.

She lived in a small rented cottage below the town square. The white rooms smelled of the flowers she had in pots in all the windows. He phoned from the low timbered entrance hall, then joined her in the front room with its children's paintings, where she had coffee waiting. Soon the conversation veered back to Mann. "What I don't understand," she said, "is why he thinks doing away with this ceremony just because it's the oldest will put a stop to all the others."

"I don't know if that's what he meant."

"Why else would it be so important to him?"

Nick couldn't imagine. "Listen, I've got to be going," he said, and scribbled his phone number on a page torn from his notebook. "If anything happens you think I should know about, give me a call, will you? And whenever you're coming to Manchester again let me know and I'll buy you lunch."

Most of the shops were open as he walked back to the car. He wondered which of the people on the streets were townsfolk, which Mann's followers, and how many were now both. As he drove away from Moonwell, down into the forest below the moor, Diana's question began to trouble him. He should have asked Mann what it was about the cave that had brought him all the way from California. He felt almost as if something had distracted him from asking.

═══════ 8 ═══════

Diana woke on Monday morning thinking about druids. She'd got onto the subject almost by accident in the Manchester library, where she'd been researching her Peak District ancestry. Her background seemed so familiar, though not the way her mother's grandfather had lived, a miner who'd carved his family a home out of the lime waste outside Buxton. But perhaps, she thought now, her sense of belonging had just been part of the peace she'd felt on the moors, the first time she'd felt peaceful since coming to England to try to adjust to the death of her parents.

Her last sight of them at the Kennedy barrier was as vivid as ever, her father giving her a hug that smelled of the pipe tobacco he always bought near the New York Public Library, her mother's cool hands on her face as she murmured "Don't worry," Diana not knowing then why she felt anxious. The glimpse of the airliner dwindling into the blackening sky had wakened her hours later in a panic that had set her praying as she hadn't since her childhood, praying they were safe. When she'd given in to her panic and called the airport, the clerk at first suspected her because she seemed to know the plane had crashed. Not until the police had questioned her at length did they tell her that both her parents were dead.

She wondered how Mann would have dealt with that—not so much that God had failed to respond to her prayers, but that if he'd wanted to take her parents he'd taken dozens of other lives just to do so. Or didn't the individual lives matter to God, just the number of lives, the statistic? All that could justify that kind of behavior by a god would be life after death.

She'd reached that conclusion in the midst of her peace on the moor. The murmur of the world had faded into the sound of the wind in her ears; the mist had withdrawn over the deserted slopes until it seemed they would never end; and as Diana had drunk in the silence and loneliness, she'd grown calm, at peace with her loss. She'd felt on the edge of passing through loneliness to whatever lay beyond.

Teaching in Moonwell had, apparently, and now Mann and his aversion to druids. On the way to the school through streets glistening with mist, pinpoint rainbows shining out of flowers, she thought how much the druids had left behind: kissing under the mistletoe, throwing spilled salt over your shoulder, gargoyles as a civilized alternative to displaying the severed heads of your enemies above your roof, even calling two weeks a fortnight, since the druids measured time by nights rather than days. Druids never wrote anything down, perhaps as an aid to memory. They often spoke in triads, since three was their sacred number. The great Celtic fear was that the sky would fall and the sea overflow. By the eighteenth century the druids had become a romantic myth, but the truth seemed to be that they had been more savage, sacrificing human beings before battle—it was hard to be sure, since no account survived of their religion. Presumably the cave had been one of their sacred places, and she wished more and more that Mann would leave it alone.

Mrs. Scragg was waiting for her in the schoolyard, which was unusually crowded. "My husband wants to see you in his office."

He was sitting at his desk, which looked absurdly large for him, reading a pamphlet called *Stand Up for God* and rubbing his hands together. His broad smile made his face look cramped between his chin and bristling eyebrows.

45

"You've some extra pupils," he said. "Godwin Mann arranged for us to take them. My wife will have the nine- and ten-year-olds and I'll have the eldest: I assume you can cope."

"No problem," Diana said, determined that there wouldn't be, even when her class lined up at the sound of Mrs. Scragg's earsplitting whistle and Diana saw their number had virtually doubled. All the new children looked bright-eyed and fresh-faced and eager, though some of them were sniffling from the chill that must creep into their tents. In her classroom Diana said, "I think you're all going to have to sit two to a desk."

Her class moved over, shuffling and grumbling. When they'd made room the new children remained standing. "May we pray first?" a boy with especially blond hair and a Southern accent said.

"Sure, if that's what you do."

The new children knelt, then gazed at the others. They were expected to kneel too, apparently, but Diana wasn't having her schoolroom routine taken over so thoroughly. "Just bow your heads," she said, and bowed her own a little.

Eventually the newcomers finished thanking God, and sat down. "Let's start by getting to know one another," Diana suggested. "Why doesn't each of you tell us your name and a bit about yourself."

"I'm Emmanuel," the blond boy said. "I come from Georgia. My daddy and my uncles worked a farm there until my uncles died fighting God's war against communism."

Two English children and two from California claimed to be fighting God's war too. Sally was bristling. Suddenly she said loudly, "My dad's in a union and he goes to church."

"You can go to church and still keep God out of your heart," Emmanuel said. "We'll pray for him and for you to show him the true path."

Sally stuck her tongue out at him and wrinkled her nose to stop her glasses from slipping. "My mum says if there's another war it'll be the last one," Jane said, "because the bombs will kill everyone."

"You shouldn't care so long as God is your best friend," said a Welsh girl. "But if He isn't you'll go straight to hell when you die."

"I won't. You don't know nowt about it. Anyway, Sally's

my best friend." She reached for Sally's hand between the desks, and Sally said defiantly, "I love Jane too."

"Girls shouldn't love girls and boys shouldn't love boys," Jane's seatmate said. "Godwin Mann says so. You have to offer up all your love to God."

"If you're going to argue I think you'd better just tell whoever you're sitting with your name," Diana said, reminding herself that it wasn't their fault they were so old before their time and so insufferable, it was the way they'd been brought up. "Now I'm going to hear each of the new children read, and the rest of you can see how much you can read by yourselves."

She'd heard two readings when Thomas's seatmate said loudly, "You mustn't say that kind of stuff. Tell Miss Kramer the kind of dirty stuff you were saying."

"Not here, okay, Thomas? We don't want to offend anyone when there's no reason to."

"I forgive you. I'll pray for you," Thomas's deskmate said, and Diana had the disconcerting impression that he was talking to her as well as to Thomas. That was the way the morning went, the new children not so much telling tales as telling their seatmates to confess whenever they did anything wrong, however trivial. She went into the schoolyard at lunchtime praying that they wouldn't be so puritanical while they were playing games.

A radio was blaring disco music, which seemed promising until Diana realized that the lyrics, repeated over and over, were "Upon this rock I shall build my church." Some of the Moonwell children began to dance enthusiastically, until the owner of the radio switched it off. "You shouldn't dance like that," she rebuked them.

Some of Diana's class were teaching the newcomers to play Harry-in-the-hole. The Welsh girl, Mary, was chosen to be in the hole, to be blindfolded and try to grab a victim from the circle that surrounded her, holding hands. If she guessed who the victim was, that child had to join her and be blindfolded, and once that process started the circle wouldn't hold for long. But before the game had even begun, Mary pulled the blindfold off. "What am I supposed to be?"

"The giant who lives down the well," Thomas said.

"He means the cave," Ronnie said impatiently. "We poked your eyes out and threw you in."

"No, we chopped your arms and legs off and rolled you in," Thomas told her with relish.

Mary looked as if she wanted to run. Diana hushed Sally and Jane, who were holding her hands and telling her secrets, and started to intervene, but the boy with the portable radio was ahead of her. "What's wrong, Mary?" he demanded.

"They want me to play at being him down the cave, Daniel."

"You mustn't play that, any of you. Don't you know who he is? He's the devil waiting down there. He'll come for you if you don't pray to God and make sure your folks do."

A cloud rose into view above the town, blotting out the sun. Its shadow flexed rapidly over the cottages and rushed into the schoolyard, evoking a sudden stony chill. "He's not a devil, he's a giant," Thomas said. "Anyway, if he gets out he'll get you first in those tents up there. He'll pick you up and turn you inside out and put you down as something else, and then you'll have to crawl about like that for ever."

Andrew spoke for the first time, haltingly. "He can't be a devil when the cave's a holy place. My granddad said they threw the giant down there because it was holy and he wouldn't be able to get out."

"Your granddad's telling lies," Mary said in her sharp Welsh voice. "You should listen to Godwin Mann. He speaks with the voice of God."

"What is he then," Andrew said, "a telephone?"

Good for you, Diana thought, and caught sight of Mr. Scragg in the school doorway. "All right now, children, don't take everything so seriously. It's only a game, after all," she said, earning herself a contemptuous glance from Daniel. For a moment she wanted to lash out at him, and was shocked by her feelings until the whistle interrupted them. As soon as there was silence Mr. Scragg said icily, "Has anyone been up on the moor today who isn't camping there?"

His gaze darted about the faces of the Moonwell children, searching for hints of guilt. "If anyone has been I'll find out, believe me. I've just been told that someone has knocked the safety wall into the cave. It'll take more than that to drive our friends away, but I'm telling you all now there'd better be no more such incidents, or as God is my witness I won't rest until I find the culprits and give them what they deserve."

When he'd finished glaring, he stalked back into the

48

building. "I was going to tell you why they were wrong to throw the devil into the cave," Daniel said, ushering Mary away, "but I think we'd better pray for you all instead." He and his friends did so, while Thomas and his group played loudly, though not loudly enough to drown out the prayers.

The new children clearly felt Diana should have kept them quiet. Throughout the afternoon she sensed their disapproval; once, when the chalk broke on the patchy blackboard and she muttered "Damn," it came at her back like a wave. Could disapproval really prevent the floral ceremony from being performed at the cave on Midsummer Eve, and if so, did it matter? Surely it stood for so much, the lost celebrations of Midsummer Day that had been disguised as St. John the Baptist Day, public bonfires, dancing in the streets. Mann wouldn't have liked those medieval rites much either, she thought wryly, feeling stifled by the threat of disapproving prayer in her classroom.

She'd never felt so in need of the relaxation classes that Helen from the post office organized each Monday evening. Walking along the High Street, which a mist was shortening, she passed strolling couples whom she didn't recognize, presumably Mann's followers. A thought stirred in her mind, something ominous about the way the town was now, but before she could grasp it she saw Helen tacking a notice to the outer door of the assembly rooms. "Why, Helen, what's wrong?" Diana said.

"Nothing at all. Everything couldn't be better." Helen's round face, which was always delicately made up, looked scrubbed raw. "But I've given up yoga, and I hope I can persuade you to. You don't need that kind of thing when you've let God into your life."

9

Geraldine was threading the last of her flowers through the perimeter fence of the missile base when the police began to move everyone back. "Come along, madam," an avuncular constable said, "you know this is government property. I hope you'll have something besides flowers waiting for the enemy."

"Anyone in particular?"

He gave her a reproving look. "I think we know who wants the whole world to be Communists. Would you like your children to grow up under a Communist regime?"

"We haven't any children," Jeremy said in a ragged voice. "The one we might have had we lost. Maybe we can thank the nuclear lobby for that. There've been a lot more miscarriages since they started testing fucking bombs."

"There are ladies present, sir, if you don't mind. Just move along now, there's a good lad."

His eyes were less patient than his words, and he seemed suddenly to have grown bulkier. "It's all right, Jeremy," Geraldine murmured, thinking that confrontations like this were one reason why some bases were being picketed solely by women. "We have to be going anyway. There's all the new stock to be checked."

They picked their way across the muddy trampled grass of the dale to their van. The eight-year-old engine only coughed and groaned when Jeremy tried to start it, but it caught first time for her. Jeremy threw up his hands. "Shows how much use I am."

"You're a lot more than useful to me. I'm all right, honestly." The policeman hadn't bothered her, even though it would have been Jonathan's birthday in just a few weeks. It was Andrew she wasn't sure about, not Jonathan. She drove fast through the mountains and up across the moors. As soon as the van was parked, she went round to the Bevans'.

"Come in then," Brian said distractedly, jutting his jaw as he led her to the kitchen where he was preparing dinner. Dried-up baked beans and sausages sputtered in a pan, soggy chips blackened under the grill above which a new plaque said "God Lives Here." "Don't go thinking I do this often," he said. "Only when she's helping at Godwin Mann's shop and I've got halfday closing."

The shop sold plaques, Bibles, pamphlets whose covers showed people beaming as if they never did anything else. "Here, let me rescue your dinner," Geraldine said laughing. "Trust a man to do nothing but open cans and defrost packets."

"June always makes this kind of dinner."

"Well, I expect it's Andrew's favorite," she said quickly, scraping chips off the grill pan. "How's he getting on? What did he make of the god show?"

"It isn't up to him to make anything of it."

"We've a few new children's books if he wants to choose something."

"If you want to go giving away books you could sell you aren't going to let me stop you." He seemed uncomfortable so close to her in the small, hot, smoky kitchen, and turned away to mutter, "We're grateful really. I know we could do with giving him more of our time and having a bit more patience. Maybe now our lives are being changed . . ."

Andrew was playing soldiers on the stairs. He'd snapped off the barrel of a plastic antiaircraft gun and was sticking his chin out like his father so as not to cry. He brightened when he saw Geraldine. "Do you want to see my these?"

"What's the matter with you?" Brian demanded. "Do you want Geraldine to think we don't bring you up to speak properly? See my these," he mimicked in an idiot's voice. "Geraldine wants to give you a book to read. I wouldn't blame her now if she gave you a baby's book."

"We'll find something to show your parents how well you can read," Geraldine said as she led Andrew into the bookshop, where Jeremy was opening cartons with a Stanley knife. "I expect you're looking forward to when they see your school work."

"They said they won't."

Geraldine thought she'd misunderstood. "They'll be going to see Miss Kramer at the open night next week, won't they?"

"My mum has to go to God's shop then because they'll be praying, and my dad has to do something at home."

Geraldine busied herself with showing him books, because she didn't trust herself to speak. When he chose *The Jungle Book,* on impulse she followed him next door. June was waiting for him on the garden path. "Thanks for seeing him home, Geraldine. Heaven knows what he'd be up to otherwise."

"No need to overdo it, June. Diana Kramer was wondering if you'll be at the open night."

"I'd love to, but I have to go to a prayer meeting, and we can't leave the boy alone in the house."

"Jeremy or I will sit, you've only to ask. Unless," she said, meaning to shame June, "you'd rather we went to the school in your place."

Brian leaned out of the front window. "Would you mind? You do know his teacher better than we do."

He looked both shamefaced and secretive, but Geraldine wasn't interested in his reasons. "I think," she said shakily, "we ought to let Andrew decide who he wants to go."

Andrew stared at his scuffed shoes. "Haven't you got a tongue?" June snapped, and he looked up at Geraldine. "You and Jeremy," he said in a small voice.

"That's settled, then," June said in what was either bitterness or triumph. Geraldine was about to retort that it was nothing of the kind when the alarm at the bookshop began to shrill.

She couldn't think for the noise. She ran back into the shop just as Jeremy switched off the alarm. "I'll call Eddings," she said, eager to deal with him, to use up some of her anger.

He wasn't at home. "I'll tell him you called as soon as he comes in," his wife Hazel said.

"Someone else's need is greater than ours, is it?"

"You might say that, yes. He's visiting our neighbors on behalf of Godwin Mann."

"I'm afraid praying isn't going to fix our alarm."

"Are you sure? Perhaps you should try while you're waiting."

Geraldine made the worst face she could manage at the receiver and dropped it into its cradle. "When he finishes God's work he'll get round to his own," she told Jeremy.

"A pity we can't ask God to guarantee Benedict's work. And what had the Bevans to say for themselves? Don't lose your temper."

"I'm not about to lose my temper. Why should I lose my temper? There's no reason for me to lose my temper just because of people." She closed her eyes and gritted her teeth and growled, almost screaming, and then she told him what had happened. He didn't seem to know what was best to do any more than she did; whatever they tried, she thought Andrew would be the loser. They argued about it all through dinner, though really she was arguing with herself. Eventually she admitted, "I can't think."

"Shall we go out for a drink or a walk or something?"

"We can't if Eddings is coming."

"Go by yourself if you like. You've had a pretty grim day one way and another. I'll finish checking the stock and maybe catch you up later."

Streetlamps were lighting up in the dusk. The jagged edge of the moor above the town smoldered against the glassy purple sky. Geraldine walked quickly up the path to shake off the growing chill. How could she make the Bevans do right by Andrew? He was their responsibility, not hers. He wasn't her child. He wasn't Jonathan.

Jonathan was safe, wherever he was. She'd told herself that in the chilly white-tiled Sheffield hospital: Jonathan was alive somewhere, and growing. She didn't need to see him, though sometimes she did, in dreams. She wished she could share her conviction with Jeremy, but the only time she'd tried he'd begun to humor her. Jonathan had felt threatened, in danger of ceasing to be, and she had never mentioned him again. She could keep him safe. It was Andrew who had to live in the real world and cope with whatever it did to him.

She stepped onto the moor and followed the path that glowed dark green in the dusk. The chill of the limestone seeped up like mist through the grass. She walked faster, hugging herself, wondering why the chill should make her nervous. She was on the bare stone above the cave when she remembered and halted, shivering.

Home from the hospital, she'd made herself give away

Jonathan's clothes at once. She'd opened the chest of drawers in the room that would have been his, she'd reached in to take a handful of baby clothes, and then she'd sucked in a breath that hurt her teeth, for the clothes had felt like ice. She could feel her fingertips aching with the cold as she'd begun to shake from head to foot. She'd stood there, unable to let go or pull away, until Jeremy had found her. Later, when he'd got rid of the clothes, she'd learned that he'd felt nothing odd about them, no undue cold at all.

The full moon trailed a rainbow halo over the clouds on the horizon. The moorland path reappeared, having faded under the sky that was now almost black. The tents on the higher slopes were chunks of ice. She hadn't known what the cold meant then, and she didn't know now—certainly not that it was so cold wherever Jonathan was—but she didn't want to be alone with that thought up here, especially when the moonlight made the landscape even bleaker. She hurried past the cave, heading for the path that led down to the far end of Moonwell. Then she faltered, for there was no longer a gritstone wall around the cave.

In the moonlight it looked even deeper. Though she was at the edge of the stone bowl, she felt too close to the gaping dark. She started away, and a fragment of rock flew from under her heel, skittered down the bowl. For no reason she could grasp, she was terrified that it would fall into the cave. She ran for the path, stumbling, almost falling.

The moonlight crept across the town below her, glinted on the roofs of cottages above the pools of streetlight. It followed her as she stepped over the edge toward the church. It glided over three faces in a narrow stained-glass window, made them appear to turn on a single neck. Among the newest gravestones, under the oak, one stone was brighter than the rest. In the moonlight it seemed almost to glow.

Moonlight gathered in the churchyard as she reached the pavement. Columns of shadow stretched across the whitened grass, blurs at the ends of the columns groped over the church wall. Geraldine peered across the road, then she crossed to the pavement bordering the churchyard. She still couldn't see the name on the glowing headstone, couldn't tell what kind of stone it was that was able to reflect the moonlight so strongly, almost as if it were shining itself. She paced along the railings and lifted the latch of the iron gate.

The gate must have been oiled recently, for there was no sound. Perhaps her straining to read the stone at the edge of the shadow of the oak was blanking out her other senses; as she stepped onto the moonlit gravel path, she wasn't aware of her footsteps. The light that seemed to have congealed into a stony stillness made her begin to shiver. She left the path and advanced between the mossy stones, her feet slipping on mounds that reminded her of beds. She was close enough to read the inscription now, the little there was of it, and her legs were shaking. She had to support herself on stones that crumbled under her fingers. When she fell to her knees in front of the glowing stone, far brighter than the stones on either side of it, it was to stop herself from trembling as much as anything. But she was shivering as if she might never stop. The only date on the unblemished headstone was eight years ago, and the only name was Jonathan.

10

"I hope I'll see you at the pub tonight, Mrs. Wainwright— Phoebe." If he called her Mrs. Wainwright, Eustace thought, she might tell him to call her Phoebe; that would help. He'd known exactly what to say to her until he'd turned the corner into Church Row, tugging so hard at his collar that the button flew into the road to be pulverized under the wheels of a delivery van. Mrs. Wainwright, he decided, and now all he had to do was walk along Roman Row, press down the latch of her bright green wooden gate, walk under the trellis of flowering vines and up the gravel path that was as good as a watchdog for letting her know someone was approaching, lift his leaden hand to the doorbell, take a deep breath that he meant to hold until they came face to face, so that he would have to let it out and ask her at once. He'd already sucked in his breath when he realized that he hadn't taken out the magazine he was supposed to be delivering. He pulled it out so hastily that he spilled half the contents of the postbag on the cottage doorstep just as she opened the door.

As he fell to his knees he thought of how he looked, a swain kneeling before his lady love who didn't even know she was. When she squatted to help him, her dress rode up her plump thighs, and he almost fell over backward. He was intensely aware of her perfume that smelled wild as heather, her lightly freckled bare arms, the bare upper curves of her large breasts, her deep brown eyes, small nose, very pink full lips, her blond hair in a ponytail that trailed down her back. Her soft, warm hand touched his as she handed him letters. "Thanks very much," he mumbled, and lurched to his feet as soon as he could, only to realize that now he looked as if he were staring down the front of her dress.

She stood up with a gracefulness that both surprised and moved him. "You can sort your letters on my table if you like."

The front room was neat as his own, a solitary person's room. Fossils were outlined in some of the stones of the fireplace that she had built herself. Eustace dropped the letters on the embroidered tablecloth and glanced away from a photograph of her late husband—long face divided by a mustache—to a photograph of Phoebe dwarfed by last year's cavedressing, a floral picture of a man dressed in gold and brandishing a sword, a halo like the sun around his head. "You'll still be dressing, will you?" Eustace said, suddenly picturing her naked and not knowing where to look.

"Don't worry, I know what you meant." She giggled, then grew sober. "Some of the people who usually help have started making excuses. I hope there'll still be enough. I wouldn't like to think our town would let itself be told what to do by someone who's never even seen the ceremony."

"Exactly." Ask her now, his voice was clamoring, so loudly that he felt as if he were wearing headphones again. But his mouth felt as if he'd swallowed superglue, and his expert hands had sorted the letters before he could say anything. He took a deep breath and heard himself say the only thing he was capable of. "Thank you."

He was heading clumsily for the door, wanting only to be out and by himself, when she said, "Did you have any reason for calling except to unload yourself on my doorstep?"

"Sorry, I've been nursing this all along." He handed her

the magazine and remembered that her husband had been a male nurse, killed two years ago as he drove off the road in the midst of an instant Peak District fog. "I don't suppose you were dying to read it," he said and wished he could bury his head in the postbag. She was both smiling and frowning when the doorbell rang.

He followed her as she opened the door to two women with bright open faces, shoulder bags stuffed with pamphlets and books. "Will you let God into your house?" one said.

Eustace slipped past them. "I'm going now so there'll be room for Him."

"You'll have to excuse me too, I'm afraid," Phoebe said to the women. As she closed the door she called after Eustace, "I'll see you later. I'm looking forward to your show at the pub."

He was so delighted that he almost went straight home without finishing his walk. He delivered the rest of the mail, then he strolled home to his cottage between the High Street and a steep slope to the moor. He lay on the couch and watched Stan Laurel burn down Hardy's house while trying to help him clear up after a party. For once he didn't even need to feel that someone was clumsier than himself.

Later he brought home fish and chips from the shop on the High Street; then he walked through the darkening town to the One-Armed Soldier. The pub was crowded, the faces under the low oak beams were mostly unfamiliar; they often were on folk nights like tonight or when Eric, the landlord, showed a film on the video screen. In a corner full of horse brasses Eustace saw the producers from Radio Sheffield; Anthony, who'd thought he wasn't worth the tape, was shaking his head on its wiry neck to fling back his graying hair. Eustace hadn't time to talk to them now, even if he'd felt like doing so—he always arrived with just a few minutes to spare so as not to lose his confidence. But when Eric bought him a pint of ale and called "Take your seats, ladies and gentlemen, for Moonwell's own comedian Eustace Gift," there was still no sign of Phoebe.

Eustace squeezed between the tables, sipping from his tankard so that it wouldn't slop over, and climbed the steps to the makeshift stage. He'd show Anthony from Radio Sheffield that he was a comedian after all. He'd found out he was the night he'd chatted to Eric about his usual pratfall-ridden week so enthusiastically that he hadn't noticed everyone was listening until they'd cheered him at the end and bought him drinks. He couldn't wait for Phoebe; the show had to go on. "That's me," he said, settling himself on the straight chair in the middle of the bare stage. "Eustace by name and Eustace by nature."

A small woman at a table by the window laughed raucously. "That's Eustace, love, meaning rich in corn," he said, and got a more general laugh, if rather a polite one. He was glancing about for someone else to chat to—make one laugh, he believed, and you've won yourself a friend who'll spread the laughter—when the door opened and Phoebe came in.

She looked breathless. Perhaps she'd been running for him. She gave him a quick apologetic smile, and at once he felt inches taller. "I deliver the letters in Moonwell, while Phoebe Wainwright there delivers the babies. Lucky it isn't the other way round or I might be delivering second-class citizens."

That brought another polite laugh, but all it earned him from the radio producers was a faint shift of the lips. It was time to give them something sharper. "Things may change now that Mission Moonwell's come to town. I believe soon we're going to have to call letter boxes epistle boxes. Don't tell me you thought epistle was what you are when you come out of a pub."

Father O'Connell, who was sitting with Diana Kramer, laughed at that, and so did the radio producers. "I hear Godwin Mann's been resting in his room at the hotel since he introduced himself to Moonwell," Eustace said with an innocent look, "but don't tell anyone, will you? Probably gives him a headache, listening to God's voice all the time. Good job that never happens to me. The way I am I'd get a crossed line, hear a voice saying 'Fasten your seatbelts' or 'What color underwear are you wearing?' . . ."

He reached for his tankard but let his hand dangle. The laughter he was leaving space for hadn't come; a few late laughs sounded encouraging rather than spontaneous. As he took a quick swallow of ale, he saw the butcher leaning against the bar, gazing at Eustace as if he wished he'd try a different style of humor. That couldn't be right, the butcher had been skeptical enough at the rally. "Now, it looks as if it's getting too crowded in Mr. Mann's room," Eustace said, "because he's sending people round town to ask if someone will let God into their house."

When Steve, the other man from Radio Sheffield, laughed at that, heads turned to stare at him. Otherwise there was silence, though surely it couldn't be as pained as Eustace felt it was. He was in danger of losing control, both of himself and the audience. Gloom & Despondency to the rescue, he thought desperately. "Hey up, Mr. Gloom, they want us to let God into our house."

"Tell them we don't take lodgers, Mr. Despondency."

"They say we can't keep Him out, He's too big."

"Great balls of fire, you know what this means, don't you? Every night loaves and fishes for tea . . ."

Nobody was laughing. Eustace found he was staring at a woman he'd never seen before, willing her even to smile. She stared blankly at him as if she wondered how much longer she had to wait for the next act, and the answer to that felt like a last-minute rescue. "Anyway, that's enough from me and the firm of Gloom & Despondency for now," he said, almost stammering. "Time for some music from—from our own Billy Bell."

So many people stared at him as if he'd meant that as a joke that he thought for a moment he'd transposed the vowels. No, he could hear what he'd said, echoing in his invisible headphones. He climbed down from the stage, his legs hindering each other, and made for a dark corner to let his face cool down. Bearded Billy, the postmistress's son, was raising his guitar above his head on the way to the stage when a young woman stood up, blocking his way. "May I tell a good joke?"

Billy hesitated. "Go on," voices cried.

She was tall and fresh-faced, with pigtails and a smile that said she couldn't wait to tell the joke. People were laughing eagerly before she sat down on the edge of the stage. "There was this Irishman called Simon O'Cyrene," she said and giggled. "And he suddenly finds he's out of work. So he says to himself, I feel lucky, I'll spend my savings on a holiday abroad instead of sitting around doing nothing. So he goes off to Israel for his summer holidays, and one day he goes to Jerusalem because he's heard there's going to be a parade. So he's standing in the crowd waiting for the parade to come along and a pickpocket steals all his money while he isn't looking. And Simon says to himself, O dare me, what's this now, I could have sworn this was my lucky day."

Eustace was bewildered. He not only didn't see anything to laugh at, especially not her phony Irish accent, but she was killing her joke by giggling in advance. Yet around him everyone was smiling, some were laughing outright as she said, "So he's looking round for a policeman when he hears the parade coming. And he says to himself he's come to see it, he may as well get his money's worth. So here's the procession coming along and Simon sees sixpence lying in the middle of the road. So he goes in the road and he's just bending down to pick up this sixpence when the procession comes along and they put something on his back. So he says what's this now, all I did was bend down to pick up this sixpence because I was feeling lucky and someone puts a cross on my back. But Jesus says to him, want to hear some good news? This really *is* your lucky day."

Eustace gaped, not just at her but at the laughter and applause that greeted the punch line. Now he noticed how many of the people in the pub were drinking soft drinks; he began to realize that he'd seen many of the faces at Mann's rally, in the choir. He must point that out to the producers from Radio Sheffield—but before he could struggle over to them, they'd sidled out of the pub.

He slumped back into the corner. They hadn't even given him a chance to redeem himself. The young woman told jokes about Doubting Thomas and Pentecost to redoubled applause, and then she said, "Would you like to hear a story now?"

"I think we'd better have some music," the landlord said, obviously unhappy with the way the evening was developing. Billy Bell had picked up his guitar when a voice beside the bar said, "There's an old song I'd like to remind you folk of before Midsummer Eve."

It was Nathaniel Needham, Moonwell's old man, who lived in a cottage on the moors. Though people claimed he was over a hundred years old, he still had most of his faculties. He raised his long wizened face toward the oak beams, his white hair trailing over his collar, and began to sing in a strong, clear nasal voice:

60

Three brave lads went walking when the sun it was high,
Swore they'd find Harry Moony and poke in his eye.

"Here's the chorus now, join in if you like:

Go down Harry Moony, harry us no more,
We've flowers to please you, to leave at your door.
Three brave lads went walking, went into the wood.
They found Harry Moony while the light it was good . . .
Go down Harry Moony . . .

He sang, but only the landlord joined in. The old man went on, smiling oddly to himself:

Three brave lads they chopped him up, limb from limb.
They rolled him down where the light it was dim . . .
Three brave lads went walking when the moon it was new.
They went back to see if their victory was true . . .
They heard Harry Moony laugh to wake the dead,
'Tha boys have my eyes but tha'll give me tha heads' . . .
One brave lad put his head down the hole.
Harry Moony he's got it, his head and his soul . . .
Two brave lads bolt their doors and locks,
But bolt and lock open to the dead man's knock . . .
'Who's that knocking? Let me hear tha hollo!'
'Tis tha friend come a-calling with nowt in his collar . . .
Jump out the window and run like a hare.
There's nowhere to hide but Harry Moony hears where . . .
Two brave lads leave their heads down below.
Two bodies walking and one more to go . . .
Old moon's a-laughing and showing his teeth.
Harry Moony he's coming from his grave beneath . . .
The priest's in the well and the night's in the sun.
And nobody leaves till Harry Moony is done.
Go down Harry Moony, harry us no more,
We've flowers to please you, to leave at your door.

Eustace came back to himself with a start. He couldn't have said how the song affected him, but it had made him forget where he was. There was a little applause, but few people seemed to have cared for the song; some looked

61

offended. As Billy Bell reached the stage at last, Diana came over to Eustace. "Father O'Connell and I want you to know we enjoyed your act so far. We could see the problems you were facing."

"Thanks," he mumbled, and was suddenly shyer than ever. Whatever instinct let him pretend in front of an audience that he wasn't shy had deserted him. He'd no chance of winning back this audience, and what would they think of him for trying? There were too many people in the pub whom he'd have to meet in the course of his work. The idea of having to face them after he'd made even more of a fool of himself was unbearable. He shoved himself out of the corner, looking anywhere but at Phoebe, and struggled to the door.

Outside he discovered how drunk he was. Most of a face appeared to be rolling about the sky above the moors, grinning at him. He stumbled home and fell into bed, and woke next morning with the sense that a joke had been played on him. The whole evening had been a joke, but he couldn't turn it into one that would make him laugh. He groped his way through the dawning streets to sort the delivery, wondering what tricks the day had in store for him. When he heard about the sheep, he thought at first that it was a sick joke.

=== 11 ===

Craig tried to keep his temper as they left the One-Armed Soldier. He'd felt like leaving once Eustace had been driven out, but Hazel and Benedict had wanted to stay to the end. The bearded youth with the guitar had received polite applause, but most of the audience had obviously been waiting for the last act, a Christian duo with an array of instruments and joyful messages. Craig resented the way they seemed to assume they had the greatest right to take the stage. He would have said so if Hazel and Benedict hadn't been with friends.

Hazel had met them at the new Christian shop, where she was helping. Mel held out his large moist hands whenever he wanted to make a point, his wife Ursula nodding her head at every claim he made. Both were bubbling over with joy, and Craig had had enough of them long before they reached the Eddingses' cottage, where Hazel had invited her friends for coffee. Halfway along the High Street he said, "You seem to have had a good time this evening."

"Didn't you?" Ursula cried. "I thought it was super."

"I enjoyed the comedian, the first one. I rather felt some of you were glad to see the back of him."

"I certainly was," Benedict said. "Moonwell can do without that sort of thing."

"Can't do without a postman though, can it? I wouldn't blame him if he decided Moonwell could."

"You wouldn't blame him?" Mel said, drooping a shoulder toward Craig. "Surely you would. It's up to all of us to blame him, to show him where he's gone wrong."

Craig breathed heavily rather than argue when he'd had so much to drink, but Vera spoke up. "You don't usually go into pubs, do you, any of you new people? Were you there tonight to spoil his show?"

"You can't spoil something that's already worthless," Benedict said.

"You were, weren't you. You went in there meaning to destroy him."

"Oh, really, now, I don't think so," Ursula said brightly. "He must be a pretty poor comedian if one failure destroys him. I hope it'll teach him to make the kind of jokes we can all laugh at. But you must remember that he went on stage tonight meaning to destroy our faith in God."

"I should think God and your faith can look after themselves. You near as damn it took over the pub so that the people who weren't on your side would be too embarrassed to laugh."

"No, no," Mel said as gently as a sickbed visitor. "The people are already with us, as you saw. They've realized they need God, not His enemies."

"Such as us, you mean," Craig growled.

"Mummy isn't, not deep in her heart," Hazel said, almost

63

pleading. "And neither would you be if you'd just take time to think."

For a moment Craig wanted to take her hand, squeeze it to let her know she shouldn't worry about him, especially not when he was trying not to worry about her. Mel and Ursula began to murmur a hymn, and the Eddingses joined in. They were still singing when they reached the cottage on the moorland road.

Craig slumped in a chair in the front room, under a mass-produced painting of Christ holding out his hands, a tasteful dab of blood on each palm. It was the lack of any painterly feeling that offended Craig, the assumption that any kind of representation ought to be enough to provoke an automatic response. He hoped Benedict had bought the painting, not Hazel.

Mel and Ursula sat down in the corner seat, and Mel read Craig's face as he looked away from the painting. "Aren't you at all spiritual?" Mel said.

"Put me down as a don't know if you like."

"Christ doesn't allow neutrality. Anyone who isn't with Him is against Him." He held out his hands as if he were offering Craig something large yet weightless. "Can you really search your heart and say there isn't emptiness where there should be faith?"

"Emptiness is good enough for me."

Mel turned to Vera. "Hazel said you were more of a believer. We believers have a duty to show others the right path."

"I believe in Pascal's wager."

"Pardon?"

"The philosopher who argued that since the existence of God can't be proved it's worth betting he exists, because if he doesn't you've lost nothing but if he does you've gained, well, whatever you've gained."

"That's sophistry masquerading as faith. The only way to believe in God is let Him rule your life."

"I think we're a bit old for that," Craig said. "We don't feel the need to be constantly told what to do."

Benedict carried in a trayful of mugs of coffee. "Some people might think that's what you want to do to us."

"What do you mean, Benedict, some people?" Suddenly

Craig wanted to get the inevitable confrontation over with. "If you've something to say, spit it out. What do you feel you're a victim of?"

Benedict set the tray down carefully next to a pile of tracts. "Excuse me. Thank you," he said as he passed the mugs round, and then he blinked at Craig. "Well, I think you need to accept the way Hazel's grown up. And I think you'd like to tell me how to run my business."

"If Vera and I were going to lend you the money you asked for we'd have wanted to."

"I suppose that's fair, to let you make suggestions, anyway."

"I said if, Benedict. If we'd been going to lend you the money."

Hazel tried to steady her mug with both hands, winced at the heat and put down the mug on the hearth. "Aren't you going to?" she said, her voice a little too high.

"We don't know how much we'll have to spare, if anything," Vera said. "We don't know where we'll be living. Not in Moonwell if it carries on the way it's going."

"What way is that?" Benedict demanded. "All Godwin wants to do is make a little piece of the world free of crime and sin and corruption. He can do it here because we're so cut off, safe from outside influences. Surely even you can't say that's not worth doing."

"Even who?" Craig felt his chest stiffening with anger. "Even someone as sinful as us? Perhaps now you see why we wouldn't feel welcome."

"Oh, Daddy, you know you're both always welcome," Hazel pleaded, but Benedict interrupted: "You haven't told me what you don't like about my business methods."

"Don't be so sure you'd want to hear. I'll tell you one thing we don't care for, and that's the way you use Hazel to try and drum up customers. We've heard some of the abuse she's had to put up with, and no wonder, the way you expect her to play on people's fears to sell your damned alarms."

"I don't mind, Daddy, really I don't. It's my duty to help."

"Oh, for Christ's sake, Hazel, when did you turn into such a bloody prig?" Craig demanded, and gritted his teeth as if he could bite back what he'd said. "I'm sorry, I didn't mean to say that. Put it down to the drink."

"I forgive you."

Craig gritted his teeth harder. "What's wrong?" Benedict asked lightly. "She said she forgives you."

"Yes, because your friend Mann says she has to, am I right? You're forgiving me because it's your duty, Hazel, isn't that so? It's got nothing to do with my loving you or your loving me or anything else that's real." He turned on Benedict. "I'll tell you what's wrong with your kind of forgiveness—it suppresses the feelings you'd have if you were honest with yourself. I thought religion was supposed to bring peace, that's the one way it might have got to me at my age, but if I lived around your forgiveness for any length of time I'd end up with an ulcer. Now, if you'll excuse me, I'm very tired and I've already said too much." Nevertheless he halted in the doorway. "As far as your business problems are concerned, I should think you ought to trust God to provide."

He labored upstairs to the bathroom and splashed water on his face, glared at himself in the mirror as he brushed his teeth. When he went into the bedroom with its twin folding beds, Vera was waiting for him. "I said we'd leave in the morning," she told him in a small voice.

"We've given up on Moonwell, have we?"

"I couldn't have stood it much longer, either." But when she came back from the bathroom, put out the light, and climbed into her shaky bed, her voice was unsteadier. "I just hope he won't stop her from coming to visit us," she murmured. "She's still Hazel, however she's changed. I still want to see her. Damn old age for not letting us drive the way we could once."

When she was asleep, Craig lay hearing what she'd said. Why couldn't he have kept quiet downstairs instead of trying to win an argument that led nowhere? The thought of Godwin Mann and his followers enraged him, the woman who'd taken the stage after Eustace most of all. Humor was a calculated technique they were using, like their imitations of every form of popular song. How could Hazel be taken in by them? Where had he and Vera gone wrong?

He felt clumsy and vulnerable, and perhaps that was why he dreamed he was. He found himself back in his childhood, found himself driven to do things for a dare he didn't even want to do. He was climbing down the rope into the disused mineshaft on the moor above Moonwell, but this time he knew what would happen, and so he was struggling to make his hands drag him up out of the dark while there was still a chance. He'd just managed to halt his descent by gripping the rope with his arms and legs when the knot that fastened the rope to a rock came loose.

He didn't fall far. Rough stone thumped the breath out of him. His friend's face appeared at the top of the shaft as if at the wrong end of a telescope, shouting that he'd go for help, and then Craig was left lying, bruised and breathless, deep in the dark that seemed to be gathering like mud in his lungs. He couldn't breathe because he knew what came next, and now he could feel it coming: something reaching for him along the tunnels of the abandoned mine, something that would drag him into the dark until he could be dragged no further, until his shoulders were wedged and his head was poking helplessly into the blackest dark. Now that was where he was, his shoulders crushed together so that he couldn't move, and whatever had dragged him there was reaching for his head. He woke with his face in the pillow, suffocating.

At least that muffled his cry. He sat up then, to free himself of the dream. Of course none of the worst had happened, he'd been rescued before it could have. It wouldn't have happened anyway, he had just been a frightened child. He must have dreamed about it now because of the song he'd heard in the pub, though he couldn't remember having heard the song before. He got stiffly to his feet and tiptoed to the window, to let the view take the place of the dream.

He pushed back one curtain so that moonlight spread into the room but stopped short of Vera's bed. He turned back to the window to find out why the moonlight was flickering, lapping the carpet. He looked up, and then he craned forward, banging his forehead on the pane. The moor was on fire.

How could fire be so white? For a moment he thought it was mist or gas, except that it moved like neither. The edge of the moor looked more charred than ever, and white flames were dancing on the stone, on the heather and the grass. Then the flames reddened and leaped higher, and Craig was shoving himself away from the window to raise the alarm when he heard a fire engine heading for the moor. He watched until the edge of the moor was still again, not even a hint of smoke under the remains of the moon, and then he went back to bed.

In the morning he learned that someone unknown had started a fire up there. The fire had driven a flock of sheep through the tents, injuring two of Mann's followers. Several of the animals had plunged straight into the unwalled cave above which Mann had held his rally. Benedict recounted all this in a tone that seemed almost to imply that Craig and Vera were somehow culpable. Apart from that, he said very little as he drove them back to Sheffield, and Craig had nothing to distract him from feeling that he shouldn't have let himself be forced out of Moonwell, though it was certainly too late now. He kept remembering that first sight of flames that had looked white as ash—white as the moon.

12

The PTA meeting seemed more than ever like a class for adults, but they weren't treated as such. As Diana followed Sally's father into the assembly hall, Mrs. Scragg remarked, "Now we can start, I suppose," as if Diana should have spent less time in discussing children with their parents. Diana took her place at the trestle table on the stage, and Mrs. Scragg slapped the table with the heel of her hand, sending a dull echo across the crowded hall. "I hope you all know what happened by the cave," she thundered.

Perhaps she didn't mean to sound accusing, but quite a few people looked away from her. "I don't know who the terrorists and vandals are who'd stoop to cruelty to dumb animals, but they'd better stay away from my husband and I if they know what's good for them. And they'd better realize it'll take more than them setting fire to the moor to drive Godwin Mann out of our lives."

She grabbed the edge of the table with both red-knuckled

hands and hitched herself forward at the parents. "Now I'll tell you what me and my husband have done to help our new friends—we've invited two of them to stay in our house for as long as they're in Moonwell. Let the cowards try to harm them now. I hope every one of you will do the same, at least all of you that own your own homes."

If that was intended to exclude Diana, that was fine by her. Mrs. Scragg sat back, snorting for emphasis, and Mr. Scragg cleared his throat minutely. "Before we move on to the rest of the business, are there any comments?" he said.

A hand waved toward the back of the hall. "Mr. Milman," Mr. Scragg acknowledged.

"I appreciate the points you were making, Mrs. Scragg, but—"

Mrs. Scragg frowned at him as if she'd never seen him before. "Stand up now or we'll not be able to hear you."

He stood up awkwardly, leaning on the folding seat in front of him. "I was saying that of course I don't approve of trying to drive people out that way, but I do think it's understandable if there's a bit of resentment about. I mean, nobody asked for the town to be changed overnight. My family and I go to church every Sunday, and we don't need to be made to feel that isn't enough."

Several people were nodding agreement, even murmuring. Perhaps this time, Diana thought, they'd speak up for themselves. "Nobody asked Mary and Joseph if they wanted to have the Christ child," Mrs. Scragg said. "If all you're wanting is to cry over the spilt milk, Mr. Milkman, I think we'll be getting on with the business of the meeting."

"It isn't all, as a matter of fact." Mr. Milman stood up straighter. "I was saying to Miss Kramer that some of your new pupils have been giving our Kirsty nightmares."

Mr. Scragg sat up on the two cushions that added height to his chair. "And what did Miss Kramer say to you?"

"She said I ought to raise the question here."

"Did she now. I hope so," Mrs. Scragg said tightly. "And how are our new friends supposed to be giving the girl nightmares?"

"By telling her the devil will get her if she doesn't confess every silly little wrong she does. Why, they even wanted her to tell Miss Kramer she'd fallen asleep one night before

69

saying her prayers. I admire Miss Kramer and I know she wouldn't want to hear that sort of thing. They've got Kirsty having nightmares about something walking down the moonlight and growing bigger and heaven knows what else. That's not what she comes to school to learn."

"If I could just explain," one of Mann's followers said. "We believe in helping one another. A sin confessed is a burden shared. Our children are only trying to help yours. Maybe you should ask yourself if God is sending your child nightmares to show where she's gone wrong."

"I'll tell you what, I know my child a damn sight better than your children do, and I don't think I'm the only one who feels that way." He glanced quickly about the noncommittal faces. "Isn't that so?"

The murmurs of assent were muted and difficult to locate. Mrs. Scragg smirked at him. "You'll have to face up to it, not all children are as perfect as yours. I reckon I'm speaking for most of us here when I say that anything we can do to improve them is worth doing."

"Not much chance of improvement with the size of your classes now," Jeremy Booth said. "You can't expect children to do their best when they're sitting two to a desk."

"They cope well enough in my class and my husband's." Mrs. Scragg craned her neck, and found him. "You aren't even a parent. What do you mean by pretending you are?"

"He's here on behalf of Andrew's parents," Diana said.

Mrs. Scragg didn't even glance at her. "Let's be hearing from someone who's got the right to speak. Who's going to speak up for the school? Our new friends will be thinking they were wrong about us."

"You have to have rules," Mr. Clegg, the greengrocer, said shyly, "even rules that don't make sense. When the children grow up they'll have to obey laws that may not make sense to them either."

Diana thought of some of the Scraggs' rules—no trousers for girls in the winter; no juice for the children to drink at lunchtime, only hot water. "Aren't you talking about training people never to want to change anything? Too much of that and we'd be training them not to think."

"They aren't here to think, they're here to learn." Mrs. Scragg looked pleased with her turn of phrase. "I want a

70

show of hands now; you've all heard the arguments. You know people who aren't even brave enough to show their faces are doing things you never thought you'd see in our town, just because they don't want to be told they're sinners like the rest of us. Now then, with all that going on, who wants to see less discipline here at the school?"

"That wasn't what we were talking about," Kirsty's father protested.

"It may not be what you wanted to talk about, but there are other children besides yours to be considered. If she keeps on having nightmares you'd best get her to the doctor. Now then, does anybody want to make our new friends feel unwelcome because they act like Christians?" Mrs. Scragg snorted when there was no response. "So who isn't happy about the discipline?"

Kirsty's father and Jeremy raised their hands at once; a few others went up tentatively. Parents were glancing surreptitiously about to see if there was enough of a response for their own not to be singled out and deciding against responding. "Not many of you," Mr. Scragg said, slapping his small hands together. "If anybody wants a word with me afterward, I'll be waiting."

But after the meeting, the rest of which was uneventful, several parents came into Diana's classroom to tell her how much they preferred her teaching to the rest of the school. Presumably they were too afraid for their children to have spoken up at the meeting. "We were thinking of moving to Manchester anyway," Kirsty's father told her, and suddenly that seemed a world away.

She walked home feeling slow and dull. The moon was out of sight behind a sharp-edged frieze of chimneys. Beyond the forest an airliner glinted like a fly, its sound out of all proportion to its apparent size. She let herself into her cottage, away from the rumbling dark, and made for bed.

She slept dreamlessly, wakened feeling refreshed and optimistic. After all, Mann and his followers would move on once he'd achieved his token victory over paganism, and she could carry on treating her pupils the way she felt they should be treated once Mann's young mouthpieces weren't there to tell tales. She'd already achieved quite a lot with her regular class, despite the Scraggs. She felt far more capable as the sun chased the shadows back under the cottages, and when she saw Mr. Scragg beckoning her curtly from the window of his office, she marched straight in.

He pushed a typewritten sheet across his desk to her. "For your immediate attention."

It was an undertaking not to teach moral or religious matters except in the manner specified by the headmaster. The teaching generally should take a Christian view of history and life today, should ensure that the children behaved like Christians to one another . . . She read on, noting misspellings and jumping letters. "What do you want me to do with this?" she said.

Mr. Scragg gazed blankly at her. "Sign it, please."

"I don't think you can ask me to do that. It isn't in my contract of employment."

His small face seemed to harden beneath the bristling gray eyebrows, yet when he spoke his voice was almost lilting. "In that case I have to tell you that this school no longer needs your services," he said.

13

As Saturday wore on, June grew impatient with Andrew. At last she gave him some Christian stickers to put up around the shop, but when he tried to climb into the display window, she threw up her hands. "What do you want to do, knock everything down? Try and have the sense God gave you," she cried, and Brian intervened: "Come on, son, you can help me in the back."

In fact there wasn't much to do in the long narrow room that smelled of boots and rope and cold Primus stoves. "What do you want to do, son?" Brian murmured.

The boy peered timidly up at him from under his eyebrows that were hardly there at all. "I can read to you."

"You've already done that for your mother. You don't

need to do any more today," Brian said, and saw Andrew suck in his hollow cheeks with disappointment. "All right, if you want to."

The boy scampered into the shop, shouting, "Daddy says I can read to him." Brian felt ashamed of himself, wished again that he'd attended the open night and talked to Andrew's teacher. He would have except that since the rally at the cave he'd been reluctant to show his face in public.

Since the rally he'd seen women looking in the shop window and pretending they weren't talking about him. Once he'd overheard a murmur about the things his poor wife had to put up with, the things he forced her to do. He'd wanted to tell them he hadn't touched June since the rally. He wouldn't while she didn't want him to, however frustrating it was for him, but he couldn't tell anyone that. No doubt the town thought even worse of him because he was too ashamed to invite one of Godwin's followers to take refuge in the house.

At least June was no longer taking Valium. Godwin's religion had done that for her. Perhaps in time she would be more patient with Andrew. He wished he could be more patient himself. Sometimes when it was just himself and Andrew he didn't feel so bad.

But when Andrew began to read him a pamphlet he couldn't help wincing inwardly whenever the boy misread a word. "Not 'Ice-ache'," he said, trying to be gentle. "You don't want to grow up not being able to read or write properly, do you? You don't want to have to work down a mine because you can't get anything better, stay down there all day in the dark."

When Andrew tried "Ice-aka" Brian wanted to shake the stupidity out of him. "It's Isaac, damn it, Isaac. See if you can read just one line without making a fool of yourself."

Andrew almost read the last sentence right, about how God wanted every child to obey his parents and teachers and anyone in uniform. He gave his father one quick pleading glance, which made Brian feel awkward and embarrassed. "That was better," he muttered. "Come on, I'll take you to watch the football for trying."

Wind herded clouds across the sun; racing shadows molded themselves to the slopes. As Brian and Andrew walked down the steepening streets to the edge of town, the wind carried the smell of charred vegetation from the moor above Moonwell. "Would Isaac's daddy really have killed him?" Andrew said.

"It's only a story, son, to show you how to behave. Or if it's true it happened a long time ago."

"Would you kill me if God said you had to?"

"Nobody's going to tell me to kill you. Now, stop being morbid and watch the game."

Two teams were playing five-a-side in the field that the school also used. Fathers and sons and old men smoking pipes stood outside the white lines, shouting. "Pass it, pass the ball," Brian yelled. "Oh, you silly bugger." When Andrew flinched, he gripped the boy's shoulder. "I'm not shouting at you. You can shout too." But Andrew stood staring, even when the ball rolled almost to his feet. "Go on, son, kick it," Brian cried.

The players were yelling at him too. "Kick it as hard as you can, son. You're not a girl," Brian told him, and the boy lurched forward. He gave the ball a glancing kick, slipped in the mud, and fell.

Brian led him home, with Andrew holding out his muddy arms on either side of his body. In the bathroom he waited for his father to undress him. "Can't you even do that for yourself?" Brian growled, embarrassed by having to touch the boy's pale skin, his penis that was shrinking back into his scrotum as if it didn't want to be seen. He needn't feel guilty, he told himself; June was embarrassed now too whenever she saw the boy naked. He ignored Andrew's protests that the bath was too hot, hauled him out when the boy lay there saying that his fingertips looked like raisins, and eventually got him dry and dressed and back to the shop.

June raised her eyes heavenward. "Where are the clothes you were wearing? What have you been up to now?"

"Someone kicked a ball at him and he fell down, love. His clothes are in the washer. He's got to get dirty sometimes if he's going to be a proper boy."

"You're no better. Look at your shoes. You don't have to roll in the mud to prove you're men, do you?" June was smiling wryly. "Never mind, Andrew, at least there are some decent children for you to play with now, not like the ones who always tease you."

"I'd rather play with you and Daddy."

"Would you?" June hugged him. "Then we will. It's about

74

time we were more of a family. I'm glad you care more for us than for your so-called friends at the bookshop."

"I think they've been pretty good friends to us all," Brian intervened.

"Oh, do you? Well, I'll tell you what I think—" She checked herself. "But not in front of Andrew, and not while we've got a customer."

A young woman was looking in the window, comparing prices. As Brian hurried Andrew into the storeroom, she came into the shop, and Brian caught a glimpse of her: large breasts, long, bare suntanned arms and legs. "Broke my flask this morning," she told June. "I'll take that green one in the window."

"You can count these for me, son," Brian murmured, opening a carton of bootlaces. He heard June say, "Have you walked far?"

"Ten miles this morning. Hey, don't think me rude, but don't go putting any of those stickers on my flask, will you? If God wants me to carry his advertising he'll have to pay me. I didn't think we had towns like this in England, God in every window."

"It's a pity there aren't a few more towns like this. Haven't you any time at all for God?"

"I've just walked away from that and my parents. Told them I was going walking for a fortnight and they mustn't ask me where. What do you call this town anyway?"

"Moonwell."

"Can't say I've heard of it. Must have overlooked it on the map. Thanks for the flask. Listen, I hope I didn't offend you with my big mouth."

"I don't matter. It's God you should worry about, and yourself. And you should think of your parents. At least let them know where you are."

"It isn't that simple," the young woman said, and Brian heard her striding away from the counter, her haversack jiggling. He imagined her bottom swaying in the tight denim shorts, her pert face that he'd glimpsed, her wide moist lips. His penis had hardened as soon as she'd mentioned her big mouth.

"What's wrong, Daddy?" Andrew said. Brian opened his eyes, quieted his breathing, and suddenly saw his chance. He had to take it, had to escape the room that had grown hot and stifling. "I've dropped some money down by the football field," he said, and as soon as he heard the shop door close, went out to tell June.

The young woman was turning the corner of Moorland Lane as he came out of the shop. She was going straight up to the moor, then, not following the main road. Realizing where she was going excited him, though he couldn't have said why. He strolled along casually to Moorland Lane, and as soon as she was out of sight on the path the side street led to, he paced to the end, to wait until she reached the moor.

A loose stone came rattling down the slope as she climbed over the edge. Brian glanced along the terraces of cottages before stepping onto the path. Nobody was about, and the street was still deserted when he reached the top. He poked his head over the edge. The young woman was striding along the path that would take her past the cave.

She was alone on the moor, or thought she was. Nobody would see or hear. Nobody would, because Brian wasn't going to do anything, only imagine what he could do. Your thoughts were your own, whatever Godwin Mann might say—Brian felt as if they were the only place he could hide and be himself. Nobody would see if he crept up behind her, unheard because of the blustering wind. He could imagine how she would struggle, how hard it would be to pin her muscular limbs. It occurred to him that all the excitement had gone out of his marriage once June always gave in to him.

As soon as the young woman was out of sight, Brian scurried across the moor. Nothing grew now between the edge where the path climbed over and the stone that surrounded the cave. Here and there charred stubs of heather stuck up from the oily black ash that squeaked underfoot. He couldn't do anything to her, he realized, because Godwin Mann came to the cave to pray every afternoon about now. All the same, he trod quietly as he paced up to the rim of the stone bowl.

The young woman was squatting at the edge of the pothole and shading her eyes to peer down. There was no sign of Godwin Mann. The sight of her, alone there at the edge of the dark, made Brian's heart pound. The wind had dropped, and he felt as if he were at the exact center of a silence as motionless and chill and deep as the cave. He felt as if the silence were seeping into him, emptying him of himself. He'd

76

begun to move his limbs stealthily, for what purpose he no longer knew, when the ash caught in his throat.

The instant he coughed he knew what was going to happen. He lurched forward into the bowl, desperate to prevent it if he could. The young woman glanced up at the sound of his cough, and made to get up as she saw him coming. She blinked, frowned, jerked her head back, her wide mouth stiffening. She was shoving herself to her feet, away from the rim, when her feet slipped and she fell.

He hadn't even time to stretch out his hands uselessly toward her. One moment she was on the edge, the next the stone was bare. Her scream plummeted into the dark and was cut short by a thud. After that there was silence except for the sound of a heavy object sliding further downward amid a shrill rattling of stones.

Brian had to force himself to go to the edge. He was terrified of falling after her. Eventually he crawled to the rim of the cave on hands and knees, feeling as if once he got there he wouldn't be able to crawl back. Silence and darkness filled the shaft, as if she had never been there at all. For a moment he thought he heard an object being dragged away somewhere, but that couldn't be below him, even if that was how it sounded. He scrabbled backward from the edge and was halfway up the bowl before he dared stumble to his feet. He turned away, sickened by the sight of the empty stone throat, and ran toward Moonwell.

He hadn't meant to harm her. She shouldn't have put herself in danger. All he'd wanted was—but he couldn't think now what he'd wanted. She must have been killed instantly, like the sheep, but he ran to the police station in case there was a chance she was alive. "I think someone's fallen in the cave," he panted.

The sergeant at the front desk of the small limestone building near the square reached for the pen behind his inky ear. "How long ago? How sure are you?"

"I was just up there walking. I saw someone go down to the cave and then I heard them scream. When I got there there was nobody. I've run straight here from there."

The sergeant was dialing the rescue team. "Man or woman?"

"I couldn't tell you. I only saw them for a moment against the sun."

When the questions were over, Brian ran back to the moor, hating himself for being tempted to wish she weren't rescued, because if she were brought up alive she might recognize him, contradict his story. One man went down, but as far as his light reached, it showed nothing. Brian retreated as soon as he could, afraid that he was going to be sick.

June gasped when she saw him, gasped again when he told her what he'd told the police. "I couldn't find the money," he said, realizing too late that the footballers might know he hadn't gone back to the field, "so I went for a walk to settle myself."

She was more sympathetic to him than he felt he deserved. She kept Andrew away from him, made him sit and rest that evening to recover from what must appear to be shock. When a policeman rang the doorbell, Brian felt pinned in his chair. But the police only wanted him to know that no sound had been heard from the cave, and nobody had been reported missing. Nevertheless Godwin Mann was going to hold an overnight vigil above the cave, so that if anyone was alive down there he or she was certain to be heard.

Later Brian lay awake, dreading the ring at the doorbell in the middle of the night and trying to define what else he was afraid of. He kept seeing the young woman falling, kept running toward her with his useless hands outstretched; his arms would never stretch far enough. "As God is my judge, I didn't want you to," he whispered. He slept at last, only to be wakened by the sensation of wearing a mask. It was the moonlight on his face. He turned away from the light, but couldn't turn away from a thought so vague as to be disturbing: that in some way, by praying at the cave Godwin Mann was making things worse.

14

On Sunday Mann called a rally at the cave. Geraldine heard hymns as she picked flowers behind the bookshop. At that distance she found the hymns moving; they made the town sound like a church. They felt appropriate as she strolled with Jeremy to the far end of the town, to the church where Jonathan's grave would be.

That had to be what her vision meant, the gravestone she'd seen in the moonlight, the stone with Jonathan's name. She'd gazed at it until the cold had driven her away, but it hadn't changed or vanished. It was real, or would be. She would make it real.

She'd wanted to tell Jeremy her vision when she'd run home in the moonlight, but Benedict had been tinkering with the alarm. The next morning she'd wakened anxious to see Jonathan's grave in Sheffield—she didn't know what she might find there. But when they'd driven to Sheffield that evening, the gravestone was still there.

Jonathan had been telling her he didn't want to be so far away. He wanted to be buried in Moonwell. She'd gone to the superintendent of cemeteries and stifled her impatience with all the paperwork, tried not to feel too disappointed that Jonathan might not be in Moonwell in time for his birthday. Jeremy assumed that she wanted the grave moved so that she could visit it more easily, and she didn't enlighten him: he might ask questions that she didn't want to ask herself, make Jonathan feel threatened. Besides, he was worrying about Diana Kramer, worrying that he'd made the situation at the school worse for her by speaking up.

They were passing the school now on their way to the churchyard. "Don't worry, she's going to see her union next week," she said, and took his hand as they approached the church.

The newly oiled gate opened silently. Geraldine remembered the silence and the moonlight, the feeling that the light had turned into white ice. She laid the flowers at the edge of the new graves, where Jonathan's would be. "Be seeing you, Jonathan," she murmured, and Jeremy squeezed her hand.

That made her feel secretive, unfair to him. Her doubts preoccupied her all the way home through the deserted town, and he didn't try to make her talk. She was still debating with herself halfway through dinner, when Andrew knocked at the door. "My mum says I have to give this back," he told her, and fled.

It was a book of fairy tales illustrated by Maurice Sendak. "What's wrong with it?" Jeremy wondered, leafing through unhappily. "I can't see anything even Godwin Mann could object to."

"We'll find Andrew something else tomorrow," Geraldine said, to cheer him up. But the next day was when Godwin Mann came to the shop.

It was almost Monday lunchtime, and they hadn't had a customer. They'd spent the morning rearranging some of the display, moving books about the Peaks to the table by the door, children's books to the far end of the shop. They'd hardly finished when June and another woman marched in. "Tell them what you told me," June said, then faltered. "They've hidden them, hidden the children's books."

"I can see it." Her companion, a lanky young woman with gray hair straggling out of a hairband, strode up the aisle between the tables. "This is what I meant. They don't let children read this where I come from."

She'd grabbed Maurice Sendak's *In the Night Kitchen*. June cried out in disgust at the page she was displaying. "I thought that kind of thing was supposed to be against the law."

"What kind of thing, June?" Geraldine asked quietly.

"Children exposing themselves. And you gave a book by this man to our Andrew. If I'd known what you were up to I'd never have let him near you."

"Now, June, this isn't like you," Jeremy said. "The little boy in the book has a penis, that's all. Little boys do have them."

"Maybe, but they don't show them to people, not in our town." June's eyes narrowed. "How come you know so much about little boys? I've often wondered why you were so interested in Andrew."

"I know about them because I used to be one."

Geraldine couldn't contain herself. "We've been showing interest in Andrew because he needed someone to, June, and it's about time you realized."

"The only people he needs are his parents," June said furiously, and fell silent as Godwin Mann strode into the shop.

He looked paler than ever, his face pared down, cheekbones thrusting forward as if his skin were being stretched by his struggle to arrive wherever he was going. "Look what they're selling to children, Godwin," June's companion cried. "They've books like this where the altar should be."

"Thank God I was called here in time." Mann sank to his knees in front of the children's books. "Forgive them, O Lord, for they don't know what they're doing. Jeremy and Geraldine aren't bad people, they don't mean to drive You out of Your house . . ."

Jeremy stooped to him. "Don't think I'm rude, but this isn't a church any more, it's a bookshop."

Mann gazed heavenward. "Nobody has the right to cast You out of a house You've been invited into, least of all one that was built for You."

"It's not just a bookshop, actually, it's our home. You can see the deeds if you like."

"We can see the evidence of your deeds right here, Jeremy." Mann crossed himself and stood up, looking saddened. "There's no more time for argument. Time is running short. Won't you invite God back into His house and into your lives?"

"Time's running short for what?" Geraldine said.

The evangelist looked suddenly wary. "I should like to tell you, but not until you've asked God back into His house."

"Then we'll do without knowing," Jeremy said.

Mann glanced at him, then made for the door. "If you won't let God's love reach you, perhaps you won't be able to ignore your neighbors." He stood on the pavement and called out, more loudly than he had at the rally. "Come and see the devil's church. Come and see the evil that's been festering in your midst."

"Damned fool," Jeremy muttered. "As for you, June, if

you're ashamed of how you used to carry on that's your affair, but you shouldn't take it out on us. I'd appreciate it if you'd just go away now."

"I've nothing to be ashamed of since I've been forgiven. You can't get rid of me that easily, nor these people either."

Several of their neighbors had come out of houses or shops and were converging on the bookshop. "What's the row?" the baker, a balding man with floury eyebrows, said.

"They're trying to make out we're a dirty bookshop, Mr. Mellor," Geraldine said, forcing a laugh. "I'll bet you didn't realize that was the sort of place you buy your wife her books."

"Why should anyone want to make that out?"

"Because every foothold you leave for evil in your town gives it more strength," Mann said behind him. "Now that we're winning it has to be more determined than ever. Why else do you think there was a fire on the moor?"

June brought Mr. Mellor the Sendak picture book. "This is the sort of thing they sell to children. This is what we let into our town because we didn't listen to Mrs. Scragg."

The other neighbors crowded round, making disgusted noises. Nearly all of them had given house room to Mann's followers, Geraldine realized, but even so—"I didn't realize," Mr. Mellor said. "A book is a guest you invite into your house, after all, and you don't expect guests to suddenly start being offensive."

"For heaven's sake, that's a book by a respected American artist."

Several people turned on Jeremy. "We know all about artists," one sneered.

Jeremy moved quickly to intercept Mann, who was stalking toward the children's books. "What are you up to now?"

"Ask yourself what Christ would have done if He'd found such things being sold in the temple."

"You lay a finger on those books unless you mean to buy them and you'll find yourself leaving very suddenly."

All the neighbors except Mr. Mellor ran to Mann's aid. "Don't you dare touch him," screeched the woman from the wool shop. "He's a man of God."

Mann held up one hand. "Thank you, my friends, but violence won't be necessary. I think I may be able to shame

Jeremy and Geraldine into realizing what they've been doing."

He strode off to the Christian shop. Mr. Mellor blinked uneasily at the others, then sidled out, back to the bakery. June went to scrutinize the shelves, and the others joined her. "So long as you mean to buy something," Jeremy said, but even when he repeated it they ignored him. They were still pawing at the shelves when Mann came back.

He marched straight to the children's books and seized the copies of *In the Night Kitchen*. "And I see *Lolita* and some drug books over there. If there's anything else that your town doesn't need, just show me where it is."

"Put those down and get out of here," Jeremy said in a quiet stiff voice, "or I'll call the police."

"They'd think that pretty strange, you calling them because someone was buying your books. Here's fifty pounds to start with and if we go over that, just tell me."

He slapped the notes down on the children's table and set off to search. Soon all his helpers were carrying piles of books: Henry Miller, William Burroughs, Von Daniken, *The Joy of Sex, A Handbook of Witchcraft, Life on Earth, A Child's Book of English Folklore* . . ."You won't get much change out of two hundred," Jeremy said, and Mann's followers stared at him contemptuously while Mann paid him the balance.

The evangelist picked up the largest pile of books and led out his helpers. As soon as they'd dumped the books in the gutter outside the shop, he emptied a tin of lighter fuel over the books and set fire to them. They caught with a whoof that brought more people out of their houses. "Shall I call the fire brigade?" an old lady cried.

"We're just burning some filth they were selling in the bookshop," June told her. "Do you know, they made Godwin pay for every book. That's money that could have been given to God."

"Maybe you should realize books that sell as well as those just did are worth reordering," Jeremy shouted, then turned away, furious with himself for having been provoked. Geraldine watched until the fire died down and Mann and his helpers left the ashes to scatter. "There they go," Jeremy muttered, "the true faces of small-town life."

"They're not like that really. I wouldn't be surprised if they apologize to us once Mann goes away, if not before."

"You've more faith in them than I have. Small-town minds that want to reduce everything to what they can cope with. The good minds go to university or just get out as soon as they can."

"I know how you feel, Jerry, but—"

"I wonder if you do know. You don't seem to care as much about our shop as you used to." His anger changed the subject. "My God, that American talks about evil, but that's evil if anything is, people trying to suppress anything they find disturbing, as if shoving it out of sight will make it go away."

"You know I still care about our shop." He meant she'd been preoccupied, but this was certainly not the time to explain about Jonathan. For the rest of the day, whenever she heard footsteps in the street she grew tense, thinking that it might be another invasion of the faithful or one of them returning to apologize. However, when closing time dragged round, nobody else had come into the shop.

Later she went out for a walk with Jeremy, though not until it was almost dark; she didn't want to meet any of the neighbors. Oily scraps of ash whispered in the gutter. She felt as if she'd been barred from all the lit houses. The High Street was deserted except for Father O'Connell, who hailed them as Jeremy started to turn away. "May I walk along with you?"

"Christ, not another sermon," Jeremy snarled under his breath.

"I was on my way to see you both. I only just heard what happened at your shop. I wish I'd been there."

"You'd have helped, would you?"

"I hope I could have made them think twice. I'll be raising the subject on Sunday if I still have a congregation. There may still be a few who prefer the church to that show on the moor."

"I misjudged you," Jeremy admitted. "I thought at first you meant you'd have helped Mann."

"God forbid, especially since he came to tell me I ought to make my preaching more like his. I don't care much for this homogenized religion, and I told him so. This notion that you mustn't think your way to faith is obviously not far from the intolerance that leads to burning books."

"May we quote you?" Geraldine said.

"By all means. It's what I'll be saying on Sunday. I don't think he'll be happy until he's converted everyone in town, or believes he has."

"He said something about not having much time. Before what, do you know?"

"Well, for whom the bell tolls and all that, but perhaps you're right to wonder if he meant something else. I'll see what I can find out, though he's difficult to pin down when he wants to be."

They were nearly at the church. "He uses words the way some doctors prescribe tranquilizers," the priest was saying when Geraldine cried out. "What's that?"

Father O'Connell shaded his eyes. "Birds. Look, there they go. I couldn't tell you what breed."

"That's right, just birds." Jeremy took her arm, having sensed her unease. "It was just the way the light caught them."

It must have been, she told herself. They couldn't have been glowing with their own pale light, even though the moonlight hadn't yet reached the church. Perhaps the light had reflected from a window opposite the churchyard and caught the birds where they stood pecking at the graves. She didn't like to wonder what they'd carried in their beaks as the three of them had risen in unison and flapped toward the moor. The moonlight must have caught them directly then, for as soon as they took flight they'd seemed even brighter. Everything was explicable, there was no reason for her to feel nervous, and yet she knew that wherever she and Jeremy continued their evening walk, she would rather that it wasn't on the moor.

15

The man at the reception desk assumed that Moonwell was a company. "No, it's where I live," Diana said. "Tell him I want to take up his offer."

Nick looked puzzled until he caught sight of her, and then he smiled broadly, his round face and large dark eyes relaxed. "I owe you lunch. Where shall we go?"

"A pub would be good. I've quite a lot to tell you."

"About Mission Moonwell?"

"Operation Moonwell would be more like it."

He frowned, rubbing his squarish chin as if he could erase the gray tinge that made it look less than shaved. "Give me ten minutes to finish a story and we'll go."

They went to a pub near the Gothic town hall, off a wide street where the buildings looked laundered by sunlight above the glacier of lunchtime traffic. They found stools near the back of the long, narrow dark-paneled room and sat down with drinks. "So what's been happening?" Nick said. "More of the same?"

"I don't know if you realized how organized it was. Mann's after the children now, with the help of the school. The headmaster tried to make me sign an undertaking not to teach anything Mann wouldn't approve of, and when I wouldn't sign, they fired me."

"Can they do that?"

"Not here in Manchester they couldn't, but you can get away with a lot in a town that takes more than an hour to reach, I guess. I've just been to my union headquarters this morning, and they don't hold out much hope."

"You're kidding. What, because they'd have to drive up there to help you?"

"No, because of something I didn't do. See, the union called a strike when I'd been at the school about six months

86

and I didn't join the strike. I thought, come on, I'm on probation here and besides, if I strike they'll bring in someone who'll treat the kids worse. I mean, I really wanted that job when I happened to read it was up for grabs, but I nearly didn't get a work permit in time. And I want to keep it all the more now I know what it entails. But the union bosses say they can't do much because I'm a foreigner and I haven't been here long enough, only I think it's because they haven't forgiven me for staying at work."

"I've got friends in the education offices. I can let you know in advance of any teaching jobs in Manchester."

"That's kind of you, Nick, but I was hoping you might be able to publicize what the school is trying to do to me." She drained her glass of beer. "My round."

When she carried the drinks to the table, Nick was looking uncomfortable. "I'll do what I can, of course," he said. "I'd certainly like to help."

"I think you'll have a story by the time I've finished." She told him about Eustace Gift's show, the book-burning, Father O'Connell's doubts. "And now Mann's going from house to house so nobody can sit on the fence. I told you it was systematic."

"The priest said he was willing to be quoted, did he? That may be the clincher. Let's eat and then I'll talk to my editor."

She waited in the lobby of the newspaper building fifteen minutes before he reappeared. She jumped up, her mock-leather chair reflating. "Do you need me?"

"Diana, I'm really sorry, not to say embarrassed. I didn't have much success."

"Maybe I should talk to him."

"I'd take you up if I thought it would do any good. You see, I did a series on Billy Graham and the rest of this fundamentalist backlash last year, and my editor's taking the line that it's last year's news—doesn't seem to see it's getting worse. He did raise an eyebrow when I mentioned your priest, though. Listen, are you free for dinner? I owe you more of an explanation, but I'd rather not go into it here."

"You needn't feel you owe me," Diana said gently.

"Well, anyway, I'd like to buy you dinner. I finish work at six."

"We'll decide who pays when they bring us the check. I still need to go to the library."

But in the high-domed reading room, where she had to apply at the desk for any book she wanted, there seemed to be no information that she needed, nothing to give her an insight into Mann's obsession with the cave. Indeed, she could find very few references to Moonwell. Then, as she leafed through the catalog again more studiedly, she found an author's name she knew.

The subject entry was for Lutudarum. The book proved to be an undated yellowing pamphlet, bound in plastic by the library. It was an essay about a lost Roman lead mine, which the writer located on a sketch map, showing Lutudarum where Diana would have looked for Moonwell. The writer's name was Nathaniel Needham.

"I should have thought of him," she told Nick over dinner in Chinatown. "He lives on the moors. If anyone but Mann knows what's supposed to be so important about the cave, he should."

"Assuming it means much to anyone but Mann. This whole idea of a deep, dark, evil well sounds pretty Freudian, don't you think?"

Her quick smile faded. "I think there's more to it. There are certainly enough stories about the cave."

"None about Mann though, I'm afraid, at least none he doesn't tell himself. His father's real name was Maniple, and I don't blame anyone for changing that."

"So tell me why you're having problems at the paper."

"Do you ever hear Radio Freedom? No, the evangelical station blots it out in your area. It's a pirate radio station I used to broadcast on, say things the paper wouldn't let me say. Only when I came back from your town I couldn't have disguised my voice enough, because my editor realized who I was."

"Oh, shit."

"He put it rather more strongly. I'm lucky still to be working there, I can tell you. And then the woman who runs Radio Freedom said I should broadcast who I was and work for the station if I cared about the truth, and that was the end of quite a good relationship, and maybe of my chance to help you. Do keep in mind what I said about finding you a job."

"I ought to take you up on that, shouldn't I? I ought to get out of Moonwell, since the parents have got what they seem to want."

He looked taken aback by her sudden bitterness. "Is it really that bad?"

"Nick, when I started teaching at that school the kids were terrified of me because they thought I'd be like the other teachers. Is that bad?"

"And when you weren't they started getting out of hand, I imagine."

"Sure, until they saw I wasn't going to hit them or send them to the headmaster for a caning. We didn't cane kids in New York, we don't need to do it here. It really pisses me off to hear parents saying it never did them any harm. I think people forget how it was for them at a school like that; otherwise they couldn't bear to send their children. And they're scared to be singled out as troublemakers even now they're grown up."

"The kind of fear Mann plays on."

"That's another thing that worries me. My kids won't say they believe his scare stories if they don't, and I'm afraid he or his followers may start some crap about how the kids are against him."

Nick drew a deep breath and stood up. "I may not be broadcasting any more, but I can still give Radio Freedom the story. Let me call Julia now."

He came back looking frustrated. "I can't get through. I'll try again in a few minutes. Julia may want to run an interview with you."

"Don't let your meal get cold. Nick, I think it'd be best if I don't go on the air. We both of us know what I really ought to do."

"Do we?" Nick said doubtfully.

"Sure. I ought to go back to the school and sign the son of a bitch of a form so that at least I'll be there to look after my kids."

Saying it made her feel even more certain, made her instincts feel as keen as they had the night they'd wakened her with the glimpse of the airplane. This time she wouldn't fail them, she promised herself. After dinner Nick suggested coffee at his apartment, but she was afraid that a sudden mist might wipe out the road back to Moonwell. She knew that if she went home with Nick, she would end up spending the night with him. In other circumstances she might have wanted that as much as she sensed he did.

She drove out of Manchester, onto the steep dark roads. Clouds hung over Moonwell, weighing down the night. She had it in her to dispel the sense of darkening and heaviness she felt as she drove toward the town, she reminded herself. The day must have exhausted her, for though moonrise wasn't due for hours, she thought she glimpsed whitish movements on the clouds above the cave. She went quickly to bed, to rest and be ready for the Scraggs in the morning.

Mrs. Scragg was at the schoolyard gate and glared at Diana as if she had no right even to step over the threshold. Some of the parents looked glad to see her, and some of the children certainly did. She had to sign. Nicholas Nickleby might have stormed into Mr. Scragg's office, but life didn't work like that, life just went on in its usual unsatisfactory way. She hurried into the school and knocked on Mr. Scragg's door.

The headmaster stared blankly at her. "I'm sorry I was hasty when you asked me to sign that disclaimer," she said, managing to smile. "I'll sign it now if I may."

"I'm glad you listened to your conscience. I hope you'll find it is its own reward." He began to shuffle papers on his desk. "But as far as your job is concerned, I'm afraid you've changed your mind too late. The post has already been filled by two of our new friends, who don't even want to be paid."

16

Andrew's head felt big and aching, his nose and eyes stuffed with tears. "But you said I could last year," he whined. "Said it was good for me."

"Well, we were wrong." His mother stuck out her hand for a clothespeg from the bag he was holding, a canvas bag with a little girl holding a handful of pegs stitched on it. "I've said no and that's all there is to it."

"But it's at the church. Father O'Connell doesn't mind."

"There's too many things he doesn't mind when he's

90

supposed to be a man of God. You're not to go near the church without me or your father, do you hear? You're not to have anything to do with Mrs. Wainwright or dressing the cave."

"But you promised you and Daddy would come and see me doing it this year."

"I was wrong, can't you understand? God sent Godwin Mann to show us where we'd gone wrong. Give the bag here if you're going to be stupid, I'll get the peg myself."

As she grabbed the bag she dropped her armful of washing on the lawn. "Now look what you've made me do, you little devil. Just you kneel down and ask God for forgiveness."

Grass blades poked Andrew's bare knees. "Please God forgive me," he muttered, and had to repeat what his mother said, "for being such a trial to my father and mother."

"Now go up to your room and close the door," his mother said, "and don't come down till you're worth knowing." Andrew felt as if that might be never. He stumbled to his feet, glancing nervously about in case anyone had heard him confessing, and saw his father in the kitchen, watching him. His father looked away quickly as if the fat gray sky meant something to him. "Just you read that story about how to obey your parents," Andrew's mother cried.

Andrew sat on his bed and stared at his room that no longer felt much like his. The bareness seemed chilly now that he couldn't have Maurice Sendak posters on the walls. He wasn't allowed to see Geraldine or Jeremy or even Miss Kramer now that she wasn't at the school, and he didn't want to play with the new children his mother liked so much, who made him feel he hadn't confessed enough. He felt even clumsier and more of an embarrassment to his parents than ever.

He began to tear the pamphlet about Abraham and Isaac, tiny pieces from the edges of the pages. He didn't dare hate God, but he hated Godwin Mann. His mother hadn't really changed except for talking so much about God, but his father had changed somehow since Godwin Mann had come to town—Andrew didn't want to think how. He couldn't help flinching when his father came into the room.

"Don't do that, son." His father collected the torn scraps of paper and flushed them down the toilet beneath the plaque that said "God Loves You." "Put that away before your mother sees what you've done to it, and we'll go out for a bit. You shouldn't be shut up on a day like this."

"Please may we go to the fair?"

"You don't call that a fair, do you? You wait and I'll give you a surprise."

People weren't supposed to have secrets once they'd confessed to God; hadn't Mr. Mann said something like that? But once they were in the street his father said, "I don't see why you shouldn't go to the church. I'll be taking you, so it's not as if you'll be disobeying your mother. No need to tell her, though, in case she doesn't see it that way."

A butcher's boy cycled along the High Street, the basket on his handlebars piled with raw deliveries. Andrew wanted to do that one day, cycle through the town like that, whistling and taking his hands off the handlebars to comb his hair. Perhaps then his parents would be proud of him.

If he wouldn't be disobeying his mother, why couldn't he tell her so that she would come and admire his bit of the cave-dressing? Sometimes thinking felt like trying to lift a weight that just grew heavier, especially when people were impatient with him. He was trying to put words straight in his head so as to ask his father in a way that wouldn't make him angry when they came abreast of Roman Row. "I'd better check with Mrs. Wainwright that someone's at the church," his father said.

Mrs. Wainwright was trimming the vines on the arch above her gate. Andrew ran to her, then faltered, for she looked as if she wanted to cry. "I'm sorry, Andrew," she said, staring at the vines. "We won't be dressing the cave this year."

Andrew's father caught up with him. "Why not? I thought you were going ahead anyway."

"There won't be enough people." Her eyes were so bright and blank they made Andrew's ache. "Anyway, I've more to worry me than dressing the cave, but I can't talk about it in front of the boy. The cave doesn't matter now."

"It does matter," Andrew blurted as she turned awkwardly and almost ran into her house. Her door slammed, and he saw that her next-door neighbor, a toothless old woman with a mustache, had been standing hands on hips in her front doorway. "Good riddance to her. The less we see of her the better," she mumbled loudly, working her lips over each other between phrases.

92

"Why, what's happened?" Andrew's father demanded.

"Haven't you heard? She lost a baby last night, and do you know why? Because the mother wouldn't have her sort in the room. 'I won't have my baby delivered by that godless woman,' that's what I was told she said. You'd think a midwife would have knelt down by the bed if it was that or lose a baby, but not Mrs. High and Mighty Wainwright. So the father tried to deliver the baby himself, and all I can say is if there's any justice that baby went straight to heaven and you know where Mrs. Wainwright ought to go."

That didn't seem quite fair to Andrew as he watched the old woman chewing her words as if she liked the taste. His father pulled him away. "Come on, I'll take you to the fair."

It was down by the playing field. Children threw quoits or rolled balls for prizes. The only ride was a roundabout, old pedal cars and bicycles bolted to a stage under a canopy like an umbrella whose canvas had blown off. Andrew sat on a rusty bicycle and pretended he was a delivery boy as the fairground man turned the rusty handle that made the stage creak round. "Look at me, Dad," he shouted every time his father went by, because every time his father was staring at the sunless sky above the moor as if it meant something to him or he wished he were somewhere else.

The fair didn't make up for his not being able to help Mrs. Wainwright. When they went home, he could tell that his mother sensed he was still disappointed, for she let him say grace before dinner. All too soon, long before dark, it was time for bed.

He lay watching shapes form and dissolve inside his eyelids, and listened to the murmur of his parents downstairs. He was waiting for his mother to demand what his father was hiding, but now that Andrew was in bed they didn't seem to be saying much. Their sounds and the long silences between felt like a storm gathering under the puffy sky. He pulled the blanket over his ear that felt swollen with trying to listen, and remembered last year—remembered fitting the lines of petals, overlapping like feathers on a bird, into his piece of the screen until there wasn't room for a single extra petal. He remembered seeing his work snap into place, his piece of blue sky taking its place above the head of the man with the sword. Light surrounded the calm face as if the head were the sun, shining like the sword he held up in one hand, the other

93

arm hidden inside his tunic made of leaves. Andrew felt cool as the church now, no longer aware of the weight of muggy heat and blankets, and he didn't notice when he fell asleep.

His dream felt peaceful too, at first. He was following the picture he'd helped create up to the cave. He couldn't see who was carrying it, not in sections as usual but put together so that it was several times as tall as he was. He ran through the dark toward the cave, over ground that felt more like ash than stone. Just as he reached the top, the moon came swooping over the jagged horizon, and he saw that the picture of the swordsman was standing over the cave. Andrew felt safe until the moon began to laugh.

It was only a fairy tale, he tried to tell himself. It was only in those books that the moon had a cartoony face with a big grin that could open and show its teeth. But it was laughing at the way the swordsman was tottering drunkenly at the edge of the cave as if he'd been moved too close. He was only a picture, Andrew told himself, and Mrs. Wainwright had said he didn't matter. The swordsman fell forward into the yawning dark, and Andrew heard him scream as he'd never heard anyone scream in his life.

Andrew lurched awake and almost screamed himself at the tarry dark. He struggled out of bed, stumbled toward the landing. Whoever he woke up would shout at him, but he couldn't bear to be alone with the dream. He inched open the door of his parents' room, and then he halted, gaping at the white statue that lay next to his mother in the bed.

The moon was shining directly on his father's face. He looked as if he were bathing in the light, soaking it up. Andrew wanted to run to him and shake him, because if the moon shone on your face while you were asleep it was supposed to drive you mad. His mother had told him that was just a story, but she always drew his curtains tight when there was going to be a moon. He would have cried out to her now, except that he was growing afraid of seeing his father's eyes open full of moonlight. Then his father's face writhed into an expression Andrew wouldn't have dreamed it could wear, and he fled back to his bedroom, hid in bed.

His father must have been having a nightmare. Only mightn't you look as terrified as that if you were going mad? What would his father do then? Something worse than the way men at football games screamed at one another, worse than making Andrew's mother sound as if he was hurting her when they thought Andrew was asleep. Andrew hadn't heard her make those noises since Mr. Mann had come to Moonwell, but now the waiting silence made him more nervous than the noises had.

He ground his knuckles into his ears. His mother always told him in the summer that he'd better be asleep before it was dark. Now he felt as if he was finding out why—finding out that everything changed for the worse. He couldn't bear waiting, couldn't bear not knowing what was happening in his parents' room. But when he made himself get out of bed and tiptoe back across the landing to ease their door open, he almost screamed. His father wasn't in the bed.

His mother was still huddled in the blankets, her back to the moon. As Andrew tried to nerve himself to wake her, he heard the front door close quietly. Suddenly he could move. He tiptoed across his parents' bedroom, knowing instinctively that he wouldn't bump into anything, and peered into the thin moonlight. His father was across the main road and loping up the nearest side street that led to the moors.

At once Andrew knew that his father had meant to leave him at the church and go wherever he was going now. Andrew wouldn't have been able to tell his mother without giving himself away. He backed out of the room and managed to close the door with his stiff, shaky hands. If his mother found out what was happening to his father, whatever it was, she might make it worse. Andrew dressed quickly and crept downstairs, put the door on the latch, and slipped out of the house.

His body heat seemed to flood out of the top of his head toward the cloudless sky. As he dodged across the High Street, the clock above the assembly rooms struck two. He ran along the side street and up the zigzag path, both exhilarated to be out so late and afraid of what he might see when he caught up with his father.

At the top of the path he poked his head gingerly over the edge. His father was loping toward the cave, ash softening his tread, under the waning moon that made Andrew blink. As Andrew ran after him, the boy couldn't hear himself. Running on the moon must be like this, running in silence, hardly feeling your own footsteps. His father was at the rim that surrounded the cave, and Andrew threw himself face down in the ash, because his father was pacing round the rim to a point almost opposite him. But his father was too intent on whatever was beyond the rim to notice Andrew.

Though he felt exposed by the moonlight and the charred landscape, Andrew began to crawl through the ash. He crawled until he was almost abreast of his father, just able to see him by raising his head. He hid his face in his hands to clear his throat, and when he looked up again, his father had gone over the rim. Suddenly terrified that he meant to throw himself into the cave, Andrew scrambled up to the edge.

The moon was almost overhead. It glared into the stone bowl and made the lip of the cave appear to glow. Beyond that, the cave looked as black and deep as the sky. Halfway between the cave and the edge of the bowl, one of Mr. Mann's helpers was kneeling, fingers interlocked, eyes closed. He must be guarding the cave, Andrew thought. Behind him, so stealthily Andrew couldn't see him move, Andrew's father came creeping. His face was a smooth, luminous white mask.

His shadow inched in front of him, as silent as he was. The praying man must see it if he opened his eyes—but no, the shadow was directly behind him, touching him now. Suppose he felt it, and turned? Andrew was as terrified for his father, terrified that his father would be found out, as he was of seeing what would happen when his father reached the man.

His father was inches short of the man when he heard something. His masklike face lifted in the moonlight; Andrew thought of a dog pricking up its ears. His father began to back stealthily away up the bowl, and Andrew fled back to his place in the ash. On his way he saw another of Mr. Mann's helpers hurrying across the moor.

The newcomer passed within a few yards of Andrew without noticing him. "I'm sorry, I overslept," he called down toward the cave. Andrew's father was already out of sight along the other path, the long way back to Moonwell. Andrew ran home as soon as the newcomer was in the stone bowl, ran slapping himself to dust off the ash, slapping harder to stop his thoughts.

He let himself into the cottage and crept upstairs. He lay in bed, hardly able to breathe as he waited for his father to come home, his mother to waken and demand to know where his father had been. At last he heard the front door close, the creaking of the stairs, then silence. His mother hadn't wakened. Andrew lay awake then until dawn, praying that whatever was still going to happen wouldn't happen.

17

"I say, I say, I say, what's this film we're watching?"

"I don't know, God told me to throw my glasses away."

"That was no God, that was Godwin Mann throwing his voice."

"Godwin Mann throwing his voice? Why should he want to do that?"

"So you can't see what an old devil his father turned into."

Nobody was laughing except Eustace. If that was laughter somewhere up on the moors, it could hardly be meant for him. He wouldn't be performing that routine when the landlord of the One-Armed Soldier showed the video in which Mann's father played the devil. He wasn't a comedian, he was just a postman who'd been talking to himself. If he weren't a postman, he wouldn't be on his way to Phoebe Wainwright's house.

He hadn't seen her since the night at the pub. Whenever he had to deliver her mail, he made sure she wouldn't hear him coming. The idea of just being a postman, nothing more than his job, was oddly comforting; the sense of being unworthy of her was, surprisingly, a relief. He was settling into not having to approach her any more when he heard how she'd been prevented from saving the baby.

What appalled him even more was how everyone he'd spoken to blamed her. He had to let her know that somebody was on her side, and today he had a reason to go to her house. He glanced along the High Street to reassure himself that nobody had heard him playing straight man to himself and turned quickly along Church Row.

He had a letter for her that had been posted locally and a

childbirth magazine that was too bulky to go through her letter box. He stepped under the viny arch and tried to think of a joke to cheer her up, something about the magazine, in case the sight of it upset her. "They mustn't have heard that God doesn't want you to deliver any more babies," he thought, and rang the doorbell.

When she peered through the front-room window, he was shocked to see how slack her face was. Cheering her up would be more of a task than he'd thought, he realized, and then he heard his headphone voice delivering the tasteless, insensitive joke he was planning to offer her. He tried frantically to think of something else to say as she opened the door.

All he could think of were jokes, even more tasteless than the one he'd suppressed, and he was terrified that they would spill out if he opened his mouth. She was gazing at him not so much patiently as indifferently, while he fumbled in his bag as though he might have more for her. He thrust the letter and the magazine at her. "For you," he mumbled, as if they were presents.

Her face turned blanker still as she glanced at the magazine and stuffed it under one arm. Now she was tearing the envelope open with one plump thumb. She must want him to speak; otherwise she would have closed the door. "I heard what happened the other night," he blurted, and floundered on: "They won't let either of us do what we do best, will they? Maybe they just can't stand creative people."

When she looked up from the single page she'd unfolded, he wished he'd made one of his jokes instead. It was a joke, of course—a joke at his expense. "Sorry," he babbled. "Nothing worse than a comedian trying to be serious, except I'm not much of a comedian, as you're painfully aware . . ."

She must be wondering if he would ever stop. Trapped with his own headphone voice, he wondered that himself. He gulped himself silent, and she began suddenly to blink, more and more rapidly. For a moment he thought she might hide her face against his shoulder, and then he found himself staring at the closed front door.

Her letter came seesawing through the air to his feet. He picked it up and rang the bell without thinking. In the seconds before she flung the door open, he saw what the letter said. The message, written in large anonymous capitals, said LEAVE OUR TOWN BEFORE YOU KILL MORE CHILDREN. Phoebe snatched it from his hand. "Can't any of you leave me alone? If I throw myself down the cave, will that make up for the baby?" she cried, and slammed the door.

He reached wildly for the doorbell, but turned away instead. Whatever he said would only make things worse. He saw himself handing her the letter for the second time, the third, the fourth. He couldn't even survive that by making it into a joke at his own expense—there was nobody to whom he could tell the joke.

He finished his deliveries and tramped home, speaking to nobody. No, he didn't want to speak to Eric at the pub. What on earth would Eric be achieving by showing the film with Mann's father? It was nothing but defiance, so trivial it was like accepting that the town was Mann's now. Eustace stalked into his cottage and locked himself in with his rage at himself. He had only just dropped his postbag beside the sofa when someone knocked at the front door.

It was the dressmaker who lived three cottages away. She squinted at him through the smoke of the cigarette in one corner of her mouth. "Well, Mr. Gift," she said, the cigarette jerking, "you've been keeping well out of our way, haven't you?"

"Where's your friend, in your pocket? Up your arse?" But all he said was "I've just been doing my job."

"So long as that's all you've been up to." She slapped her breasts vigorously to dislodge a worm of ash. "Well, are we going to see you up there on Sunday?"

He felt close to laughter, or something more violent. Someone like her had sent Phoebe the letter. "I don't think you'd want to see me," he muttered.

"Oh yes we would, my lad. Do you know you're the only one in the street who wasn't up there last Sunday? You're not going to say we're all deluded, are you?"

"I'm not going to say that, no."

"I should think not too. Do you know that every single person in both of the next streets was up there? Just you make sure you are on Sunday. We don't want our street shown up." She trod on her cigarette and peered at him.

"You aren't scared to go, are you? No need to be. We all know what you have to confess. Do yourself some good for a change."

"It doesn't seem to have changed you. Now, if you'll excuse me," Eustace said, and closed the door, "while I play with myself, or get ready for a black mass, or stick pins in my Godwin Mann doll." His urge to laugh went out with the words, leaving him more furious than ever. He went back to the sofa and watched the dressmaker stump away down his path, and suddenly he had to force himself to sit down rather than chase after her, grab her, drag her—where, he didn't know. Somewhere he was almost sure he heard laughter, deep and hollow, growing.

=== 18 ===

PRIEST DEFENDS SEX BOOKS, the headline said. Given the lack of detail in the report, you might well assume that the bookshop was a sex shop. The name of the town—"a small town near Sheffield"—was apparently Moonwell. It wasn't Nick's fault, Diana told herself; he'd done his best, and now she must do better. She dropped the newspaper on the hall table and stepped out of her cottage.

The afternoon was gray and muggy. Diana's thin dress clung to her as she made for the hotel. The round-shouldered man at Reception, who wore a Sacred Heart badge in his lapel, referred her to one of Mann's helpers when she asked for Mann. "If you need counseling, perhaps I can help," the young, wide-eyed, smiling woman said. "Godwin is resting just now."

"I thought he was available to anyone who wants to talk to him."

"Usually he is. Right now he's preparing," the young woman said, and went on quickly: "Miss Kramer, isn't it? I'll tell him you were asking for him. He'll come to see you as soon as he can."

Then Diana would talk to Nathaniel Needham. Indeed, that might better equip her to talk to Mann. Townsfolk watched her suspiciously as she headed for the nearest path to the moors. This morning the woman from whom she rented the cottage had wanted to know how much longer Diana would be staying now that she had no job. "For a while yet," Diana had told her—for as long as she felt the children had to be protected. It didn't matter that she'd seen parents telling their children to stay away from her. Her instincts told her she had to stay, and that must be to protect the children, even though she had a vague, uneasy notion that she was underestimating whatever she had to protect them from.

She climbed on the moor and hurried across the dead ground, the ash that muffled her footsteps, and the oppressive silence that seemed to surround the cave, above which one of Mann's followers was kneeling. From the top of the slope where Needham had stood at the rally, she surveyed her route. The slopes beyond were thick with grass and heather, but there was no sign of a cottage, nor of a path. A mossy concrete slab showed her where an abandoned mineshaft was. She avoided that and trudged up the next slope, fanning herself. There was a cottage two slopes ahead.

She ran down into the next hollow and made her way between the abandoned shafts, left uncovered this far from town. Tussocks and heather slowed her down, grass concealed ankle-deep puddles. The silence seemed to have followed her from the cave; no bird was singing. Not until she climbed the next slope did she realize the silence was mist.

In the few minutes she'd spent in the hollow, the adjacent slopes had all but vanished. A clump of trees looked like stitching on gray velvet. The mist unveiled a glimpse of the cottage a few hundred yards ahead, then wiped it out. She made for the cottage, the only landmark.

At the bottom of the slope, darkness lay under the grass. She avoided the dark widely wherever she saw it, even if it was only puddles. She felt as if the ground were gaping at her, opening its mouths. One detour took her to the edge of a shaft, which she almost didn't see for tall grass. She recoiled, heart pounding, and stumbled up the wet grass of the nearest slope. She was safe on an island in the midst of a still, gray sea, but she no longer knew where the cottage was. She was preparing to wait until the mist lifted when a man's voice said, "Who's there?"

"I'm lost. Can you help me?"

"Wait there where you are." The mist fell silent, and Diana's eyes began to sting as she tried to see where the voice had come from. When it spoke again, it was farther away. "If you want to be found, keep talking," it growled.

"My name's Diana Kramer. I was looking for Nathaniel Needham's cottage. I almost had it when the mist came down."

He appeared suddenly at the foot of the slope, a tall man leaning on a stick. He levered himself through the mist and towered over her. He had white hair that spilled over his collar, a long face wizened as a monkey's, and large, veinous, knuckly hands that gripped his stick as he leaned at her, his gray eyes staring blankly. "Well, you've found me," he said.

"You're Nathaniel Needham."

"That's who I am. And if you've come looking to save my soul, you've got yourself lost for nothing. I'll make my own peace with God when the time comes."

"I haven't come for that. I've nothing to do with what's happening in Moonwell. I read your pamphlet about the Roman mines, and I heard the song you sang the other week at the pub. I guess you may want to see traditions preserved, like I do."

He shrugged, apparently because he felt cold. "Take my arm," he said, and began to descend the slope. "You Americans are fond of our traditions, aren't you? My da used to say that's because you've got none of your own."

"I ought to tell you I'm not a tourist. I taught school in Moonwell until I refused to be a mouthpiece for Godwin Mann. I love the town and I don't see why someone else should cross the ocean to change it."

"Happen there's traditions you wouldn't want to keep." He raised his stick to point at an open shaft they were avoiding in the murk. "Who do you think used to live down one of those?"

"Miners?"

"Think a man who spent his working life down there would

102

want to live down there as well? No, love, not bloody miners. A family who'd wait for someone like you to get lost on a day like this."

"Robbers, you mean."

"Happen they started off that way, but what they needed most was food. And they'd plenty of that once they dragged some poor lost fool into their lair. My da heard tell how they were caught when someone from Moonwell was missed. They'd cut out his tongue so he couldn't scream for help, and cut bits off him, but he was still alive. My da heard tell they gave their kids the eyes for supper," he said, and with less relish, "I suppose you'd better come in till the mist lifts."

He'd brought her to his cottage, when she'd thought he was leading her back to Moonwell. He unlocked the small front door, which was thick with red paint that had splashed onto the limestone walls, and stooped in. The door opened into the main room. A double bed stood against the far wall; a bookcase full of dusty books leaned in one gloomy corner; two faded easy chairs faced a hearth on which stood a toaster-shaped radio that must have been at least thirty years old. Needham stooped slowly to the hearth and began to build a fire with chunks of wood. "You're here in my house where you wanted to be," he said, "and I still don't know what you're after."

"I'm trying to find out the truth about the cave. Godwin Mann keeps claiming that there's something evil there, something that's spreading evil I don't know how far."

Needham reached for a box of kitchen matches beside the radio and lit the fire. As it began to crackle, he rubbed his hands close to the flames, then reached behind him and lowered himself into the right-hand chair. "I think Godwin Mann is on the right track."

Diana couldn't keep dismay out of her voice. "You agree with him?"

"I don't agree with what he wants to do, no. I think he should leave well alone, but you can't reason with his sort. Only I don't think he knows the half of what's down there in the cave."

Diana felt as if the chill were seeping through the small window from the mist that crept across the grass. "Why, what do you say is down there?"

"Come and sit by me before I get a crick in my neck." He settled back, closing his eyes, as the fire flared higher. "What do I say? The man in the moon."

"Oh."

"The man in the moon came down too soon and asked his way to Norwich," he chanted like a grandfather to a child. "But I don't reckon you'd know that song."

"Sure I do. One of the children I taught used to sing it. And I know my Shakespeare. The man in the moon was supposed to have a bundle of sticks on his back because he'd been exiled to the moon for cutting wood on the Sabbath."

"Aye, that's the story." He sounded grudgingly impressed. "And you hear tales of people bringing the moon down to earth and waking up the dead, and St. Peter having to put it back. And wishing on the new moon brings you luck, and babies born at the new moon are healthiest. Happen you don't realize those are the kind of story people make up about things they're afraid of."

"Used to be afraid of, you mean."

"Not so long ago either." He turned his head toward her, flames flickering in his slitted eyes. "I remember my da sitting where you're sitting now, in a muck sweat because the radio was saying they'd put a man on the moon. It did for his heart, and I've lived alone here ever since."

"I'm sorry," Diana said, though he sounded as if he would resent sympathy. "But did he really have a reason to be afraid?"

"No, and I told him so." He breathed hard through his nose, and then he said, "I told him what he was afraid of on the moon was already on the earth."

Diana made her face blank. "The man in the moon, do you mean?"

"God help us, you sound like a nurse. I haven't had one in my house yet, and I'm damned if I'll have one now. Didn't I just tell you the man in the moon was a story folk made up to hide the truth from themselves? When folk knew the truth they kept it to themselves, the druids did. Happen that's why they never wrote anything down."

"Godwin Mann mentioned the druids," Diana said, telling herself that there might be a version of some truth in the midst of all this.

"Aye, and what does either of you know about them?"

104

"Quite a lot," Diana said, provoked. "I do, I mean. I know some historians say the Romans occupied your country in order to destroy the druid religion. It was either religion or politics."

"It was religion right enough." He was quiet for so long that Diana wondered if he were nodding off. Suddenly he said, "The druids made their last stand here at Moonwell. They did what they'd never dared to do—they called what they worshiped to come down from the moon and stay on the earth."

"I thought they worshiped the sun."

Needham thumped the arms of his chair. "They had a god of the moon all right, they just didn't dare give it a name. They sacrificed people to it, but the priests didn't stay to see it come for them. They used to throw people down shafts like the one your gospeling friend wants to tamper with. That way it had to go down out of the light to get its sacrifices."

If there was any logic to his argument, it wasn't clear to Diana. "Seems strange they'd try to use the moon against the Romans."

He sighed like a long-suffering teacher. "The Greeks and Romans worshiped the moon, and the druids reckoned their months and years by the moon, and I keep telling you that was just to keep it happy, don't you understand? They all knew it had no love for us. The druids were only the last of an older religion, if you didn't know. There's something about it in those books."

Diana took that as a hint that she could look at them. Mist surged against the windows as she crossed the dimming room, scraps of carpet shifting underfoot, to the light switch. The bare bulb lit, though feebly. "Could you show me where?"

"I could have once. Look if you want to."

The books weren't merely dusty; above the illegible spines, the tops of the pages were furred with gray. "Just because I can't see any longer," Needham growled, "doesn't mean I can't think."

She thought of living up here alone and blind, miles from the next house, surrounded by the gaping shafts. "I wasn't thinking that," she said.

"And it doesn't mean I can't remember." He drew himself up in the chair and recited: "'. . . sustulere monstra, quibus

105

hominem occidere religiosissimum erat, mandi vero etiam saluberrimum . . .' Know what that means? A monstrous cult who thought murdering someone was the height of religion, especially if you ate him afterwards. That's what old Pliny said about the druids."

"But it wasn't so long since the Romans gave up human sacrifice themselves."

"They were never like the druids. There was a book, fifty volumes of it, written before Christ was born, that told all about the druids. 'To fear the moon, to feed her as she must be fed, and never to look upon her feeding'—I read that somewhere, quoted out of one of those books, the thing the druids used to believe. Those books were lost because they told too much about the druids. And Moonwell was lost because of what the druids brought to it."

"You mean its Roman name was lost."

"Aye, you said you'd read my pamphlet." The thought seemed to mollify him. "The Romans couldn't have known this was the ideal place for the druids to call on their god that wasn't a god but a monster."

"Why was it ideal?" Diana asked, and then her instincts told her. She didn't need to hear him say, "Because we see less of the sun here than anywhere else in the country."

The shapeless movements at the window were darkening. "But is there really any story about the druids using magic or whatever it was against the Romans?" Diana said.

He turned his head and stared at her with nothing in his eyes. Eventually he said, "I'll tell you what I know, and if you don't believe it, suit yourself. But you won't like what you hear."

At least she wouldn't have to touch the fattened books. He waited for her to sit down, and then he said, "Happen you know the Romans never gained much ground up here. A military dictatorship was all they could manage, and not much of that this far into the Peak. Half the Peak was forest then. Where we're sitting now was the edge of a forest of oaks."

Mist stirred like foliage at the window. "Well, the Romans cut down trees for their furnaces and worked the natives in the mines," Needham said. "And at first they didn't notice if the odd child or old person went missing. Even when a Roman patrol did, the commander of the garrison thought they'd got lost in a mist that was lasting for days. But then he thought of sending a patrol into the woods to see what the natives were scared of.

"The woods went down past where Moonwell is now, for miles. You can still see some of the old trees. Whenever the trees had to be felled for fuel the natives had to be forced to do it. The Romans thought they were just being superstitious savages until they noticed that the natives were most afraid of the woods when the moon was up.

"Well, the commander knew that meant druidism, and he sent a patrol into the woods in daylight, and they found the cave you're so concerned about. It was in a glade of oaks then, and all the oaks around it were carved. Some of them had three faces, and some looked like men with their innards hanging out, the way the druids used to cut them open as part of their magic. Some of those carvings must have been hundreds of years old even then. And caught on one of them they found a bit of a tunic that a soldier in the missing patrol had been wearing.

"The commander didn't let on to the natives that he knew anything. The Romans just kept watch until the next full moon, and then they saw a few of the natives sneaking off into the forest. One of them was carrying a newborn baby. The Romans followed them to the cave and saw them throw the baby down, and they were just going to seize them when the thing that lived in the forest came looking for its food."

His eyes were brighter, as if he could see what he was describing. "The Romans ought to have noticed there was more to the place than superstition. Happen some did. Some of them thought on the way to the cave that there was more moonlight under the trees than there ought to be. One soldier even thought that the rays coming down through the branches looked like a spider's web, the way they kept crossing. He thought the light seemed to get hold of your feet when you stepped in it, but happen that was the ground or the undergrowth. Only there must have been more to it than moonlight, because they saw the thing in the forest running across the web the rays made, to get to the baby in the cave. You don't want to hear what it looked like, do you?"

Diana nodded, then had to swallow in order to say, "If you know."

"They could never agree on what they saw, not that they

107

talked about it much. The light got brighter as it came nearer, for a start, until the moonlight hurt their eyes. It looked like a spider as big as a man, a beautiful spider made out of moonlight, or it may have looked like a maggot that was growing more legs than a spider, or a man with arms and legs that stretched out over the forest and a face just like the moon's face except it was moving. The druids were running away from the cave as they saw it coming, and they ran straight into the soldiers. But the soldier who'd seen the light turning into a web saw it scuttle over the edge of the cave, down to the baby, and the light seemed to flare up out of the cave as if the moon had fallen in.

"The Romans marched their prisoners back to the village, and executed all of them except the head druid, who was an old man they'd hardly even noticed. They wanted to find out from him what they were up against, and he wanted them to know. He'd done what the druids never dared to do, he'd used magic so old it was almost forgotten not just to call their god they mustn't name but to keep it here on the earth instead of coming down on the moonlight for its sacrifices. He believed the whole forest was its place now, the druids' last refuge where nobody else would dare enter.

"Well, the commander didn't know if burning down the forest would help. So he tried to starve the thing into the open. He set a guard around the village so that nobody could get out. A few nights later they saw the moonlight coming through the forest and trying to reach out for people, and sometimes they saw a man made out of moonlight standing just inside the forest, beckoning. Some of the soldiers almost went to him, except the others held them back. One of them thought that when the man went back into the forest just before dawn he got taller as he went away, until he was as tall as the trees.

"The commander had the notion that the thing got weaker as the moon waned. Of course the druid priest made out it wasn't so, but he must have realized the commander was waiting until it was weakest before he attacked. So one night, just before dark of the moon, the druid escaped, ran into the forest. He came back at dawn, or something did."

"Meaning . . ." Diana said.

"Meaning it looked like him—it mostly *was* him. He'd made the ultimate sacrifice, and he almost managed to let it

108

come among them before they realized. Only the Romans saw how all the villagers backed away when the druid came out of the woods. So they tied him until he couldn't move a muscle, and waited until nightfall. And they saw him start to glow as if he'd swallowed the moon.

"The next day they made the villagers cut down the trees around the cave, all except the one where they'd found the bit of uniform. And then they crucified the druid on it and piled wood round it and set fire to it. In the morning the fire was ash, but the druid or the thing that looked like him was still alive and crawling about in the hot ash, though all that was left of it was a head on a few charred bones."

For an instant Diana saw that as clearly as if she'd once seen it herself. She snatched her mind back to the flickering room, the windows patchy with moisture. "The pain must have trapped it," Needham said, "or going inside the druid; otherwise it would have got loose from the tree. So the soldier who saw clearest drew his sword and went into the hot ash and chopped off its head and arms and legs, and then he kicked all of it down into the cave. Except he picked up the head—happen he was showing he wasn't scared to. And the moment he touched it, it was part of him.

"He went and stood on the edge of the cave, and he cut off his own arm. And then he stepped off the edge himself. That same day the Romans killed all the villagers and burned the village and most of the forest to the ground."

Even as a story, that dismayed her. "But why?"

"So the place would be forgotten—so that the rest of the druids wouldn't gather here. And they knew something was alive down there that might get a hold over people who settled near. Presumably Rome wasn't happy about what they did, because there's no record of it or the garrison as I know of. Though I wonder if the thing down there wiped out all memory of the place until it was ready to come back."

"But if the memory was wiped out—"

"How can I know about it? Say I dreamed it. Say I dream because I can't see. I told you you wouldn't believe me."

"I didn't say that. But I don't understand how, if all that was forgotten, the dressing of the cave got started."

"I think the druids still knew where to look. It would have wanted them to. I think Moonwell was settled by druids, people with some of the old beliefs anyway, after the Romans

109

left Britain. Happen they thought they'd revive what was in the cave until they realized what they'd be reviving. What do you think it'd do if it ever got loose? Think how much it must hate mankind for crucifying it and burning it and chopping it to bits and leaving it down there in the dark. The figure they made out of flowers wasn't a tribute, it was meant to guard the cave. I heard tell that once it didn't just have a halo round its head—its head was the sun."

"The sun god," Diana realized. "That's why they put it there on Midsummer Eve, only now they pretend it's for St. John the Baptist Day and make it look like a saint."

"Aye, but do you know why it was Midsummer Eve? Because that's when the nights start getting longer and the power of the sun begins to wane, which is like saying the power of the moon gets stronger. In Rome it was the feast of your namesake, the goddess of the moon."

"No, I'm the other one, the huntress," Diana said almost without thinking. "If Mann stops them dressing the cave, how much do you think it will matter?"

"Not much by itself." Needham's eyes were suddenly more lifeless than ever. "If that was all he planned to do."

"Why, what else?"

"You'll have to ask him that." Needham pushed himself to his feet. "Now, you'll have to excuse me. I haven't talked so much for years. I'll see you part of the way back if you like."

Glancing at the window, Diana saw that the mist had vanished as unexpectedly as it had appeared. A waning moon was high above the moors. "I'll find my way," she said. "Thanks for putting up with me."

Moonlight coated all the slopes, turning heather into white lace, grass into spikes of ice. From the first slope Diana saw Needham in his doorway, his eyes like globes of marble. She looked back again from the top of the slope. His door was closed, his window was dark.

She made her way down the slope toward Moonwell. Doughy clouds rose over the horizon, but the moon showed her every open shaft and made them look deeper and blacker as the light probed into them. Could any of them be connected with the main cave? The breathless silence isolated her with the moon, tilted coquettishly above her as if to display how little of its face was left, half an eye gaping at her, the top of the head missing. However fast she walked, it hovered over her. Once she thought three shapes were fluttering above her high in the sky, but when she looked she saw only the white, decaying mask.

On the edge of the ashen land she faltered, for stars were glimmering in the heather, five-pointed figures in a dozen places. She was spellbound until she realized they were spiders' webs. She ran through the ash to the path down to Moonwell, not sure yet how much she believed of Needham's story. She couldn't expect Nick to take any of it seriously, and certainly his newspaper wouldn't. Once she was home she could ponder what she'd heard, but there was no doubt in her mind what she must do now. She had to confront Godwin Mann.

19

The second newspaper to pick up the story was a tabloid. PRIEST IN SEX AND DRUG BOOKS SQUABBLE, the headline said. Jeremy flung the paper on the table that had ousted the altar and waited while Geraldine read the report. Because of a printer's error, the town wasn't named. "At least people won't know it's us," she said.

"You should have seen their faces when I bought the paper, Gerry. Everyone in Moonwell must be rubbing their hands over it, except Father O'Connell and Diana Kramer and one or two others."

"So let them. They can't do us any more harm. They'll have to accept eventually that we aren't going to budge."

"My God, what more harm do you think they *could* do? When did you last see a customer step through those doors? What do you want us to do, stay here just to prove a point while the books gather dust and the bank manager comes for us?" He went round the table to her and held her shoulders

111

gently. "Some of the bookshops in Hay-on-Wye are supposed to be falling vacant. We'd have the Welsh mountains there and neighbors who care about books."

"And what about Andrew? Are we just going to abandon him? You heard the way he was screaming last night."

"He must have been having a nightmare, and no wonder, but what are we going to achieve by staying? June and Brian aren't going to let us anywhere near him."

"I'm not so sure about Brian," Geraldine said, knowing that Jeremy was probably right—but of course it wasn't only Andrew who made her feel compelled to stay in Moonwell.

She wished they could leave as much as Jeremy did. Whenever she met people in the street, she couldn't help wondering what they thought of her. Her yearning for their good opinion dismayed her even more than their contempt, and sometimes, when people spoke to her as if they were doing her a favor, she was barely able to restrain herself from flying at them.

Why couldn't Jonathan make himself clear? If she had him buried wherever they moved to, would that satisfy him? Or had the shining gravestone meant that he wanted to be buried only in Moonwell? She had to let them know in Sheffield soon if she didn't want his grave moved here. Perhaps she didn't need to be alone with her doubts; if Jeremy saw the stone he would have to believe, whatever arguments that might lead to. "Come with me tonight," she blurted out, "and I'll show you why I don't know if I want to leave."

"Why tonight? Why not now? It's not as if there's anyone to keep the shop open for."

"You never know, we might be lucky today. Wait until tonight, Jerry, all right? I've a reason."

They'd see nothing in daylight at the graveyard: she never had. Perhaps sharing her vision would help her understand why. Did Jonathan's life after death mean there had to be a God, or would life after death exist without religion, whatever the religions claimed? In time she might talk to Father O'Connell. As for Godwin Mann, she suspected that he would regard her belief in Jonathan as something she ought to confess, not discuss.

Nobody came to the shop that day. She wondered if Mann's followers were putting off potential customers. Jeremy tried to conceal his impatience with having been made to wait. The thought of feeling trapped in the shop until dark didn't appeal to her either. "Let's go out and I'll buy you dinner," she said, remembering that she'd said that the first time they'd gone for a meal.

They drove to the Snake Inn, all by itself in the pines on the Manchester road. After dinner they sat outside, watching mountains glow in the twilight and grow dim, and Geraldine realized how peaceful she felt now that she was out of Moonwell. Suppose Moonwell was where Jonathan wanted to be, and Mann and his followers were driving him out? She could imagine how their children would treat him if he were alive, the child of the disreputable Booths. She felt as if Mann couldn't even leave him alone where he was.

As she drove back to Moonwell, the moon appeared above a reservoir, a lopsided crescent skimming the water. Toward Moonwell it seemed to grow brighter, icing the ridges. The signpost for Moonwell dripped with rain like whitewash, the town's name hardly legible. As she turned the van onto the side road, she felt herself grow tense with wishing. All the way up to the crest that overlooked the town and down the last stretch of streaming tarmac, she was wishing that there would be something for Jeremy to see.

The van coasted down to the church. Railings and tree-trunks fluttered by, blurring her view of the graveyard. As she parked the van, Jeremy stared about, obviously disappointed by where she'd brought him. He was blocking her view, but she suddenly felt sure that the stone would be there. She turned off the engine and slid back her door. "Come and see," she murmured.

Jeremy dragged his door open, the sound harsh in the silence. She splashed through a puddle to take his hand as he climbed down. Beyond the dripping railings, the moonlit grass was almost as white as the memorials; she was surprised how bright the remnant of moon was. At the forefront of the newest graves, where she'd left the flowers for Jonathan, a stone was glowing.

She tugged at Jeremy's hand. "Look," she said urgently, and pushed open the gate that was beaded with rain. Under their feet the soaked gravel made a sound halfway between a squeak and a squelch. She stepped onto the soggy lawn, and then she missed a step. Not all the stone was there.

It was certainly Jonathan's, for she could read most of his

name. NATHAN, it said, but would that be enough for Jeremy? Why wasn't it all there? The stone was mottled now, as though it were aging. The marks reminded her of the markings of the moon, and she had an odd momentary notion that the stone was incomplete because the moon was waning. "Come on," she whispered, pulling Jeremy onto the grass, but this time it was he who made her falter. He was staring at the flowers she'd left where the stone was. In the moonlight they were moving perceptibly, opening.

"What's that?" Jeremy demanded in a small choked voice. He peered at the flowers, stumbled forward.

"Look at the stone," Geraldine urged him. Under the mottling it showed not only the year of Jonathan's stillbirth but also, very faintly, the month and the day. "The stone, Jeremy," she cried, just as the moonlight vanished.

She moaned in frustration and dismay. Clouds that would go on for minutes had closed over the moon, and the stone was no longer glowing; it was barely visible in the barred light through the railings. Jeremy was stooping to the flowers, reaching for them, and then his hand flinched back. "My God, they've taken root. They're growing."

"It doesn't matter. Jeremy, read the stone." She wanted to fling herself at him, hold his head so that he had to see. How might Jonathan be feeling because his father wouldn't look? But Jeremy was tugging at the flowers, one of which tore free of the wreath, spattering the headstone with moist earth. She stepped toward him, and then headlights swept into the graveyard and pinned them both.

Jeremy leaped up, almost falling. Geraldine glanced at the stone and saw that now it was blank. Beyond the headlights a sliding door slammed open. "In the name of God, what are you doing there?" Benedict Eddings cried.

Geraldine turned toward him, then looked back at once at Jonathan's stone. But there was no stone, only bare grass and her flowers, which were curling up, withering. "It's this place," Jeremy said hoarsely. "There's something wrong with it. Things growing that shouldn't be growing."

"What business is it of yours? Nobody of yours is laid to rest in there." Benedict flung open the gate with a clang that dislodged a shower from the railings. "Come out of there at once. Haven't you committed enough sacrilege? You'd stoop to desecrating graves, would you?"

114

Windows lit in the cottages behind him; a sash slid up. Jeremy lurched toward him as if to manhandle him into the graveyard. "I told you, something's happened to the flowers. Take a look for yourself."

Benedict retreated hurriedly. "Have you been taking drugs as well as selling books about them? Leave our graveyard this instant or I'll call the police."

"You'll call the fucking police, will you? Maybe I should call them to you and your shoddy workmanship, you pious little hypocritical bastard." Jeremy took another step, then burst out laughing mirthlessly as Benedict retreated further. He grabbed Geraldine's arm so hard she almost cried out. "For Christ's sake, let's get home," he muttered.

Faces peered out of windows opposite the church as Jeremy started the van. When he swung the vehicle away from the pavement, she realized he was shaking. "What did you see?" she said, as gently as she could. "Did you see the stone?"

"I don't know what I saw, and I don't want to know." He slowed the van and clenched his hands on the wheel as if that would quiet him. "But I'll tell you one thing—I wouldn't have a child of mine buried there if it was the last graveyard on earth."

20

June was full of righteous anger when she came back from the Christian shop. "Hazel didn't want to say much, but I got it out of her. He found them dancing on the graves and throwing the wreaths about. Either they thought they could get their own back on the town that way or they were high on drugs. I've never heard anything so pathetic."

Brian blinked at her from where he sat hunched behind the counter. "I hear they're planning to move."

"Good riddance. They'd better not try to say goodbye to

Andrew." She glanced around the shop. "Why are you sitting dreaming in the gloom like I don't know what? You'll have people thinking we're shut."

When she switched on the fluorescent tubes, the interior of the shop jerked forward, closed around him as the street under the padded sky fell back. "Sitting in the dark like an old spider," she said, and brushed away a star-shaped web between two stoves in the window. "What's been wrong with you these past few days?"

"Some kind of summer germ, I expect. Maybe I need more fresh air."

"You can collect the boy from school, then. He was saying you don't any more just yesterday. Take him for a walk if you like, while I've time off from the other shop. And if you don't feel any better, go to the doctor. Even Godwin does."

Brian closed his eyes, but her voice probed the nervous orange dimness where he was trying to hide. "You'd tell me if there was anything else, wouldn't you? Godwin says we mustn't keep things to ourselves. Bring them out into the open where they can be dealt with, that's what we're supposed to do."

"I know what he says," Brian mumbled, feeling as if she kept dragging him out of a long, dim tunnel that was himself. If only he could go all the way down there, he might stop remembering for at least a little while.

"You aren't blaming me, are you? I know you must be frustrated. It's only that I'm afraid Andrew might hear us. And I still think he's backward because God was punishing us for what we used to do."

The shop bell rang. Brian's eyes twitched open. A young woman wearing a loose overall with a crucifix stitched on the front was striding up to the counter. "Mr. Bevan? Godwin says would you come and see him now if you don't mind."

Brian thought of hiding in the tunnel of himself, of hunching himself up so tightly that they wouldn't be able to ferret him out. Once they went for help he could make a run for it, onto the moors. But June was watching him, not knowing whether to be proud of him or nervous, and it seemed he could only do what he was told.

He followed the young woman into the street. Her overall sketched her body, and he felt his groin stirring until the sun broke through the clouds. He had almost to close his eyes as

116

she led him to the hotel. He could feel his skin stinging wherever it wasn't covered.

The relative dimness of the hotel felt like ointment on his skin, soothed his eyes. The young woman announced them at the reception desk, then took him up to Mann's room. At the moment when he had to leave the rickety lift, Brian's steps grew heavier, as he remembered all that he'd done and felt and would have to confess.

"Okay," Mann called when the young woman knocked at his door. She stood aside for Brian, who stumbled into the room more quickly than he meant to. It must be one of the smallest bedrooms in the hotel, just a single bed and a sink under a mirror bolted to the wall. The bareness made him think of an interrogation room.

Mann was sitting on the bed. His angular face looked thinner than ever, tight and ready as a fist. He sat forward, blue eyes gleaming. "Close the door, Brian. I'd appreciate your help."

This was so unexpected that Brian had to lean against the door. "What can I do?"

"I need rope, all you have. Better still, rope ladders."

"You'd be better off with the mountain rescue people. They'd be able to see you were safe, as well."

"They don't want me to do what I have to do. They say it's too dangerous. Seems like they don't trust in God as much as they should. Won't you do this for God? I'll pay for everything you provide."

Brian wanted to help, yearned to if that would relieve him of his guilt, but it wasn't that simple. "I haven't any ladders at the shop. I'd have to order them."

"I'd need them early next week."

"I could drive over to Sheffield." If Mann trusted him so much, perhaps he wasn't as guilty as he thought he was.

"Would you do that? I'd be most grateful, and you don't need me to tell you God would be." He glanced down at his clasped hands, then at Brian. "I want to ask you one more favor. Don't tell anyone what you'll be doing for me, okay? I don't want our enemies to learn of it and try to stop me."

"Stop you doing what?"

Mann gazed at him until Brian wished he hadn't asked, felt as if he'd betrayed himself by asking. But Mann was only deliberating, apparently. "I mean to take God down into the cave," he said, almost to himself. "Whatever is there is no match for God."

His eyes focused sharply on Brian. "I told you that because you'd agreed not to say anything. I'll see you Sunday at the rally," he said with the hint of a warning in his voice, "or before then if you get to Sheffield first. Here, let me give you a hundred pounds, and if you spend more, just show me the check."

Brian stuffed the notes deep into his pocket. Mann was already sinking back on the bed, folding his hands on his chest, his face relaxing a little, perhaps as much as it ever did. Brian closed the door quietly and strolled along the corridor, the wad of notes brushing repetitively against his thigh. It seemed a token that he could redeem himself, or even that he'd been judged and found worthy. Surely Mann could tell if anyone could.

He hadn't meant her to fall, he reminded himself. He wished he could believe he'd dreamed her fall, as he'd dreamed the other night of going up to the cave and creeping behind Mann's sentry there. Perhaps that dream was a symptom of the fever he'd caught, some midsummer illness worse than hay fever, for even the thought of the dream made his skin crawl. He still felt in danger of confessing if he didn't keep tight control of himself, and if he confessed to making the young woman fall he was sure he'd be suspected of far worse. At least there would be only one more rally before Mann went down the cave.

Clouds had closed over Moonwell again. The subdued light allowed him to step confidently into the square. He'd take Andrew for a walk on the moors. He waited by the main door of the school while the children swarmed out. The last few came out by themselves, their faces sullen or smiling at a secret or bright with faith. Brian kept glancing up in case the clouds were about to break, and so he didn't notice Andrew until the boy had walked past him to Katy at the gate.

Katy spent most of her time at the Christian shop now, perhaps atoning for having stolen from the Bevans. Her presence at the school made Brian feel as if June didn't trust him. "Here, Andrew," he called. "It's your dad. Here I am."

Andrew turned clumsily, his schoolbag bumping one scabby knee. "It's all right, Katy," Brian said. "I'll take him."

118

"Mrs. Bevan said I were to bring him home. She said you had to go and see Mr. Mann."

"He needed my help," Brian said defensively, and reminded himself that he wasn't supposed to tell. "You can say to my wife I took the lad. We're going for a walk. You'd like that, wouldn't you, son?"

Andrew nodded so feebly that Brian could almost have hit him for making Katy think he didn't like to be with his father. "The rescue man said it were going to be misty on the moor," Katy said.

"I didn't say we were going there, did I?" Brian felt found out, as if he were the criminal, not her. "All right then," he muttered at Andrew, "we'll go home."

"I'd better come," Katy said. She must be afraid that June would think she wasn't to be trusted even to collect Andrew, but it seemed to Brian that she was making sure he didn't go on the moors with Andrew. What business was it of hers? The boy had to do what his father told him. Brian was tempted to take him up anyway, except that she would only go telling tales to June, upsetting her. He walked faster instead, making Katy pant and stumble to keep up as he dragged Andrew along by one hand.

"Thanks anyway, Katy," June said. "I'm sorry, I didn't realize."

She sounded to Brian as if she were apologizing for him. "I'll be going to Sheffield tomorrow, if you're interested."

"What are you going there for?"

"On Godwin's behalf."

He'd expected that to drive her doubts away, but she was still trying not to frown. "Why?"

"I'll tell you later," he said, and thought of another way to justify himself to Katy. "Listen, Andrew, you tell your new teacher that if she wants a bit more room than she's got at Mrs. Scragg's, we'd be happy to have her."

The moment June nodded he realized that would give them even less opportunity for sex. He felt as if he'd tricked himself. At least June's doubts should vanish once she knew what Mann had asked of him, but when he told her after Andrew was in bed, she still looked dubious. She must be worried on Mann's behalf, not suspicious of Brian's story. He was glad to go to bed, to hide in his sleep for a while, until he

119

woke shaking uncontrollably because of what he'd seen: the moon's new face, hatching.

It was more than a full moon. It was swollen and trembling, almost filling the sky and touching the moor. It had more than one face, it had three, one of which vanished before he could glimpse it as the white globe began to turn. It wasn't just trembling, it was cracking open, hatching three shapes the color of the moon, shapes that unfurled their wings and glowed brighter as they flapped away across the moor. He could still see the new face as they burst forth from it, the face that had been hidden until the familiar markings turned away. The new face was his own.

Of course it was the dream that was making him shiver, not the frosty light of the remnant of moon outside the window. All the same, he felt as if the light were making his body uncontrollable, hardly recognizable. He was tempted to go to the mirror to prove to himself that he didn't have the moon's face, however unfamiliar it felt, but he would be bound to wake June. Here on the edge of nightmare he felt vulnerable again, at the mercy of whoever might find out about him. If Mann found the hiker's body, he would never be able to keep from confessing. But Mann needn't find the body—at least, he needn't be able to tell anyone about it. His safety would be in Brian's hands.

21

"Bit summery today, isn't it?"

"Too bloody summery by half. And there'll be more of it before the year's over."

"Look at them all grinning like idiots. You'd think the sun was shining just for them."

"More like they think it's shining out of Godwin Mann's arse."

"One of them won't be grinning when we've finished with them. Are you ready then, Mr. Gloom?"

"Let's join the happy throng, Mr. Despondency."

Eustace stepped out of his cottage when he saw that the crowd was thinning. A few stragglers hurried along the High Street on their way to the cave. Hardly anyone chatted to him on his rounds since the fiasco at the pub. Maybe they'd rather God delivered their letters. "Like pigeon post, only holier. Pentecostal post," he muttered as he closed his gate.

He made his way through the deserted streets and climbed toward the sky. Large white clouds unfurled across the sun and drifted onward. An old man who lived in Kiln Lane was struggling up the last few yards before the moor. When Eustace offered him a hand, he grumbled, "I can manage." For years Eustace had been Moonwell's unofficial social worker, checking that old people didn't need help while he was on his rounds, but now some of them wouldn't even open their doors to him. No wonder someone must have been delighted to make him deliver the letter to Phoebe Wainwright—but before today's rally was over, he'd blow their halo off if he could. He owed Phoebe that much.

The choir was singing as he stepped onto the charred moor. He followed the path of blackened stubble through the ash to the stone bowl. All of Mann's followers, which seemed to include virtually the whole of Moonwell, stood above the cave. "About time you joined us, Eustace," Mrs. Scragg said loudly from where she stood, watching the children as if their parents weren't with them.

"Mr. Gloom to you," he almost said. She'd always told him he was slow at school, the old bitch. Maybe it wasn't such a bad thing if Phoebe didn't deliver so many children for the Scraggs to cow, but he still meant to expose the writer of the letter. He walked faster, staring at hundreds of faces he'd seen at their front doors in answer to his knock, every one of them sealed into the same pious blankness now. "Just enough masks to go round for God's matinee . . ." Even the dressmaker's look of contemptuous triumph as she realized he'd come to the rally seemed preferable, though he would have liked to spit in her face.

He came to rest opposite Mann as a large mottled cloud closed over the sun. Though he was beyond the crowd, he felt

121

unsettlingly close to the cave. Perhaps he'd walked around the bowl too fast; the crowd seemed to be turning in a slow dance, a whirlpool whose center was the cave. He closed his eyes to try to regain his balance, to be ready to prowl in search of faces that looked guilty when Mann started urging them to confess. He'd know which one to stare at until they couldn't keep quiet any longer, he was sure he would. But he was still trying to settle himself when the choir fell silent. In the stillness, which the faint sound of church bells was too distant to trouble, Mann said, "I won't ask anyone to confess here today."

Eustace's eyes snapped open. "I know you're all here because you believe," the evangelist was saying. "God's love is in every one of us now, and we've only to try our best to be worthy of it. He loves you for offering this place back to Him. Now I want to ask you all to do Him one more favor. I want you all to join me here at noon on St. John the Baptist Day to help me make this God's place forever."

His voice echoed from the monotonous bare slopes and resounded in the cave. "I know that ordinarily it would be a day for trading, but I want to ask you as you love God to close your shops that day and join me here. All you'll have to do is pray. I'll do the rest. My faith tells me I can."

Eustace remembered what Mann had said to him the day they'd met on the road into Moonwell: that Mann was facing his greatest challenge. He struggled to control his dizziness, his sense of being drawn down toward the hub of the whirling. He was afraid to walk in case he fell over, but he still had to search for whoever didn't want to be noticed.

"I guess there are still a few people in Moonwell who aren't with us," Mann said. "A very few. There's surely no reason for them to be up here St. John the Baptist Day, and I'd appreciate it if someone who knows them would tell them so." Without more ado, he sank to his knees. "And now—"

Now, Eustace thought, there would be prayers and hymns, and he would have lost his chance. Rage shuddered through him at the thought of the letter-writer hiding in plain sight, praying. His head was swimming so much that he didn't realize at first he was speaking aloud. "There's someone here who's not a Christian," he said.

Every face turned to him. He had the largest audience he'd ever had, and it froze him, his mouth hanging open, his body swaying uncontrollably as it fought to keep its balance. It took him a moment to realize what they were all thinking. No, he tried to say, I don't mean me, I'm not the one who has to confess. But their gaze and their feelings—contempt, encouragement, impatience, reassurance—sucked him in, and he was falling into the dark.

At least, his awareness was. His body was still standing, and he could hear his voice, distant and unstoppable. He didn't know what he was saying; all he knew was that the only way out of the dark was to fight his way back to his voice. Now he could almost make out what it was saying, and he was suddenly desperate to stop it. But when at last he struggled out of the dark and back into control of himself, back to feeling the ashen wind in his face as a cloud dragged across the sun, the look of the crowd told him it was too late.

"We forgive you," Mann said. "We'll pray for you." Some of the crowd nodded and fell to their knees, but even they looked disgusted and appalled until they rearranged their faces into piety. When Eustace stumbled forward inadvertently, a woman shrank away from him as if she couldn't bear the thought of his touch. "What did I say?" he wanted to demand, but he didn't dare ask. As Mann started to pray— "We ask Your forgiveness, O God, for this sinner"—Eustace lurched toward the path to the town. In the midst of the chorus of prayer that followed him across the moor, he thought he heard dry, croaking laughter.

22

The thing in Needham's story was like Br'er Rabbit, Diana thought. At least you had to wonder why the Romans were supposed to have thrown it down the very cave where it had been wont to receive its sacrifices. You might suspect that it had influenced them to do so, like a subtler version of Br'er Rabbit's pretense that he didn't want to be thrown into the briar patch. You might wonder if it had been able to blot out the memory of Lutudarum and of all that the druids used to do. You might think a whole lot of damn fool things, Diana reflected, and there didn't seem to be much else she could do while she was refused access to Godwin Mann.

He'd no time now to talk to unbelievers, his minions had told her at the hotel. She might have gritted her teeth and pretended to accept his faith if that would let her in, but then she realized how little that was likely to achieve: she needed more than the old man's story to confront him with. She'd driven to the library in Sheffield and spent a day poring over books.

She'd come away with a great deal of information and a sense that parts of it could be put together to prove all sorts of things, the way you could claim to show that God came from space or that the end of the world was near. Take Guy Fawkes Night, which it had been illegal not to celebrate in Britain until 1859. Of course it celebrated the failure of the Gunpowder Plot to blow up the Houses of Parliament, but the bonfires people lit to celebrate were at least as old as Samhain. That was the druid festival marking the death of the sun, and it is known as Halloween now. Their other major festival was Beltane—May Eve, Walpurgisnacht, the date of Hitler's death. Beltane had celebrated the return of the sun with huge bonfires and human sacrifices. Men had passed firebrands from person to person, and whoever was holding the brand when it went out had had to go down on all fours and have his back piled with rubbish. That reminded Diana of the man in the moon with sticks on his back, just as the guy on top of the bonfires sounded like the man who wasn't a man who'd been burned at the cave. Even Mann couldn't stamp out Guy Fawkes Night, she told herself.

As for the moon, it had always meant magic, often black. Worshiping the moon had been condemned as evil at least as far back as the Book of Job. Lunacy, lycanthropy, and mooncalves, inhuman things that grew in the womb, were all blamed on the moon. Hecate, goddess of the witches, had originally been a moon goddess with three faces, who had been accompanied by a pack of infernal dogs. Witchcraft was supposed to be the remains of shamanism, and apparently the druids had been shamans, wearing pelts to communicate with those species of animal. Shamans were led away by dreams into the wilderness to meditate and experience many lives, life out of the body, visions, ecstasy. The Satan of the witches was identified with Cernunnos, god of the druid underworld. It seemed odd that his name was so like Cerberus, guardian of the Roman underworld, a dog with three heads, three being the magic number of the druids. The pentacle had been involved in druid magic, which was why it was nicknamed the druid's foot. How far might the druidic influence extend? Perhaps it had something to do with the three wishes in fairy tales, but surely not the three persons of God or the three victims on Calvary. There were too many questions and glimmering connections; she felt stifled, unable to think. She stepped out of her cottage, to breathe.

Patchy clouds lumbered across the sun. The sky flickered like a smoky fire. The broken promises of brightness made Diana feel frustrated, impatient to do something, but what? A phrase of a hymn drifted down from the moor, together with a smell of ash. It wasn't worth her trying to confront Mann now. She ought to be visiting the Booths, to reassure them that someone didn't believe the nonsense they were being accused of.

Nothing but a sluggish breeze moved in the High Street. Windows of shops and cottages gleamed emptily at her; a pig's plastic head stared at her from the butcher's. With nobody about to disapprove of her, she felt a touch of that sense of homecoming she'd experienced the first time she'd seen Moonwell, yet she felt as if she'd forgotten why she was needed here or didn't even know. The streets seemed to ache with the absence of children, the silence where there should be shouts, the sounds of play. It didn't matter what they were led to believe so long as they were happy, she tried to tell herself; they'd grow out of it, some of them anyway. But she wasn't convinced they were happy, didn't want to imagine how school might be for them now. Her thoughts shut off the streets from her, and so she was halfway across the town square before she noticed she was being watched.

It was the sound that alerted her, a faint soft tearing mingled with snarling. She couldn't locate it in the square or the empty streets. The hotel and the ponderous clouds stood over her. She took another step, and then she happened to glance past the side of the hotel, down the alley that sloped steeply past the kitchen. Six eyes met hers.

She saw the eyes and teeth first, the jaws ripping at a piece of meat as red and bloody as the lolling tongues. There must be three stray dogs in the alley, Alsatians with matted fur and dangerous reddened eyes, but she could see only the heads watching her over the slope of the alley. If she moved, she thought, they would come leaping, and she would see if they really had three bodies or only one. The thought was so absurd that she stepped toward the alley to see.

As soon as she moved, the three heads began to snarl in unison, baring their gums like charred gray plastic, their stained yellow teeth. She mustn't back away, or they would attack. She'd halted, willing them to slink away so that she could watch, when the clouds parted overhead. Instinct made her step forward as the sun blazed straight in their eyes. They flinched back, whimpering, and fled down the alley.

Diana reached the alley in time to see them turn the corner, three stray dogs. She'd known all along that they were, she told herself. But her chest was tight, her heart was jumping. Maybe she'd be able to laugh at herself when she reached the bookshop, cheer up Geraldine and Jeremy. She hoped they would be there. Moonwell felt like a ghost town just now, forgotten by the world.

The thought stopped her breath for a moment. "My God," she whispered, staring along the empty High Street, wondering which way to run, who to tell. It was true, then. It was happening again, and nobody had noticed. Perhaps she had realized too late.

23

That Sunday evening Vera was leafing through a will when she said, "Something's wrong."

Craig put down the *Telegraph* and reached for his pipe. "I thought it seemed like a straightforward legacy."

"I don't mean this, I mean Hazel. I feel something's wrong."

He bent over his pipe and thumbed tobacco into it, feeling as if someone had pinched his stomach. "Go ahead and call her. She won't want to hear from me."

"You know she does," Vera said fiercely, and hurried to the phone. She must be anxious because she hadn't spoken to Hazel since they'd left Moonwell. If she blamed Craig for that, she was concealing it well, but he wished he'd never had that argument at Benedict's. He'd come away disliking not only Benedict but his own daughter.

At breakfast on his last day in Moonwell, Hazel had turned on Craig, accusing him of leading Benedict to expect a loan and then letting him down—of doing so because he didn't care for Benedict and his faith. "Faith that we'll bail him out, you mean? Faith that people won't have heard about his shoddy workmanship?" Craig had managed not to say, but the sight of Benedict looking injured yet forgiving had proved too much for him. Hazel was just looking for a substitute father, wasn't that so? Someone to tell her what to do, forgive her when she confessed she'd done wrong, make her feel safe from the world? "If that's the kind of father you want you're welcome to him," he'd growled, stalking upstairs for the luggage. Only when she wouldn't look at him as he climbed into Benedict's van had he realized how he'd injured her, and the worst of it was that he'd experienced no surge of love for his hurt child, he'd disliked her for not being able to cope with the truth.

It wasn't up to him to judge her. They'd always encouraged her to be herself, and now she was. She wasn't their little girl any longer. After she was married, her room had felt like a wound in their house that had taken months to heal, and when Benedict was courting her, Craig had grown impotent with Vera—fathers often went through that, apparently—but they'd adjusted to all that, or thought they had. Now parenthood seemed to have all the anxieties with none of the rewards, and he hated himself for taking out his feelings on Hazel.

Vera was dialing. When she'd failed three times to make the connection, she called the operator. "Moonwell," she explained, and had to repeat it twice. "Look, never mind the name, I've given you the area code. Don't try to tell me there's no such place." She beckoned Craig, her voice shaking. "You speak to him."

But when Craig took the receiver, the phone at the other end was ringing. As Vera sank into her chair, one hand over her eyes, a voice said "Peak Homecare."

"Hello, Benedict. Is Hazel there? Her mother would like to speak to her."

"Not just now."

Craig tried to keep the stiffness out of his voice. "Will she be home soon? Could you ask her to call then?"

"She won't be home till late. She's out praying."

For a moment Craig heard that as "playing," as if Hazel were indeed a child again. "They're holding a prayer meeting at the shop," Benedict went on. "I wouldn't be surprised if they go on all night."

"Praying for what?"

"Oh, there's always plenty to pray for, though I don't suppose you'd think so."

"Yes, but they don't usually go on all night, do they? Why now?"

"I'm afraid you wouldn't believe me if I told you."

His smugness infuriated Craig. "Well, if you won't tell me what's going on and Hazel's mother can't talk to her, it sounds as if we'll have to come and see you."

Vera nodded vigorously, smiling. "It wouldn't be possible just now," Benedict said. "I've had to move all the alarms into the spare room and store the rest of my materials in the shed. I can't afford to rent space any longer."

"I'm glad to hear you've found a way to cut your costs. We can always stay at the hotel. Don't be surprised if you see us soon."

"The hotel's full," Benedict said, too readily. Craig dropped the receiver into its cradle. "What do you think?" he said to Vera. "Shall we go and see what's up?"

"Oh, yes please. Shall I call Lionel or will you? I'm sure he won't mind holding the fort for a couple of days."

Lionel was their partner, who would take over the practice if they moved. "I didn't mean right now," Craig protested. "I was thinking more of the weekend."

"I don't want to wait until then to find out what's wrong. You think something is too, I can tell."

"But it may not be serious by our standards. Anyway, it's really up to Lionel when we can go."

Lionel said he would be happy to fit in with whatever plans they made. "Go tomorrow if you like." When Craig found the phone number of the Moonwell Hotel in the AA book, having searched so hard his eyes began to ache, the receptionist told him somewhat reluctantly that a reservation hadn't been taken up. "We'll take it," Craig said, and immediately felt dubious. "Hazel may not thank us for this, you know," he pointed out to Vera.

"I'll chance it. She needs me, I can feel it."

"Let's hope she realizes she does," Craig said, earning himself a reproachful look.

Later he tried to make love to Vera. At the end of half an hour his arms were trembling from supporting himself on the bed. He felt as if age had withered his penis. "Never mind," Vera said, stroking his sweaty forehead as he abandoned the task. "We'll pretend we aren't married when we're staying at the hotel."

He slept eventually, and wakened refreshed. That lasted until they were a few miles out of Sheffield and he had to slow down on the tortuous road. A reservoir glared in his eyes, a sports car edged up behind him until their bumpers were almost touching, then swung round him and at once was braked so sharply at a bend that Craig almost rammed it. There wasn't a bus to Moonwell on Mondays, but he spent the rest of the journey wishing he'd insisted that they take the bus tomorrow.

The sky turned gray as the road climbed through the wild

129

fields toward Moonwell. Tension and lack of sleep must be catching up with him, for as the Peugeot coasted up the long slopes of the moors, he felt as if each crest concealed a drop. The feeling was uncomfortably reminiscent of his childhood fall into the mineshaft. Damn Benedict for making him feel this way. Even the sight of the blank sky above Moonwell gave him a twinge of panic. He willed himself to stay aware of the road. By the time they reached the hotel, his head was throbbing so much he could barely see.

Their room was cramped under the eaves, its window protruding through. Craig sank on the bed, which exuded a faint smell of detergent, and closed his eyes. Vera drew the curtains and went out to the chemist's, while Craig lay listening to the quiet of the town, hardly the sound of a car. When Vera came back, she gave him a glass of water and a brace of paracetemol tablets; then she said, "Of all the people I could have done without, I bumped into Mel and Ursula."

"Remind me," Craig said, trying to relax so as to give the painkillers a chance.

"Benedict's holy friends. They've gone to warn Hazel we're here."

Five minutes later the lift came creaking to the top of the hotel, and Hazel knocked at their door. "Oh, Mummy, why have you come back now?"

"I'm sorry we did if that's how you feel. I thought you might even have been glad, but I obviously don't know much."

"Mummy, I *am* glad. I never would have wanted us to part the way we did. But Godwin's called a special rally for tomorrow, and I'll be busy until then."

"What you mean is, unbelievers aren't welcome."

"I just mean you'll have the town almost to yourselves and nothing to do," Hazel said unconvincingly.

"We'll be going nowhere while I feel like this," Craig growled, resting one arm on his closed eyes.

"What's wrong with Daddy?"

"He doesn't like driving on these roads, that's all. Just leave him alone and he'll be all right. We'll be in the bar," she told him, and when Hazel demurred, "I want a drink even if you don't. We've got to talk."

Craig heard their voices swallowed by the creaking of the

lift, then the hush closed round him. He took two more pills as soon as he dared, and reached for the controls of the bedside radio. He'd forgotten the evangelical station, but in fact even that wasn't coming through. All he could hear, until he turned off the radio and lay back, was static that sounded unpleasantly like dry, inhuman laughter.

24

Monday was half over before Diana managed to contact Nick. He sounded delighted to hear from her. "Are you in town? Free for dinner? How are things in that town of yours with the strange name?"

"What name is that?" she said, trying to sound casual.

"To tell you the truth, I can't remember. Blame last night's heavy drinking. I remember you, though. I was sorry you had to dash off last time."

"So was I, Nick. But listen, you asked how were things here. I'm afraid they're getting worse."

"In what way?"

She closed her eyes and took a breath and willed him not to be incredulous. "Moonwell's supposed to be a tourist town, a center for hikers, right? But the only visitors the town has had for months are the people who Godwin Mann sent ahead. And what worries me even more is that nobody seems to have noticed."

"Moonwell, that's the name, of course. So are you saying this is Mann's fault somehow?"

What else could she claim that he might even consider trying to slip into print? "It sounds that way, doesn't it? Even I didn't notice until yesterday. Whatever's happening is getting to me too."

"Some kind of mass hypnosis, religious hysteria, that kind of thing, you mean? If you're being affected by it you should get out straight away. I can put you up if you like."

He was making a play for her. In other circumstances she might have responded. "I can't just leave all those children in the midst of it, with nobody to care how it may be affecting them," she said, and suppressed the thought, which would neither define itself nor go away, that she was here for another purpose entirely. If she left she might forget the town, just as Nick had forgotten the name. She mustn't brood about staying and being forgotten. "I have to see what happens tomorrow. Mann's going to do what he came to do," she said.

"Let me know what happens, or if you change your mind about leaving," he said, and she realized he was more anxious about her than eager for a story. "I wish I could promise you some coverage."

"Aren't you still in touch with that radio station?"

"They closed it down last week." He was silent. Then he said, "If you're as worried as you sound and won't leave, I should at least come and take a look."

"Oh, would you?" Perhaps he'd notice the effect that had on him. "When?"

"I'll have to let you know. Not for a few days, but soon. It's your turn to buy dinner," he said, and more seriously, "Remember, call me any time you feel you need to."

At least someone else knew now, she told herself, even if she'd had to blame Mann in order to convince him. Being alone in her knowledge had dismayed her, especially when the Booths had told her they were moving to Wales. If only she could talk to someone less skeptical than Nick—and then, slapping herself on the forehead, she realized that she could. She went out at once, to the church.

Sunlight flickered on the thick walls and seemed to shrink the gargoyles. Mistletoe gleamed like scales on the trunk of an oak among the headstones. Father O'Connell was praying silently in front of the altar. When he stood up, dusting the knees of his cassock, she went along the aisle to him. "Why, it's Diana," he said, and took her hands. "Have you come to swell my dwindling flock?"

"Not exactly, Father O'Connell, I'm afraid. I just wanted a word with you."

"Always glad to see you. And listen, call me Bob so you don't have to put on such a glum, respectful face. Come with me now and we'll have ourselves a pot of the Earl Grey you like so much."

He ushered her across the High Street to the presbytery, a cottage where an Alsatian dozed on the hall carpet and pricked up her ears as the door opened. "Are fewer people coming to church, then?" Diana said.

"Fewer of my congregation since I told them what I thought of what happened at the bookshop. Some of Mann's flock stray in now and again, but they always seem to find it wanting." He patted the dog absentmindedly. "Good girl, Kelly. Still, if I'm to tell the truth, maybe they've reason to have their doubts about the church. Seems as if it may have a bit of a Celtic fort in its foundations."

"I thought you believed taking over traditions was one of the strengths of your church."

"Yes, but there's traditions and traditions. I found out that when they built the fort they may have buried a child in the foundations—supposed to make it impregnable, you see. But you don't want to hear such things about children. Go in the front now and sit down, and when I've made tea, we'll talk."

Diana sat in the front room and glanced about at Irish landscapes, a family album on a table next to the electric fire, a Morris West novel sprawled on a chair. Kelly padded in and laid her head on Diana's lap, nuzzled her hand until Diana stroked her. By the time the priest wheeled in the trolley, Diana was impatient to talk. "I've been looking into our traditions too," she said.

She told him how Lutudarum had vanished from the map, how the same was beginning to happen to Moonwell. "When I first came here the streets were full of hikers and tourists like myself, but where are they this year? The streets are full of new faces, and maybe that's one reason we didn't notice, but they aren't tourists." His eyes were telling her to go on, and so she said, "I think Godwin Mann has stirred it up, whatever's making the outside world forget about us. And another thing it can do is prevent us from noticing."

"Well," he said, and the doorbell rang. "Excuse me a minute," he said.

She could have wept for having been interrupted when she was almost sure he'd been sympathetic. He came back along the hall with someone and put his head round the door. "You

133

can stay a few more minutes, can't you? I'd like to hear what else you have to say."

She'd said all she could. Presumably he'd gone up to his study to counsel one of his parishioners, and what she'd told him might fade from his mind. Quite soon, however, she heard him and his visitor on the stairs again. They halted outside the front room, and Father O'Connell pushed the door open. "Diana, I think you ought to hear this."

His visitor, a thin, pale, awkward man in his thirties, sidled timidly past him into the room. Diana had seen him before— in the lobby of the hotel, she realized. He looked on the edge of fleeing, even when the priest said, "Miss Kramer shares your doubts. I'd like you to tell her what you just told me."

The pinched man only stared at her. "Delbert here has been watching over the cave on Godwin Mann's behalf," the priest explained. "I think you meant to say, Delbert, that he's more worried about what he's up against than he lets on."

"I didn't mean to say that." Delbert dragged his chapped fingers through his graying hair. "He believes he can do anything. He thinks he's been called here as God's champion. He thinks his father playing Satan in that film was a sign to him that he had to stand for God. He's high on faith, gets that way at the rallies. He's even having visions now."

"Then you're saying," the priest said with a hint of nervousness, "you don't think he's equal to whatever task he's set himself."

"Didn't I already say so? Oh, you want her to hear, as if any of us can do anything now." He gave Diana a mistrustful sidelong glance. "I know about these things. I was a Satanist in California until they put me in the bughouse and Godwin brought me out. I'm telling you, what's down there in the cave is older than Satan. It's what cavemen were afraid of in the dark, and it'll turn us into cavemen if he stirs it up, it'll have us how it wants us."

Something dark pressed against the window, molded to it like a snail: the shadow of a cloud. "Does anyone else feel the way you do?" Diana said, and found her voice was stiff.

"They'd rather believe Godwin will save us all. But I'm telling you, I looked down into that cave last night and I heard something laughing. It's ready for him, it's eager to meet him. Maybe it even put the thought in his head to come here in the first place. I told him what I heard down there, and he figured Satan was making me tell him to try to faze him. So now he's even more set on going down there tomorrow."

"If people could be convinced in time that it's dangerous—"

Delbert interrupted her. "The more opposition he runs into now, the more he'll be convinced he's right. I told you, there's not a thing anyone can do."

Deep down she felt he was wrong, but that wasn't reassuring either. "You said he'd had a vision," Father O'Connell prompted.

"That's the worst part. He believes everything's a sign he's going to win on God's behalf." He glared out at the clouds looming behind clouds and muttered, "He told me he dreams every night of a calendar with a devil's face, a calendar for June. And after tomorrow's date the calendar is dead blank."

25

Someone was knocking at the front door. Brian forced his sticky eyes open and threw off the humid sheets. It must be the police, and all he felt was relief that they'd found out what he'd done to Godwin and the hiker. He swung himself out of bed and stumbled blinking to the window.

He pulled the curtains open and levered up the sash with the heels of his hands. As the sunlight struck his hands, they felt as if they were shrinking. He leaned out of the window, his shoulders bumping the sash. The two people on the path weren't policemen, they were Godwin's messengers.

June was closing the front door. The rattle of the sash made the messengers look up. "Nearly time," they called to Brian, smiling brightly, and trotted to the next house to spread the good news. Godwin wasn't dead, then. Brian had only dreamed of disguising the flaw in one of the ropes he'd brought back from Sheffield, and you couldn't be held responsible for dreams.

In the bathroom he bathed and shaved, cutting himself twice because the light over the mirror stung his eyes and skin. Surely it was guilt that made him feel like this, gave him a feverish impression that his body was no longer quite his. Perhaps Godwin wouldn't find the hiker, perhaps she'd fallen farther than Godwin could climb. It wouldn't be fair if helping God and Godwin caused Brian to be found out, to betray himself.

When he was dressed, he ventured downstairs, nervous of encountering Miss Ingham, Andrew's teacher, who was lodging with them now. But she'd gone ahead to help at the cave, leaving June flapping her duster at corners of the front room. He'd never known such a spidery summer, nor had he ever seen five-pointed webs before. June half turned toward him as he came into the room. "How are you feeling? We were going to let you sleep."

"What do you mean? There's nothing much wrong with me as I know of."

"You were tossing and turning half the night. Once I woke up and you weren't even in bed. I'd have come looking for you, but you'd got me so exhausted I just went back to sleep."

"I must have gone to the toilet," he said hastily, rather than admit that he couldn't remember getting out of bed at all. "That's where you'd better go now, Andrew, and then we'll be off."

June went back to peering into corners of the room. Her back to Brian, she murmured, "You seem very eager to go."

"Shouldn't I be?" She couldn't know about the cave— there wasn't much to know. "I thought you'd be glad I'm helping Godwin."

"Of course I'm glad." But then she looked straight at him. "I just wonder why you're suddenly so anxious to please him."

"Who says I'm anxious? I didn't ask to help, you know. He asked me." Thank God, here was Andrew to save him from further awkwardness. "Hurry up, son. You're going to see Godwin Mann climb down the cave."

"You're not to go anywhere near, Andrew, do you hear?"

"You just keep hold of my hand while we're up there,

136

son," Brian said with a touch of defiance, and took one clammy hand, thrusting his fingers between Andrew's so that the boy's ragged, bitten fingernails couldn't scratch his skin.

The High Street was crowded with people converging on the paths up to the moor. June caught up with Hazel as they climbed the nearest path, the limestone houses huddling together as the town fell away. Hazel chatted brightly, though she seemed preoccupied, while Benedict wondered aloud if Brian might like a security check at the house or the shop: God had enough to look after without keeping burglars away. He had to raise his voice to be heard over the sound of hammering ahead, and he fell silent as they stepped over the edge of the stone bowl.

Several of Mann's followers were standing just above the cave by two pitons driven into the rock. Mann was going to abseil down, Brian thought, and felt proud of himself for having helped; he smiled at the sky masked by clouds. He'd already told the police about the hiker, he reminded himself to quell his waves of nervousness. Whatever Godwin found down there, surely it needn't trouble Brian.

All the same, Brian flinched as the crowd in the bowl began cheering. Godwin had arrived. He stood for a few moments on the edge of the stone bowl, hands spread on either side of him. Perhaps they were meant to deprecate the cheers, but they gave him the look of Christ blessing a multitude. Some of the older people in the gathering dabbed at their eyes. The cheering intensified as he came down into the bowl, the gold cross stitched on the front of his overall catching the muffled sunlight, a whistle dangling from a string around his neck. In the midst of the cheers, the screech of a bird somewhere on the moors sounded like laughter.

The cheering faded as Mann reached the pitons. He knelt above the cave and closed his eyes. A wind stirred the ash on the blackened slopes, setting charred stumps of heather trembling. Sunlight fluttered over the landscape and made the mouth of the cave appear to shift, stone lips working. Brian saw June grip Andrew's hand with both of hers.

Mann crossed himself eventually and stood up. "I want to thank you all on God's behalf for coming here today. I guess He thinks of you the same way I do—you're a living act of faith. I can feel your faith giving me the strength to do what I was called here to do."

Brian willed himself to believe with his entire being. He was sure he could feel what the evangelist felt, the energy of a faith that was urging Godwin to succeed. Brian couldn't be singled out in the midst of that, it couldn't be directed at him to make him speak. Perhaps it was just his restless night that was making him still feel nervous.

The wind caught Mann's voice, swelling it like a voice that was being tuned on a radio. "You'll pray for me, won't you? I know God wouldn't have sent me here if He didn't think I could do it, but right now, deep down I'm scared. I know I won't be scared if I can hear you all praying and singing God's praises while I climb."

His voice grew thin as the wind rose. "Today God will heal this festering wound in the earth," he said, unfolding one fist toward the cave, "and then I believe this whole country will begin to turn away from superstition and the occult back to God, when it hears what I'll have to tell."

Several of his followers brought him his equipment and helped him put it on: a miner's helmet, a kit bag loaded with rope and metal that clinked. Two of them fixed the ropes for him to abseil. He stood on the edge of the cave and glanced up as the sun burst through the clouds. "I think God wants us to know something," he said smiling, and swung himself out over the edge, began to walk straight down the wall of rock.

It didn't feel like a good omen to Brian. The light seemed to make the cave gape wider, brought the charred slopes lurching forward as if the low, swollen clouds were forcing them. "He's going down to pray," June murmured to Andrew, "to make this into a holy place."

"Why?"

"Because bad people used to use it for evil things. They didn't know any better. They weren't like us. They weren't civilized."

"Like apemen, Mummy?"

"Something like that. Nobody had told them about God," she murmured, sharing a smile with Hazel and Benedict at his questions. Brian willed her to shut up so that he could think. Why was the sight of the ropes jerking as Godwin climbed down making him so nervous? Godwin had obviously learned how to climb in preparation for his task, and Brian had put aside the faulty rope. The sun glared down on him like a lamp in an interrogation room. He'd only dreamed of

138

disguising the dangerous rope, he'd actually put it . . . He drew in his breath, a gasp that made his mouth taste ashen. He couldn't recall putting it anywhere.

He stepped forward inadvertently, bumping into two people in front of him. The rope jerked beneath the clouding sky, and every jerk might worsen the flaw in the rope. "Let's pray," one of Mann's watchers by the pitons said. Brian stepped back, trying to pretend he hadn't moved. As the prayers began, he joined in fiercely, almost shouting, and then he glanced sideways at June. His body stiffened, prickling, although the sun had clouded over. If he hadn't glanced at her like that, she might have told herself that he'd only stumbled, but now he was sure that she knew.

26

Late that afternoon Diana found she could no longer bear the waiting. She'd walked the length of the empty town twice, listening to hymns that drifted from the moor, telling herself that as long as the rally was singing, nothing could be wrong. She'd looked into the church and rung the presbytery bell, but there was no sign of Father O'Connell. She rather hoped he'd thought of someone in the church hierarchy to consult, though she suspected he felt bound to stay to see what happened. It seemed that Delbert's warning had come too late.

Delbert had left them with Mann's vision of the calendar and sidled out of the presbytery, glancing fearfully about to make sure that nobody saw him. "He did say he'd needed psychiatric treatment," Diana had commented, but she'd seen in the priest's eyes that he didn't think the warning could be explained away so simply, any more than she did. "All we can do for now is keep watch," he'd said.

Her frustration dogged her through the deserted town and sent her at last toward the moor. The hell with being told to stay away—she couldn't bear not to know what was happening. The ashen sky was growing darker; clouds like veils of sooty cobweb drifted across the gray, seemed to cling overhead. Above the path the sun was a blurred patch of white, a spider's cocoon embedded in the clouds. Wind flaked ash from charred stumps of heather. She was intensely aware of the moors, the unchanging lonely slopes stretching beyond the horizon to the roads where traffic might be passing, unaware of Moonwell. Perhaps nobody knew it was here any longer. She wished she'd called Nick to remind him. Surely it would still be here tomorrow.

The charred path was trampled black as oil. The closer she came to the sound of praying, the more of an outcast she felt. Couldn't they all be right, and Diana mistaken? After all, there was a word for people like her who were convinced they knew some truth that nobody else could see—but the trouble was that she would be happy to be proved wrong, hardly the attitude of a schizophrenic. She crept up to the edge of the stone bowl and peered in.

"Though you walk through the valley of darkness you needn't fear any evil," the crowd that surrounded the cave was praying. Diana glanced about for Mann, hoping that she couldn't locate him because he hadn't arrived yet—and then she saw the ropes hanging slackly into the dark.

The sight dismayed her even more than she could have predicted. If it was so easy to climb down there, why had nobody done it before? Surely not because climbers had been turned away until the time was right, yet the sight of the cave growing darker under the darkening sky filled her with a sense of dreadful imminence, until she could hardly breathe. The crowd, the children especially, looked vulnerable, too close to the edge, too close to flee if anything rose from the dark. Her panic sent her around the bowl, craning her neck to see more of the ropes, of the gaping cave. She didn't realize how visible she was until the crowd turned on her.

Their hostility felt like a blast from the cave. The children's faces were the worst, all of them wishing her away as if she had no right to be there, even Sally blinking through her precarious spectacles at her, even Ronnie, who'd clasped his hands together as if he'd rather hide them in his pockets. Perhaps she really shouldn't be there, she thought, retreating awkwardly toward the path. Perhaps all she was doing was undermining their prayers. It was St. John the Baptist Day, she reminded herself, not Harry Moony's—and then she remembered what John the Baptist's fate had been. She stared about at the blackened, lifeless slopes, and realized something that she needed desperately to feel: she wasn't entirely alone. There was still Nathaniel Needham.

She left the burned slopes behind as quickly as she could, but that wasn't especially reassuring. Green slopes glowed sullenly around her beneath the stifled sky, and she was uncomfortably aware of the dozens of abandoned mine-shafts, the maze through which she was picking her way. They led her thoughts straight to the cave through which Mann was venturing. She could almost see the dripping walls, shifting as the light from his helmet swayed; she could almost feel how his feet slithered on the mud that coated the floor of the passage. She let out a gasp of relief at the sight of Needham's cottage.

He was standing in the doorway, his knuckly hands gripping the stick that supported him. His long, wizened face was upturned, listening. As she approached, it swung toward her, his stick pointing at her like a dowser's rod. "Who's there?" he cried.

"It's Diana Kramer, Mr. Needham."

"Did you come past the cave? What are they doing there?"

"Praying and singing hymns," she said, and with an effort, "Waiting for Godwin Mann to come back up."

"He's done it then, has he? The damned fool. What kind of a preacher is he if he doesn't even realize he's putting his own soul at risk? Who does he think he is?"

"I'm not quite sure what you mean."

"Didn't I tell you one reason the druids feared the moon so much was that anyone they sacrificed to it would never go on to the afterlife? Didn't I tell you they'd be part of that thing down there for ever?"

"Well, no, you didn't," Diana murmured, rather wishing that he hadn't now. "But then he's not a sacrifice."

Needham gazed blankly at her. If she could read terror in his eyes, perhaps it was her own. "Just about everyone in town is up there praying for him," she said. "That must count for something."

Needham's eyes flickered nervously. "Not enough."

A phrase of a hymn came drifting, blurred as mist, across

the slopes. Nothing could have changed yet at the cave, but the sound, thin and lonely on the moor, made her shiver. "I wish I knew what he was doing," she blurted.

"Then you should be there watching, not bothering me."

"Mann doesn't want anyone there who isn't totally for him."

"They'll blame you anyway," Needham said with a doleful smile. "Are they all up there? Hasn't anyone gone down with him?"

"No, it's just him and his miner's helmet and all the faith he can carry."

"Thinks that's enough, does he? Happen he thinks he's God," Needham said with a furious contempt that she thought concealed fear. Or perhaps she was projecting her own fear, because she was wondering how she could know Mann was alone or what he was wearing.

"At least I imagine he's on his own," she said, reminding herself that it was just the impression she'd had on her way across the moor. The trouble was that the more she tried to deny it, the more real it seemed. "If he gets into difficulty, I'm sure someone will go down after him."

"Bloody useless if they do, and they won't like what they find."

"What might that be?"

His face seemed to shrivel. "I reckon we'll all see soon enough."

He was making her feel worse. "Well, I just came to let you know what was happening," she lied. "I should be getting back."

"Aye, someone ought to be there who can see what's really going on."

The wind had dropped. Layers of cloud that looked progressively blacker were gathering over the moors. The dimness made the green slopes appear to tremble, to start forward as if the earth were shifting. On the horizon the mountains had begun to disappear into the clouds. It was early evening, but it felt more like dusk. She made her way between the open shafts as quickly as she could for fear of being trapped by the dark.

The sky sank toward her as she descended the slope. The clouds were so dark now that she couldn't see their movement; the mass of blackness seemed to have stopped overhead, filling the sky. The lurid glow of grass and heather made her eyes ache. The restless mouths of shafts led her thoughts back to Mann. She couldn't help reluctantly admiring him: if she felt so vulnerable in the dark up here, how much worse must it be for him? He was alone with his light down there under the moors, the light groping toward whatever had been thrown down there, and what would happen when the light found it? She ground her knuckles into her lips, for she could see the light swaying on the roof above her, not of clouds but of rock.

She glared desperately at the dimming slopes. She had to go home, lie down. The silence and darkness might just be the threat of a storm, and surely the light had been lightning. Her mouth was parched, her skull felt soft and throbbing. The moors shuddered whenever she glanced at them, as if the ancient rock were shaking off its vegetation, breaking through. Whatever happened at the rally would have to take place without her. But she was congratulating herself on having found her way between the shafts and back onto the path when she heard a shout from the direction of the cave.

Over there the clouds piled above the jagged rock were almost black. A movement bright as knives against the clouds made her start, but it was only a flight of birds, three of them above the cave. Silence held her unable to stir, and then she heard the voice again. "Are you all right down there?" someone was shouting.

It was nothing to do with Diana, they'd told her to stay away—but she began to run toward the cave, her feet skidding on the ash. She wished she knew where the sun was behind the overcast. The stone bowl was so silent that she thought the rally had broken up. But no, the cave was still surrounded, the crowd peering down into the mouth that was even darker than the sky. Movement drew her eyes to the near edge, where several of Mann's followers were hauling on one of the ropes. They were pulling someone up out of the dark.

The shout jerked at her heart. One of Mann's helpers was leaning down toward the cave, so precariously that she was terrified she would see him fall. "Godwin, are you all right?" he shouted.

The hollow croaking must have been Mann clearing his throat, for the next moment they heard his voice. It sounded gigantic in the cave. "Never better," it called up. "It's done at last. Praise God now as much as you like."

Someone began to sing "Jesus Loves Me," and the crowd took up the hymn. Their voices sounded muffled by the black sky, cut off by the stone bowl. They ignored Diana, who watched Mann's helpers hauling on the rope, the pile of it behind them writhing slightly. There couldn't be much left to haul, she thought, just as a dark object rose into view over the edge of the cave.

It was Mann. He was wearing an overall and boots, but nothing else that she could see: no helmet, no rucksack. How long had he been without a light down there? The front of his overall was bulging and muddy; whatever had been stitched on it was indistinguishable. He turned his head, surveying the rally as the hymn gave way to cheers and deafening applause, and Diana saw that his eyes were almost shut. Perhaps even the darkness up here hurt them after he'd been down in the utter dark. He began to smile—she saw his teeth glint—as his helpers pulled him up to the edge, and then the rope gave way.

The crowd screamed. Those nearest the cave surged forward, and Diana was terrified that some of them would fall. They stumbled back to safety as they saw Mann grab the edge and haul himself lizardlike up the last few feet of rock, out of the cave. Perhaps he bruised his chest in doing so, for he was clutching it as he stalked away from the edge, gazing across the mouth to that part of the crowd where Andrew and his parents stood. Diana told herself that it was only the growing dark which made his smile look so ominous. The crowd was silent, waiting to be sure he wasn't injured. They began cheering again as soon as he said, "Don't you worry about me. I'm back."

27

Some of the oaks below Moonwell were so old they had taken root more than once. Branches thick as Craig's paunch had stooped to the soil and rooted themselves. He and Vera spent the afternoon strolling through the tangled woods. They felt more like a church to him than a church would have, especially since the foliage cut off the sounds of gullibility from the moor. Eventually he sat with Vera on a rock upholstered with moss beside a stream that ran through the roots of oaks. The calls of birds pierced the hushing of leaves. When Vera had gazed into the water for a while, he said, "Remember Hazel didn't know when we were coming back."

"I know I shouldn't feel they were trying to make sure there wasn't room for us. But I do."

"They were just being Christians, taking in the homeless."

"Then why didn't Benedict say they had when you rang him?"

"Maybe he realizes we wouldn't want to be reminded of his priggish friends."

Mel and Ursula had been staying with the Eddingses since the fire on the moor had driven them out of their tent. Vera had learned that, and other things she liked no better, from Hazel yesterday. "Well," Craig said, "this is very pleasant, sitting here like this by the babbling brook, but it won't get our work done. I'm ready to leave whenever you are."

"I want to have one more good talk with them first, without anyone losing his temper. There has to be something to like about him or our Hazel wouldn't have married him."

"He probably feels the same about us. Listen, while I was recuperating yesterday I thought of something we might do for them. See what you think," Craig said, and told her.

Vera's eyes widened in the growing dimness. "We could,

145

couldn't we? Why didn't we think of it before? Come on, let's see if they're back yet."

In any case, the gathering dark would have driven them out of the woods. There must be a storm on the way, and Craig told himself that was why he felt nervous, in case lightning struck the trees anywhere near. They picked their way through the gloomy woods that were growing silent and chill. Roots that he couldn't see tripped him. He hadn't noticed on the way into the woods that so many trees were overgrown with mistletoe; he kept feeling he'd lost his way, especially since they'd strayed out of sight of the road. The soft dim ground hindered him and Vera as they climbed between the looming trees, but surely climbing must lead them back to Moonwell. At last they emerged from under the vault of foliage, two fields distant from the road.

They followed the drystone wall to the road as soon as the aches in their legs began to ease. They climbed the road to the first sight of Moonwell, and Craig experienced a hint of the panic he'd suffered while driving. Darkness was thickening above the town as if it were flooding there from all directions at once. It seemed to shrink the buildings, huddling them together, small and fragile under the oppressive sky. The rally was over, for they could see a crowd on the charred edge of the moor.

Hazel and Benedict must have gone straight to the hotel. They were waiting in the lobby when the Wildes limped in. "Hazel thought you'd got lost," Benedict said reprovingly, raising his sharp chin and gazing down his long nose at them. "Let's go up to your room. We don't want to be overheard."

They all stood in the lift and watched the lit numbers that counted the floors. Nobody spoke until they were in the room beneath the eaves. Then Benedict said, "I must say you could have chosen your time better. Things are difficult enough for us just now without Hazel being upset further."

"Oh," Craig said heavily, "I thought Godwin Mann had put your world to rights."

"Craig," Vera murmured, reminding him what they'd agreed. He went over to the window, walking away from the argument as far as he could. The dark and the last of the rally were coming down from the moors. "Your mother has something to say to you, Hazel," he said.

"Hazel, what do you want more than anything else in the world?"

"Nothing for myself. Benedict's business to improve, I suppose. Things really aren't too good, Mummy, even though we're doing all we can. He's having to go further and further afield to find work."

Going where his reputation hasn't reached, Craig thought, pressing his lips together and gazing down into the square. Here came Godwin Mann, supported by two of his followers. "Perhaps you'll benefit from some of the goodwill your evangelist is spreading, Benedict," Vera said. "Leaving aside business, Hazel, what do you and Benedict and, let me be honest, your father and I hope you'll have one day?"

"Well, a baby, of course. One day."

"I knew it," Vera cried. "We've been talking it over, and we've decided that's how we want to help you financially. We'll draw up a deed, and we'll buy things for the little one as soon as we know it's on its way."

It must be the overall that made Mann look bulkier than his two helpers as they progressed along the line of street-lamps, which were lit despite the early hour. Craig turned away from the window. "We certainly will if you'll let us. What do you say? Will you accept this as our peace offering?"

"You ought to know you don't need to offer us anything except not being angry with us," Hazel said, and pulled him away from the window so that she could hug them both.

"We're very grateful," Benedict said hastily. Craig disengaged himself from the women and went over to him, shook the man's limp, clammy hand. "That's settled, then," Craig said.

"You must come home tonight and eat with us," Hazel cried. "We'd better hurry home and tell Ursula. She's making the dinner." By now her tone was apologetic. "I don't think she and Mel will be staying much longer now Godwin's done what he came to do."

Craig heard the lift. "Here he comes now."

He hadn't meant to stop them talking. He wanted to ask what precisely Mann was supposed to have achieved. They listened as the doors of the lift creaked open, as the three came slowly down the carpeted hall past the Wildes' room.

Mann's door closed, and his helpers took the lift down. "We'll see you in about an hour," Hazel said then.

Craig wished there were more lights in the room. The idea that Hazel had been nervous about talking while Mann was in the corridor annoyed him, made him uneasy when, damn it, there was no reason to be. He shaved in front of the mirror above the washbowl, changed his clothes, and lay on the bed, but he couldn't relax. All he could do was resolve to have a good time, for Hazel's and Vera's sakes.

He was glad to reach the cottage, even though the cloned Christ was waiting over the hearth. He was glad to be out of the thick gloom under the sooty sky, when by rights it shouldn't even be dusk for hours. He made appreciative noises over Ursula's cooking, spaghetti of various consistencies heaped with charred or almost raw lumps of indeterminate meat. He managed to smile when Mel clapped his hands at the news that Hazel meant to have a baby, cried "Another life for Christ," and insisted on leading prayers for the birth.

When Craig raised the question of the rally, he couldn't get a satisfactory answer. "Godwin was super, just wondrous," Ursula told him, ladling out a second helping of spaghetti despite his protests. "He carried God down into the cave, and God drove out the evil. There'll be some changes round here yet, and that can only be good news." Craig caught Hazel's eye just then and was rewarded with a grimace of sympathy at the way his plate was being loaded. Maybe there was hope for her sense of humor after all.

When he and Vera left, hours later, Hazel gave him an impulsive kiss over the garden gate. He remembered how she'd had to stand on tiptoe to kiss him all those years ago. The impression lingered as he made his way back to the hotel, gripping Vera's hand for fear of being separated from her in the dark that was thicker than ever, breathless as the approach of a storm, even between the streetlamps. He hoped the storm would break and relieve the sense of imminence that set his skin crawling.

He felt a little better once he was in bed with Vera, one arm around her waist as she fell asleep, and yet he had the notion that if he slept the storm would waken him, or something would. He needed rest before he drove home tomorrow. At least Mann was inaudible. On his trip down

148

the corridor to the bathroom Craig had passed Mann's room and heard a low sound that must have been the evangelist's voice, no doubt thanking God for the day's work. For a moment Craig had thought the moon had risen, but it had only been the light from Mann's room.

28

The radio alarm wakened Eustace with static. He forced his eyes open and peered into the dark that was hissing at him, and eventually found the clock. "Go on, you might as well go wrong," he snarled at it, "everything else has." He was burrowing under the tumbled sheets, away from the panicky sense of not knowing what he'd said on Sunday in front of the crowd, when through the open window he heard the rattle as an awning was pulled out. Someone was opening a shop.

He squirmed unenthusiastically out of bed and groped his way to the window. The chilly dark felt heavier than sleep. He pushed the halves of the window wider and craned his neck to see the clock above the assembly rooms. The lit face was dim as a smoldering fire, and he had to strain his eyes to convince himself of what it said. Though the hour felt like four in the morning, the clock out there agreed with his that it was half past six.

"Stare all you like," he muttered at himself. "That won't make it go away. Reality's right and you're wrong." He withdrew his head, feeling like a tortoise, sluggish and crusty, and collided his way across the room to the light switch. The light here and in the bathroom was muffled, brownish. Breakfast could wait: the sooner he finished at the sorting office, the fewer people he'd encounter on his rounds.

He shivered as he stepped out of the cottage, for the street felt dank as mist. The unbroken clouds overhead looked like a starless night sky. Bedrooms and kitchens were lighting up,

149

but they and the streetlamps on their pedestals of light seemed isolated by the dark. He kept his head down as he hurried to the sorting office.

It was a small room behind the post office. Usually the driver of the delivery van from Sheffield would let himself in by the back entrance and leave the sacks of mail, but today the room was bare. Eustace sat on his stool and closed his eyes; staring at the pigeonholes under the fluorescent tubes made him feel he hadn't slept enough. The dark gave him the impression that no time was passing, but when he next glanced at his watch it was almost eight o'clock.

He couldn't get through to Sheffield. Though the phone wasn't dead—he checked that by dialing to make it ring itself—he could reach nothing but a hollow stillness that made his ear tingle. He was still trying when the postmistress looked in from the shop. She lowered her round head as if she were preparing to butt him with her curly, sheeplike scalp. "What's holding you up?"

"Not a thing, I'm self-supporting." Aloud he said, "There's been no delivery, and I can't raise Sheffield."

"Ridiculous," she said as if she meant him. She dialed Sheffield and thrust the earpiece up beneath her white curls, took it away from her face to glare at it for not responding. She tried the phone in the shop and came back looking unhappier with him than ever. "It must be something in the atmosphere. No wonder it's so dark," she said, a connection he failed to grasp. "But that's no excuse for lateness, no excuse at all."

She'd had little time for excuses even before she'd stood up for Mann. Since he'd said whatever dreadful things he'd said in front of them all on Sunday, she'd missed no opportunity to show her contempt for him. Next week he had to take her assistant from the counter on his rounds, obviously to train the burly youth as a replacement for himself. "Well, what are you going to do now?" she demanded.

"Maybe I should go over to Sheffield and find out what's wrong."

"And how will you get there, may I ask? There's no bus on Wednesdays. I've been thinking for a while that what your job needs is someone who can drive."

"At least I can go down to the main road in case the van's broken down." And maybe he could hitch a lift and never come back. They'd been glad enough of him yesterday, when he'd made his rounds instead of going up to the cave, but now they wanted to see the back of him. Maybe that was one prayer of theirs he could make sure was answered.

The High Street was crowded now, people going to work or to the shops or taking the children to school. Everyone was complaining about the weather. "Which damned fool called this midsummer?" Eustace heard someone say in a voice like Mr. Gloom's. He rushed himself past Phoebe Wainwright's street, past the thought of telling her he meant to leave or at least apologizing for having delivered the anonymous letter. He had a sudden panicky notion that whatever he'd said at the rally had been about her. He didn't want to think about that just now. He wanted to be out of Moonwell, out of the town's disapproval and the dark.

Past the bookshop, which was lit but closed, the lamps gave out as the road climbed toward the ridge that overlooked the woods. He hoped that when he reached the ridge he would see sunlight on the horizon. As he made his way upward, keeping to the middle of the dim road, the tiers of street-lamps fell away behind and below him, toward the playing field where the goalposts looked like matchsticks now.

When he made the ridge, he couldn't help sighing. Behind him the lights of Moonwell huddled together under the black sky. Around him the dark extended as far as he could see; he couldn't even distinguish the sky from the edge of the moor. He was seized by a yearning to go back to Moonwell, where at least there was company, however reluctant. He was going to look pretty odd to any drivers on the main road, a hitchhiking postman in uniform. Maybe that was how he should go on stage, give himself another chance where he might be appreciated. "Maybe that's just what I've been looking for, but don't tell anyone, will you?" he said loudly, the dark closing in his voice, and stepped down toward the woods.

Two steps and the slope cut off the lights of Moonwell. There was only the dark and the trees, still as fossils. Masses of foliage hung silently over the road, which grew much darker as soon as it led into the woods. The sooner he was through the woods, the sooner he'd be on his way—but he faltered to a standstill as he came abreast of the trees.

He had to go on. The other road out of the Peaks was miles

151

beyond the town, across the moors. The woods were the same old woods, he told himself, the dark was only another sunless day in the Peaks, even if unusually so. But the stillness of the woods made him struggle to breathe, and he could imagine how the road in there must sink into blind dark. "What's up," he growled at himself, "afraid of a few falls in the ditch?" He lurched forward, but a shudder halted him. Nobody in his right mind would venture in there.

Not without a flashlight, anyway. It wouldn't take him long to go back for one. He tried to ignore how relieved he felt as he turned away from the woods, told himself he was only in a hurry to get the flashlight. But he hadn't reached the top of the slope when he heard a car on the road.

The dark disoriented him. At first he thought the car was coming through the woods. When the headlights appeared above him, he dodged hastily out of the way, forgetting to stick out his thumb. Nevertheless the car jolted to a halt. "Want a lift?" the driver called.

He was a man in his sixties with large ears, pouchy eyes, a few strands of gray combed over his skull in memory of his hair. His wife looked younger, jet-black hair, dark eyes in a face like china, but perhaps she wasn't. "We saw you on stage at the pub," she said to Eustace, pushing the passenger seat forward so that he could climb in the back. "We liked your act, didn't we, Craig?"

"Definitely," the driver said with a reminiscent laugh. "Hop in if you're bound for Sheffield."

"That'll do me." He ought at least to find out what was hindering the mail. He tripped over the woman's seatbelt and almost ripped it out of its housing as he tried to disentangle himself. She and her husband watched with faint encouraging smiles that seemed to say they appreciated his inventiveness but would rather savor it under more appropriate circumstances. By the time he managed to tumble himself into the back, he felt like hiding under the seat.

The car coasted forward under the cavernous arch of the oaks, and Eustace was disconcerted to find that he didn't feel much more at ease with venturing into the woods this way, trapped in the car, his eyes straining to see beyond the headlight beams as they poked jerkily at the dark. As soon as the beams passed the mouth of the woods, the trees on either side of the opening seemed to lurch forward. The chill of the dark settled into the car, and he saw that the driver was shivering as he craned over the wheel, staring at the rising banks that constricted the road as it grew steeper. Suddenly the car skidded to a halt, slued across the road. "I can't go this way," the driver muttered. "We'll take the other road."

He turned his head to see where he was reversing, and Eustace was dismayed by the hint of panic in his eyes. The car bumped into the yielding bank at the side of the road. Grass and ferns scraped the paintwork, and then the car was screeching back the way they'd come. Though the car was going faster, it seemed to take longer to drive out of the woods than it had to come in.

The car raced up to the ridge, Moonwell glimmering ahead. The driver dragged at the handbrake and leaned over the steering wheel, one shaky hand covering his eyes. "I'm sorry, I get like that sometimes. I thought I'd grown out of it. Sorry." Eventually he straightened up, breathing deeply. "You don't mind if we go the long way, do you? I'd like to get a newspaper to see what the weather's up to."

His wife massaged his shoulders as he drove down into Moonwell. Eustace might have cracked a joke to cheer them up if he'd been able to think of one. He felt redundant, and shyer than ever. At least the driver seemed happier once they reached the lit streets. He parked by the first newsagent's he saw and hurried in. Moments later he reappeared, frowning. "I might as well not have bothered. No papers were delivered anywhere in town today, and nobody knows why."

29

There had been a moment when Craig thought they would never be out of the woods. He wouldn't be able to turn the car, he'd drive in search of a lay-by as the road grew steeper until the car went off the road in the dark, off a sheer edge, and they would be falling, falling . . . It had just been his old fear, he told himself as he went into the newsagent's. It ought to leave him once he was out of this wretched local weather.

The proprietor's pipe-stained smile faded as he watched Craig survey the counter. "If it's a paper you want you're out of luck. Buggers who deliver them are on strike more than likely, only we can't check because the phones and radios don't work. We're used to freak weather round here, but never anything like this."

"So you don't know how long it's likely to continue, I imagine."

"All I can tell you is if there's going to be a storm, the sooner we get it done with the happier I'll be."

Craig went back to the car and announced the news to Vera and the comedian dressed as a postman—Eustace, that was his name. Behind the wheel again, he switched on the radio in the hope that he could prove the newsagent wrong, but when he tuned across the dial there wasn't even static, just a silence so hollow it felt capable of swallowing all sound.

He drove past people gossiping in the light from shop-fronts. The long thin windows of the church shone through the trees. Beyond the chain of streetlamps, Hazel's house was dark. Craig wondered what she was doing. Living her own life, that was all he needed to know. So long as it was hers and not just Benedict's.

A few yards past the cottage a sign indicated the end of the town's speed limit, a white disk crossed by a black bar like the pupil of a sheep's eye. The car climbed between ferns still as photographs to a ridge that overlooked the moors. Ahead the road meandered over slopes so smudged by the dark that he couldn't tell which was grass, which heather. The thought that this was late morning of a midsummer day weighed on him, made him feel desperate to be out from under the dark sky that seemed almost to touch the moors. "Never mind," Vera murmured, "it can't go on forever," and at that moment he thought he saw the faintest glimmer several slopes ahead.

He sent the car forward as fast as he dared, not least because the sight of the headlights finding nothing but the road made him feel the dark was closing in. Tussocks blazed at the edge of the ditch, a sheep stared with yellow eyes. The road sloped up, the car raced over the crest, and Craig braked. There was sunlight on the farthest slope.

It was only a strip on the horizon, as if the curtain of dark had been lowered all but an inch. That thought made Craig feel microscopic under the enormous blackness. The edge of the far slope shone green as new wet grass, so luminous it appeared to start forward from the dark, beckoning him. "That's what we're looking for," Eustace said, and coughed as though he'd spoken out of turn.

"It certainly is," Craig said, smiling at him in the mirror as the car gathered speed down the slope, past a sheep that was staring over the edge of the ditch, its chin resting on a tussock. The next upward slope was longer. He braked instinctively at the crest. For a moment, as the headlight beams jerked over the edge, he'd felt he was racing straight for an unfenced drop.

The distant strip of light looked thinner. Never mind, it was only the edge of the sunlight, the promise of sunlit fields and roads and houses beyond the bleak, dark slopes. The splayed beams wobbled downward. Were they failing, or was there mist ahead? Certainly a chill was seeping into the car. He eased off the accelerator, and it seemed to take far too long for them to gain the top of the next slope, as if they were caught in a marsh of darkness. But when the car lurched over the rise and the moors opened around them, there was no sign of sunlight at all.

"Good night," Eustace muttered, presumably as a joke. Vera laughed, whether politely or nervously Craig couldn't tell. Either this rise wasn't as high as the others or the storm clouds or whatever they were had advanced a little farther, he told himself. He made himself press the pedal, though as soon as the car nosed downward, the headlight beams appeared to shrink. It wasn't mist, and he didn't think it was his vision. Best to drive as fast as he dared to recharge the battery—he would rather not get out of the car up here on the dark moors. Never mind that each jerk of the beams made him think he was driving off the road, over a sudden drop; he wasn't going that fast, not quite. The beams wavered up from the roadway and flashed the face of another sheep, peering over the edge of the roadside ditch.

Vera stifled a cry. Surely it had only been the unexpectedness, Craig thought fiercely, hoping she hadn't noticed that the jaw was resting on the tarmac, the bulging yellow eyes not moving as the light swept across them. The sheep must have died in the ditch, the body must have been down there out of sight. The other sheep hadn't moved either, he remembered, and all he'd seen of it had been its head at the edge of the road. Maybe there was a killer dog loose on the moors. He shoved his foot down on the pedal, and the headlight beams scooped at the bare road, then shot over the top. His whole body jolted, and he dragged at the wheel, trod with all his weight on the brake. There was nothing beyond the crest of the road but dark.

There must be. A road couldn't just stop in midair. It must be a sharp bend, unmarked or divested of its warning sign. He rolled his window down and craned out to look; then he made himself open his door and lean his shaky body out into the hollow stillness, the chilly dark. He could still see nothing beyond the small lit patch of road and the dim tussocky banks on either side of it but darkness that looked solid as black ice.

He slammed the door and pressed himself against the driver's seat as if that would make the car more real, make his panic give way to reality. Perhaps if he switched off the headlights he might be able to see what really lay ahead. He was reaching tremulously for the switch when Vera said in a pinched voice, "You're running the battery down. Let's go back."

He let the car coast backward down the slope at once, before he tried to turn it. He was dismayed to realize how welcome the excuse was that Vera had offered him. He glanced at her, then he looked over his shoulder while he reversed toward the ditch. As soon as he caught sight of Eustace, his panic flooded back. Eustace was as scared as Craig knew Vera was—as he was himself. This time it wasn't just his childhood fear that he was retreating from. Whatever was out there, they had seen it too.

30

Throughout that morning Diana felt as if she hadn't woken up. However many lights she switched on in the cottage, it still seemed too dark. The lights could neither drive away the thoughts that had kept her awake half the night nor clarify them. When she opened the front door, hoping that fresh air would clear her head, the darkness settled over her like a fall of dirty cobwebs. She went back to the percolator in case coffee might free her from her prickly stupor, her sense of being unable to organize her thoughts.

The first black gulp seared her throat, but that was all. Perhaps she needed her yoga techniques to help her sleep. The trouble was that when she'd tried them in the early hours, she'd felt on the edge of something much larger than relaxation, much larger than the glimpses she'd had of Mann in the cave. Nathaniel Needham had hinted that he'd experienced visions, but could Diana be that Celtic just because of her ancestry? She felt in danger of coming face to face with something she dreaded without knowing what it was.

The shrilling of the doorbell almost jerked the mug out of her hand. Jeremy Booth was outside, shading his eyes with one hand as if to ward off the dark. "What do you think about this, then?" he said, rolling his eyes to indicate the sky.

"I don't know what to think about it," Diana said, more certain every moment that she did. "Time for a coffee? I've been drinking alone all morning."

When she brought him a mug in the front room, he was gazing at the children's paintings, months old now. "So what will you be doing when the summer's over?" he said.

She wished the question didn't seem so ominous. "I still haven't decided. I want to see how the kids are."

"You don't mind staying, then."

"Somebody has to."

"We would if there were anything to stay for," Jeremy said, obviously feeling rebuked. "But between ourselves, I don't like the way things have been affecting Geraldine. It was starting to get through to me as well."

"In what way?"

"My youthful excesses catching up with me, I think." He gave a token laugh. "My psychedelic past. I'd have thought it would have worked itself out of my system by now, but it must have been the pressures we've been under. I started to see things."

"Do you mind if I ask you what sorts of things?"

"I'd rather not talk about it, Diana." He drained the mug and stood up. "Don't think me rude if I scoot away. I don't like leaving her alone while it's like this, it's making her nervous."

"Were you here for a reason?"

"Well, yes. Gerry tells me you'll be staying for a while, and we both admire you for it. If we leave you the key, would you mind keeping an eye on the shop? We're going up to Wales to look at some new premises."

"Now?"

"Tomorrow, but I thought I'd better ask you now in case you'd rather not."

"There's nobody else if I don't, is there?"

"To be honest, I don't think there is."

Committing herself to staying on behalf of one more person hardly mattered. She'd already been singled out by her ability to see more than the townsfolk could, and there was no point in resenting having been chosen like that without being asked. "Leave me an address where I can get in touch with you if I need to," she said.

She watched him as far as the lamplit corner. The moors loomed above the town as if the black sky were solidifying. The massive blackness overhead took her breath away, made her body shudder with a frustrated urge to tear the blackness open. A line of Needham's song ran through her head and let the chill seep into her, but she was damned if she'd hide in her cottage. She grabbed a coat and made for the shops.

"Not blaming Godwin Mann for that as well, are you?" the newsagent growled when she wanted to know why there were no papers. She was tempted to say that she was, but she went out to the hotel instead. At least she wasn't totally alone in what she suspected. She had to know the worst, she told herself, before she could begin to plan.

She was crossing the lobby to the reception desk when a beaming young woman headed her off. "Godwin knows you want to see him. He'll come to you as soon as he can."

Diana suppressed the nervousness that made her feel. "Do you know someone called Delbert, a thin guy, Californian?"

"Oh yes, we all know Delbert." The smile didn't change, yet it suddenly looked smug. "Did you want a word with him?"

"If he's here."

"He'll be where he's lodging. He's been a bit excited since yesterday. Godwin thought he needed to stay with someone who could take care of him, so he's staying with Mr. and Mrs. Scragg."

Surely the Scraggs wouldn't refuse Father O'Connell access to him. She left the lobby, where the dark seemed to turn the ceiling into a void above the chandeliers, and headed for the church. As she passed the school, the children were singing a hymn. The sound brought tears to her eyes, but at the same time it made her uneasy: were they celebrating Mann's triumph or singing to make the darkness go away? People had halted under streetlamps and were smiling toward the school, and Diana felt more outcast than ever.

The lit church was deserted. The interior felt cold and stony. She couldn't help faltering as she came out of the porch: the graveyard, steeped in darkness, seemed larger; the gravestones looked like rocks sprouting jaggedly from the unkempt grass. The children's voices drifted to her along the High Street, but the line from Needham's song was louder in her head. "The night's in the sun," the voice repeated as she hurried across the road between the meager streetlamps. Her footsteps sounded small and flat as she went up the path to the presbytery and rang the doorbell. Something thudded against the other side of the door, scratching at the wood, snarling.

Of course it was Kelly, the priest's Alsatian dog. She stepped forward from where she'd flinched back, heart lurching. No wonder the dog was on edge with the dark. Could Father O'Connell be asleep? The noise the dog was making should wake him. She glanced round in the hope of seeing him on his way to the church or the presbytery, and as she did so she glimpsed a light on the moor.

She ran to the gate for a clearer view, cupped a hand next to her eye to block off the glow of the streetlamp. She was beginning to think she'd imagined the light out there when it flared again, nearer. It was a car. Surely it was coming from beyond the dark, which meant the dark had an end, and she could ask the driver where. She opened the gate and waited for the car.

It swung into view at the top of the slope above the church and came racing down, too fast. When she stepped onto the pavement and waved urgently, the brakes screeched, the car slued across the road toward her. She dodged back into the presbytery garden as the tires scraped along the curb with a tearing sound and a stench of rubber, and then the passenger window was rolled down. "What is it, Miss Kramer? Why did you want us?"

It was Eustace Gift. His small mouth under his large nose was screwed smaller, but he didn't mean her to laugh. "Where have you just come from?" Diana said.

His eyes went blank. "You'd better ask the driver."

The driver, a balding man, climbed out of the car and rested his folded arms on the roof. Diana saw that his arms were trembling. "I don't know where we got to," he muttered. "A couple of miles or so. The road's blocked somehow. No way through."

His companion, a woman with a delicate face, went round the car to him. "It's something to do with this dark," she said defiantly.

"Blocked how?" Diana said, glancing at each of them in turn. Nobody seemed to want to answer. Eustace looked away from her as she glanced at him. "You've left the door open," he said.

Diana looked back. The presbytery door was ajar. "The dog must have clawed it open," she realized.

"That's the priest's house, is it? I wouldn't mind a word with him," the driver said, and strode up the path. "Be careful, Craig," his wife called and ran after him, Diana at her heels. Eustace came up to them just as the driver eased the door open and dodged aside, pulling his wife with him. "Careful," Eustace stammered, "look at its eyes."

160

He meant the dog. It was cowering in the hall, glaring terrified out at the dark, its raw tongue lolling between its teeth. "Come on, boy," Craig said, stepping forward minutely, and then the dog leaped past him, fled whimpering along the path as Diana shoved Eustace out of its way. She saw it clear the fence and race toward the moor, and felt as if it had infected her with its panic. She made for the lit hall of the presbytery, so as to be out of the dark. She was the first to see what the dog had done to Father O'Connell, but it was the driver's wife who began to scream.

31

When the hymn ended Andrew went on singing by mistake. Some of the children giggled—not the ones who'd come to Moonwell just last month. Miss Ingham gave him a smile, the one that stayed on her face whatever she was saying. "Let's kneel down now and talk to God," she said.

Andrew squeezed his eyes shut until they filled with swelling light and prayed as hard as he could, though not in the words she was using. He prayed so hard he ceased to feel the floorboards bruising his knees. He was praying that his father was cured now that Mr. Mann had made the cave into a holy place.

Whatever was wrong with his father, it had something to do with the cave. He'd seen his father creeping up there in the moonlight, he'd felt his father growing tense when Mr. Mann went down the rope. His father must have been asking God to go down with him, to kill the giant or the devil that had heard Andrew's parents the first time Mr. Mann had called everyone to the cave. If Andrew's mother hadn't spoken up that time, it wouldn't have singled out his father. But Mr. Mann had done what he'd been called to do and come back safe, he'd said so. The trouble was that since then Andrew's father had been more secretly nervous than ever.

He mustn't be sure that the demon was dead. Maybe he was afraid to look over the edge of the cave to make sure, or afraid that someone would see him looking and want to know what he was doing. That was why Andrew had to go and look, to make sure it was a holy place now so that he could tell his father. "Please God," he said, for everything to come right, and joined in as the crowded class said, "Amen."

"God see you safely home," Miss Ingham said, which meant they could all go. Andrew thought of joining the others as they swarmed out, of inventing a reason on his way to the cave why he hadn't waited for her—but she was smiling at him, and the only way he could move was toward her big, wide face, her broad shoulders that made her look like a triangle balanced on thin legs. He still wished she were Miss Kramer. "Don't forget to say your prayers before bedtime," she called after the children. "Remember, God likes to look down and see you on your knees."

"I don't know how He can see anything with all this dark," Sally murmured to Jane.

At least Andrew could ask the teacher one of the questions that were troubling him. As he followed her into the school-yard, he said, "The dark's the bad coming out of the cave, isn't it?"

Miss Ingham smiled at him with a frown above her eyes. "What do you mean, Andrew?"

"Mr. Mann killed the demon in the cave, didn't he?"

"He did what God sent him here to do."

"Then is the dark all the bad coming out and going into the sky?"

"Do you know, I think maybe it is." Her smile had turned generous. "That's why God makes children like they are, because they can see more clearly than us sometimes," she said, and to him, "And maybe people aren't praying hard enough. Tomorrow we'll all pray for a wind to blow the dark away."

He hadn't quite meant that. Looking up at the black sky, which seemed lower and more solid every time he saw it, he wondered if it could really be that simple—just a wind and all the cold, dark stillness that made the town feel like a ghost of itself would be swept away. He had a sudden sick feeling that her smile was meant to pretend that everything was all right, the way all the people he saw in the dark street seemed to be pretending. Now God had come into their lives, mustn't it be true and not a pretense? He wanted to believe that, and perhaps he could once he knew that his father was just his father again.

His mother was at the shop, poking a brush at the dim corners of the ceiling. "Has Andrew been good today?"

"He's been a credit to you, Mrs. Bevan." The teacher took the orange comb that made Andrew think of a centipede out of her hair, which fell blackly over her shoulders as she dropped the comb into her canvas bag. "If you give me the key, I'll take him home and start dinner."

"You needn't do so much for us, Miss Ingham, really."

"That's right," Andrew's father said, coming out from peering round the stockroom door. "You've been working hard all day. We're glad to have you staying with us. You don't owe us anything."

"Think nothing of it. I love cooking when I'm using ingredients fresh as God made them. I really do believe it's a way of praising God."

"I hope it isn't a sin to open a can occasionally," Andrew's mother said, so sweetly that he winced.

"Oh, I'm sure God understands," the teacher said smiling. "I could show you some recipes one evening if you'd like."

Andrew looked nervously out of the window, for he felt as if they'd forgotten the dark. Maybe they preferred to behave like this so as to distract themselves, or didn't they even realize? He felt all the more nervous when he saw one of Mr. Mann's helpers coming toward the shop.

She was looking for Miss Ingham. "The pub is going to show that video tonight, the one where Godwin's father plays the devil."

"You'd think they'd have something better to do," Andrew's father said loudly. "Childish, that's all it is, just because they don't agree with Godwin."

"We want to make sure there'll be plenty of us there to show what we think of it," the woman with the cross on her front said.

"We'll tell some people to be there, shall we?" Andrew's mother suggested.

Andrew almost couldn't speak for eagerness. "I will."

163

His mother opened her mouth, then glanced almost imperceptibly toward Miss Ingham. "All right, seeing it's for God. Just tell the people in Roman Row and come straight back."

"Two streets," Andrew pleaded.

She stared at him as if he were showing her up, and he was terrified she'd say he couldn't go at all, ruin his plan. "Just Roman Row and Kiln Lane, then," she said in a voice that promised she'd have something to say to him later. "But don't you dare cross the big road."

Why was she anxious that he shouldn't cross the High Street when there hadn't been any traffic along it for days, maybe longer? He ran out of the shop and round the corner into Roman Row and dashed from house to house. Every time a door opened he was already on the next path and ringing the next doorbell. He called his message over the hedge or the fence and raced on. He'd rung Mrs. Wainwright's bell before he realized that she would hardly want to help Mr. Mann. He dodged next door, hoping she wouldn't appear. But her door wavered open as he rang the neighboring bell.

"Sorry, Mrs. Wainwright," he said and gawked at her. She no longer just looked plump, she looked puffed up. Her cheeks were dragging her mouth down, or her body was. She peered at him as if she didn't know him in the dark, then turned away painfully, trailing the door shut behind her. He was still staring at it when the old woman whose bell he'd rung poked him with a bony finger. "Well?"

"They're going to show a video tonight at the pub with Mr. Mann's father in it, and I'm supposed to tell people who don't want them to."

She pushed her lower lip over her mustache as if to show Andrew what she could do with no teeth. "All right, my lad, you run along home. I'll give the street their marching orders."

"I'm supposed to tell them in Kiln Lane too."

"You leave them to me," she said in a voice that warned him not to argue. Nothing was further from his mind. He thanked her, dashed back to the High Street, and dodged into Kiln Lane. In a minute he'd run to the end of the terrace of cottages and was at the path to the moor.

The light of the last streetlamp didn't reach far up the path. He blinked at the looming sky and reminded himself that he was here for his father. He remembered treading on the eyeless lizard that day at the cave with Miss Kramer, remembered wishing his father could see him tread on it so that he'd know Andrew was starting to be a man. Now Andrew had to be more of one, had to let his father know there was nothing at the cave to be frightened of, nothing to make his father crazy as he'd looked the night he'd sneaked up to the cave. Andrew closed his eyes and prayed, and then he started upward.

Once he was above the lamps, they showed him the edge of the path. He stayed well back as he clambered toward the unmoving sky. He felt as if it were pressing down on him, lowering itself spiderlike to meet him. He grabbed the charred edge of the moor and hauled himself onto the moorland path.

When he stumbled to his feet, he saw how alone he was. The ashen moors stretched around him, while below him the lights of Moonwell looked like matches stuck upright in the dark to smolder. He'd hoped to see cars on the Manchester road, but it was out of sight beyond the woods. He felt as if the world had gone away, abandoned him on the dead moor.

He was shivering, worse when he tried to stop. If it was dead, he told himself, it couldn't hurt him. All he had to do was look in the cave. How could he tell his father not to be frightened if he was scared himself? He took one faltering step along the path, a darker band through the sullen dimness that coated the slopes, and suddenly his shivering turned into running, just as uncontrollable. Heather crumbled underfoot with an unpleasant oily softness whenever he strayed from the path. He ran up the slope to the stone bowl and fell to his knees at the top.

Ash crawled on his legs and scratched in his throat, made his mouth taste smoky. He rubbed his stinging eyes and peered down toward the cave. It looked just as it had since the wall had fallen in, except darker beneath the black sky. He couldn't make out more than a large dark blotch without depth at the center of the bowl. It didn't seem enough to tell his father. He had to go closer, look in.

As soon as he stepped into the stony hollow, he felt he was going to slip. He sank to his knees again and began to crawl backward to the cave. As the top of the slope rose above him, the sky seemed to close down like a lid. Now he was afraid of crawling too far without noticing. He hitched himself round, trembling with the stony chill, and went down head first toward the cave.

There was no sound except for the scrape of his toecaps on stone, the dragging of his body as he inched forward on his stomach. Near the cave the slope grew steeper—too steep for him to cling to while he craned over the edge. He lurched to his feet and ran around the cave, a few feet from the edge, to where the slope was gentler and the cave went straight down. He threw himself on his stomach again, gasping and shivering, and shoved himself forward. Five shoves that bruised his chest, and he was at the edge. He levered himself another few inches with his elbows and gripped the edge with both hands, then he leaned over.

There was nothing but dark below him, a dark that felt much closer than the sky and colder. He pushed himself forward a last inch to make certain. As his eyes adjusted, he made out the far wall of the cave, stretching down into blackness. It didn't feel especially like a holy place, but was he sure he knew what a holy place was supposed to feel like? Surely all that mattered was that it was empty, cleared of all the bad that filled the sky. He was raising himself on his elbows so as to inch backward when he thought he saw a movement in the cave.

He craned out further, his elbows trembling with the strain. Perhaps it was just the way things sometimes seemed to move about in the dark when you couldn't see them properly. Then the movements clarified and separated, and he saw that there were three shapes, three insects crawling up the rock. Why should the sight of a few insects make him feel he couldn't breathe? His head was swimming by the time he realized that since the pale, thin shapes were crawling on the wall where it merged with the dark, they must really be larger than he was.

He jerked forward with the shock of it, and almost lost his balance. The rim of the cave cut into his hands as he saved himself barely in time. He was praying that he wasn't really seeing what was down there, but every second made them clearer. They were the color of the lizard he'd trodden on, the color of things that lived in the dark. They had long fingers they were using to climb the rock, slowly but relentlessly. Two of them were raising their smooth heads toward him in a way that made him think they had no eyes, while the one in the middle seemed to have no head.

That was the sight that convulsed his body, threw him back from the edge so violently that he had no grip on the stone for a moment, almost slid down the slope and over the rim. He staggered dizzily to his feet and fled sobbing up the stone bowl. All the way along the charred path he kept glancing back in terror of seeing the pale shapes crawling after him over the dead slopes beneath the black sky.

He fell several times on the path down from the moors. He had no idea how long he'd been up there, how long his parents might have been waiting for him. He couldn't even tell them what he'd seen, or his mother would want to know why he'd gone up to the cave, and that would make his father worse. The cave wasn't holy, it wasn't even dead, unless the things he'd seen were breeding in it like maggots. All Mr. Mann had done was drive them out, and where would they go now? He was terrified of blabbing all this to his parents because he couldn't stop himself. But when he fled along Kiln Lane and into the shop, his parents weren't there. "We have to stay here until your mummy and daddy come back," Miss Ingham told him. "Something's happened at the priest's house and they've gone to see if they can help."

32

Father O'Connell must have been trying to open the front door. His blood was on it, and on the walls and carpet just inside the presbytery. Perhaps his dog had only leaped at him to stop him from opening the door, perhaps she hadn't attacked him until he tried to fight her off, unless she'd been so maddened by the dark she had gone for him at once. He must have fled along the hall to grab the phone, presumably to use as a weapon, the way he was holding the receiver. If he hadn't, Diana thought with a clarity that threw the horror into sharper relief, the dog might not have come after him to finish him off.

The driver's wife was digging her nails into her cheeks while she stared and screamed as if she would never stop. "All right, Vera, come away now, don't look any more," Craig said, putting his arm round his wife's shoulders as Diana coaxed her out of the presbytery, away from the sight of Father O'Connell, of the remains of his hand that had clung to his throat as he'd died, trying to hold his throat together. "There's nothing we can do here," Craig murmured, and Diana felt more alone than ever.

Vera balked as soon as she was out of the presbytery. She stared at the sky and began to shake, gripping her hands together. She was moaning now, small distressed sounds. When Craig murmured, "Let's get you to a doctor," she gazed at him with icy contempt. "There's only one place in this town I want to go."

"I'll get the police," Eustace said hastily. He sidled past the onlookers who were gathering outside the gate, but the dressmaker who lived in his road stepped in front of him. "Not so fast. What's up?" she demanded.

Eustace sidestepped. "Father O'Connell's dead," he threw back.

The woman nudged the gate open with her stomach. "His dog turned on him," Diana explained, but the woman ignored her until she'd stepped into the presbytery and seen for herself. She swung round, looking grimmer. "What's it got to do with you?"

"I found him," Diana said, which was all she intended to say except to the police. She watched as people ventured up the path to the front door and recoiled, and she was thinking of forbidding anyone else to gawk, closing the door if she had to, when the police car drew up at the gate.

The inspector had a long, bony face, a thin, silvery mustache, prim, almost invisible lips like an old woman's. He gestured the onlookers back from the gate with a single precise wave, then he marched up the path, his head lowered slightly as if he was determined not to be distracted by the blackness overhead. "Please wait here," he said in a quiet, clear voice to Diana and the elderly couple, and went into the house.

The crowd was drifting back toward the gate, perhaps to be

near the streetlamp. Diana noticed Andrew's parents frowning at her. She turned her back on them as the inspector came out of the presbytery. "Which of you found the body?"

"Technically I did," Diana said.

There was a murmur from the crowd, which he ignored. "What do you mean, technically?"

"I was the first person into the building. As soon as Father O'Connell's dog ran out, I went in to see what had happened to him. As you saw, he—"

He held up one hand almost negligently, as if she ought to be alert for his cues. "How did you open the door?"

"Why was she here at all?" someone in the crowd—she thought it might be Andrew's mother—said loudly. "She never even goes to church."

"Perhaps if a few of you had kept on going to his church . . ." Diana shouldn't have responded; she was losing the control she'd been exerting over herself ever since she'd found Father O'Connell. "How did we open the door?" she said to the policeman. "He must have been trying to open it when the dog attacked him. It wasn't locked."

"Are you saying it was wide open?"

"No, I'm saying it was ajar and we pushed it open when we couldn't get an answer, and that was when the dog ran off."

"Ran where?"

"Up there," Diana said, glancing at the moors, which loomed closer as the black sky pressed down.

"As Postman Gift told me," he said, as though at least the confirmation was something he could approve of, and addressed the crowd. "Please don't approach Father O'Connell's dog if you should see it. I have an officer searching for it now." To Diana he said, "I think you should tell me why the four of you were coming to see the priest."

She felt as if the dark were hovering closer in case she even thought of telling. Not here, she decided, not now. "We weren't coming to see him. I heard the dog and it sounded as if something was wrong. I'm afraid I stepped straight in front of these people's car. It was my fault it skidded."

Craig was beginning to confirm her story when Vera interrupted. "It isn't that simple," she cried. "It was the dark."

The policeman raised his eyebrows. "What was the dark?"

She seemed to swallow what she'd meant to say, perhaps

because he looked suspicious of her, not recognizing her. "It made the dog attack Father O'Connell," she stammered. "The dog must have been driven mad to attack him, a priest."

"A funny kind of priest that preached against another man of God," someone in the crowd said, just loud enough to be heard. "Maybe God wouldn't have let him die that way if he'd supported Godwin."

Diana swung round, glaring at the crowd. "Why don't you say what you really mean, that you think he deserved to die? He was a damn sight more tolerant than any of you, and a lot closer to God if anyone is. Maybe that's why you're glad to see the last of him."

Vera seemed to have thought better of swallowing her words. "I didn't mean only the dog," she blurted out to the policeman. "We've just come back from trying to drive home to Sheffield. We couldn't get past the dark."

"You mean you hadn't enough petrol."

Vera clenched her fists. "No, I don't mean anything of the kind. We came to a place on the road where there was nothing but dark, no way to the main road. We were cut off."

The policeman glanced at Craig, as if for sense. "That was how it seemed to me," Craig admitted.

"And the phones don't work," Eustace put in. "We're cut off that way too."

"Please keep your voices down. I'll have to have all this looked into." The policeman's lips looked even primmer, as if he were offended by the complications. He went to the gate to clear a path through the crowd as the town ambulance drew up. He wanted to believe that the dark was nothing more than a freak of the weather, Diana thought. What would it take to persuade him otherwise, and everyone else? She had a sudden terrible suspicion that something soon would.

"I feel as if nobody knows we're here," Vera said in a choky voice, then she rallied. "Come on, Craig, I don't want to stay here. Take me back to the hotel."

"We'll have to find someone to fix the tires," Craig said as if defying any of his listeners to contradict him, and ushered her away as the stretcher-bearers went into the presbytery. Eustace stayed near Diana. "Please let me know if you plan to leave town, in case I need to question you further," the policeman said to her, and she heard her unspoken cry trailing away in the dark inside her skull: "I can't leave, don't you understand? None of us can leave . . ."

33

All the way back to the shop June was growing angrier. "The nerve of that Kramer woman, telling us we should have gone to church. Just what did they all want with Father O'Connell, four of them without a crumb of faith among them? The police want to question them a bit more closely, if you ask me . . ."

Brian murmured wordlessly and nodded as he loped along beside her. He didn't know if he agreed with her or not, but her being suspicious of someone else was an enormous relief. He might be able to think over what he'd done without feeling she was watching him. Her anger with Miss Kramer and the others was almost as much of a relief as the dark.

He couldn't help it, he welcomed the dark. What he needed to do was go up on the moors and think. Maybe he could take Andrew for a walk up there; June wouldn't like it, but she wasn't so ready to disagree with him now that Miss Ingham was lodging with them. Once he was out in the dark he wouldn't feel as if she were still watching him, as he'd felt ever since Godwin's rope had given way.

Perhaps she thought Brian had stumbled forward at the cave because he was concerned for Godwin. Perhaps she was even ashamed of having been so suspicious of him lately, but that only made Brian feel worse. She'd reason enough to suspect him—Godwin's face had made that clear when the rope had given way. He hadn't just dreamed he'd disguised the faulty rope, he couldn't just have dreamed he'd crept up behind Godwin's watcher in the moonlight, though he didn't dare think why. He was even more afraid to wonder how much Godwin knew.

He averted his face as they passed the hotel. At least the woman's screams at the presbytery hadn't brought Godwin out. Since yesterday every footstep near the shop or the house had set Brian's heart lurching. Maybe he didn't need to feel like this, maybe Godwin had forgiven him. He'd be able to think clearly once he took Andrew up on the moor.

Andrew was crouching under the fluorescent tube inside the display window, his face pressed against the pane. When he saw his parents he dodged back into the shop, bumping into a Primus stove. "You were told not to go in the window," June cried. "Just because we've no customers at the moment doesn't mean we can afford to have things wrecked."

"I think he was anxious for you," Miss Ingham intervened. "You got a bit nervous when you were going round the houses, didn't you, Andrew?"

June took a loud breath and released it as a sigh. "That's the last time you go out by yourself while it's dark, Andrew. I should have known you'd end up scaring yourself."

"I'm not sure it was quite as simple as that," the teacher murmured.

"Don't think me rude, Miss Ingham," June said sweetly, "but I've known him a few years longer than you have."

Andrew had shrunk back against the counter. "What scared you, son?" Brian said, taking pity on him. "Did you think you saw something?"

The boy stared miserably at him, then looked away. "There, you see," June said. "He knows perfectly well he was just being silly. The best place for you is bed, my lad, so the grownups can talk."

"I'll start dinner," Miss Ingham said.

"I'll come with you." June turned to Brian as she reached the door. "You might as well lock up. If anyone wants anything from the shop, they know where to find us."

She was going with Miss Ingham to tell her about Father O'Connell. Brian wondered if he had time to take the boy up on the moor before he followed the women home, but he wouldn't be able to think while Andrew was in such a state. "It's all right, son, no need to be frightened now," he said roughly. "Daddy's here."

Andrew blinked at him, then ran and hid his face on Brian's chest. Brian's hands wavered near the small hard

172

head; he wasn't quite able to stroke the boy's hair. Andrew was hugging him fiercely, yet Brian had the fleeting impression that he was doing so in order not to flinch from his father. It started his feverish nervousness crawling, as if his skin were coming alive in an unfamiliar way. "Want to tell me what happened now that the women aren't listening?" he suggested.

When the boy began to mumble, Brian made to push him away so as to hear, until he realized that Andrew was praying—Brian couldn't tell for whom. "We'd better be on our way home if you've nothing to say to me," Brian said, embarrassed, and had to coax the boy out of the shop. All the way home Andrew hung onto Brian's hand, more tightly between the streetlamps. Whenever they passed a road that led to a path up to the moors, Brian felt him shiver.

June was mutely angry when they arrived home. Once Andrew had picked at his vegetarian dinner and been bathed and put to bed, she spoke up. "Do you know what we heard while you were bringing the boy home? They're still going to show that video."

At first Brian didn't understand what the new objection was. "Oh, you mean even though—"

"I mean even after Father O'Connell died so horribly they're going to watch their devilish film. They're saying Father O'Connell would want them to show it, he was going to see it himself. I don't believe for a moment that's true, but if it was, it's no wonder his dog went for him."

"We ought to go and show them we're on Godwin's side," Brian said.

"You and Miss Ingham go if you like. I'll have to stay with the boy. He won't even let me switch his bedroom light off. Someone needs to stay who won't stand for his nonsense."

Could she be secretly jealous because Brian was going to the pub with the teacher? He hadn't thought much about Miss Ingham except to find her presence in the house inhibiting, but when she came downstairs wearing perfume and one of her long dresses, he found her unexpectedly pleasing. The way the dress kept hinting at her body warmed his groin. "Call me Letty," she said, and he wondered if she might agree to a stroll after the pub.

The One-Armed Soldier was packed with Godwin's followers. Brian bought Letty an orange juice, a pint of strong ale for himself. "It's a treat to see you, I thought you were dead," Eric, the landlord, remarked in a voice that carried across the room. Brian muttered as neutrally as possible and joined Letty and her friends, who were talking about how Godwin had been resting in his hotel room ever since he'd braved the cave. Letty's face was why he hadn't taken much notice of her before, he realized, her large, plain face with its permanent smile. Put a bag over her head, he thought automatically, and was restraining himself from glancing at the outline of her thighs when the teetotalers began demanding to see the film.

"Whatever you think of it, keep your hands off it," Eric said, slipping the cassette into the player. "And don't be shy about coming to the bar."

The film was called *The Devil's Well*. Brian wondered if that had made Godwin think of Moonwell, though it was about an industrialist who drilled for oil where he'd been warned not to. Most of the swarthy actors didn't seem to be mouthing English. From the groans and the shaking of heads around him, Brian gathered that the industrialist was played by Godwin's father.

The drill dug deep into the earth, and then oil filled the screen, except it wasn't oil: it was too black, too purposeful. The industrialist turned to the camera, grinning diabolically, and everyone around Brian began to sing a hymn as demons swarmed out of the gushing muck. The dripping demons that looked like men ripped the doors off houses and killed the townsfolk, pulled handfuls out of their throats, held them up screaming, and smashed them against walls. . . . Father O'Connell mightn't have liked this after all, Brian thought; he wasn't sure he liked it much himself, especially when the victims came back to life and went in search of the few survivors. He especially disliked the sight of a young woman dressed in a T-shirt and denim shorts stumbling through the town in search of her husband although she no longer had a head. He joined in the hymn so lustily that people glanced at him.

His thoughts crowded the hymn out of his head. Of course, the young woman reminded him of the hiker who'd fallen down the cave. But the sight of the headless body on the move recalled to him how he'd felt as he'd watched the hiker

174

on the moor. God help him, he was feeling that now. The spectacle of the headless body was jerking at his groin.

He felt sick with self-loathing and at the same time almost uncontrollably excited. He tried to think of June, but couldn't even see her face. Letty Ingham was closer, and he tried to concentrate on her, to distract himself from the flickering screen that was making his eyes seem to swell. He could imagine lifting her long dress, parting her thighs, thrusting himself into her, if it wasn't for that maddening flat-faced smile of hers. Suddenly he saw the teacher and himself lit by dazzling white light, his hands closing around her head, twisting it, lifting it clear of her shoulders . . . He had to struggle not to seize his rampant groin under the pub table. He sang louder, almost bawling.

Demons and corpses overran the town, and Godwin's father grinned out through a repetition of the title. The audience began to clap in time with their hymn. As Eric pulled the cassette out of the player, he glared at Brian as if he'd let Eric down. "Thank you," people said innocently to him as the pub emptied. Brian would have liked to stay for another drink—the pub felt like a refuge from the dark— except that he would feel bound to apologize to Eric, maybe to explain too much. He followed Letty Ingham, his penis shrinking from the chill and the dark. He couldn't help thinking how satisfying it would be to have the strength he'd glimpsed, dazzled by himself and the white light. It was only a fantasy, he told himself, but it made his skin feel unstable, too alive. He averted his face as he passed the hotel, and then he realized that he couldn't hide it from June. He had even more secrets to keep from her now.

Thank God she was in bed, Andrew snuggling against her, where he must have pleaded to go. Brian crawled into Andrew's bed and wondered nervously how long it would be before he betrayed his secrets. He heard Letty humming a hymn downstairs, and all at once he knew that he had things the wrong way round. No wonder he felt like this when he'd somehow managed to forget what Godwin had told them all. There was only one way to get rid of his feelings, however painful it might be. Father O'Connell was gone, but he could still confess to Godwin Mann.

34

On her way home from the presbytery Diana felt as if the dark had won. Perhaps she was exhausted, but she had the impression of shrinking as the dark grew larger, until she and the town meant nothing at all. She did mean something, she told herself fiercely, but what? Maybe she would know once she'd had a good night's sleep.

Something rustled on the hall floor as she unlocked the door of her cottage—two pieces of paper. They were paintings, which she recognized even before she read the children's names on them. Sally's painting showed climbers on a mountain, stick figures with beaky noses, heads the size of dimes; Jane's was of a carnival in which all the rides had to be crammed into the space left by her carousel. Both of them were paintings Diana had put up on the classroom wall.

Their teacher must have given the children their paintings to take home because it was nearly time for the summer vacation, however it looked. Diana imagined the two girls discussing what to do, Sally fiddling with her patched spectacles, Jane agreeing solemnly that they should post the paintings through Diana's letter box. She felt like weeping. They hadn't forgotten her, but she had nearly forgotten them. "No you don't, damn you," she hissed at the dark.

She made black coffee and drank it as hot as she could, walking back and forth through the cottage to try to wake herself up. When she went out, she still felt as if she hadn't wakened—as if she needed to waken so as to understand what she could do about the dark. Finding out from Mann what had happened at the cave must be a first step, she told herself. At least now she had an excuse to go into the hotel.

The large, dim lobby under the dusty chandeliers was a relief after the streets, the dark lurking between the street-lamps, leading to the sunless moors. She went to the reception desk, where the manager stood looking harassed, his oval forehead gleaming through what remained of his red hair. "Are the couple who were in a car accident here just now? Craig and Vera somebody."

"Mr. and Mrs. Wilde." He glanced about for a receptionist, then peered at the board where the keys hung. "Yes, they're here: 315."

"I'll go up, shall I?"

"You may as well," he said, sweeping back his sparse hair with both hands in a despairing gesture. "Top floor."

When she stepped into the elevator, the doors closed, but she had to press the button twice before the lobby fell away. The elevator faltered at each level, giving her a view of deserted corridors through the small square window. At the top, the doors staggered open with a muffled squeaking. Either the central heating didn't reach up here or it was turned off. Perhaps it was the chilly stillness that put her in mind of a cave, for the gloomy floor with its eighteen bedrooms felt larger than it should. She went quickly along the right-hand corridor and knocked on the door of 315.

Craig opened the door and smiled rather shakily at her. "Miss Kramer, it's good of you to look in. If you're blaming yourself for the accident, please don't. It was entirely my fault, me and my neuroses."

"I thought you showed a whole lot of presence of mind. Is your wife okay now?"

"I'm sorry, I didn't mean to be rude. Please do come in and say hello to her. We're just making coffee, if you'd like some."

Vera turned from staring at the electric kettle as if at some vitally important task. "Miss Kramer, I don't know what you must think of me after all that fuss I made."

"I might have behaved that way if I'd been through all you'd been through," Diana said, probing gently.

"Oh, I think we just let this dark get on top of us," Vera said with an awkward laugh. "I don't like it, I won't pretend I do, but that's no excuse for my carrying on that way, as if that poor policeman hadn't enough to do. I don't mind telling you, Miss Kramer, I'm ashamed of myself."

"We managed to find someone to fix the tires," Craig said. "The car should be ready tomorrow. I hope this wretched weather will have improved by then."

"I thought," Diana said carefully, "you thought the dark wasn't just bad weather."

She was speaking to both of them, and it was Vera who responded. "I told you I was ashamed, Miss Kramer. I'm not as young as you, you know. Finding that poor man's body preyed on my nerves, that's all."

But you talked about the dark before you saw him, Diana thought. It was no use; she would only disturb them if she persisted. The kettle began to steam, and she stood up. "Won't you have coffee?" Vera said plaintively.

"Thanks, but I have to speak with Godwin Mann. I don't suppose you know which room he's in."

"Yes, I'll show you." Craig let her out of the room and pointed down the corridor. She was moving away when he cleared his throat. "Our daughter, Hazel, was telling us you've been ousted from your job because of differences over religion. If you should feel in need of a bit of free legal advice, please don't hesitate to contact us," he murmured, and closed the door.

Diana felt both touched and dismayed: he was talking as if life were going on as it always had, or as if pretending would make it so. Mann's wasn't the only unquestioning faith. But it was Mann's that had caused whatever was happening to Moonwell, and now she must see what had happened to him.

She started along the corridor, away from the elevator and the stairs. Craig had pointed to the room at the end, next to the bathroom; what could be more banal? Never mind that the shaded wall lamps seemed small and fewer than she would have liked, never mind that the low corridor felt colder and more largely empty as she ventured forward, but she would have welcomed a sound or two in the total stillness; she couldn't even hear Craig and Vera, though surely they'd be talking. She resisted a crazy urge to stamp her feet on the faded brownish carpet, to have at least some noise for company.

She stopped in front of the door to 318. She was raising one hand to rap at a panel when her gaze wandered to the foot of the door. Whatever light Mann was using in there, it was unpleasantly white. Her hand was inches from the panel when she heard Mann's voice in the room, gentle yet penetrating, if rather forced. "Don't worry, Miss Kramer, I

178

haven't forgotten you. I'll be coming to you soon. I'm looking forward to meeting you face to face."

She found she was backing away from the door as she stared at it, realizing that there was no spy hole, no way he could have seen her. She turned and walked very fast to the stairs; if she'd run she would have lost all control. She was through the lobby, past dozens of Mann's aimless followers, and out of the hotel before she remembered that the elderly couple were still up on that floor.

She couldn't go back now. Perhaps they would be able to leave tomorrow, allowed to leave since they were determined not to notice what was happening. No, she couldn't let them go into the dark, unless the police who were investigating it managed to get through and come back. Just now it was more urgent to make sure that Jeremy and Geraldine didn't leave tomorrow unless it was safe. She ran from streetlamp to streetlamp, faster when she came in sight of the bookshop. She hammered on the door, but it was no use. Through a newly broken window she could see that the shop was unlit, deserted. The van had gone already, and so had the Booths.

35

Geraldine had been sitting on a carton of books, leafing through a picture book of sunlit Wales and feeling as if she hadn't seen the sun for weeks, when the stone smashed the window. By the time she'd dragged the doors open, the street was deserted. Whoever had thrown the missile could have dodged into a house or be hiding nearby in the dark.

She went back to Jeremy, who was reading the note that had been wrapped around the stone. "Don't you worry," he was muttering. "But it won't be because you want it, you bastards."

Geraldine put one arm around his shoulders and read the

childish handwriting. DONT STAY WHERE YOUR NOT WANTED, the message said. "I don't want to wait until tomorrow," Jeremy said.

"Suppose they don't stop at throwing stones? Suppose they set fire to the shop?"

"Let them, if that's how small their minds are. The shop and the stock are insured, anyway. Bastards!" he shouted without warning, and lurched toward the door, then halted. "They wouldn't let us see their faces? So much for the openness Mann's supposed to have brought to Moonwell. So much for their so-called faith."

"Never mind, Jeremy. I agree with you, we might as well leave now." Surely the gravestone had meant simply that Jonathan wanted to be near them, and she didn't like to think of his being anywhere in this dark that made her feel she was asleep and about to start a nightmare. The sooner they were out the better, for Jeremy's sake too. "We'd better tell Diana we're going today."

"We can tell her on the way."

They went through the shop and their rooms to check sockets and locks, and Geraldine was saddened to realize how little she regretted leaving. Jeremy went to the van, while she locked up. "We won't stop to talk," he said as he drove to Diana's.

Diana wasn't there. Perhaps she was up by the church, where quite a few people were heading. Whatever noise had drawn them had been blotted out by the sounds of the van. "Anyway, she's got the key," Jeremy said, and swung the van round, back toward the bookshop and the road beyond.

The lights of Moonwell shrank into a huddle as the road swooped up into the dark. It wasn't like driving at night, and not only because she knew it was still afternoon. The dark seemed thicker than night, and somehow closer—like being slowly frozen in black ice, she thought. When the headlights reached the top of the slope, the dark seemed to collapse toward them from all sides, from the horizon. But the van was speeding onward, down toward the woods.

Two oaks reached across the road, their branches tangled so inextricably that it looked as if they'd grown together. The van sped under the tangled arch, and at once the dark seemed even closer, trapped under the trees. Jeremy leaned over the steering wheel. "The sooner we're out of here the better," he growled, and she wished he wouldn't say what she was trying not to think.

She glanced back as the van reached the first curve of the forest road. Compared with the dark in here the sky looked lighter, almost gray. The next moment it was gone, and ahead was only the cramped patch of lit road, trees seeming to step forward on cue as the edges of the headlight beams touched them. When the road dipped, it felt as if the dark were dragging the van down. "Well, we're on our way," she said, to cheer them up.

The road curved, curved again. The trees leaned closer, linking branches overhead, then fell back for a lay-by. As far as Geraldine recalled, it was the only one on the forest road. It would be harder to turn the van now, though why should they want to? Each curve took them closer to the main road, and surely that meant out of the dark. Once they were out, they would laugh at their fears, laugh so much they might have to stop the van.

Jeremy had rolled his window down, despite the chill, and was listening for traffic ahead. Geraldine wished the forest wasn't quite so still; she couldn't recall when she'd last heard birdsong. It must be the stillness that was making her glimpse movements, not only the trees stepping forward into the light and falling back into the dark but movements behind the trees, as if the light were drawing creatures to it. The dark was working on her, she told herself; her yearning to see was making her think she saw. There could hardly be something behind every tree, peering out as the van passed like those faces in picture puzzles she'd never cared for as a child, drawings of forests where you had to find hidden faces. There couldn't be so many creatures in the woods, and certainly not just a few that could dodge from tree to tree as fast as the van was moving. They must be bushes or undergrowth, of course, and the headlights were making them look paler than they should.

Jeremy was peering ahead as if he didn't want to glance aside. "What the fuck is this?" he muttered. He meant the dark, Geraldine told herself, not the things she wasn't really seeing, shapes scuttling from tree to tree, their heads that looked dismayingly blank emerging from concealment far too high on the tree trunks. She would have told him she didn't mind if he drove faster, except that then he might realize she was nervous too, and each one's nervousness would feed the other's. Best to keep quiet, remembering that they were closer to the main road every moment, surely almost there now. "Is that the main road?" she blurted.

"Where?" Jeremy craned himself over the wheel so eagerly that the van swerved, and she wished she hadn't spoken: it couldn't be the main road ahead, for what she thought she'd glimpsed, a large shape moving across the forest road just beyond the curve, hadn't carried any lights. It must have been a tree that had appeared to move because the van was moving. The van swung round the curve, and both she and Jeremy cowered back in their seats, gasping, as the headlights lit up what was standing in the middle of the road, thrusting forward its white eyeless face that bore a gaping smile, its outstretched arms touching the trees on both sides of the road.

"Fucker!" Jeremy screamed, and drove straight at it as though that would make it disappear, its long, oval body the color of a dead fish, its penis dangling like a withered umbilical cord down one fleshless leg. It only smiled more widely, a smile that seemed totally devoid of emotion on the flat, shiny, featureless face, and let go of the trees, ready to reach for the van with its huge splayed hands. At the last moment Jeremy cried out with loathing and despair and swung the van toward the edge of the road, slued it round, tires screeching, back toward Moonwell.

He almost made the turn. He would have if he'd slowed even slightly. Geraldine thought of treading on the brake herself, too late. The van bumped off the road, swaying violently, throwing Jeremy against her, their heads cracking together. He was still clutching the wheel, but his feet had been dislodged from the pedals. "The brake, where's the brake," he moaned as the van plowed through the undergrowth between two trees. The van was still speeding when it crashed headlong into an oak.

All the lights went out, the dashboard as well as the headlights. Geraldine was hurled forward against her seat belt in the dark. The belt almost dislocated her shoulder before jerking her back against the padded seat. She slumped there, stunned almost beyond being terrified, listening to the stillness through the inflated jagged drumming of her heart. Somewhere in the engine, cooling metal ticked. Or did the sound mean that the engine was getting ready to explode? "Jeremy," she whispered in a voice that seemed stuck in her throat, "are you all right? Are you there?"

Silence. She reached for him, afraid to find he wasn't moving, afraid he would be wet with blood. She touched his leg and felt it flinch, heard him moan. A moment later his hand groped for hers. "It's happened," he said in despair. "Something must have happened at the missile base. That's what all this is."

"We have to get out, Jeremy. Can you walk?"

"Walk where? What's the point? Didn't you see that thing on the road? A nuclear mutation, that's what it was. Radiation must be affecting us right now."

She didn't know if he was correct, and hadn't time to wonder: the thing on the road might be coming for them now, its long, pale fingers groping through the trees for them, its featureless head nodding forward. Wouldn't it be preferable to die in the fire if the petrol exploded rather than fall into those hands? But if they fled now, they might still have a chance. "Come on," she whispered, "before it explodes."

"It already has, don't you understand?" But she heard him struggling to open the door on his side of the van, which was higher off the ground now than hers. It creaked and then slid open squealing, and she wanted to tell him to hurry, not to let go of her hand, in case the smiling eyeless thing was making for the sounds. He let go of her hand in order to haul himself out of the van, and she heard him climb painfully down onto the grass. "Take my hand," he said shakily, urgently.

She grasped it and climbed blindly down onto yielding earth. She was trying frantically to judge how much the van had swerved among the trees. The road was behind her, she thought, the road and whatever was there. "This way," she hissed and stumbled forward, her free hand outstretched, until her fingers bruised themselves against a tree trunk.

It was wider than her arms could reach. She pulled Jeremy round it until she thought she'd placed it between them and the van, then she slumped against it, slid down with Jeremy until they were sitting among the roots. The crusty bark scraped her shoulders on the way down, but its solidity felt reassuring, as familiar as anything could be in this dark. She held her breath and waited for the van to explode.

She was breathing faster than she liked by the time it became clear that the van wasn't going to. The silence was no relief. She'd known woods to be still, but never like this: not the creak of a branch or the whisper of a leaf—no sign of life, except for the thing she'd seen on the road. Though it must be at home in the dark, wouldn't it have to make some noise, however slight, if it were creeping toward them? She squeezed Jeremy's limp hand. "The van isn't going to blow up," she whispered. "Maybe we can fix it if the damage isn't too bad. There's a flashlight in there somewhere."

She ought to have grabbed it before they'd left the van. She couldn't see Jeremy, couldn't see the trees, couldn't even see any part of herself. Pale blurs swarmed on her eyes from the strain of trying to see, and every one of them made her think it was the smiling faceless shape, the long hands reaching for her. Even if they couldn't fix the van, the flashlight would keep back the dark and help them get back to the road. Perhaps they could try for the main road, even though she couldn't hear it; surely it was closer than Moonwell. "Come on, Jeremy," she whispered, pulling at him.

He stood up reluctantly, his hand tightening on hers. She sensed that he was staring at the dark. She wondered what he thought he was seeing, how the images his eyes manufactured looked to him. She could tell he was close to panic, even closer than she was. "This way," she murmured, guiding him while she knew which way to go.

She had a moment of panic when she let go of the tree. No need to hurry, the van should be almost directly ahead, give or take a few feet on either side; she was sure that they'd fled almost straight from the van to the tree. She strained her ears in case the engine was still ticking, and her senses intensified: there was something large just ahead of her that she was about to touch—the van, she told herself fiercely, not something that would reach for her. It was neither. It was a tree.

"What's wrong?" Jeremy demanded, feeling her recoil from bruising her fingertips on the rough trunk.

"It's all right, nothing." She willed him to keep his voice down, told herself that they must have passed the tree without her noticing on the way to taking refuge. She guided him past, over the fleshy ground that swallowed their footsteps. Not far now, it couldn't be, and almost at once a shape loomed on whatever sense she was using instead of sight.

Before she could find it, Jeremy jerked back. "Jesus, what's that?" he nearly screamed. "What did I touch?"

She made herself reach in front of him, her fingers tingling with readiness to flinch. It was another tree trunk. "Just a tree," she murmured.

"Not just a tree, there's a face on it. Or maybe I hallucinated it. Christ, what a time to have a flashback after all these years."

The derision in his voice failed to disguise his panic. "Someone must have been carving on it, that's all," Geraldine said, dreading a recurrence of the time she'd had to help him through a bad trip, the endless hours of reassuring him that it would stop eventually, that he wasn't going mad; they would seem even longer out here in the dark. "We'll go this way," she whispered.

They must be almost level with the van by now. She'd been veering to the left when they encountered this tree, and so she led him to the right, over earth that felt so soft she had to reassure herself that it wouldn't give way, through the silence that clung to her ears as the dark clung to her eyes. The next thing she touched would be the van, she decided; there couldn't be room for anything else in the space she'd glimpsed in the moment before the crash. An object that she sensed was higher and wider than herself blocked their way, and she stretched out her hand at once for the feel of metal. But her hand groped over deep-set eyes and a mouth with jagged teeth.

She bit her lip to keep back a cry. It was a tree, with more than one face carved on it. Her fingers touched something higher on the trunk, something cold and waxy that grew where the hair of the face would have been: long, oval leaves—mistletoe. Her hand ranged about with a desperate aimlessness, trying to distract her from what she had to say. "I don't know where the van is."

"Never mind. Can't be helped." Jeremy sounded almost relieved that she was admitting what he already knew. "Let's just find somewhere to sit and wait. Maybe it'll get lighter or I'll feel better. Someone's bound to drive by eventually."

He was coping by telling himself that the shape on the road had been a hallucination, she realized. What would he do if she told him he was wrong? She'd never taken psychedelics, but she'd seen it in the headlights, and it was still somewhere

185

in the dark. She wanted to drag at his hand and run, anything rather than wait blindly, but running would only betray where they were, if indeed the smiling white thing with the elongated arms didn't know already. Perhaps it was waiting for them to run into those arms. "Please," she murmured so intensely that it made her shiver, yet so quietly that she couldn't hear herself, pleading for any kind of help. She felt Jeremy tugging at her hand, guiding her forward to the tree where he mustn't have noticed the carved faces, urging her to sit among the roots and wait in the utter dark. She was letting herself be urged, since any other course seemed even more dangerous, when fingers closed around her free hand.

Her mouth gaped, her throat shrank, until she thought she was going to choke on the scream she couldn't release. "What's wrong? What's wrong now?" Jeremy demanded as he felt her grow tense and shuddery. The next moment she managed to slacken her grip on him and let out a long breath. The hand that had taken hers was a child's.

She wanted to let go of Jeremy, reach for the child's face and trace the features with her fingertips, but she was afraid that if she let go of Jeremy she might lose him in the awful dark. She didn't need to, she told herself. Only one child could have found them in this. The small hand was squeezing hers as if to tell her so, to encourage her to trust him now that they were together at last. She felt like crying out with joy, but then she would have to explain to Jeremy, and she mustn't risk an argument now. She pulled him to his feet among the roots as the small hand tugged gently at hers. "One more try," she whispered.

"For Christ's sake, what now? What are you trying to do when we can't even fucking see?"

"Trust me, Jerry," she murmured, squeezing his hand as the child's hand was squeezing hers, until Jeremy stopped trying to pull free, making her dread that he would stumble away from her in the dark. He lurched in the direction she was guiding him, and she heard him cursing monotonously and almost inaudibly, as if he could curse the darkness away. The small hand led her gently around obstacles that she couldn't even sense, over the loamy earth. When without warning the earth hardened underfoot, she couldn't help crying out. Jeremy said "Christ" in a voice that sounded drained of feeling. It wasn't hard earth, it was tarmac.

The child's hand led her into the middle of the road. They'd ventured a few yards before she realized that she and Jeremy were being guided back toward Moonwell. "Wouldn't it be better if—" she murmured, and fell silent for fear that Jeremy would want to know who she was speaking to, refuse to believe her, refuse to go on. She might have guided his hand to the child's, except that he would think he was hallucinating, and panic. Best simply to follow where she was being led; she was too overwhelmed by joy to care much where she was going. Her cheeks were wet, and she couldn't dab at them. Her head, her whole body, felt light enough to fly. She was hardly aware any more of the dark.

Jeremy was silent as far as the ridge that overlooked Moonwell, but the sight of the lit streets started him stammering. "Gerry, you're a miracle. How did you do it? Only I didn't realize we were heading this way or I'd have suggested we go down to hitch a lift on the main road."

She barely heard him. The moment the lights had come into view, the child's hand had let go of hers. She swung round, strained her aching eyes at the ridge that was just visible. She and Jeremy were alone. "Jonathan," she whispered.

"Jeremy, you mean," Jeremy said with a hint of impatience. "Never mind, there's a breakdown van in town, near the playing field, I think. Let's go and get ours towed back." He was obviously anxious to be among the lights. As she stumbled with him, she stared desperately over her shoulder at the woods. Jonathan was in there, or somewhere in the dark, and there was nothing she wouldn't do to get him back.

36

"This is the weather for us, eh, Mr. Gloom?"

"Too many bloody lights about for my taste, Mr. Despondency."

"Give the folk time to get used to the dark and happen they'll put out the lights themselves."

"If they keep us waiting much longer, it'll be me who'll be putting out their lights for them, you can bet your eyes on that."

"I'll bet theirs if it's all the same to you. But they're an adaptable lot round here, I reckon. They'll change for anyone who brings a bit of light into their lives, change into anything. All except the likes of that Eustace Gift."

"Don't tell anyone, will you, but I think he's listening."

"If you ask me, he's sitting in there by himself still wondering if they kept the post away from him because of what he said in front of everyone up there last Sunday."

"Aye, and sitting brooding about how nobody will give him the time of day after that."

"Even if they knew it any more."

Eustace had had enough. He switched off the videocassette of *Sons of the Desert* and darted to the window. "Hey up," a voice warned, and there was silence in the street, where he could see nothing but two streetlamps and the segments of terrace and front gardens they illuminated. He ran to the front door, down the path to his gate.

Three figures stood just outside the glow of the lamp at the end of the lane. The lamp lit an almost vertical slope of the moor, spiky with grass. Had he been hearing three voices? Perhaps they hadn't said all that he'd seemed to hear, but he was sure they had been talking about him. He stepped onto the pavement for a better look at them, and they turned toward him.

He couldn't help recoiling. Their faces looked blank and white as eggs. It must be the dark, for he couldn't even see what they were wearing; it must be the dark that made them seem thin as insects. The dark was behind everything, and he couldn't bear the way it had trapped him in a town that loathed him. It felt like the embodiment of that hatred, a medium that wanted to blind and suffocate him, wipe him out altogether. He backed away from it, into his cottage.

He'd hardly closed the door and stumped into the living room when the voices recommenced beyond the open window. "Didn't dare come near us, did he, Mr. Gloom?"

"Wasn't even sure he could hear us, Mr. Despondency."

"Keep them confused, that's the ticket," the third voice said. The others sounded like the voices Eustace used in his routines, but this was very much like his own, like the voice that had come back to him through the earphones, far away beyond the dark. He glared at the window, clenching his fists. "Then we'll have them where we want them," the voice said.

"Get them huddling round the light the way they used to."

"And then—"

"Hang on, don't forget the clown is listening. You're all mouth."

"Listen who's talking. Anyway, nobody would believe him. He's still not even sure we're here."

"Know what I'd like to do?"

"Tell us, tell us."

"Let him hear what he said up there at the rally."

"You're a clever one. You ought to be on the stage. You mean let him hear what he said about his friend the midwife?"

"No friend of his after what he said, I reckon."

"Even though everyone thinks she is. Happen they think she might have a few of those kids he said he wanted to give her."

"The ones he was going to throw down the cave so they wouldn't have to go to school in Moonwell."

"Aye, and throw the other kids in after them."

"He sounds a bit mad if you ask me."

"Must be, to be hearing voices."

This time Eustace almost fell as he ran along the hall. He pulled the front door open so furiously that it bruised his left foot. He hopped along the path, cursing in a muted screech, and hobbled along the pavement toward the streetlamp. But there was nobody. For a moment he thought he saw movement above him, except how could the three shapes be climbing straight up the almost vertical slope to the moor? What he'd seen or thought he'd seen concerned him far less than what he'd heard, for he knew that he'd heard the truth.

He glared at the dark and felt as if it were flooding through him, sweeping away all that he'd taken for granted about himself, leaving him only the memory he'd been straining for days to grasp. The rally had made him blurt out his feelings about the way the Scraggs treated children. He'd known already that he felt that way, but what he'd said about Phoebe Wainwright came from somewhere deeper in him. He'd been shown a part of himself he didn't recognize, and so had virtually the whole of Moonwell.

He had to talk to Phoebe now, or he never would. He hobbled back to his cottage and slammed the door, closing himself out in the dark; then he made himself hurry to Roman Row, to give himself no chance to falter. The cottage next to Phoebe's, where the toothless, garrulous old woman lived, was unlit, thank God. He limped under the arch of vines that looked withered now, and up the path. Before he could reach for the bell, his gravelly footsteps brought Phoebe to the window.

His toes curled in dismay, his bruised foot throbbing. Perhaps she'd been eating heavily because she was depressed. She blinked slowly at him and shook her head on its rolls of neck. "Go away," she mouthed through the glass. "I don't want any visitors."

"Please come to the door, won't you? I've something to say to you."

"You've said enough," she told him, more indifferently than angrily, and shoved herself away from the window, plodded across the room, and switched off the light. He heard her laboring along the hall and up the stairs. He wanted to ring the bell, but the sight of her as she crossed the room had dismayed him so much that he limped home as fast as he could, to be out of the dark. There was nothing he could do about her overeating. Surely it must be overeating that had made her belly swell that way.

37

When Brian heard the timid knocking at the bedroom door, he fought his way awake. "Get back to bed," he snarled.

"It's Letty Ingham, Mr. Bevan. I'm sorry to trouble you. I wondered if you could tell me what time it is."

"The middle of the night," he growled, and then remembered about the dark. "Just a minute," he said, murmuring too late to avoid waking Andrew, who was sandwiched between himself and June. "Don't want to go back to my bed," the boy whimpered.

"Keep quiet then or you'll wake your mother." Brian peered at the bedside clock, forced his eyes wider. "I'm afraid I can't tell you, Miss Ingham. The damn thing's stopped."

"So has my watch, and the town clock doesn't seem to be striking either. I don't know how I'll be able to tell when it's time to take Andrew to school."

"You go ahead if you like and I'll bring him." The sooner she was out of the house, the sooner Brian might be able to banish her from his thoughts.

June woke then, and sat up straight as a knife blade. "Why can't Miss Ingham take him?"

"We were just trying to decide what time it is, Mrs. Bevan. What I'll do, I'll go to the school and find out what's happening."

She went back to Andrew's bedroom, which she was using now that the boy wouldn't sleep alone. "Don't want to go out in the dark," the boy whimpered.

"You won't have to until it's time for school. You don't mind going out in the daytime, do you?" June said heartily, and glared at Brian across the pillow. "I'd like to know who's been filling your head with this nonsense."

Brian lay back and closed his eyes, to hide. If the boy was

frightened because of him, it must be that he sensed how uneasy Brian was. In his sleep Brian had thought he was pulling Letty's head off, making her giggle, as he dwindled inside her. He heard her go out of the house, and kept his sigh of relief to himself. But he'd hardly begun to relax when she came back.

"People are taking their children to school," she said through the door. "Their clocks and watches aren't working either. I'm told it's some kind of magnetic effect to do with the weather."

"It must be morning," June decided, and swung her legs out of bed. "I can feel it is. No more of your nonsense, Andrew. Miss Ingham will be taking you, so you've nothing to worry about. Quickly now, I've the shop to open."

By the time Brian came out of the bathroom, she'd bustled Andrew away with the teacher. "Your breakfast's on the table," she called up the stairs, and left Brian surrounded by stickers and plaques that said "God Lives Here" or "God's Room" or "On Loan from God," though they might as well all have said "God's Watching You," the way they made him feel. He gobbled his breakfast and headed for the shop.

On the High Street everyone was bidding good morning to everyone they met. If they all thought it was morning, did that make it so? June was counting the cash in the till, though nobody had bought from the shop since the young hiker. Her routine was a way of pretending that nothing had changed, he realized, but that didn't explain the way she'd glanced at him. "What's wrong, love?" he said.

She mouthed her counting and then said flatly, "What could be wrong?"

"If it's that I went to the pub with Letty Ingham, I only went to show whose side I was on."

"Miss Ingham! You think I'm worried about her, do you?" She slammed the cash drawer so that the till rang. "No, I don't think you've been up to anything with Miss Prim-and-Proper-Healthy Ingham. You wouldn't get far if you tried to make her do any of the filthy things you used to make me do. But you won't be surprised if I wonder what you get up to now that I won't do them."

Brian forced himself to respond while he could. "I'm not with you, love."

192

"Aren't you? Then maybe you can tell me why you're so eager to take Andrew out since it's got so dark."

"Why shouldn't I? He's my son, isn't he?" Brian had to restrain himself from grabbing her across the counter, he was suddenly so furious. He stepped back, well out of reach, his arms tingling. "Just what did you mean by saying he'd have nothing to worry about with Letty Ingham as if he would with me?"

"You tell me, Brian. Tell me why he's so frightened of you."

"I'll be buggered if he is. He's frightened of this dark, and no wonder."

"Isn't it?" June gave him a bitter smile. "The dark's been sent us by God just like everything else. It's meant to guide us back to Him like all the troubles He sends us. If you ask me, it's a sign that there are still a few people in Moonwell who aren't on His side."

"I've already told you I am."

She ignored that. "There can't be any reason for a child to be frightened of God's dark, can there? That isn't what the boy's frightened of."

"So it must be me. Do you know, love, I think the dark's getting you down, confusing you."

She leaned toward him across the faded guides for hikers. "I realized something this morning. You were the one who started worrying about whether Andrew was a pansy. Who'd have made him that way if he was? The only man he's spent much time with is you."

Brian had a sudden feverish impression that his arms could stretch to her, grab her from halfway across the shop. "I'm not arguing with you when you're like this. You pray a bit and maybe that'll get you thinking straight. I'm going to see Godwin."

"Going to tell him what you can't tell me?"

"No, of course not," he said, turning to the door for fear that his face would betray him. "I want to ask him how long he thinks this is going to last and what we ought to do."

He went quickly out, before his rage could turn him back. She'd no right to say such things about him and Andrew. What was she trying to do, leave him with no sense of himself at all? The only way to get rid of all the guilt that was

193

festering in him and regain himself was to confess to Godwin. He hardly saw the people in the dark streets as he made for the hotel.

A beaming woman with a cross on her front met him on the chipped steps of the hotel. "Godwin says we can have a service at the church," she told him.

"You mean he's conducting it now?"

"No, he's delegated someone. He'll be leading us again in worship soon, but going down the cave took a lot out of him. There'll be lots of hymns and praying at the church. You should come."

"I'll try and get along later," Brian said and sidled past her into the lobby, which was almost deserted. The receptionist looked half asleep. Brian hurried to the lift and stepped in, shivering. He'd grown almost used to the chill of the streets, but each floor that sank past the small window seemed to lower the temperature. The lift wavered to a halt on the top floor. The doors staggered open, and the cold reached for him.

It must be all his guilt that made the corridor seem so cold and huge and daunting. He'd been down it once before, past the same anonymous doors, the same dim lamps on the walls. He drove himself forward, feeling as if he were tiptoeing because he couldn't hear himself, to Godwin's door at the end. At least it would be brighter in there, he saw. Part of his mind noticed how the brown paint had speckled the door-knob when the door was painted, how the door didn't quite fit the frame, and he found those details somehow reassuring as he knocked on the panel in front of his face.

He had to swallow then, because he couldn't hear for the drumming of his heart. The lift started down the shaft with a groaning of metal, and Brian glanced along the empty corridor, which looked suddenly longer and dimmer. Was the whole top floor deserted? The voice beyond the door made him flinch. "Come to me," it said.

It was just the suddenness that had startled him, not the tone, which was gentle, almost coaxing. He wished he were going to confess to a priest so that they couldn't see each other's faces, but there was only Godwin. Before he could tell it to, Brian's hand grasped the doorknob and opened the door. He had to force himself not to shut his eyes against the brightness as he lurched into the room.

194

Godwin was sitting on the bed, his legs stretched out, his upper body against the headboard under the bright lamp. His eyes were closed, his hands were clasped on his chest. He must be praying, though for a moment Brian thought he was supporting something on his chest. Unless it was inside his loose shirt, there was nothing. More than ever his face had the look of thrusting forward into an icy wind, the skin stretching, turning almost white. His stillness made Brian feel he couldn't move, until Godwin's face turned slowly toward him. "Shut us in," he said softly.

Brian reached behind him, pulled at the door, and then he stood wondering what to do. Should he kneel down, close his eyes? The light overwhelmed him with Godwin's presence, the thin, almost-lipless mouth, the sharp bones, the closed, flat eyelids. The light clung to him like frost, made him shiver. He opened his mouth to speak, to regain some control of himself, and all his guilt rushed into his head, choking him. He was struggling to speak when Godwin's unseeing face lifted toward him. "You've something to say to me," the evangelist said.

Brian's words came tumbling. "I need forgiveness. I wanted to help you, I did try to help, only something, something inside me—"

"Quiet now. No need to talk. I know." The pale mouth smiled. "You did help me, Brian, and not only when you brought the rope. Without you, I mightn't have succeeded."

Brian was swaying, dizzy with relief. "You really think so?"

"Would I lie? Come here, put your hands in mine. Let's rid you of your doubts about yourself. Until you're clear on who and what you are, you'll never be able to do what you're capable of."

He must mean things that Brian could do for God. Brian stumbled forward and put out his hands timidly. The evangelist's hands reached unerringly for them, closed over them and held Brian there, stooped awkwardly toward the bed.

When Brian began to shudder from head to foot, he thought at first it was because of his posture. Or perhaps this was what faith healing felt like, yet he couldn't help blaming the icy light for causing him to quake, turning his limbs into soft objects that no longer felt like arms and legs. He glanced away from Godwin's masklike smile and up at the lamp, to see what kind of bulb could emit such a light. But the holder was empty. There was no bulb.

His body tried to fall back, away from the evangelist, but he couldn't move, not even his numb hands at the ends of his unfamiliar arms. He was helpless in the white light that was streaming into him, not from the lamp but from Godwin himself. "You're the first of my true followers," Godwin said softly, opening his eyes at last. Deep in the white sockets, reptile eyes no larger than shirt buttons gazed into Brian's.

=========== 38 ===========

Diana was on the plane to New York when the windows filled with white light and the passengers began to scream. She woke in the dark of her cottage in Moonwell, and in a way the dark was worse than the dream. By her watch it wasn't even time to get up. The dark pressed in silently all around her, and she couldn't help drifting away from that, back to New York to stroll in Central Park, where all at once something huge and pale appeared above the skyscrapers, laughing with vast, cruel delight. Then she didn't know where she was, just somewhere gray and desolate under a sun like a lump of ash. People were dancing in a ring as wide as the horizon, but when she approached them she saw they had no heads. She woke feeling that it could be anywhere—could soon be anywhere, if she didn't stop it. Perhaps the dreams were meant to show her how she could.

She tried to relax as she'd learned to do at yoga. She sensed dreams waiting just beyond the edge of her conscious mind, waiting to lead her away, presumably back to the vision she'd glimpsed on the moor. Or might she be led physically up there? So long as she had time to grab a flashlight, she thought, already feeling more nervous. She couldn't relax while there were things she ought to learn. Surely it was time to go to the police station, she thought, having realized that her watch had stopped. At least that was something to do. At least she wouldn't feel she was waiting for Mann to find her in the dark.

She washed and dressed and made herself a meager breakfast, feeling as if she were performing rituals whose meanings were almost forgotten, more irrelevant every time she repeated them. On the wall of the front room, Sally's and Jane's pictures were drooping. She fixed them back up and made for the High Street, and wondered why all the shops were shut, until she heard the singing at the church. As she crossed the square, she saw a whitish glow beyond the curtains of Mann's room at the hotel. The curtains looked like clouds over a full moon, she thought uneasily, and hurried to the police station beyond the square.

The policeman with a face like an old maid's except for the silvery mustache was behind the counter, frowning at Craig and Vera. "You don't mean to tell me we can't leave Moonwell," Craig was saying.

"Just until we've ascertained precisely what the conditions are, sir. You must understand it's for your own safety."

Vera turned as Diana came in. "They won't let us go home," she complained.

"Maybe it's for the best," Diana said, and reached for the bell push on the counter. The policeman glared at her. "Just wait, please," he snapped.

"You aren't on your own, are you?" Her sympathy turned to dread. "They didn't come back."

"Who?" Vera demanded.

"It's entirely possible that my officers decided the best course was to abandon the car and continue on foot. The electrical conditions out there may have caused engine failure—they certainly cut off our radio contact. Perhaps now you'll understand why I'd like you to delay your journey, Mr. and Mrs. Wilde. The mountain rescue team have enough people to search for."

His rapid speech must be intended to convey an impression of efficiency, but to Diana it sounded defensive. "How many police were there in the car?"

"Two in the first." Suddenly he turned on her. "For reasons of your own, Miss Kramer, you seem to have set out to undermine people's faith. If you've none of your own that is your lack, but I warn you officially now that under the

197

present conditions your behavior may be seen as likely to lead to a breach of the peace. Now, what can I do for you?"

What peace? she wanted to shout at him. It wasn't peace, it was apathy, lack of awareness, a refusal to look. "Did you find Father O'Connell's dog?" she said, having learned everything else she'd come to learn.

"I fear not. I suspect it's far away by now. If you're worried, I should keep inside your house." He swung away from her. "I'll make sure you know as soon as the roads are declared safe, Mr. Wilde. I take it you'll still be at the hotel."

Outside, Vera said "I don't want to stay at the hotel."

"I really don't see what alternative we have."

"Something about the hotel you don't like?" Diana suggested.

"Just the feel of it up there on the top floor. It's too cold, for one thing," Vera said resentfully. "I don't expect luxury in a place like this, but it's like being down a cave."

"You could stay at my place," Diana blurted.

"That's most kind of you, Diana." Vera came forward impulsively and kissed her on the cheek. "Would you mind if we let you know? Our daughter lives in town, you see. Perhaps her lodgers could have our room at the hotel."

"Presumably another police car went looking for the first," Craig said, to carry them past the awkwardness. "Not the most intelligent response."

"I'm sure they're doing what they think is best," Diana said, already regretting having invited the Wildes to stay. She was taking on more and more responsibilities, yet they felt like a substitute for the real thing. Deep down she knew that if she was ever to do what she felt capable of doing, she would need to be utterly alone.

39

"God see you safely home," Miss Ingham said, and Andrew began to pray harder, inside his head. He was praying that his parents were somewhere safe and well lit. It must be the light that was keeping the things out of Moonwell, the things he'd seen crawling up the cave, the evil things that had lived down there until Mr. Mann had taken God to them. Now they were crawling out like maggots out of a dead bird, and Andrew couldn't understand why God hadn't killed them all down there.

Maybe they weren't coming. Maybe they had to stay down there until it killed them, now that it was a holy place. Surely God wouldn't let them come down to the houses. Yet when Andrew thought of some of the things God let happen in the world, things that were nobody's fault except God's, he didn't feel sure at all.

The other children were flocking out of the classroom as if the dark was nothing to be afraid of, grumbling or fighting when Miss Ingham wasn't looking, behaving worse than they used to before it got so dark. They wouldn't believe what he'd seen at the cave. He wished he could tell Miss Kramer, but just today in the assembly hall Mr. Scragg had said that nobody was to speak to her, because she didn't believe in God; she was only staying in Moonwell to try and turn people away from Him. Andrew still liked her, but there was no chance he'd be able to talk to her now. All he could do was talk to God and hope that God was listening, except that God must have zillions of people more important than Andrew to listen to, and why should He listen to Andrew when nobody else did? Andrew prayed a last prayer and stumbled to his feet, and realized that Miss Ingham was staring beyond him, at the classroom door. His heart was jumping painfully before he turned and saw his father.

His father stepped forward, beaming. Under the fluorescent lighting his pale face looked almost white, except for the shadows under his eyes. His cheeks seemed hairier than ever, his chin was sticking out so far he reminded Andrew of a cartoon. It was as though he were trying to look more like himself, Andrew thought, as his father gripped his shoulder. "Come on, son, we've a special surprise for you."

"You'll be taking Andrew home, will you, Mr. Bevan?"

"That I will, Letty. No objection, I suppose, seeing as he's my son?" He was still beaming, showing all his teeth. "We'll see you later."

"Miss Ingham took us to church today," Andrew interrupted. "There were lots of people."

"Have a good time, did you?"

"Of course we did, Mr. Bevan. There's nothing that's more fun than praising God."

"Just you wait, Andrew. Someone very special wants to see you." His hand tugged at Andrew's shoulder, turning him. "Going to church, that's nothing."

Miss Ingham smiled at him, but her eyes looked hurt. "May I know?"

"Well, I wanted it to be a surprise for the boy. He hasn't much excitement in his life." He leaned past Andrew and whispered, "Godwin Mann."

Miss Ingham's face brightened. "Wants to see Andrew?"

"Wants to see a good boy, and I don't know any better."

"Neither do I. You go with your father, Andrew. You'll be glad you did."

Andrew thought he might be. He could ask Mr. Mann what God was going to do about the dark and the things in the cave. If anyone could stop him being frightened, surely Mr. Mann could, particularly since going to see him seemed to have cheered up his father; Andrew had never seen his father so bright. He was suddenly so eager that he followed his father as far as the schoolyard before remembering that he would have to go into the dark. "Take my hand, son," his father said.

Andrew grabbed his hand and stepped into the yard. They passed through the light of the first streetlamp, and beyond it his father gripped his hand more tightly. He didn't need to hold on to Andrew quite so hard, but perhaps he'd forgotten how strong he was, or perhaps it was his way of showing he loved Andrew. They hurried past a line of lit shops that made Andrew think of tanks in an aquarium, and he bit his lip. His father's hand was tightening on his every time they stepped out of the light, tightening so much it didn't feel comforting. All at once he wondered if his father were holding his hand not to reassure Andrew but to try to reassure himself.

Andrew peered nervously at his father's face as it came out of the dark. His father was still smiling, baring his teeth, which the streetlamp made gleam. Could he be smiling so that Andrew wouldn't see how he really felt? Andrew tightened his own grip, to tell his father not to be afraid. They were going to see Mr. Mann, and then they wouldn't need to be.

As they came in sight of the hotel, Andrew's father raised his head. He was gazing at the brightest of the windows under the steep roof. It must be Mr. Mann's room, Andrew realized, a beacon in the dark. His father was beaming so hard that Andrew could see his gums; his mouth looked like a dog's, all teeth. They were both so intent on the window as they almost ran across the square that they didn't notice Andrew's mother until she stepped in front of them.

She stared at Andrew's father as she often stared at Andrew. "Where have you been?"

"I told you where I was going."

"You aren't telling me you've been with Godwin all day."

"You don't notice time passing when you're with him."

"I had to ask Katy to look after the shop," she complained, and frowned at Andrew. "Where's Miss Ingham? Where were you going with the boy?"

His father hugged him. "We're going to see Godwin, aren't we, son? That'll show anyone who thinks you're not as good as their kids. We'll give them something to think about."

"He's going to see nobody while he's looking like that. Have some thought for me if you've none for yourself. Do you want Godwin to think we can't even keep him clean? Cleanliness is next to godliness, my father always said."

Andrew was trying not to pull away from his father just because his father's smell had changed. It must be something his father had handled in the shop that gave him a cold, stony smell. "Godwin won't mind," his father said, hugging him.

"He mightn't, but I do. Do you want us to be the talk of the town? Just you come with me this minute," she said, and

Andrew didn't know if she was speaking like that to him or to his father. Couldn't his father wash his face in the hotel? But then she demanded, "Anyway, what does Godwin want with him?"

Andrew almost cried out, almost pulled his hand away from his father's. She'd halted under a streetlamp, leaving him and his father outside the sanctuary of light. He was scared of the dark, that was all, and troubled by the smell that made him think of the reptile house at the zoo. His father's hand couldn't really feel as it seemed to. "I couldn't tell you," his father said.

"Well, he won't be going until I know. And if he does I want to be there to make sure he's on his best behavior."

She turned her back on them as if they could only follow. They stepped through the light of the streetlamp, and the shadow of Andrew's father reached for her. It couldn't hurt her, Andrew told himself, any more than his father would. He clenched his hand on his father's as if that would make it feel as it ought to. He was just being silly, the way his parents said he was. He was too big to be scared of things that weren't true, especially when there was so much to be scared of that was.

His mother swung around again as his father's shadow shrank away from the next lamp. "The Booths are back in town, as if they didn't know where they're not wanted. Don't you dare go near them, Andrew."

"I promise." He wouldn't have time to see Geraldine and Jeremy, not while he was looking after his father. He tugged his father toward the shop. He was praying that his father would be better once they were out of the dark, but if something was still wrong with him—if the demon from the cave could still influence him—then Andrew had to make sure they went to Mr. Mann. Then he wouldn't be even a little bit afraid of his father, wouldn't imagine he could feel his father's hand growing long and cold and stronger every time they stepped into the dark.

40

When Diana concluded that the Wildes weren't taking up her offer of accommodation, she felt so resigned it was almost like relief. She was on her own, as apparently she needed to be. There was no use telling herself she wasn't all that Celtic: the depths of her mind knew better. There was no point in wishing someone was with her to make sure she didn't endanger herself. She could only trust her instincts, and hope it wasn't too late.

She went round the cottage and made sure all the windows and outer doors were locked. She peered at all the light bulbs to see if any looked close to failing, then she climbed the stairs to her bedroom. Already she felt as if she'd been asleep for days and needed to relax in order to wake up, to see what was there to be seen. She lay on her bed and went through her relaxation exercises, tried to empty her mind and let the awareness in.

It didn't work. Random thoughts kept drifting through. The night's in the sun, she thought, but at least Father O'Connell wasn't in the well, though did that make a difference? Could this dark be what the druids had meant by the fall of the sky? She wondered if she ought to switch off the light to help her mind go blank, and was nerving herself to do so when someone knocked at the front door.

She shrank back against the headboard. Had Mann sensed her trying to recapture her awareness and come to deal with her before she could? "Jump out the window and run like a hare," she thought, "there's nowhere to hide but Harry Moony hears where . . ." She went downstairs as if her exhaustion was dragging her; there was no point in delaying the confrontation. But when she opened the door, she found the Booths.

Jeremy looked harassed; Geraldine seemed oddly calm. "May we come in?" Geraldine said.

"Sure, of course," Diana said wearily. "I didn't mean to be rude."

They followed her into the front room, where Jeremy stared at the picture of the sticklike mountaineers as if it made him nervous. He cleared his throat. "We didn't get very far."

"What stopped you?"

"The van went off the road in the woods, and now we can't get it repaired. Nobody seems to want to go down there."

"Why not, do you think?"

"Well, it's this wretched dark, isn't it? No wonder it makes folk nervous, preys on their minds. Mine too. At least we managed to find our way back. Luck was on our side for once."

"I'd say we were guided," Geraldine said quietly.

"Yes, well, let's not argue about that in front of Diana, all right? If that's how you felt, Gerry, then it's right for you."

"I don't want to cause an argument," Diana said as casually as she could, "but who did you feel you were guided by?"

Geraldine looked defiant. "There's only one person it could have been—our unborn son."

Whatever Diana was expecting, it wasn't this. Jeremy took her silence for embarrassment, and intervened hastily. "Anyway, we just wanted to get the keys back from you and tell you we're back at the old place if you're feeling lonely."

Diana reached for her handbag and found the keys to the chapel. "I wouldn't go out of the town if I were you," Geraldine said, "not while it's like this."

"Why not?" Diana demanded, more sharply than she would have wanted to.

"I think we're safe where there are lights. We must be, otherwise we wouldn't have been brought back."

Safe from what? The more Geraldine said, the harder it might be for Diana to do what she was determined to try. She gave the keys to Jeremy, who stood up at once. "Any time you want company, Diana, just come round. We unbelievers need to stick together."

Diana watched them climb the alley toward the High Street, their arms around each other. She remembered the broken window at the bookshop and told herself they would look after each other. She hadn't time to worry now, but she knew she would if she tried to relax. She had to try something else—go where she'd experienced her glimpses, up on the moor.

As soon as the Booths were out of sight, she locked the cottage and took her flashlight from the car. She was tempted to stay well clear of the hotel, but she ventured as far as the corner of the square. Mann's window was still lit, with that pale light that made her think of bones, of death, of the skin of the eyeless lizard that had crawled out of the cave. She dodged into the nearest alley, even though there were no lamps in the narrow cobbled passage.

Though the High Street was deserted where she crossed it, she hid the flashlight under her anorak and kept it there while she hurried to the moorland path. She climbed the path quickly, above the shrinking lamps, and switched on the flashlight as she reached the top. The oval of light spread across the charred moor, grew paler and vaguer until it petered out a couple of hundred yards away. She took a breath that tasted ashen, and climbed onto the moor.

She'd hoped to feel her awareness stir, but there was only a blurred apprehension, as if the dark were creeping closer. The town was a few handfuls of light below her, a lit miniature that might as well be miles away. Around her was nothing but blackened stalks and bare black earth, not a hint of green. Trying not to breathe the ashen air too deeply, she set out for the cave.

As soon as she left the edge above Moonwell, she wanted to look behind her. It was only her sense of the moor's cutting off the light of the town, she told herself. She switched off the flashlight to let her eyes adjust and to save the batteries. The dark rushed at her, filled her eyes, and then something else came, a glimpse of a face with eyes far too small for their sockets. She fumbled the flashlight on, so wildly that she almost dropped it in the blind dark.

For a moment, or much longer, she didn't know where or who she was. The dark had turned into a cave, just too large for her light to reach the walls or the roof. It seemed like that because she'd felt as if she were in a cave when the shrunken face with tiny eyes far back in the sockets had reared up, out of a mass of decay that was still moving. She'd felt as if it

205

wasn't happening to her, as if she was sharing someone else's experience; yet it had been appallingly vivid, the face that looked withered into the misshapen bone, clenched around its own intense evil, as it had pressed its lipless mouth onto hers. Was that what Mann had found in the cave?

She bit her lip and said a silent prayer—she wasn't sure to whom—and closed her eyes as she switched off the flashlight. The dark crowded around her, chill and massive. It was all she could see now, even when she opened her eyes; at least, if she could make out the edges of slopes against the sky, they were so dim that she might as well have been imagining the sight. When she switched on the flashlight, she took her time about it, to prove that she could.

The dark fell back—only the dark. She'd have to keep the light on; she would never find her way otherwise. Once she was above the cave, in the stone bowl, she could dispense with it, she told herself. She picked out the trampled path and started along it as quickly as she could, though the swaying oval of light made her feel as if shapes were dodging out of sight wherever it touched, closing in behind her as soon as the light had passed. She mustn't look back. Whichever way she turned, the dark would be behind her.

She was on the slope up to the stone bowl when she halted, swallowing the taste of ash. She'd thought she heard a charred twig snap, a sound so minor it wouldn't have been audible except for the utter stillness. It might have been a breeze: how welcome that would be in this stillness! Or perhaps she'd snapped the twig herself, though she couldn't see any when she swung the flashlight beam around her feet. Perhaps she hadn't even heard the sound, she thought, and made herself follow the beam up the slope. By the time she reached the top, she'd managed to convince herself she was alone at the cave. But as the flashlight beam wavered up from probing the gaping stony mouth, it picked out a shape that stood on the far side of the bowl.

41

That was the day Nick realized more was wrong in Moonwell than he knew. Religious hysteria had overtaken the town, some kind of trance which, if he understood Diana correctly, made people unaware that the town was even on the map. That didn't quite make sense to him, but certainly nobody outside Moonwell seemed to want to know about Godwin Mann. His editor didn't and sent him to cover the latest outbreak of picketing in Lancashire. Julia was setting up a pirate station in a different suburb of Manchester, but she wanted nothing to do with Nick or any story he might offer her. All he could do was go to Moonwell to see for himself what was happening as soon as he had a day off.

He'd told Diana he would, and he'd broken his promise. More disturbing, he hadn't realized until today that he'd let the chance to visit her drift by, when the early morning silence of the streets outside the newspaper building had reminded him of Moonwell—reminded him that he hadn't even thought of her for days. More was wrong than she had told him, and it seemed to be wrong with him as well.

When he couldn't reach her by phone, he set off for Moonwell. In the midst of the Peak District he found he couldn't recall the route or locate Moonwell on the map. The sight of the forested slopes ahead reminded him of the route he'd once taken, and he'd driven into the forest, switching on his headlights as it grew cavernously dark under the trees. It was just the trees, he told himself; he would see daylight once he was out of the woods. And indeed he did: he saw racing clouds above the ridge that overlooked Moonwell. Then the clouds stopped, the daylight went out, as if the landscape were a slide that had been snatched from the viewer of his eyes.

Before he could brake, the car ran off the road. The road

must have curved—to the right, he seemed to remember. He swung the wheel that way, the only instinct that was left him in the dark that had taken the use of his eyes. Either his memory had tricked him or he'd passed the curve. The car tilted so violently he thought it was going to turn over as it continued down the unseen slope.

All this felt like a dream, too abrupt to be real. The dark couldn't really be out there when he'd only just seen daylight. His foot was stamping on the brake, but it didn't seem to have much to do with him. He was going to find out at last what it was like to be in a car crash, he mused; he'd wondered ever since he'd had to visit accident victims as a cub reporter. You should let out your breath so as not to be winded by the impact, he thought, but he couldn't see when the impact was coming, could see nothing but the headlight beams jerking in space, as unable to grasp the dark as he was. His consciousness lurched then, and he realized he'd seen daylight, clouds, the ridge, only because he'd expected to. It was the dark that was real.

He trampled harder on the brake, desperate to feel he had control of something. The car began to skid. The rear end slued into what felt like space, like the edge of a sheer drop. Nick gulped and felt his bowels loosening. He released the brake, and the car slithered over the grass. A jagged rock broader than the windscreen seemed to leap into the headlight beams an instant before the car rammed the rock.

The sight had made him suck in his breath. The air rushed out of him, bruising his throat and chest, as the seat belt snapped taut across him. Though the impact with the rock wasn't as vicious as he had feared, it put out the headlights.

He reached blindly for the handbrake and pulled it as hard as he could, hardly knowing why; then he rubbed his chest with his shaking hands and tried to swallow while he stared vainly at the dark. He rolled down his window eventually, as if that might help his eyes. There was nothing but darkness and hectic afterimages, no sense of distance, not even a glimpse of the car or the rock. He fumbled under the extinguished dashboard for the flashlight and found it at last on the mat beside the gear lever. It was smashed, useless.

The one thought that held him back from panic was reminding himself that he hadn't gone blind. He'd seen the headlights until the crash had put paid to them. The dark was only dark, however unexpected at this time of day. Would he be better able to cope with it if he knew what was causing it? Sitting brooding about that wouldn't help at all. He groped for the door release and eased himself out of the car.

He had to grip the upper edge of the door frame in order to lever himself to his feet. The slope was so steep that his heels slipped on the tilted floor of the vehicle. As he hauled himself upright, gripping the roof, he felt the car shift an inch. For a nightmarish moment he thought it was balanced on the edge of a sheer drop, thought that his movement had pushed it over. Then it stabilized, and he eased some of his weight off the roof, straightening himself gingerly until both feet were firmly planted on the grass.

He waited until the dark stopped turning jerkily red in time with the thumping of his heart, then he closed his eyes and counted one hundred. When he opened them, he still couldn't distinguish his surroundings, not even the ridge that must be above him, against the sky. It didn't matter, he told himself. The road was up there, and once he reached it he could feel his way to Moonwell. All he needed to do was let go of the car and pick his way up the slope.

It took him a long time to push himself off into the dark. He was tempted to wait until he saw lights on the road and then start running, but how long might he have to wait? Suppose whatever had made him and the rest of the world forget Moonwell had stopped the outgoing traffic? "Get going, you damn fool," he growled, to stop himself brooding over the cause of the darkness, and shoved himself upward, out of reach of the car.

His voice sounded flattened and shrunken, and unnervingly separate from him. He resisted the impulse to retreat to the car while he could still find it. The sooner he saw Diana, the happier he'd be. He should have done more to help her before it grew as late as it seemed to be now. He turned and, stretching out his unseen hands, took his first steps up the slope.

A minute's oblique climbing brought him to a gentler incline where he could walk upright, moving one foot at a time, placing the heel of one against the toe of the other. He estimated that he'd climbed fifty yards or so in what he judged to be a straight line when a mass rose in front of him. He sensed it a moment before he touched it, fingertips prickling: heather. Above it the slope was too steep to be climbed blindly. Had it been as steep where the car had left the road, or was he losing his way? He groped his way along the bank of heather, bruising his fingers on chunks of rock, to the grass, where the slope was almost level. He halted there, listening.

Shouldn't he be able to hear the occasional sound from the town? The stillness was total except for the noises of his own body: he'd never realized they were so various. The dark clung to his eyes like tar. He must be nearly at the road. He held back from walking faster, striding to it—the corky ground was by no means even, and he could sprain an ankle even if he didn't break his leg in a ditch. A hundred steps or less, he promised himself, and he'd be back on the road.

Apart from a clump of heather that would have tripped him if he hadn't been walking carefully, there seemed to be nothing for the first hundred steps except the gentle slope. Of course he'd no reason to suppose a hundred steps would take him to the road, no reason to feel betrayed by himself or by anything else. Another fifty steps should do it, or if not, a few more. He obviously wouldn't be returning to the same point on the road. He wasn't sure how many steps he'd taken, having stopped counting because it made him feel tense, when he realized that the gentleness of the slope had lured him away from the road.

He managed not to turn. He might forget which way he'd been facing, and be totally lost. You already are, a voice at the back of his mind complained, as he craned his head over one shoulder and then the other in the hope of somehow sensing the road, his bones creaking loudly. All he could sense was the dark that swarmed with his yearning to see. The road must be to his right, but how far? About ninety degrees, he figured, and set off at that angle. He'd taken three paces when he trod in a puddle under the grass.

"Shit," he muttered, sniggering at himself as he seesawed his arms to keep his balance while he pulled his foot out of the mud. Of course it was only his own laughter he was hearing. He inched forward, poking the ground with his toes before setting his feet down, until suddenly his foot groped into space. For a breathless moment he thought it had taken him over the edge. He threw himself backward and was sitting on wet grass. "Bastard," he snarled.

At once he wished he hadn't spoken. It felt too much like acknowledging the laughter that could only be in his head, however real and vindictive it sounded—acknowledging it as though it were out there in the dark. He stretched out a hand before he could panic, to find out where he'd almost stepped over. It was a hollow, no wider than his arm could stretch. In finding that out he slipped forward on the grass, his hand sliding down the far side of the hollow, moist earth collecting under his fingernails, bulging them to the quick. His fingertips came to rest on a cold, slimy root at the bottom of the hollow, a root that felt like a misshapen hand. He was about to heave himself away from the hollow when the root moved.

It squirmed and stretched along his hand and then, before he could recoil, it wasn't there. Nick scrambled backward out of the hollow. It must have been a lizard, he thought, trying to ignore how it had felt. It had felt as if the long cold hand he'd first taken it for had clasped his, momentarily, before withdrawing into the hollow.

He stayed on all fours, glaring blindly about him. He felt like an animal at bay. He mustn't give in to that feeling; it was like giving in to the dark. He forced himself to reach for the hollow again, to be sure of avoiding it when he stood up. It was ridiculous to dread touching anything alive—the lizard must have been far more shocked than he was. He moved crabwise away from the hollow, and got quickly to his feet. Something was standing in front of him, waiting for him. He felt its cold breath on his face.

"Just the wind," he muttered, shivering, and wished again that he hadn't spoken; it made him feel surrounded by listeners. If it had been the wind, why hadn't he heard it in the grass? Why had he felt it only on his face? It had smelled like soil and decay, and made him think of a mouth that was yawning too widely. He would rather not put a face to such a mouth. "Just wind," he whispered, feeling as if he was trying not to be overheard.

He tried again to visualize Diana: long legs, black hair streaming in the moorland wind. The memory felt like a promise of light, and helped muffle his dread of moving from where he was standing. He sidled a few feet—to sidestep the hollow, he told himself, not the thing which he'd imagined had breathed in his face—and then ventured forward. He'd taken two paces when something cold and smooth that

211

smelled like a dank cave leaned over his shoulder and whispered in his ear.

He never knew what it said. He swung round, lashing out blindly at whatever was there, his body blazing with fear and rage and a loathing of how his fist might feel when it landed. It plunged into air, and he went with it, fell to his knees again, bruising them and his hands on the rocky earth under the grass. He leaped up at once and realized he had no idea which way he'd been heading. "Bastards," he whispered, though really he wanted to scream the word to stop himself from weeping, whether with contempt for himself or horror at the nightmare he was living. He stood glaring so hard at the dark that not only his eyes but the skin around them stung, his fists trembling with readiness to lash out at anything that touched him, trembling like the onset of a convulsion that would shake him from head to foot. Every false image his eyes manufactured looked as if it were coming at him, grinning facelessly. He was sure he could sense presences creeping closer to him, surrounding him. He thought suddenly that they meant to drive him toward a sheer drop, make him take that last blind step. He swung round, fists raised, ready to defend his spot of ground where at least he was safe from falling, even if his mind wasn't safe from the dark and whatever might be reaching for him. Then he halted so abruptly that he wrenched his neck. He'd glimpsed a light somewhere.

For a moment that felt like the edge of a drop; he suspected his eyes of playing tricks, in league with the dark. But no, there was a light, a distant glow to his left that outlined a ridge. He stumbled in that direction, would have run if he had been able to see the ground, however faintly. He trod in puddles, tripped over stones, and almost sprawled headlong several times, but it didn't matter: he was heading for light. It must be Moonwell—nothing else could make a light that wide up here. The promise of the distant glow made him feel as if the whisperers with their long hands and gaping mouths were close behind him, but he mustn't look round. He stumbled up the steepening slope toward the glow.

When he reached the top, the light was beyond the next ridge. He limped downhill toward it, his ankles throbbing. Here and there he could just distinguish irregularities on the

212

almost invisible slope—rocks, not crouching figures with pale, blank heads. He tried to remember where they were as he lost sight of them in the trough of dark. He was fighting for breath by the time he reached the upward slope.

He almost groaned when he came over the ridge and saw that the glow was at least one more ridge distant. Perhaps it wasn't the town after all—it seemed too white for the glow of streetlamps—but it was light, that was all that mattered. He stumbled downward on his aching legs, into the drowning dark that was full of the threat of a whisper in his ear, and up the next slope. This one was so long that he was convinced it must lead to the glow or at least to a clear view of its source. He was almost at the top when the light went out, leaving him in the blind dark.

He didn't know how long he stood there, willing the light to come back. Eventually he inched, heel to toe, as far as the crest of the ridge. He was on bare rock now. The slope below him seemed quite gentle, at least at first. He was venturing gingerly downward when a flashlight beam glided over the rock at his feet, up his body, and blinded him.

<hr />

42

When Diana saw Nick in the flashlight beam, at first she didn't believe what she was seeing. She'd come up on the moor because she needed to be alone, and now, when she least needed him, here was Nick. Then she realized how he was faltering in the stone bowl, how near he was to the brink of the cave. "Nick, stop!" she cried.

He was shading his eyes to try to see through the beam; now he smiled uncertainly, blinking. "Diana? Is that you?" he said, and took another step forward.

"It's me, yes. Don't move whatever you do." She swung the beam to show him where he was heading, and the cave seemed to gape wider. "Careful," she cried, for the sight of the cave had made him stumble backward, so hastily that she thought he was going to lose his footing on the bare rock.

He shook his head to clear it, closing and opening his eyes, and met her as she went round the stone bowl to him. When they put their arms around each other, it seemed inevitable, long delayed. It would have been the start of something immediate under more favorable circumstances, she thought, gazing at his round face that looked even less shaven than usual, at his broad mouth that was no longer sure of itself. He stared about as if waking up from sleepwalking. "My God, we're above the town, aren't we," he muttered. "I don't know how I got here. It must have been your light."

"What must, Nick?"

"The light I saw that brought me here." His eyes were narrowing, wincing at the dark. "Only it didn't look like yours. It wasn't that color, wasn't any color, come to think of it."

She sensed he had more to tell her, but she didn't want to learn it up here in the dark. "Where's your car, Nick, on the street somewhere? Come on, we'll go back to my place."

She felt him begin to shiver. "The car went off the road. I drove out of the woods and it was as dark as this. How can it be when it's—whatever time it is?" He raised his wrist into the flashlight beam and consulted his watch. "That's just great, isn't it. It's stopped."

"They all have," Diana said, steering him toward the path to Moonwell. "I'll tell you what's been happening as soon as we're at my place."

That froze him. "You know what's happening? I wish you'd tell me. There was something in the dark. Don't think I've gone mad, Diana, but it spoke to me."

"I don't think you have, Nick, but I'd really rather not talk about it until we're home."

His eyes turned bright and blank. "I don't know what I've been thinking of, keeping you talking up here when we could be—" He obviously didn't want to say "safe." "Let's be off," he said.

When they came in sight of the lights of Moonwell, she felt Nick shudder, a suppressed sigh of relief. He squeezed her waist and then let go so that they could climb down the narrowing path. On the High Street he glanced nervously

214

about at people gossiping obsessively in the shops and under the streetlamps. "Good God," he said softly.

None of her windows was broken; no hostile messages waited beyond the front door. The low-timbered hall felt snug, a cranny out of the dark. The children's paintings sagged in the living room, which smelled of the flowers wilting in vases. She'd been replenishing the vases from her garden, her own unacknowledged ritual to stave off the dark.

Nick drew the curtains without being asked when he'd carried mugs of her coffee into the living room. Still at the window, he said, "Do you mind if I sit by you?"

"I wish you would."

He sat by her on the settee and seemed not to know whether to touch her until she took pity on him, held his hand in both of hers. "It's all right," she murmured, not quite knowing what was.

"Sorry. I'm not this awkward usually, but everything's got through to me, I didn't realize how much."

She rather liked him that way, less confident of himself than she imagined he'd been in the past with other women, except that he was trembling, reminding her of the dark and whatever was there. "We're safe now," she said as convincingly as she could, and put her arms round him. She did feel safe for the moment, felt drowsy and warm and comfortable as he stroked her hair. Then he took a determined breath and muttered, "All right, tell me what's happening."

Perhaps because she'd been alone with the truth for so long, she felt unexpectedly tongue-tied. "You didn't finish telling me what happened to you."

"Just that I got lost in the dark and somehow ended up at the cave. I feel as if I was lured there." He was gazing at her for her reaction. "You don't seem surprised."

"I believe you, Nick. What else can I say?"

"Only what you think is happening, what this dark is. You tried to tell me something of the kind was imminent last time we spoke."

"I may have hinted at it. Is that what brought you here?" she said rather sadly, feeling responsible.

"Diana, what brought me here was that suddenly nobody seemed to have heard of Moonwell. You tried to warn me about that, only you had to play it down so I'd believe you. It's part of the same thing as the dark."

215

"I think so."

"Go ahead, Diana, I can cope with it. Tell me what it is."

She gave him a resigned glance that made him smile uncertainly. "I think it's whatever was in the cave, the thing Mann came here to destroy. It was too much for him. Maybe it even lured him here to let it out."

"You still haven't said what you think it is."

"Something that was here when the Romans were here something to do with the moon. The story goes that the druids called it to help them. And maybe the dark is a kind of revenge for having been left down there in the cave all these centuries. Or it could be," she said, remembering Delbert in the presbytery, "a way of trying to reduce people to a primitive state."

"It did that to me all right, up there on the moor. I wish I thought we were both crazy, but I believe you, mostly. Damn little use that is to you now with me stuck here," he said bitterly, and then rather plaintively, "Maybe I'll be missed."

"Does anyone know you're here?"

He grimaced. "They'll probably have forgotten where I was asking about by the time they realize I'm missing."

"I'm afraid you're right, Nick. That's part of what's happening."

"And the things I thought were around me in the dark . . ." He glanced uneasily at the window, but there was only the streetlamp beyond the low hedge. "All right, Diana, what are we going to do?"

The question jerked her back to full awareness, from feeling almost comfortable now that she was able at last to talk and be believed. What could she tell him? Whatever she had to do, she didn't see how he could help—she only hoped he wouldn't try to stop her. She was still wondering how to answer him when he said, "Whatever it is, we'd better decide fast."

The change in his voice made her twist round, her pulse jumping even before she realized why he was staring at the window. Beyond the glass, one by one, the lamps were going out.

43

They were safe now, Andrew told himself. His father was safe. They were home in the light, and his father looked just like his father, except perhaps for something about his eyes. He was no longer grinning the grin that had made Andrew think of a dog's; in fact, every time their eyes met across the dinner table as they ate Miss Ingham's omelettes, he smiled at Andrew. Yet the smile troubled Andrew, made him think his father was telling him a secret he was too stupid to understand. At last Andrew thought he did, and bowed his head quickly over his plate so that his mother wouldn't realize. His father must be telling him they had to slip away to see Mr. Mann.

Perhaps his father had thought of an excuse to get them out of the house, and that was why he'd wolfed down his omelette as though he could scarcely taste it and looked as if he was still waiting to be fed. "You made a meal of that all right," Miss Ingham said. "Have you room for another?"

Andrew's mother intervened. "I think that had better do when there's so little food in the house, and the shops for that matter. It's about time they organized the deliveries. Good heavens, you'd think they were scared of the dark." She turned to Andrew's father and at the same time leaned away from him. "What's that smell, by the way? Have you been getting something on you in the shop?"

"Not as I know of."

"Well, it's horrid. The best place for you is a bath."

Andrew knew what she must mean, though he'd stopped noticing it once they were in the light—the smell of dark zoo places, places crawling with reptiles like the one he'd stepped on near the cave. Was it the smell of the dark? "I can't smell anything, Miss Ingham, can you?" he blurted.

"Maybe Miss Ingham's too polite to say." His mother looked as if she wanted to knock him off his chair. "Anyway, I'm the one who has to deal with smells in this house. Now I don't want to hear another word about it. It's a disgusting subject for the dinner table. I don't know what this family is coming to."

Miss Ingham smiled understandingly at her and cleared up after dinner, which only seemed to irritate Andrew's mother further. His father retreated to an armchair and gazed out at the three streetlamps that could be seen from the window. Andrew hovered between the rooms, getting in the way. He hoped his mother and Miss Ingham would be friends, because he'd had an idea: the teacher could ask Mr. Mann to come here—he was supposed to like visiting people. Only if Andrew suggested that now, his mother was sure to lose her temper, but she might be in a better mood when they'd finished praying.

"I'll lead prayers, shall I?" Miss Ingham said. Andrew knelt quickly by his father's chair, and his father slipped to his knees beside him; the glimpse from the edge of Andrew's eye made him think of something slithering off a rock. "We thank You, Lord, for all Your promises," Miss Ingham began, while Andrew thought that the only promise he wanted was for the dark to go away and let his father be himself. He squeezed his eyes tight and prayed for that fiercely inside his head while he mumbled in response to Miss Ingham, and then he risked opening his eyes in the hope that God might have answered his prayer. His praying hands clenched, his chin dug into his chest as if that could change what he'd seen. Only two of the lamps beyond the window were lit now.

He shut his eyes so tightly that they stung, and tried to take his prayer back. Don't make the dark go away just yet if it's too hard or you're busy, he prayed, only don't put out any more lights, please don't. . . . He felt as if he'd made the lamp go out himself by looking to see if the dark had gone, by testing God when Miss Ingham had told the class you never should. I do believe in You, he prayed, I believe You can do anything, only don't let any more lights go out; I'll pray every night for ten minutes if You don't; I'll pray until I go to sleep. He kept his eyes shut as long as he could; then he sneaked them open a crack. He closed them at once, praying desperately. All three lamps had gone out, and the dark was pressing against the window.

He bent low over his clasped hands as if that might hide him. He wished he could keep his eyes shut forever—at least the dark inside his eyelids was his own. Then his mother screamed, and all at once it seemed too dark in there. He forced them open so that he could see the grownups, who had stopped praying. But he couldn't see anything. The light in the room had failed too.

"It's all right, Mrs. Bevan. God is with us. Let's pray for guidance," Miss Ingham murmured somewhere in the dark.

"Where's the boy?" Andrew's mother cried. "Get hold of my hand, Andrew. Be quick and don't fall over anything."

Andrew reached across darkness that felt like the mouth of the cave and found her hand, which shook as it groped for him. She grasped her wrist with her other hand to keep it still, but it flinched as his father spoke, his voice magnified by the stillness. "Keep calm," he said. "I know what to do."

He was rising to his feet, Andrew told himself, not growing to a new height in the dark. Beyond the window were screams and cries of panic; the lights had failed in all the houses. Then Andrew realized that nevertheless he'd seen his father get up. Was his father glowing in the dark? No, the glow was seeping through the window and outlining the women and Andrew too, so faintly that it was hardly like seeing. "Follow me," his father said.

Andrew's mother pulled the boy to her in case he tried to join him. "We're safest here. Where are you going?" she demanded, her voice tight and stiff.

"Can't you see?" Andrew's father strode along the hall as if he could see in the dark and opened the front door. "Look if you don't believe me. Everyone's going. They know there's only one place to go now."

Eventually Andrew's mother went warily along the hall, her hand bruising Andrew's arm, ready to drag him back. Beyond the front garden he could just see the High Street, the houses dim as the shapes he'd glimpsed crawling up the cave, the windows like pieces of slate. The sight of the unlit houses and streets terrified him. The High Street was crowded with figures that were making their way toward the center of Moonwell, where the glow was coming from.

"It's a sign," Miss Ingham whispered, though surely it

must be the floodlights they used to light up the front of the hotel. When Andrew's mother saw people leaving the houses opposite and joining the crowd, she pulled Andrew toward the gate. "Hurry up then if we're going. We don't want to be left behind in this."

Perhaps she didn't want to be left out of the singing in the town square, where everyone was heading. Andrew tried to believe that the hymn would keep them safe as he crept forward into the dark. The hymn spread back along the crowd to them, his mother tugging at his hand to make him join in. "Nearer my God to Thee," he sang as loudly as he could, as if that might blot out his sense of the lightless side streets, gaping like caves. Being carried along by the dim crowd made him nervous too, even though they must be heading for the hotel, where Mr. Mann was. He'd stop being scared as soon as they were there, he promised himself.

His father was loping beside him, his face turned up toward the glow. Andrew saw his teeth gleaming darkly, his lips drawn back as he bellowed the hymn. Somehow Andrew didn't find that reassuring, any more than the blurred heads bobbing all around and above him. At least the light was growing, and soon he could see the faces nearest him, some of which looked almost as fearful as he was. The crowd slowed as they neared the square, people at the rear shoving forward with impatience or nervousness toward the light. Andrew saw people ahead of him on the edge of the square look up and fall to their knees as they saw where the light was coming from.

The kneeling people had to shuffle forward to let the rest of the crowd file around the edge of the square, and so minutes passed before Andrew saw what they were seeing. "God save us," Miss Ingham murmured as his mother began weeping. The teacher must mean that God had done so, Andrew thought, watching his father, who was gazing upward with an expression that seemed to mingle awe with a secret terror. His father's face filled with the light as he lifted Andrew up, his arms feeling stronger than they had when Andrew was little, and Andrew saw.

It wasn't the floodlights. The big square lenses at the foot of the hotel were dark. For a moment Andrew thought the full moon had come up, though surely it shouldn't for days, and then he realized that the light was streaming out of Mr.

Mann's window, which was wide open. Mr. Mann stood there, leaning on the sill. Andrew gasped, because it looked as if the light was streaming out of him.

Mr. Mann leaned forward as the hymn came to an end. At that distance Andrew couldn't make out his face; it looked blank as light, shining whitely. Mr. Mann held out his hands as if he were cupping the light as it poured down into the square, and those who weren't already kneeling sank to their knees. As Andrew's father set him down, his mother cuffed the boy's head to make him bow it and stop staring. In a voice that seemed as close to Andrew as his parents were, Mr. Mann said, "We must pray now—pray for light."

Andrew clasped his hands together so hard that his fingers ached. He could tell by the murmur that passed through the square that everyone wanted the prayer to be granted as much as he did. His father had already closed his eyes and was muttering fervently, almost growling. He glanced about warily as he realized everyone else was silent, and hushed himself. There was utter stillness as the crowd waited for Mr. Mann to speak, and he was lifting his face to the sky when Miss Kramer ran into the square. "Don't listen to him," she cried.

44

When the second lamp went out Nick ran to the window and pushed up the sash. A third lamp failed as he leaned out to see. He felt as if the dark were flooding down from the moor to find him, to teach him not to think he'd got away. He turned to Diana, almost hoping she would be as nervous as he was so that he could cope with his own feelings by trying to calm her. But she looked resigned, which was even more disturbing. "The lamps are going out," he said harshly—anything to make her speak.

"I know."

Her unexpected gentleness made him feel more trapped than ever. "What are we going to do?" he demanded.

"What do you want to do, Nick?"

"Something, damn it. Not just wait for it to come for us." He wished he hadn't said that, especially since he wasn't sure what he meant: surely only the dark. He craned out of the window again, and realized he was staring at Diana's car. Couldn't they outrun the dark that way? He was about to propose it when the car vanished.

For a moment he thought he'd gone blind, and then he knew that the light had failed in the room behind him. The lit windows of the cottages across the road turned black, and people screamed. Diana was suddenly beside him, reaching for his hand. "It's all right, Nick. This had to come. It's been too late to stop it for a while, I think."

"Your car's still going, isn't it? Give me the keys if you don't want to drive," he said urgently. "If we get out we can bring people back. We can't save your kids all by ourselves."

"I wish it were that simple." She was holding his hand in both of hers as if that might reassure him. "People have tried to drive out, but they've had to turn back. You had a taste of why up on the moor. And those who were supposed to come back haven't—I hate to think why not."

He felt worse than helpless, he felt crushed by the dark. "Christ, Diana, this is just fucking ridiculous," he said, a curse seeming the nearest he could get to a prayer.

"Poor Nick. I'm sorry I made you feel you had to come here. Maybe when we see what's going to happen . . ." Her voice trailed off. "I want to know why it isn't darker."

How could she want it to be darker? She leaned out of the window, and Nick saw what she meant—saw the street and the houses, so dimly that at first he thought he was hoping rather than seeing. People were opening their front doors as they realized that their neighbors' lights had failed too. Somewhere a man shouted impatiently, "Try it now. They're new fuses. It must work." Now the people from the cottages opposite Diana's were stepping forward on their paths to gaze along the street, and Nick craned past Diana to see.

A glow bright enough to outline the roofs sharply was rising from the town square. Doors were slamming, towns-folk heading for the square, almost the whole streetful as they saw the light. He thought of moths heading for a flame, and the paleness of the glow made him even more dubious. "It's like the light I followed on the moor."

Diana's hands tightened on his. "Of course, *that's* what the dark is meant to do—make people desperate for light, any light. Come on, or stay here if you'd rather," she said, peering apologetically at him. "I have to try and stop this."

"You know what the light is, then."

"Yes, but I've no time to explain now." When he wouldn't let go of her hand she leaned close to him. "Really, Nick, you don't have to back me up."

"Try and stop me." He let go of her only while they felt their way along the hall and stepped out of the cottage.

All the streets were emptying, the townsfolk heading for the sound of a hymn. An old man stood on his doorstep and tried to light a candle to see by, cursing because matches wouldn't stay lit, although the air was still. Diana avoided the crowd and headed for the square along a street that was already deserted except for a workman who was fiddling with the timers in the streetlamps, his face so determined it looked like a mask. Nick found the sight incongruous and touching, but it made him feel vulnerable, nervous that the glow would go out as it had on the moor and plunge them all back into the dark.

But the glow was stronger when he and Diana came in view of the town square. The square was already full of people, most of whom were kneeling. The glow made their faces look carved out of ice, their eyes too, staring up at something he couldn't yet see from the side of the square he and Diana were approaching. "You'd think the moon was up," he muttered in a rage at the way the spectacle dismayed him. "They used to say at this time of year the moon could drive you mad." The closer he came to the light, the more he felt he might almost prefer the dark. At least the way the glow filled the eyes of the crowd, they were unlikely to notice Diana.

He and Diana hadn't reached the square when the hymn ended. Those who were still standing fell to their knees as the silence drained of echoes. Had the light intensified? Ranks of faces, bloodlessly white, stared up at it. Nick told himself fiercely that he'd wanted to do something—maybe now he had a chance. But when he edged round the corner of the hotel and saw the source of the light, he could only gape.

223

For one reassuring moment he thought that someone had managed to run power from a generator in the hotel to a spotlight in an upper window, and then he saw the figure in the window, a figure that looked thin as a filament from which the light was streaming. He saw the face thrust forward almost fleshlessly, as though the icy light were searing it to the bone. It seemed less like a human face than like the lingering idea of a face. "Is that Mann?" he said incredulously.

"I don't think it is," Diana whispered, "not any longer."

Nick wasn't sure that he wanted to know what she meant, and this was hardly the time to ask. She took a step forward as the figure in the window spread its shining hands. The stillness made the soft voice sound so close it might have been behind Nick. "We must pray now for light," the voice said.

"That's it," Diana cried. "God, of course." She lurched into the square, in front of the crowd. "Don't listen to him," she shouted.

Every face turned instantly to her, the light going out of their eyes. Nick had stood in the midst of waves of hatred between police and pickets, but he'd never felt a flood of hostility as dangerous as this. He went forward quickly to stand beside Diana, not so much from the absurd notion of protecting her from the crowd as in the hope that someone else might join them.

For a few moments nobody moved, though there were mutters of hostility that Nick thought could rise to shouts and then to violence. Diana ignored them and gazed up at the figure in the window. She drew a breath Nick could feel in his own chest, and said loudly but evenly, "Tell them what light you want them to call."

The figure craned its head forward. Nick didn't remember the evangelist's neck as having been nearly so long. "Miss Kramer the schoolteacher, isn't it? I'm sorry if losing your job to someone more godly has made you bitter. All light is God's light, Miss Kramer."

"Which god?" Diana challenged, and faltered as a chorus of hisses and groans rose from the crowd. "You know what I mean," she said defiantly, "even if you've got these people so they can't tell the difference."

Mann folded his arms across his chest, almost as though he was holding a burden there inside his voluminous jacket. "If

224

you feel you can enlighten us, Miss Kramer," he said in the soft voice that seemed to glide like mist into Nick's senses, "I'm sure we can take time to listen."

Titters went through the crowd, and sounds of impatience. Diana glanced about at them and waited until they petered out, as she might have done in a classroom. "I want to tell all of you one thing first," she said. "I'm as much a victim as you are."

That earned her blank, hostile stares. "We're trapped here," she said, and glanced up at Mann. "Something has us where it wants us."

"Something called the devil," a large red-haired woman shouted, "that's as anxious to see the back of Godwin as you are, but neither of you will."

"It isn't as simple as that, Mrs. Scragg, and I can't believe that everyone here thinks so. Some of you must have noticed what's happening. You shopkeepers must have, you've had no deliveries for days. And we've lost most of our police and the mountain rescue team out there. We're being systematically cut off from the world and losing all the people who might have taken charge."

"That's a cheap trick, even for you," a man leaning on a stick said, his face darkening with anger. "Trying to use our losses to win your argument. I haven't given up my son for lost yet, and if he is then it was in the course of doing his duty, just like the rest of the police."

"We don't care if we are cut off from the world," a young woman cried. "The world is evil. If it's trying to isolate us then that's the devil's doing, to make us give up our faith. It doesn't realize we know we're better off. We can be self-sufficient; there's enough livestock and farmland if it comes to having to survive."

Some of the crowd looked taken aback. Now's your chance, Nick thought fiercely at Diana, and wondered if he should speak up himself. Then a woman shouted, "And we don't want our children taught by unbelievers. We don't want them going out of town and mixing with the faithless. Godwin brought us all the teachers we need."

"Real teachers, not like you," an old woman yelled at Diana, to the support of a chorus of jeering. I thought you were supposed to be Christians, Nick thought angrily, and would have said so except that the soft voice came seeping

225

down. "It looks as if all you have to offer is doubts and darkness, Miss Kramer."

"I'll tell you one thing I have my doubts about." Diana's voice rang out, clearer and calmer than ever. "Perhaps it's all that stands between me and believing in you. I'd like to hear what happened when you went down the cave—what you found there and what you did."

Quite a few faces turned toward Mann's window. Perhaps they were curious rather than doubtful, but wasn't that preferable to blind faith? The figure in the window drew itself up. Surely it was a trick of perspective that made the evangelist look taller than he had been at the rally, but it made Nick feel as if Mann was preparing to show them something in response to Diana. He could almost believe that as the light appeared to swell, the figure had begun to swell too.

Then Mrs. Scragg intervened. "Anyone with an ounce of godliness in them can see what happened plain enough," she cried. "Our man up there's a saint if ever I saw one. Now that's enough. We're here to pray, not listen to your godless prating, *Miss* Kramer. If you don't shut your lying mouth there's plenty of us here to shut it for you."

Nick stepped closer to Diana. "Perhaps there are folk who'd like to hear her out. You'd be well advised to listen."

"Her bodyguard," Mrs. Scragg sneered, as a policeman with a long, prim face and a thin moustache pushed through the crowd to Nick. "Who are you, may I ask," he demanded, "and where have you come from?"

"I'm a newspaper reporter, a friend of Diana's. I'm here because—"

As soon as he mentioned Diana, there was uproar. "Another outsider come to try and shake our faith," cried the young woman who didn't need the world, and someone yelled across the square, "Or tell lies about us to outsiders so they'll try and corrupt us."

"I must ask you to leave," the policeman said to Nick. "You're likely to cause a breach of the peace." He must have seen how uncooperative Nick felt, for he raised his voice. "Otherwise I shall have to ask you to accompany me to the police station."

"I'll help you." A beefy man who smelled of raw meat

226

swung Nick round before he knew what was happening and wrenched his arms up behind him, almost dislocating them. "Move," he growled. "Any trouble and I'll break your arms easy as wringing a chicken's neck."

45

Diana watched the butcher drag Nick away, the police inspector striding alongside, and wondered desperately what she ought to do. She wanted to go with Nick to make sure he wasn't harmed, but she couldn't shake off the impression that she was being lured away from the square. The face in the shining window turned toward her, and for a nightmarish moment she saw the moon where the head should be, a smiling moon with pits for eyes. Was Mann's face a mass of blotches behind the light? All she could be certain of amid the pale glare was his smile, a victorious smile that might look like a benediction to the waiting crowd. She ran after the three men and dodged round the inspector, into Nick's path.

Nick was being forced forward, head down, arms twisted up to his shoulder blades. When he saw Diana, he tried to look as if the butcher weren't hurting him. "Sorry I wasn't much help," he muttered, peering at her from under his brows. "I didn't realize things had gone this far."

The butcher jerked Nick's arms. "No talking."

"I don't think that's necessary," the inspector intervened. "Just ensure he doesn't try to give you the slip."

The butcher eased his hold on Nick, slightly and reluctantly. They had to trust the policeman, Diana told herself—had to believe there was some decency left in him. "Go with them, Nick. Don't make any trouble. I'll know where to find you."

"What about you, Diana?" he said, wincing as he tried to raise his head. "Where will you be?"

"I just want to watch what happens. I won't put myself in any danger," she lied. The butcher shoved him toward the police station, and Diana turned back to the square.

Those who'd stood up during the altercation were on their knees again. The square was full of rapt white upturned masks and black shadows, motionless as ice. If she tried to interrupt again they would only silence her; sooner or later Mann would have his prayer. She could only watch and hope that the awareness that was hovering at the edge of her mind might prove to be of some use. But she hadn't stepped into the square when Mrs. Scragg heaved herself to her feet and bore down on Diana. "No you don't, miss. I knew you'd come sneaking back to try and spoil things."

"I've said all I had to say."

"And a load of rubbish it was. I think we'll just make sure you aren't heard from while we're praying. Are there two strong men who'll help me put this perverter of our children where she can't do any harm?"

Two men stood up next to their sons, Ronnie who'd always had too much in his pockets, Thomas who'd been full of feeble jokes that only Mann's brood could object to. Both boys were staring at Diana with loathing. They'd been made to feel that way, she told herself, glancing about for others of her pupils, but the children she could see didn't want to see her. She felt suddenly beaten and hopeless, at the mercy of the pale shape perched above the square, and then the fathers grabbed her, bruising her arms. "You don't need to do this," she said as calmly as she could. "This is England, right? You don't do this to people just because they disagree with you."

"Not to our own," Ronnie's father said, leaning so close to her that she could smell sour milk on his breath, and the other muttered, "You want to stop people praying, stop our lads praying. We aren't having that, so shut your gob."

"My God," Diana cried in a voice that sounded far too small, "can't you see anything wrong with what's happening here?"

Mrs. Scragg struck her across the face. "Don't you be soiling the name of the Almighty. That's the kind of blasphemy she was teaching your children. Bring her to my house now and I'll keep an eye on her. I've dealt with her kind before."

The men shoved Diana out of the square, so violently that she would have fallen except for their grip on her. She had to run in order to regain her balance, her toes scraping on the tarmac; there was no use struggling. She twisted her head round to look back at the hotel. Again the face in the window looked blotchy as the moon, but it was smiling, a smile that seemed almost as wide as the head. Presumably only she could see that, for a murmur of relief went through the congregation as the soft voice said, "Now there are no unbelievers here, let's make an act of faith that the dark will become light."

Mrs. Scragg glanced back, then glared at Diana. The woman must resent not being involved in the prayers. The crowd was chanting, blotting out the voice that must be leading them. "God of our ancestors, lighten our darkness," they prayed three times. "We offer ourselves to you."

Diana tried to struggle free then—anything to stop what she sensed approaching—but the men dragged her out of the High Street into a lane that faced the school. It was much darker here, out of sight of the hotel. Her captors tightened their hold on her, and Diana thought they weren't just making sure she didn't slip away but taking out on her their unacknowledged dread of the dark. Then Ronnie's father looked up beyond the looming blocks of darkness that were cottages. "God be praised, do you see that?" he whispered.

Diana raised her head, and her heart faltered. She could see the roofs and chimneys, outlined whitely. It wasn't just the glow from the hotel; the dark was drawing back like a fraying veil, revealing a night sky stuffed with dark clouds. A white blur crawled behind the clouds, creeping toward a gap of clear sky. She knew it was the moon, but deep down she was afraid to see Mann's face peer gigantically between the clouds, grinning triumphantly at her. There was no need to invent nightmares like that, she realized, trying vainly to relax so that her captors might slacken their grasp. The moon would be just as terrible.

"Show us your light, O God of our fathers and our forefathers," the crowd was chanting, excited now. Mrs. Scragg stared at the sky, where veins of white light were stretching out from the gap, outlining the clouds. Diana poised herself to jerk free and run—she would have only one chance—and then Mrs. Scragg turned on her. "Let's get this one locked away safe and then we'll have time to give thanks."

She stumped along a short path between flowerbeds crushed by concrete slabs and unlocked the cottage at the end of the lane. "Bring her here to me now," she said. The men marched Diana up the path just as the whiteness broke free of the clouds. As Mrs. Scragg slammed the door behind them, the moonlight reached into the cottage.

46

Geraldine snuggled against Jeremy on the couch at the end of the bookshop and listened to the dark. The screams in the streets had turned into hymns and moved away into the town, which meant that there shouldn't be any more dog turds or threatening messages through the letter box for a while. The dark had driven their tormentors away, and now she hoped it would do more. If Jonathan was still too shy to let them see him, perhaps the dark would bring him back.

More than anything else now, she wanted Jeremy to accept him. She mustn't let Jeremy recoil from him, scare him away. She could feel how Jeremy was striving to breathe regularly, to keep from shivering. She listened to the distant hymns and prayers and gazed at the dark that made her eyes feel out of focus, drained of sense. She'd heard nothing but the faithful when, without warning, light spread across the floor in front of her.

The sight made her forget to breathe. After so long in the dark she felt as though the patch of lit floor were being created before her eyes, intensely detailed as a photograph but infinitely more real. The moonlight traced the grain of the bare boards and plugged a knothole with black dark; even a splinter stood up starkly in front of its matchstick shadow. The longer she gazed, the more luminous the patch of floorboards seemed to grow. Then Jeremy began to tremble; he must think he was hallucinating. "It's really here," she whispered. "Come on, let's go and see."

She led him across the shop, whose bare shelves were just visible outside the path of moonlight, and opened the front door. The paint of the cottages was black now on white walls, as if the street had turned Tudor. The spectacle of the bright deserted street made her feel like dancing under the moon. She hurried with Jeremy along the path, and the moon flew over the roofs.

At first she didn't know why the appearance of the moon made her falter. The clouds seemed almost to be driven back by it, clearing the sky in all directions, but that must be winds, too high for her to feel them. As for the brightness, no wonder the quarter moon seemed brighter than usual after so much dark. None of that troubled her—but then she knew what did. The new moon must have come and gone beyond the clouds and the dark. It was later than she'd realized: Jonathan's birthday had gone unnoticed. She felt worse than thoughtless, as if she'd left her only child alone in the dark. "Jeremy, I want to go somewhere," she murmured.

"We haven't got the van."

He'd relaxed once he saw that the moon was out, but now he sounded frustrated. "I don't mean that, not just yet anyway," she said, taking his hand. "I want to walk."

He stared toward the center of Moonwell, where the whole population seemed to be cheering and whooping and singing a hymn. "You mean while there's nobody about to stop us?"

"I suppose so."

"Fine, let's do it. It's our town too while we're living here, so let's see if any of these bastards have the courage to tell us different to our faces. Where do you want to go?"

"Just to the end and back."

"You mean the graveyard?"

"I'd like to spend a little time in there, yes."

"Gerry, if this is more of that stuff about Jonathan leading us back here . . ."

"I thought we'd agreed not to mention that, since we only argue. I just feel I'll be closer to him there, all right? I wanted to remember him on his birthday, but it looks as if I'm too late."

"I'm sorry," he said as though she'd made him feel responsible for that, and held onto her hand as they stepped off the garden path.

Apart from the celebration in the square, they might have been alone in Moonwell. The High Street seemed like a dream of itself, newly colored and preserved by the icy light. They stayed on the main street until they were in sight of the square, of the crowd singing joyfully and brandishing their clasped hands at the luminous smile that was tilted almost coyly in the sky. Jeremy hurried through the narrow lanes whose upper windows glittered with the moon that swam through them, leaving the roadways steeped in shadow. He was hurrying in case an unexpected cloud should blot out the moon, she realized. She mustn't mind that it wasn't because he shared her feelings about Jonathan: he shared the loss, he just coped with it differently. The trouble was that having done so, he seemed unable to accept that there could be any way besides his own.

They came up out of the silt of darkness onto the High Street a few hundred yards short of the church, and she wondered why she had suddenly grown tense. The church looked whitewashed, moonlight flooding down the high steep roof. Shadow filled the small peaked porch and bruised the faces of the gargoyles; moonlight had blanked out all three faces in each tall, thin, arched window. The church no longer had a priest, Geraldine remembered—but it couldn't just be the desertion that made Jeremy suck in a breath.

She glanced at his shocked face, then peered ahead at the churchyard, where he was staring. Lumps of shadow lay in the grass among the gleaming headstones, spidery shadow nested in the roots of the willows and the oak, but there was nothing that didn't belong in a graveyard unless Jeremy had glimpsed something through the railings that she was unable to make out. Now that she strained her eyes, wasn't there a pale shape on the grass between the railings and the head-stones? Before she quite knew why, she was running.

Jeremy mumbled a protest and tried to grab her, but she shook him off. He caught up with her as she reached the gate. She halted there, her hand falling short of grasping the latch, her heart pumping faster, not only from her run. A small white naked shape lay face down on the grass beside the churchyard path.

She gazed through the bars of the gate at it, her throat growing parched with emotions she couldn't begin to define, while Jeremy tugged at her arm. "Don't look, come away," he muttered nervously, but she snatched her arm free. The small naked body was so still that she hardly dared go closer to find out why it wasn't moving. Though it looked like marble in the moonlight, she knew it was alive, or had been. "Let me alone," she cried as Jeremy reached for her, and the shape on the grass raised its head.

"Oh Christ," Jeremy breathed. This time he grabbed her arm for support, not to drag her away, but she realized that only when she'd turned furiously toward him. His eyes bulged as he stared through the gate. She drew a shaky breath and made her head turn, to look the naked figure in the face.

It was a child, a boy. At first her mind seemed unable to grasp more than that, though later she would tell herself she'd been afraid to believe what she was seeing. The boy gazed at her as if he was too exhausted or too afraid to show emotion, except for a faint plea in his moonlit eyes, or was she imagining that? He raised himself feebly on all fours, damp grass twitching upright where he'd been lying on it, and she saw that his eyes were blue as Jeremy's, blue eyes in a square face that was a smaller version of Jeremy's except for the lips, which were more like her own. An irresistible surge of emotion carried her forward, unaware of bruising her elbow on the gate. She was so intent on reaching the child that at first she didn't understand why she couldn't—didn't realize that Jeremy was holding her.

"Let go, Jeremy." She made herself stay calm, for her emotions felt like a bomb. "It's all right if you don't want to go in. Just wait here."

"Are you crazy? Can't you see it?" He seemed almost incoherent with panic, his hold on her tightening as a substitute for words. "I was afraid it might come when the lamps went out. I thought the moonlight would keep it away."

"Jeremy." She stroked his hands that were gripping her shoulders, she kneaded his fingers to make them relax. "Look again. It isn't anything we saw on the road, it's a child. Can't you see who it is?"

He peered unwillingly past her, his hands growing rigid.

When he spoke his voice was shakier than ever. "It isn't . . . I thought it was . . . Christ, I don't know what I'm seeing any more. Whatever it is, I don't like it. Leave it alone, Gerry, for God's sake."

The child sank back onto the grass, still holding up his head feebly to watch them. Were his eyes dimming, or had they only ceased to catch the light? She loosened Jeremy's grip on her, gently but firmly. "He's a child, Jeremy, a living child alone out here in the cold and the dark. You wouldn't leave him to that, I don't believe you could."

"Ask him where he lives, then." Jeremy sounded close to hysteria, though he'd lowered his voice. "Or tell him to go to the square and let them take care of him. You needn't think he's coming home with us."

"I didn't hear that, Jeremy. You didn't say it, it was someone else, someone I couldn't have married. I couldn't live with anyone who felt like that about children." She gave him a warning glance and turned her back on him, stepped through the gateway.

The boy began to smile timidly as she went along the path, unzipping her jacket. Her breasts loosened inside her T-shirt now that the jacket was no longer supporting them, and she felt momentarily like a mother about to feed her baby. The boy struggled onto all fours again, his skin gleaming white in the moonlight, and she noticed that the grass where he'd lain was glistening. It must have been the weight of his body squeezing the moisture out of the ground. Wondering how long he'd lain there on the chill, damp earth, she felt like weeping. He stumbled to his feet as she reached him, his long fingers dangling beside his penis that looked drained of blood. He was about Andrew's age, but nothing like Andrew: he seemed empty of emotion—too exhausted, she told herself. "Come here," she said with fierce pity, and wrapped her jacket around him.

As she zipped it up to keep him snug, her fingers touched his neck. She couldn't help shivering, he was so cold and damp. Impulsively she lifted him in her arms rather than lead him, and was dismayed to find he weighed even less than she'd expected; there seemed to be hardly any flesh on his bones. She pressed her lips to his cold forehead, which was as high as Jeremy's. "We'll feed you," she whispered.

She was almost at the gates when Jeremy lurched into the

graveyard. "They've stopped singing in the square," he mumbled, his eyes turning reluctantly to the face of the child in her arms. "I think the prayer meeting's over."

"We've got to get him home before they see us."

"Gerry . . ." he pleaded, refusing to look again at the child's face.

"You can't stop me, Jeremy, and neither will they. We've given up enough." She was already running to the nearest lane. As she dodged around the corner, she heard the crowd beginning to stream out of the square. "Don't go down there alone," Jeremy called desperately, and ran after her, down into the dark.

The child's face gazed up at hers as she hurried through the empty lanes. Once she had to hide in an alley to avoid a family as they strode home, singing a hymn. Jeremy was first into the High Street, and gestured her back wildly until it was deserted enough to cross. He ran to the chapel and let her in just as the Bevans appeared at the end of the line of failed streetlamps under the smiling sky.

Geraldine carried the boy through the bookshop, where moonlight filled the shelves with volumes of shadow, and through the inner hall, up the stairs to the guest room. The small room was full of whiteness, brightest on the bed. She put the boy down on the sheets and stepped back to gaze at him as Jeremy ventured into the room. The boy's face seemed to come alive in the moonlight, and his mouth opened smiling. She gripped Jeremy's hand as a wave of anticipation made her dizzy. The boy's eyes brightened as he gazed at them, standing hand in hand beside his bed. "Mummy, Daddy," he said.

47

Nick didn't try to reason with the policeman until the butcher had left them alone, by which time he was locked in a cell. Perhaps he should have struggled free as the butcher marched him into the dark, but he would have been no use to Diana if his captor had rendered him incapable, as the man was clearly eager to do, muttering "Go on, try it" in Nick's ear like a Lancashire comedian doing an impression of a tough cop. Nick allowed himself to be marched to the police station, which surely would be all the inspector required of him.

A curve of the High Street cut off the police station from the town square. A small building with double doors in a porch, narrow windows in thick walls under a peaked roof, it reminded Nick of a village school. The policeman swung his flashlight beam from wall to wall beyond the porch. Furniture sprang up on shadows: a counter, empty desks. Dog-eared notices pinned to a board started forward like birds out of a nest. The policeman unbolted a flap in the counter and motioned the butcher to bring Nick through, but Nick balked at the sight of the short corridor that led to a cell. "Surely that isn't necessary," he said between his teeth, tears starting from his eyes as his arms were forced farther up.

"You aren't necessary," the butcher snarled, butting his head against the side of Nick's. "Just be thankful you aren't being treated how you deserve."

The policeman unlocked the barred door and stood aside without speaking. The butcher shoved Nick along the corridor, then swung him violently into the cell. Nick lowered his head just in time, and only his shoulders smashed into the wall beside the single bunk. He glared helplessly at the lamplit key as the inspector locked him in. "If you want me to keep an eye on him, just say the word," the butcher said eagerly.

"No need, thank you. I can manage now."

"You know where to find me if you change your mind." The butcher sounded piqued by the hint of reproof in the inspector's voice. He marched out, slamming the porch doors.

Nick limped to the bars as the policeman went into the main room. "Inspector," he called.

"I haven't left you, never fear. I'll want your details for the records."

The light bobbed away among the desks, which shifted as if the dark were a flood. Nick grasped the bars to keep back an impression that the dark was drowning him. Eventually the light shrank into the corridor and poked at him. "Your name, please."

"Nick Reid. But look, surely you don't think I meant to break the law. Can't you let me go now? I give you my word that I don't want any trouble."

The light swung up into his face. "Your address."

"I can't give you that until I know what I'm charged with."

"I've already made that clear. Breach of the peace. Your address, please."

"I want to keep the peace as much as you do. I'm here to help, can't you understand? But I'm worried about Diana Kramer—that's why I came here in the first place. If you won't let me out, then for God's sake go and make sure they don't harm her. Don't just stand there doing your paperwork."

"If you're so anxious about her, you should have kept her quiet, shouldn't you? The sooner you give me your details the sooner I can get on with the work I should be doing."

"My God, you're trying to police this town all by yourself. What happened to the rest of them?"

"It's quite possible they're on their way back to Moonwell with help. You got here, after all. You had no trouble finding your way here, presumably."

"Let me out of here and I'll tell you."

"I think not," the inspector said with a short mirthless laugh. "Your address, please, if you want me to see to your teacher friend."

237

How much paperwork might he need to persuade himself that he was still in control? "I nearly didn't get here at all," Nick said, "and I don't believe anyone else will. Now I can give you some idea of what it's like out there, but I'm damned if I'm going to while I'm locked up like an ape in a cage."

There was silence, and then the light drooped. It looked like an admission of defeat, or at least as if the policeman were considering Nick's ultimatum. Then the light went out.

"Bastard," Nick snarled in his throat. But the light hadn't been switched off to cow him, for he saw the policeman's face, barred with shadow, gazing past him at the small window of the cell. Moonlight was streaming in. Nick felt limp with relief at the overcoming of the dark, and then his instincts caught up with him. It was too reminiscent of the light he'd seen on the moor and then at the hotel.

In the square the townsfolk were cheering. At least that should mean they weren't harming Diana, but it didn't help him. The policeman shone the flashlight on his notebook. "Whatever you were going to tell me, I think it's beside the point now. All I want from you is your address."

Nick would have grabbed him through the bars if he hadn't been out of reach. "Do you really believe everything's all right now?" he said desperately. "Aren't you worried at all by how your town's changed?"

"Undoubtedly I would be if I didn't believe in God." The policeman frowned at him. "Authority comes from God, you know. That's a grave responsibility that I hope I'm worthy of. If that won't keep me from error, I'd like you to tell me what would, you and the rest of your subversive brethren. Now—"

He was going to ask for the address again, Nick thought wildly. But the inspector turned away from him, toward a noise at the porch doors. "It's open," he called.

Only the sounds of celebration in the town square answered him. The shadows of the bars stretched along the corridor into the crowded dark of the main room. Then the noise at the doors came again, a scratching that sounded urgent. The policeman trained the flashlight beam on the porch. "Come," he shouted.

When there was still no response, he tramped along the corridor. Desks swam out of the dark as the flashlight beam expanded into the main room, but was it the light that made the doors appear to shake? "Wait," Nick said, suddenly more

238

nervous. "Better make sure you know who's there before you open the doors."

The inspector threw him a contemptuous look. "Your lady friend's got you as hysterical as she is. Or are you suggesting I should let you out in case I need help? You'll have to get up earlier than that to catch me, my friend." He pointed the flashlight at the doorknob and threw the doors wide.

What had been waiting in the shadow of the police station came in so fast that at first Nick couldn't see why the policeman staggered backward, dropping the flashlight, which careened off the leg of a desk and lay on the linoleum, spinning crazily, turning the room into a nightmare carousel of glimpses. Nick saw the policeman hurl himself at the doors, slamming them just too late. As the man swung round and made a dash for a cupboard where Nick saw truncheons beyond flashing glass, three shapes leaped on him.

They were dogs—mad dogs, to judge by the sounds of snarling and cloth tearing. The flashlight beam swung toward them, and Nick saw them bring the policeman down, one slavering red mouth burying its teeth deep in his thigh, another ripping at his fist as he tried to defend himself. The man screamed once, and then there was only an agonized gurgling. The next swing of the flashlight showed the third dog on top of him, paws on his chest, worrying his throat like a rat. He must have been as good as dead when his free leg kicked out, his boot smashing the flashlight against the wall. Then there was darkness in the main room, and the sounds of panting and snarling and teeth ripping flesh.

48

The Scraggs' cottage was huddled at the foot of the moor, in sight of the school. Diana had often thought that it looked like a guardhouse, the curtains always open on the windows that faced the school, and now she was inside she found that

239

it felt as it looked. Though it was too cluttered for its size—a coat stand took up half the width of the narrow hall, which meant she was crushed between the two men who'd marched her crabwise into the house—it felt like the annex to an institution, cold and unwelcoming. Ronnie's father dug his fist into the small of her back and shoved her into the living room.

It was full of furniture and stank of stale tobacco. Diana thought the smoke had blackened the pictures on the walls until she realized that must be shadows the moonlight was casting. The paintings and the wooden fireplace were too large for the room, as if they'd been brought in from another house to make this seem more like a home, and so was Mrs Scragg. "Put her there," Mrs. Scragg ordered, snapping her fingers at an armchair near the window.

They slung Diana into the moonlit chair, which creaked and wobbled and exhaled the stench of stale tobacco. "You treat my furniture with respect," Mrs. Scragg snarled at her. "That was my grandmother's chair, I'll have you know. So now I suppose I've got to stay here and miss all the hymns. I've a good mind to have you put on your knees and made to join us in offering up our thanks."

"We'll make her show a bit of respect if that's what you want, Mrs. Scragg," Ronnie's father vowed. "About time someone taught her how to behave after the way she let our lads run wild."

"The way I heard it, she was letting my Thomas waste all day telling jokes that weren't fit to hear. Maybe they call that education where she comes from. I taught him a lesson he won't forget, but it should have been her, not him. She's not too old for it either, if you ask me."

"I'm grateful to you both," Mrs. Scragg said. "It does me good to know you parents support our methods. You go now and pray with your families. I'm more than a match for Miss Permissive Ungodliness."

"Happen you are at that," Ronnie's father said, laughing. "And if we should hear her wailing, we won't be coming back to see why."

Diana sat and let them rant. Thomas's father shook his fist at her, his shirt pulling out of his trousers and exposing his navel. She could just see it in the gloom, a blind wrinkled socket in the midst of a mat of hair. It seemed distant and meaningless; everything did. She felt as if being talked about in the third person had absented her, removed her so far that the threats couldn't bring her back. She seemed to have left her emotions behind, and she felt she could go further if she could just think how.

Thomas's father made a disgusted sound and flung himself away from her. Moonlight flooded over her again. She felt almost resigned to it: what could she or anyone else do to put out the moon? The men went out, the front door slammed, and she was alone with Mrs. Scragg.

The woman closed the door of the room and pushed an armchair against it, then she stuck a cigarette in her mouth and dropped herself in a chair opposite Diana, one hand straying negligently toward the heavy poker to make sure it was within reach. When she'd spent half a dozen matches in trying to light the cigarette, she glared at Diana. "Not a word out of you, miss, or I'll give you something to shut you up. We'll just sit quiet until my hubby brings Delbert home and then Mr. S and I'll decide what's to be done about you."

Quiet was all Diana wanted. She felt more than ever as if she weren't there or soon wouldn't be. The moon shone in her face, the tilted slice of moon hovering above the roof of the school that looked tipped with ice. If she gazed at it, there seemed to be nothing but her and the moon, no window framing it, no town. She didn't feel quite ready for that; when she began to shiver, she glanced away. Mrs. Scragg twisted round to look out of the window, and presumably saw only the lane, resounding with the singing in the square. "Not your kind of music, isn't it? You'd better get used to it for as long as you're here, miss. It won't be going away."

Her voice and the sight of her face thrusting forward, unlit cigarette poking from one corner of her mouth, seemed less menacing to Diana than absurd, a nuisance that she wanted to flick away, an interruption to whatever she could do if she relaxed enough. The moonlight crept up the wall above the hearth and began to unveil the painting over the mantelpiece, a dark, bleak view of the empty moor with a mound of clouds overhead. "Meets with your approval, does it, miss?" Mrs. Scragg said furiously. Diana wondered why she should be so resentful, until she noticed the Scragg signature in one

241

corner of the painting. Neither that nor the woman's fur
could distract her now; she couldn't look away from the view
of the moor, she could hardly breathe. The moonlight spread
over it and filled the frame, and at the precise moment when
the entire painting was moonlit, Diana saw that it was no
longer a view of the moor, nor even a painting. It was a
window giving onto where she had to go.

49

Craig and Vera were in their hotel room when the lights of
Moonwell began to fail. Hazel had insisted she would have to
ask the people who were lodging with her if they'd mind
moving to the hotel, and Vera had turned huffy, as if she was
using this as an excuse not to invite her parents, or Benedict
was. All this picking at motives, family life at its pettiest and
most neurotic, made Craig feel more trapped than ever; he'd
never been able to cope with it, and now, isolated at the top
of the indifferent hotel by the dark, he liked it even less. How
much more time were they going to waste here, when they
should be back at their office dealing with legal matters
which, however complex, they knew how to disentangle?
This frustration was one more reason why Vera had grown so
touchy and looked suddenly years older. "Never mind,
love," he said inadequately, and sat by her on the bed, where
she was gazing from the cramped window. He'd begun to
massage her shoulders when the square went dark.

"Good God," he said in empty disgust, and was standing
up to see what had happened when the room went dark too.
For a moment he was back in the abandoned mineshaft,
falling into blindness. He stumbled against the bed and found
Vera again, held onto her. "What's happening now?" she
cried querulously.

"Just the electricity, love. Best to wait until someone fixes it. We're safest where we are," he said, feeling as if the dark were robbing them of all their capabilities, their lifetimes of experience blotted out in a few moments. She sat forward abruptly, as if she'd grown impatient with his hand on her shoulders, and then he realized what had changed. "There, you see," he said, wondering why he felt the need to tell her, an old man's redundant description of the obvious. "They've already fixed the lights."

"What is it? Where's it coming from?"

"We'll take a look, shall we?" It must be moonlight, streaming from above and behind the hotel, turning the streets that led to the fields below Moonwell into an amphitheater of shadow, though shouldn't moonlight be able to reach the fields too instead of leaving everything outside Moonwell in pitch darkness? Craig pushed up the sash and leaned out while Vera clung to him. The light was streaming from the hotel itself.

He was still trying to make out the source when the townsfolk began flocking into the square as Mann's followers crowded out of the hotel singing hymns. Hundreds of people fell to their knees and gazed up. Absurdly, Craig thought they were gazing at him until he realized that they couldn't even see him. "Why, it's the evangelist. He's fixed it up somehow. Look at them, the fools, just because he's got the only light in town."

"Moths," Vera murmured.

"Sheep, more like. Maybe you can't blame them with all this dark, but even so . . ." He drew in his head to peer at her face, pale in the indirect glow. "Who made the lights go out, I wonder? How come he's managed to get one working there and nowhere else? By God, I think he's rigged all this to get them where he wants them. Just look at them, they think he's a saint now, they'd do anything for him. I've a damn good mind to go along to his room and have it out with him right now."

"Don't, Craig, please." She clutched at his arm. "They might turn on you, the whole town. For heaven's sake don't interrupt them while they're praying."

"I'm going to take a walk down the corridor and see if I can get a glimpse of what he's up to, at any rate."

"I won't come with you," Vera said desperately.

"That's right, love, you stay here. I shouldn't be long."

He stepped out of the room before she could say anything else. Since the corridor wasn't entirely dark, he closed the door. A glow was seeping out of Mann's room, frosting the carpet on the sill, glinting faintly in the wall lamps. It made him oddly nervous, but he was damned if he'd let himself be daunted by any of Mann's tricks. He tiptoed along the corridor, his fingers groping over the stubbly pattern of the wallpaper. He was halfway to Mann's room when a door opened behind him, making his heart jerk painfully. "Craig, come quickly," Vera hissed. "It's the teacher who wanted us to stay with her. She's telling them not to listen to him."

"Good for her."

"We ought to do something, Craig. It's just her against them."

He went reluctantly back to the room. The teacher had left the square, but soon she came back. She hadn't spoken when a large red-haired woman stepped into her path. Two men stood up from kneeling and grabbed the teacher's arms. "Leave her alone, you brutes," Vera cried, beating her fist on the window ledge.

"My God," the teacher protested in a voice the Wildes could barely hear, "can't you see anything wrong with what's happening here?"

"Yes," Craig said loudly but unheard, and the red-haired woman slapped the teacher's face. Vera raised her fist shakily. "I'm going down. Let's see if they dare treat me like that too, at my age."

"They might, Vera. Remember we're outsiders."

"We're Hazel's parents, aren't we? Though you wouldn't know it, the way we're put up here in the attic as if we're no more use. Where is Hazel, anyway? Is she down there in that mob? Why isn't she doing anything?"

She was ranging back and forth across the room, her helpless fury growing. She'd opened the door, but now she stormed back to the window. The teacher and her captor had gone. Vera was craning out, trying to see them or Hazel when Mann spoke. "Now there are no unbelievers here, let's make an act of faith that the dark will become light."

Vera pressed her knuckles into her mouth. The soft voice seemed to be in the room with them, to be addressing them

244

directly, warning them not to intervene. It was all rot, Craig told himself, more of Mann's oratorical technique, yet he couldn't help feeling as if the voice had found them in the dark.

"God of our ancestors, lighten our darkness," the crowd began to chant. "We offer ourselves to you." Staring down at the mass of tiny white mouthing faces, Craig felt dizzy and nauseated, as if he were about to fall into their midst, their chant dragging him down, blotting out his senses. When Vera wouldn't come away from the window with him, he had to close his eyes. He thought he'd kept them closed for some time before Vera demanded, "What's happening now?"

The crowd had fallen silent. The mass of faces seemed to be gazing up beyond the hotel. Their anticipation unnerved him. "Show us your light, O God of our fathers and our forefathers," they chanted, and Craig wanted to yell at them not to be superstitious fools, to get rid of the apprehension that was building up in his throat. Then light flooded over the town, and he felt as if he'd lost the power to speak.

It was the light from Mann's room, he told himself, appalled by the jubilation that swept through the crowd, people cheering, waving, leaping. He craned out of the window, Vera clinging to his waist. When he realized it was moonlight, he had a moment of befuddled panic before disgust overtook him. How could he have allowed the notion that Mann was somehow responsible for the moonlight even to suggest itself to him? He wasn't that old, by God, or that gullible. He was breathless with rage, at himself for having been vulnerable and at Mann for taking advantage of the moonlight and the crowd. Hardly knowing what he meant to do, he squeezed Vera's hand and left her in the growing moonlight as he stalked out of the room.

His eyes were dazzled as he stepped into the dimness. It didn't matter, he knew his way along the corridor by now. He wished his tread could make more noise on the carpet, to let Mann know that someone was approaching who wasn't in awe of him. The cavernous stillness made him feel hardly there at all, but Mann would soon know that he was, by God. He'd see through Mann's mumbo jumbo if he could, and maybe bring a few people to look behind the stage show to see where the light that had lured them all was coming from.

Either it or moonlight still outlined Mann's door. Craig put one hand on either side of the doorframe and stooped painfully to the keyhole to peer in.

At first he could see nothing but a white glow. He couldn't make out what the glow was showing. He glimpsed movement before his neck twinged and he had to straighten up, but whatever he'd seen, it wasn't Mann; in fact, his brain couldn't grasp it at all. Was it an animal, a guard dog? Didn't that prove Mann had secrets that he didn't want made public? Certainly there was a smell that reminded Craig of a zoo. The crowd was cheering and shouting for Mann to come back to the window, and Craig wondered if the evangelist might not even be in the room. The quicker he looked, the better. He lowered himself groaning to his knees and closed his left eye as he pressed the right against the keyhole. It took him a few moments to focus, and then he felt as if a grip as cold and unyielding as metal had seized the scruff of his neck. Something was squatting on Mann's bed.

It was naked. That shocked him so badly that at first it was all he could comprehend, and then he tried to deny what he was seeing. It couldn't really look like a gigantic spider crouching in the nest of the bed, thin limbs drawn up around a swollen body that was patchy as the moon. The patches resembled decay, but they were crawling over the bulbous body, over it or under the skin. He wasn't seeing this, Craig's mind screamed, if he just shoved himself back from the door he would stop. Then the hands and feet of the shape on the bed gripped the sheets, wrinkling them in the light that shone brighter than the moonlight streaming through the window, and the limbs raised the body unevenly, the long neck stretched toward the window. The smallness of the hairless gibbous head in proportion to the body made the shape look even more like a spider. The head turned as if drinking in the jubilation of the crowd, and Craig glimpsed its face, not smiling now but sneering with a mouth that widened hungrily. It was still just recognizable as Mann's face.

In that moment Craig felt his mind begin to close down, everything that was bright and alive in his skull going dark, everything he thought of as himself. One thin white arm came groping negligently off Mann's bed as though Craig had been sensed beyond the door. Perhaps it was growing, for it looked capable of reaching the door, so that the long hand could snatch it open and drag Craig into the room. He fell backward choking and sprawled on the floor of the corridor, out of reach of the glow that seeped around the door.

As the dark filled his eyes, he felt as if his mind had gone out. He scrabbled backward, away from the glowing outline of the door that might burst open; then he heaved himself to his feet, his fingernails scraping the pattern off the wallpaper. He didn't know where he was stumbling, except away from the room that was the lair of the shape with Mann's face. When a door swung open, dashing moonlight over him, he flinched wildly before he realized Vera had opened the door.

She ran to him and seized his arms as if to support him. "Craig, what happened? What's wrong?"

"I'll tell you later," he said in a voice that kept sticking in his throat. "Let's get out first, now, quickly."

"Thank God we're doing that, anyway. Just let me throw our things into the cases."

"No, no, no time. We'll come back when it's lighter. Let's just find Hazel now."

"What about the stairs?" she complained, peering toward the dark by the lift. "There aren't any windows. We'll fall."

"We can keep hold of the banisters and each other. Come on, I thought you wanted to see Hazel. She'll be down there now."

His lips were stiffening, trembling, not least because Vera looked capable of waiting for Hazel to approach her. Then she shook herself and grimaced ruefully. "All right, let's see what they have to say for themselves," she growled, and closed the bedroom door.

He felt her shiver at the dark. "Leave the door open if you like," he murmured.

"Perhaps we should. Oh, God, the damn key's in my handbag, in the room. That's what comes of your hurrying me. I wouldn't want to leave our things not locked up, anyway," she said with what sounded like bravado, and turned toward the stairs.

In a way the darkness there was reassuring, if anything could be. It meant that the door of Mann's room hadn't opened, that the shape with the distorted grinning face wasn't scuttling out of the room. He couldn't have seen anything like that, Craig told himself wildly, though the door was bursting open again and again in his mind, brightness and a swollen object spilling forth. He groped desperately toward the staircase, his fingertips stubbing themselves on door-frames, his nails aching as they dragged him along the wall. When his fingers touched the lift doors, he almost cried out, the metal was so cold. At least that meant he and Vera had reached the stairs, which were beside the lift shaft. She led him then, and he felt her groping in the total darkness for the banister. "There it is," she muttered, and stepped down, pulling him with her. He lurched into bottomless dark.

He grabbed the wall, dragging Vera away from the banister. "What's wrong now?" she cried. "What are you trying to do?"

"I'd like to keep hold of the wall," he murmured, willing her to keep her voice as low as his without having to be told why, dreading her asking on the way down what he'd seen in the room at the end of the corridor, in case even mentioning it made it aware of them. "I don't feel safe the other way."

"Go on then, if you want to do it all yourself. Just go slowly. You don't care whether or not *I* feel safe."

He needed to feel in control of the situation as much as he could, needed to believe he was leading them out of the hotel with the urgency Vera couldn't know was required. She let her hand lie stiffly in his as he rested his free hand on the staircase wall and took the first step down.

Ten steps and the staircase turned a corner. Seven more led the stairs across the width of the lift shaft, and then it turned again, toward the next floor down. The darkness thickened as it grew more confined, and Craig could no longer hear the uproar in the square, heard only his own labored breathing that the darkness seemed to hold against his face. Then Vera halted, a few stairs short of the second floor. "What is it?" he gasped, panic almost choking him.

"I thought we were the only people left in the hotel."

"I'm sure we are," he stammered, suppressing the thought of the opening door, the dreadful brightness. "They'll all be out there praying. Come on, let's find Hazel."

But she stood where she was. "I heard something, a door, I think. Maybe someone's in here thinking he's all by himself in the dark."

She was going to call out. Craig's hand jerked up. Only if he tried to cover her mouth she would struggle, and they would be lost, the thing with Mann's face would know they were there. Then she giggled. "Of course, it's him, isn't it," she said, sounding close to recklessness. "Godsgift Mann. Maybe we ought to ask him to show us the way, since he thinks he can do that for everyone."

"We can do without him." Craig glanced up wildly, but the darkness was still total. "We'll show him," he said as convincingly as he could manage.

"You're right, we don't need him. You and I are enough for each other if that's the way they want it," she said with a fierceness he wasn't prepared for, and stepped down with him.

He stumbled when his foot touched the floor of the corridor. His fingers groped around the corner, over the chilly doors of the lift shaft. Only two floors to go, the mocking thought came. He was one floor distant from Mann's room, he told himself, and it was just a hotel, however dark, a hotel that smelled of metal polish and carpet cleaner and unemptied ashtrays. Surely he was imagining that underneath these was a reptilian smell. His shaky fingers led him across the metal doors to the stairs.

Stairs creaked under Vera's tread but not under his, presumably because he was closer to the wall. He sensed that she wanted to speak, and he squeezed her hand in the hope that would forestall her. His ears throbbed with straining to hear if there was movement anywhere in the hotel. He stepped down faster, holding on to the corners that boxed in the lift shaft, taking the last flight as quickly as he could without causing Vera to protest aloud. He faltered at the landing, but now there were just three more flights of stairs between them and the lobby, less than that to seeing the end of the dark. He groped quickly for the metal doors, and his arm plunged through the opening where the doors should be, into empty dark.

His panic made him do the worst thing he could do: he let go of Vera. He was tottering on the edge of the open shaft, flailing his arms wildly, when he felt Vera stumble against him, grabbing at him, pushing him over the edge. Then the knuckles of his right hand knocked painfully against the edge

249

of the open door, and he shoved his fist against the wall there, flinging himself and Vera back.

"We're all right," he muttered, panting with the pain of his bruised hand and his heart. "It's the lift, the doors are open. Keep well back." The shaft must go down at least thirty feet to the basement, but it wasn't the mine, he wasn't back in the nightmare of falling. He could hear it was the lift shaft, hear the faint creaking of the cable. He was standing there to give his heart and his breath time to calm down when he wondered what was making the cable creak.

That was the sound he'd heard on the way down, not the stairs under Vera's feet. Perhaps the door she'd heard had been the doors onto the lift shaft. He had the sudden thought, so dreadful that he almost stumbled forward without realizing, that something had been opening doors so as to lie in wait for him and Vera, something that had climbed spiderlike down the cable and was waiting now for them to step blindly into its long arms, its hands. A reptilian smell drifted toward him out of the dark, and he felt as if the blackness had frozen around him, holding him fast, unable to move or speak. Then Vera spoke, so loudly he was terrified for her. "Don't let's stand here, it could be dangerous."

A thought paralyzed him—the thought of her being dragged into the dark without ever knowing what had seized her, or worse, finding out in hideous detail—and then it sent him lurching toward the stairs. He stepped into gaping emptiness. It was the staircase, he realized as he found the wall. He hurried blindly down, colliding with the corners around the lift shaft, almost falling.

Vera's protests at his haste subsided as the last flight of stairs came in view. A carpet of moonlight was laid out from the glass doors of the wide lobby to the foot of the stairs. Vera must think they were safe now, but Craig felt vulnerable as china, even once he was past the closed lift doors that gave onto the lobby. He was struggling to convince himself that his eyes must have tricked him as he'd peered through the keyhole, serve him right for doing so, but he felt as if the shock of that sight hadn't caught up with him. Out in the square the crowd sang and waved their hands and cheered, and what appalled Craig as much as anything he'd witnessed was the expression he saw everywhere. Hundreds of moonlit faces were turned worshipfully upward, willing Mann to give them another glimpse of himself.

50

"This ought to bring out the loonies, Mr. Gloom."

"It's what they all asked for, Mr. Despondency."

"All except the ones who think there's nothing to believe in."

"They're in for a surprise that'll make their eyes pop, then."

"Especially him in there who doesn't even know whether to believe in us."

"Happen we're him throwing his voice, he thinks."

"Bloody cheek. I'm Useless Eustace, and I'm out here with you."

"More useful than he is, all the same."

"The only joke he's got left is himself, and nobody wants it."

"Happen he thinks if he stays in there long enough the world will go away."

"He may not recognize it, right enough."

"If he ever dares look out at it, you mean."

"He's afraid to look out."

"Afraid to go out."

"Afraid to come out and see us."

They were chanting, and now they began to dance. From the way their moonlit shadows bobbed on the curtains, Eustace thought they'd linked arms. At least that meant he didn't have to see how long their arms were—long enough, he thought, to reach into the corner where he was crouching in an armchair, as far from the window as he could manage. He mustn't fear that: they only wanted to taunt him—they kept virtually saying so, if he was really hearing their voices.

251

If he just stared at the shadows and let his mind go blank as it wanted to, he could believe he was seeing the shadows of bushes.

Except that there were no bushes in his garden. He could only maintain that the shadows were natural so long as he stopped remembering. First all the lights had gone out. The dark had seemed almost welcome, an excuse for inaction, an enemy too vast to struggle with. He'd felt peaceful, no longer compelled to make up stories about everything that befell him. The cries of panic in the streets had nothing to do with him. He'd been sitting calmly in the dark when the moonlight had come poking in, and when he'd gone to pull the curtains and shut out as much of it as he could, he'd seen three figures climbing head first down the side of the moor.

"I saw three shapes come crawling down," he sang to himself to blur the memory. They must have been crawling on their backs, for he'd seen their faces, white and featureless as snails' bellies except for their grinning mouths. They must have wanted him to see that, to appall him or perhaps to bewilder him, for how could they sound as they seemed to if they looked like that? He mustn't wonder about that, it would let them reach him, break through his calm. If he couldn't both think and be calm, he was happy to give up thinking.

"Afraid to look out, afraid to go out, afraid to come out and see us." They were waving their arms like gospelers now, and he had to shut his eyes; he couldn't cope with the sight of even the shadows of the arms that could reach across the room for him. The voices already seemed more distant, excluded by his own dark. Maybe they thought he didn't want the world to go away, but for him that wasn't a taunt, it was a promise.

Then a thought stirred in his head, although he tried to lull it back to sleep. Suppose he was giving them what they wanted, withdrawing into himself so that he would truly be of no more use? He already was, he tried to tell himself: useless to everyone, especially Phoebe Wainwright. But he might be the only person in Moonwell who suspected that she needed help.

Perhaps nothing more was wrong with her than with him: a lack of nourishment now that he'd finished the little food he'd kept in the house and the shops would hardly favor him even if they hadn't run out too; a sense of meaninglessness now that he and Phoebe no longer had jobs, nothing to help them pretend that life was going on as normal. But the difference between her and himself, he thought suddenly, was that she was worth saving—and maybe that was why his tormentors were trying to lure him into forgetting her along with everything else.

He didn't want to open his eyes and leave his comfortable dark. If he starved to death, that didn't seem to matter. But letting it happen to Phoebe did, if indeed that was all that was happening to her. He shifted in his chair, suppressing an urge to scream at the dancing, chanting shadows to leave him alone, and then he smelled himself. He stank of days of not washing, and at some point he seemed to have wet himself. He shoved himself out of his chair, his whole body itching with self-disgust, and ran upstairs to the bathroom.

Moonlight filled the bath, shining it whiter. The water spluttering out of the taps looked like milk. He stripped naked and prepared to step in, forgetting that there was no electricity to heat the water. He grabbed the soap and managed to work up an icy lather, and was rubbing it over himself when he heard a noise at the bathroom window.

He didn't look. He knew what the soft thumping was: the hands reaching up from the garden, beating time to the chant. He joined in the chant, suppressing the wild laughter that threatened to shake his voice out of control. He was singing so loudly he couldn't tell when they stopped. Their fingers slid down the window with a squeal like wet rubber on glass. Maybe that was all, he thought, and tried to ignore the fact that he was hoping it was.

He stood over the bath and splashed water on himself, gasping; then he toweled himself vigorously and raced to his bedroom to dress. In the dressing-table mirror he caught sight of his silhouette, spiky with uncombed hair. He stooped to pick up his comb just as something thumped the window.

"Run out of ideas, have you?" he muttered. "Old joke, not funny any more, go away, we'll let you know." He tugged at his hair with the steel comb, scratching his scalp; it took him minutes even to drag the comb through. He tidied his hair as best he could, cursing monotonously at the reflection of the window and the shape he glimpsed there. It wasn't a hand this time, it was too rounded. He thrust the comb into his pocket and swung round, and then he began to scream.

Most of the nose was missing, and one eye. The hand that was displaying it to him had poked a finger in the socket, like a long white worm. The hair resembled wet grass, trailing over the patchy forehead. All the same, he could see it was Father O'Connell's face.

Eustace's scream of rage and horror scraped his throat raw. He lunged toward the window, then veered out of the room, almost falling downstairs, almost blind with the storm of his emotions. He struggled with the latch and wrenched the front door open, lurched onto the path.

The garden was deserted. He glanced wildly about the street, cottages like cardboard in the moonlight, and caught sight of three pale, thin figures under the moor, one of them brandishing an object like a ball. Outrage drove him toward them, but as he trod on the pavement he faltered. Were they trying to lure him away?

Though he was shaking with hatred and dismay, he forced himself to turn his back on them. He'd never catch them, and perhaps they would do worse than taunt him if he chased them onto the moor. Let them follow him if they dared, then the people who were returning home from the town square would see them. He had to find out how Phoebe was.

Shock caught up with him as he turned toward the main street. His legs began to tremble, and he had to lean over his garden wall and wait to be sick. When he managed to swallow instead, he stumbled along the terrace and into the High Street, into the crowd. People glanced at him, pityingly rather than with hostility; others were too wide-eyed to notice. He hurried shakily past the shops, which were being unlocked, and dodged into Roman Row.

Phoebe's front door was wide open. He saw that before he reached the gate. Moonlight lay like a welcome mat in the hall. Perhaps she'd just stepped out. Eustace turned under the trellis of rotting vines up the squeaky gravel path.

He knocked twice at the door, but there was no reply, no sound at all from the house. Eventually he took a breath that made his head swim, and went in. The front room was deserted; moonlight crept over the fossils embedded in the fireplace, made them appear to stir; in the dead light, the

254

floral figure that had stood guard over the cave last year looked withered. He stared at the photograph, wondering why that made him even uneasier, and then he searched the house.

It was empty. It smelled cold and stale, except for a hint of her wild perfume in the bedroom. Her weight had left a dent in the mattress of the double bed. Eustace avoided the gaze of her late husband's photograph and went to the window, hoping to catch sight of her. Then he flinched back, afraid to be seen in her house, appalled at how habitual his reactions were even after everything that had befallen Moonwell.

He had to find her, or have her found. The cottage felt as if she'd been gone for too long. He hurried back to the High Street, where the townsfolk were queuing outside the shops, complaining about the rationing of food, too much like bloody wartime. "The farmers are having a meeting now to see what they can do," the butcher announced from his doorway as Eustace ran into the square.

The tilted moon hung in the cloudless sky. One upper window of the hotel looked full of its light, though none of the others did. Eustace went as straight across the square as he could, then round the curve to the deserted stretch of the High Street where the police station was. He reached for the handles of the porch doors and hesitated, hearing dogs growling somewhere. Hardly in the police station, he thought as he opened the doors and stepped into the dimness.

========= 51 =========

At last the sounds of snarling and soft tearing gave way to silence. Nick resisted the urge to press closer to the bars of his cell, to try to make out what was happening in the room beyond the corridor. He was afraid that the dogs might leap out of the darkness, fasten their teeth in him before he had time to dodge back. Being unable to help the policeman as

255

the dogs savaged him to death had left Nick feeling weak and vulnerable to all his fears, his helplessness. He was standing a foot or so inside the cell, peering through the bars that flickered and shook with his peering, when the dogs padded out of the dimness.

They stopped at the end of the corridor and lay down. The moonlight through the window of the cell gleamed in their eyes. They were licking their lips, which were wet with a liquid that the light turned black. Apart from that, they were monumentally still.

Nick glared about the cell for a weapon. Of course there was nothing; even the bed was bolted to the wall. In his pockets he found a comb and a pen. If he couldn't harm the dogs, at least they couldn't harm him. He stepped close to the bars and stared the dog at the center of the trio in the eyes. "If I had a gun I'd learn to use it just for you," he whispered.

The dog stared whitely back at him. Nick gripped the bars and stared at it until his eyes stung. Dogs couldn't outstare human beings. "What's wrong with you?" he snarled. Whatever happened, he wouldn't be the first to look away. He was still staring, and beginning to feel as if he were being hypnotized or hypnotizing himself, when he realized that the celebration in the square was over. Reality jerked into place around him. How long had people been walking past the police station without his noticing? He began to shout for help.

The voices in the street faltered momentarily, then they broke into a hymn. The louder Nick shouted, the harder they sang. He fell silent suddenly, not only because of his rage at them, which was making his head throb worse than his bruised shoulders. He'd realized that despite all the noise he was making, the dogs hadn't stirred.

He lunged forward to make them move, shook his fist at them through the bars. Their stillness enraged and terrified him. He kicked the bars and roared at the dogs, until he became aware how grotesquely he was behaving. He felt at the mercy of his lack of sleep, couldn't recall how long it had been since he'd slept. He stumbled backward and sat on the hard bed.

The street sounded deserted now. He was alone with the dogs. Their sides heaved slightly as they lay waiting. He didn't want to wonder what they might be waiting for. He was tempted to throw the comb or the pen at them, except for a dread that they might not move even then. He'd been gazing at them for so long that his exhaustion made them appear to be creeping toward him when, without warning, all three stood up.

Nick shrank back inadvertently, but they weren't coming for him. They slunk away into the main room. At first he could distinguish them from the dimness, three shapes like mist drifting to different corners of the room, and then he lost sight of them. He pressed his face against the bars, and realized that the porch doors were opening.

"Look out," he shouted, "dogs loose in here!" But the man had already stepped into the police station. He glanced about rather timidly, small mouth open under his broad nose, and took a step forward. "Where are you? What did you say?" he called, and the dogs leaped.

Their snarling had warned him. Nick saw him cross his arms over his face to protect it, and lurch toward a desk. "Not that way," Nick groaned, dragging helplessly at the bars, and almost shut his eyes. The man went down on all fours and squeezed under the desk just as the dogs reached him.

Perhaps he'd dodged under there to confuse them, but the back of the desk was solid, no way out. He couldn't even turn around beneath it. Nick thumped the bars and yelled hoarsely at the dogs as they paced snarling toward their victim, and then he remembered the comb and the pen. He tore out the comb, which had snagged on the lining of his pocket, and flung it like a knife.

Though the bars helped line up his aim, the dogs were at least twenty feet away. He'd missed, he thought numbly, just as the comb sailed past the desk and struck one dog in the eye. The animal backed off, yelping and snarling, shaking its head to try to shake off the pain. As if that were a signal, the desk under which the man was crouching heaved up, spilling papers and metal, and was driven blindly at the dogs.

It caught one of them against the wall. The animal's frenzied yelping and the sound of snapped bone made the man falter, then he raised the desk and smashed it down with all his force. "Go on," Nick cried as the man stared about in search of a weapon, as the two remaining dogs converged on him, almost crawling on their bellies, their blackened lips stretched back over their gums, exposing dripping teeth. Then the man gave a shaky laugh and grabbed the handle on the desk against the wall.

Was he hoping to find a weapon in the drawer? But the drawer was stuck. The man shoved one foot against the desk and tugged as the dogs closed in. The drawer came loose suddenly, strewing stationery over the floor, and the man was left holding an empty drawer. "Christ, no," Nick whispered, and was drawing a breath to shout to him to run when the man went berserk.

The corner of the drawer caught one dog on the side of the head. The splintering impact was so loud that Nick thought it was the drawer that had broken until he saw the spray of blood the animal left in the air as its legs crumpled. The third dog was already backing away, baring its teeth until it seemed its lips would tear, as the man rushed at it, scything the drawer in front of him. The edge of the corridor blocked Nick's view, but he deduced that the man was driving the animal into a corner. He heard a dull blow and a yelp, and the dog staggered back into view, its head split open. The man followed it, and the drawer came down, again and again. From feeling appalled yet exhilarated Nick turned nauseated, and looked away until the butchery was over.

The man dropped the drawer and came rather shakily toward the cell. "I've never done anything like that before," he muttered.

Nick couldn't tell if he was boasting or justifying himself. "You had to do it. Can you find the key and let me out?"

The man halted at the end of the corridor. "Depends what you're in for."

"Didn't you see me at the prayer meeting? I didn't understand what was going on, that's all."

"That makes two of us. Locking people up for not believing now, are they? I'm surprised I'm not in there with you. Just tell me where to look for the key."

Nick hoped the man could deal with it now that he was obviously shaken by his encounter with the dogs. "I'm afraid it must be on the policeman. He's in there. The dogs got him."

"Oh, dear." The man hung on to the edge of the corridor with one hand and wiped his forehead with the other, then he pushed himself away from the wall, into the main room.

258

"Oh, God," he murmured, "look at this . . . Oh, my God, that's his . . . I can't, oh . . ." Eventually Nick heard him run to a corner and vomit. At last he brought the key and fumbled it into the lock, and stared white-faced at Nick as together they opened the door. "Where will you go now?" he asked plaintively.

"I've got to find Diana Kramer. They may have locked her up somewhere too. She was arguing with an Irishwoman with red hair."

"Mrs. Scragg from the school. She might have Miss Kramer at her house. I can take you there and anywhere else you need to find." The man gave him a tentative smile that looked inappropriate to his round blood-spattered face, his hands smeared with blood. "I'm a postman," he declared.

52

The painting on the Scraggs' wall filled with moonlight, and it was no longer a painting. The signature vanished as the light reached into the frame and beyond it; then a mist began to drift forward across the slopes of the gloomy moor. But it was moving too quickly for mist; it was rushing over the slopes toward Diana, who felt herself rushing to meet it though her body was still sitting in the shaky armchair by the dead hearth. She couldn't help holding back, trying to cling to her sense of herself, not least because she knew that whatever was beyond the white mist, it was no longer the moor.

"Don't you be criticizing my painting, miss. You save that for your pupils, if anyone anywhere is fool enough to let you teach." Mrs. Scragg's furious voice was falling away behind and below Diana, who felt insubstantial as mist now. She couldn't remember when she'd last eaten. No wonder she felt so light-headed. Or had she been fasting without planning to, preparing herself for this? The thought seemed to release her, or overcome the last of her resistance. The whiteness reached beyond the frame for her, blotting out Mrs. Scragg's harsh voice. Diana was flying, plunging forward through the frame.

It seemed as if her plunge would never end. There was no sense of up or down, only a feeling of indescribable vastness. She was glad she couldn't see beyond the mist; instinct told her that even a glimpse would be more than her mind could cope with. She felt utterly vulnerable, even so, rushing with the mist wherever it was going. She wasn't even sure it was mist. It seemed more like gas, the gas of an explosion spreading across vast emptiness. It felt like the birth of everything.

If it was, why couldn't she have seen it begin? Was a consciousness directing it, or was the explosion only the imperative of the surrounding void? She couldn't hold on to her thoughts any more than she was able to control her headlong rush or her sense of herself. She felt both shapelessly vast and dwarfed by the distances she was traveling. The gulf of time she was crossing, and the awesomeness of her pace, shrank her life to less than a moment from birth to death. Her memories were left behind across an abyss of space and time. Only her awe and terror distinguished her from the churning gaseous matter she was part of, spreading across infinity.

Time had no meaning for her now, and so she couldn't tell how long it was before the rush began perceptibly to slow. She didn't realize that the incandescent mass had begun to coagulate until she saw the void beyond it, unobscured by the gas. The sense of the enormous dark through which other clouds of gas were racing, vaster than galaxies yet so distant they were hardly visible, shrank her further, threatened to blot out her awareness. She was profoundly grateful when her awareness turned to nearer things, still vast but, by contrast, almost comfortingly awesome. The mass in whose center she was hovering had begun to form into stars.

Again she had a piercing sense that time was meaningless. She was experiencing a process that had taken millions of years. The massive violence of the process, dust and gas being sucked into cores of incandescence whose heat she flinched from imagining, touched her on some level deeper than consciousness, her whole self opening flowerlike toward that fiery power. She became aware that the galaxy was spinning majestically in the void, stretching out its spiraling arms beyond the reach of her senses—one hundred million light-years beyond, she thought, a last echo of learning from the life she'd left behind. The awareness drew her outward, toward a young star.

Though it seemed to be nowhere in particular, she could tell that it was closer to the center than the edge. A nebula spun around it, lumps of matter colliding and growing, drawing more matter to themselves as they grew, creating raw worlds. She settled through the void toward the third planet and its satellite, and time quickened again. Earth and moon convulsed as the sun brightened; both globes broke out in volcanoes, flaring wounds. Clouds closed over the planet then, and Diana thought she saw glints of water on the moon, perhaps even the shimmer of an atmosphere. For the first time she tried to control the vision she was experiencing, tried not to be drawn toward the moon. Perhaps it was the way it appeared to seethe, to stir wakefully under the bombardment of chunks of the nebula, matter left over now that the worlds were formed, but there was something about the satellite she didn't like.

Was her apprehension carrying her toward the moon? The earth had more gravity, she told herself desperately; it ought to be able to capture her, to pull her away from the moon. But that didn't work for whatever she was, nor did trying to shift her awareness to the nebula around her, the galaxy, anything that could hold her back from the moon. The moon was beneath her now, and she was tethered to it by forces as invisible and insubstantial as she was.

The moon was already dead, she saw. Water and atmosphere had evaporated, and the globe seemed dry and hollow as a husk in a spider's web. Meteors still dug into the surface, causing it to erupt in huge volcanic craters. The bursting of the surface made her think of corruption, life growing in decay, hatching. But that wasn't what terrified her, made her struggle to draw back from the moon while there was still time. She sensed that however dead the globe was, it harbored awareness. The earth was being watched.

She could only pray that the watcher wasn't aware of her. Surely she was too insignificant to be noticed. She was

261

intensely relieved when her perceptions turned toward the earth, which was changing more rapidly now, though each change lasted millions of years. Meteors still rained down, but caught fire in the atmosphere. Huge continents were splitting, drifting apart as storms picked at the world. Mountains reared up, seas flooded into gaps that were beginning to outline continents she could almost recognize. There might soon be life as she knew it—and then she realized what she had known instinctively. Life on earth was what the watcher on the moon was waiting hungrily for.

Her terror turned her to face the moon, the dead surface that was nonetheless violently alive, lava exploding from raw craters, falling back more slowly than it could on earth. All her being cried out for the bombardment of meteors to stop, to leave alone whatever was lurking in the dead globe, but her will was powerless against the mindless forces of the universe. The movements of the crust were only geological, she tried to reassure herself. Perhaps at least there would be nothing worse to see. She tried to forget how life must be crawling out of the seas of earth by now, evolving on the land into creatures large enough to attract notice. How soon would dinosaurs appear? She felt as if her dread were rushing time forward toward what she feared, and terror overwhelmed her as she saw the change that was creeping over the moon.

At first she took it for an eclipse, the shadow of the earth turning the satellite black. But the blackness wasn't advancing like an eclipse, it was crawling over the entire rim of the moon. She had a vertiginous impression that the moon was shrinking. If it was, then something was eating it away— something that was rising into sight from the dark side of the moon.

She was suddenly afraid that the moon would turn black, leave her in the dark with whatever was approaching. Even that might have been preferable to seeing. As she watched helplessly, long pale tendrils, eight or more of them, reached over the rim of the moon. One stretched to the edge of the immense dead crater above which she was hovering. It was only when it gripped the edge of the crater that she realized it was more solid than the fissures she'd thought the tendrils were. The dark at the rim of the moon was the shadow the globe cast on whatever was behind it—whatever had climbed out of the dark side and was clinging there spiderlike with legs that stretched around the globe.

As Diana's consciousness struggled to recoil, she grasped that dreadful as it was, the sight was nothing but a censored image of the reality, an image that was all her mind would let in. Perhaps even that was too much for her to cope with, the sight of the bloated body, white as only something that had passed all its hideous life in darkness could be, that heaved itself over the rim of the moon.

Her glimpse must have lasted only an instant, though it felt like an age. The sight would have destroyed her, left her insane in the void, if she had had to bear it any longer—if she had glimpsed its face. Then the body that was bigger than the moon seemed to pour itself into its tendrils, which were already merging with the moonlight. Diana saw the light stream down to the earth, saw it touch the ground and take shape.

She felt as if she'd passed beyond horror. She watched the shape stalk the new lands, the steaming forests. As the moonlight strengthened, it grew. The towering famished trunk reminded her of a maggot, the way the skin moved ceaselessly. The head was too large for the body, and she managed not to make out its face, except as a mask like the markings of the moon. When it opened its mouth wide and reached its arms as long as trees into the lairs of its prey, pulled its prey out struggling and shrieking in its long hands, she managed almost to blot out what it looked like. Already its prey was far larger than a human being, but she sensed that it wasn't satisfied. It was hungry for more than food.

Days, months, years, centuries flickered across the earth. The time of her vision might have been speeding to assuage the hunger. Seas opened, continents collided, mountain ranges heaved up jaggedly, almost as if the planet were troubled by the parasite that ranged over it whenever the moonlight was strongest. Then time began to slow, and she knew the hunger was close to being satisfied. She was trapped in the vision, drawn down toward a speck of red light in the midst of a jungle. It might have been a signal to the thing that climbed the moonlight, though it could never have been intended that way.

It was a fire in a clearing. Around it crowded creatures that walked on two legs. Diana felt pity rather than recognition; they didn't look much like human beings. It wasn't their smallness she pitied so much as the way they still seemed so animal, so vulnerable. But when they raised their eyes and saw what was lowering itself hungrily toward them, surrounding them with all its legs, their terror was far too human.

She watched it feed, since she couldn't turn away. She learned what it was hungry for: whatever distinguished the human from the animal. She suffered helplessly through the centuries of its triumph, as the race became more human. She watched it stalk through the last ice age, its swollen body lighting up the icy wastes. That must be where the tales of giants originated, in the sight of the spidery legs that reached into the sky, growing taller as it strode away from feeding. Perhaps it was where religion was born too, the first priests supplicating the sun to return, to save their people from the hunger of the moon, a plea which flared through her like a reminiscence of the power that had touched her as the stars were born. But the moon had its conciliators, prototypes of the druids, men articulate enough to call the stalker into human form, the form of a man so brightly white they couldn't look directly at him. They promised it their cannibal sacrifices, promised to hold the moon sacred, and it lent them the powers to change and grow stronger to hunt when the moon was full, so that it could take what it wanted from their feeding. Diana wanted to cry out to the conciliators not to bargain on behalf of humanity, but the bargain was already past; already the dreadful purpose of the rites was being forgotten, glossed over as the centuries advanced. Only the hunger the rites assuaged and the inhuman power they fed would never change.

Humanity advanced. Civilizations grew up. The worship of the moon was tamed, civilized. People who ran with the full moon were outcast or treated as mad or put to death. The old religion survived in the least accessible places, where the moon thing fed, driven out by the brightness of cities. Glimpses of it gave rise to legends of ogres, of monsters that stalked the empty ocean. Then the druids had called it to Moonwell, and the Romans had tried to destroy it while it was trapped in the druid priest's body. All they had done was to enrage it, provoke it to plan a revenge that had festered over the centuries, a revenge on the human race.

The utter dark of the cave hadn't quelled it. On the contrary, it had gained power over the dark. Before the druid's body had finished decaying, it had called up blind creatures from the deepest caves to heap the pieces of the corpse together with the body of the Roman soldier who had sacrificed himself, never realizing he was to feed the very thing he'd meant to destroy. It had slowed the decay, transforming it into a kind of life that brooded through the centuries of darkness, a makeshift body it could inhabit while it waited. Over the centuries its eyeless servants had become more like itself. In the upper world the moon was still worshiped, the worship giving power to what waited in the cave. Sometimes it reached up and grasped minds in which racial memories of the old worship were buried, and then they went mad or changed with the moon. If they hunted, it shared their feeding, fed on the spirit as they fed on the flesh.

It still lacked the strength to climb back to the moonlight. Once its eyeless servants had borne it toward the upper shaft, but the makeshift body had fallen apart before they had crawled more than a few yards. Besides, it wanted a human being to be its bearer, the first of its triumphs. Perhaps the time it waited in the blind dark was nothing to a being that couldn't die, but to Diana the years felt like the centuries they were. All the same, she couldn't help wishing for them to continue when, far along the cave, she saw a light descending the upper shaft. God help her and everyone, the waiting was over. Mann was coming.

She saw him reach bottom and venture along the passage, paying out rope behind him. His face beneath the helmet looked drawn taut by his resolve, the skin over the cheek-bones almost translucent. She felt grudging admiration and, most of all, terror for him. The light of the helmet found what was waiting in the blackness, and she saw Mann's face fill with loathing and shock.

Perhaps he was most shocked by how small the thing was. The haphazard body had withered almost to nothing over the centuries. The smallness of it must have made him feel safer, for he approached, Diana pleading mutely with him to go back. The thing had gathered itself, and as soon as he was within reach it leaped, the leap it had been preparing for centuries. It closed all its rotting limbs around him, pressed its lipless mouth over his, cutting off his shriek.

Loathing had paralyzed him. Diana could only watch as the crumbling limbs plucked at his clothes, as the pale misshapen body molded to his chest. She couldn't even turn away as the body began to merge with his. His face was last to be invaded, its features swelling poisonously around his look of utter horror, then subsiding into a mocking replica of Mann's face, of his smile.

It was almost a relief for Diana to be left in the dark as the thing that had been Godwin Mann flung its lit helmet aside and strode toward the upper shaft, toward its worshipful prey. Around her in the dark, eyeless creatures waited for its call. All this was only the preamble, and everything that had happened in Moonwell since the thing with Mann's face had emerged from the cave was just cruel play, the thing rejoicing in its powers, testing their limits. Soon it would tire of being worshiped by mistake, soon it would have its revenge. The dark seemed to close around Diana, trapping her in the vision, as she realized how complete its feasting and its revenge would be, realized what it planned to do to the world.

===== 53 =====

Something dropped on Phoebe Wainwright's foot and brought her back to herself. She was slumped over an unyielding ridge in a cold, dim place. Her arms dangled beyond the ridge, her breasts ached against it, her distended belly dragged her down. When she heaved herself upright and twisted round to peer at the fallen object, she found it was a hymnbook. She had been slumped forward against a pew. She was in church, and waiting to die.

She managed to raise her ungainly body, her wrists trembling as she gripped the ridge in front of her, and sat back on the hard bench. If this was dying, it didn't seem too bad, and why should it? She believed that natural death was like stepping through a doorway you didn't even notice. Even her inflated belly didn't disturb her since she'd realized it must be swollen by hunger. Her starving body would let her out soon, and she would see Lionel again, not just the photograph she kept by her bedside. She would learn the secret he'd promised to tell her when he came home that day on which he never had. "Just you wait and see, my love," he'd said, kissing her on both cheeks before the real kiss on the mouth, and she'd been waiting all day to learn what had made his eyes sparkle so brightly when the policeman with the prim face had come to her door, looking so untypically saddened that she'd hardly needed him to speak. Now the sadness, the emptiness within her, was nearly done at last. She'd come to the church to make her peace with God in her own way, and she felt as if she had.

Why then did she seem held back by having to complete a task? Of course, she remembered sluggishly, she ought to have told Eustace Gift she forgave him for what he'd said about her at the rally, since it certainly no longer mattered to her. She was sorry he hadn't been able to tell her to her face how he felt about her, rather than suppress it until it burst out of him in such a warped form. She wiped away a tear: she'd always been fond of him—she could have told him so if he had given her the chance. She hoped he would find someone to be happy with.

Why did she still feel troubled? A memory plucked at her nerves, but it must have been a dream. Soon after she'd learned what he'd said about her, she'd dreamed of Eustace on her, his face changing into Lionel's and then into no face, just a smiling blankness out of which peered tiny gleeful eyes. She'd awakened lying naked on her bed, the moonlight covering her and pouring between her thighs. Just a dream, she told herself again. No, what bothered her was the way Eustace had been made to confess his feelings.

Godwin Mann had done that, Mann and the hysteria he'd brought to Moonwell. Her body stiffened, her hands propping her on the bench became fists. Mann's influence in Moonwell had made her lose the baby, the first she'd lost in ten years, the first ever that had died because the parents had refused her services. That was why she felt she'd left a task unfinished. She wanted Mann to face up to having been responsible for the baby's death.

Moonlight crept over the pews toward the altar, trailing faint distorted outlines of stained glass. Did Mann feel any responsibility for the grief he caused? No doubt he told himself it was God's will. The thought enraged her, made her body ache with a yearning to confront him. She wouldn't feel at peace now until she did.

She levered herself to her feet and glanced wistfully about the church. There no longer seemed to be much to make her wistful. The figures crowded into the long windows looked unnaturally thin and faceless; the moonlight made one group appear to have a single body, the shadows of willows set all the figures dancing grotesquely. It couldn't only be the light that made the church feel cold, dusty, abandoned. Mann had done that too, by claiming that Father O'Connell was less godly than himself. She could almost believe he had somehow been responsible for the priest's death.

She'd do herself no good by letting her imagination roam, especially not when she was so shaky with hunger now that she'd stood up. Moonlight touched the altar as if to display how empty it was, and she saw a large spider scuttle off the altar cloth. She stumbled along the pew, supporting herself with both hands, and handed herself from pew-end to pew-end as far as the back of the church.

She wouldn't get far without a stick. She limped past the willows in the churchyard and stopped at the oak. By hanging onto a low branch, she broke it off, so immediately that she fell against the rough trunk. At least she had support and was glad to be able to leave the church behind: she was beginning to imagine that one of its heads, even patchier and less complete than the other gargoyles under the sloping roof, had Father O'Connell's face, grinning down raggedly. She didn't think she would return to the church after she'd confronted Mann. She would feel more peaceful at home with Lionel's photograph.

She hobbled down the High Street toward the hotel, her stick creaking whenever she leaned on it. People stared out of shops at her, but nobody offered to help. She had to rely more on the stick once she was in the deserted square. Just as she lurched onto the pavement in front of the hotel, the stick broke.

She floundered through the doors and onward. The lobby was crowded with Mann's followers, one of whom jumped up with an outraged squeak as she saw Phoebe reeling toward her chair. Phoebe plumped herself down, panting open-mouthed. Eventually she heaved herself to her feet and limped over to the reception desk, where the manager was gazing glumly at the moonlit shadows the crowd was making on the carpet. "Could you tell me Mr. Mann's room number?" she murmured.

"Nobody can go up." He raised his head from the crutch of his cupped hand, oval forehead gleaming through strands of red hair, and peered blankly at her. "He's got the whole top floor to himself now. As long as their rooms are paid for, that's their business."

A matronly woman with a cross in the shadow of her breasts tapped Phoebe on the shoulder. "Godwin only sees people by appointment now."

"He's changed his tune then, hasn't he?"

"I'm sorry, madam, there's nothing I can do," the manager said, and turned toward the switchboard as it emitted a hiss like an indrawn breath. She saw him stiffen as a soft voice spoke through the headphones. "Please send her up."

"Mr. Mann, is it?" The manager stooped gingerly toward the microphone; he was clearly bewildered by how the switchboard was behaving. "Send whom up, sir?"

"The midwife."

He must have seen her crossing the square and then overheard her through the switchboard, Phoebe thought, disgusted by the awe on the faces of his followers. "Can I have a word?" one murmured.

"Help yourself," the manager said, shrugging.

The young man crouched before the microphone, almost kneeling. "Godwin, are you sure you wouldn't like some food brought up to you? We'd all be glad to do without a little."

"I appreciate your loyalty," the soft voice said. "Don't trouble yourselves. Nobody need go without. Please have my visitor helped up to my floor."

So many people crowded around her that Phoebe thought

they meant to carry her bodily upstairs. Eventually two men took her arms and steered her away from the counter. One switched on a flashlight as they reached the edge of the lobby, and they followed the patch of lit carpet upstairs.

The murmur from the lobby faded as the men heaved Phoebe onto the first floor. They supported her up to the second, between walls that seemed to swell like flesh as the light almost reached them. The landing felt padded with silence, a respectful hush Phoebe yearned to break. She stumped toward the third floor, but the men had to grab her arms as she stumbled inadvertently backward down the stairs. "I don't suppose he'll mind if we just help you to the top. He told us all to leave him alone unless he asked for us," the man with the flashlight said.

They let go of her as soon as she stepped onto the top floor. She clung with both hands to the end of the banister rail and watched them retreat, the glow of the flashlight bobbing around the corner, gone. She heaved herself away from the stairs and almost choked with panic, for she was swaying about within arm's length of the open lift shaft. She staggered to the wall across the corridor and leaned there panting.

This floor of the hotel was full of moonlight. It was brightest at the end of the corridor where her guides had told her Mann's room was, and now she saw that it was streaming through an open doorway. Surely it couldn't all be coming from there? She hadn't time to ponder that, the way she'd begun to shiver. Perhaps that wasn't only weakness; her breath was misting the air in front of her. Realizing that revived her a little, and she began to waddle along the corridor, one hand on the wall. She'd passed one closed door when the soft voice said, "Glad you could make it, Mrs. Wainwright. I wanted you to come of your own free will."

Phoebe's distended belly tightened. "You took the trouble to find out my name, then. Had a guilty conscience, did you? Think you're the one who needs to ask forgiveness for a change?"

The soft voice laughed, so cruelly that Phoebe's breathing faltered. She heard boards creak in the open room; it sounded as if the entire floor was creaking. "Why Mrs. Wainwright, that isn't why you're here."

Phoebe doubled over the sudden twisting pain in her belly. "You may be able to predict your followers," she said through clenched teeth, "but don't be so sure you can do it to me."

"I know everything there is to know about you, Phoebe. I've taken a special interest in you ever since you took charge of dressing the cave."

"What do you mean, ever since? That was years and years ago." She straightened up, eyes streaming, and what the voice had said seeped into her like the chill. She stared along the blanched corridor. "Who are you?" she blurted.

"Don't you know who I am after I've been waiting for you all this time? And yet here I am knowing so much about you," the soft voice said with grotesque coyness. "Why Phoebe, you and I want the same thing, and that's why I've given it to you."

Phoebe slumped against the wall and clutched her belly. The pains felt so nearly familiar, and yet they couldn't be. What are you raving about, you fanatic?" she groaned.

"Exactly what you're feeling now. It's what you think it is. What you always wanted but thought you couldn't have because you'd lost your husband."

Phoebe began to drag herself backward along the wall, one arm pressed against her belly. She would have to let go of the wall to reach the stairs, shove herself toward them. Best to cross the corridor beyond them rather than risk the gaping lift shaft. But she was only abreast of the shaft when the hand came out of Mann's room.

It wasn't a hand, her mind tried to plead. Hands weren't so pale, or so restlessly patchy; fingers shouldn't move like worms. Besides, it was too large even in proportion to the arm, which she realized numbly was reaching halfway down the corridor. But when it spread its fingers, it looked all too like a hand, until the light she'd thought it was holding blazed up so fiercely that the fingers seemed to turn into rays of light, white light which felt like spears of ice as it fastened on her distended belly. She reeled backward, arms flailing, and sprawled on the floor opposite the lift shaft. "Come to me," the soft voice said.

It had tricked itself, she thought wildly. By making her fall over it had rendered her incapable of obeying. She closed her eyes and willed herself to die before the voice could claim to know any more of her secrets, before the spasms in her crotch and belly could prove to mean what the voice had said.

"Come to me," the voice said peremptorily, and Phoebe wa
about to give way to hysterical laughter when she realized
was no longer talking to her.

She squeezed her eyes shut tighter as if that might make th
outrage go away, but she felt long fingers or the icy light o
her. Her clothes tore suddenly, and something squeezed ou
of her between her legs. She shoved her wrist in her mout
and bit until her teeth crunched on bone, and then she force
her eyes open.

A baby was crawling away from her down the corrido
toward the open door. It was fat and unhealthily pale, but
was managing to crawl. Its cord was tugging at its twin, o
however many were still inside Phoebe, kicking impatientl
now. It was crawling toward the light that streamed into th
otherwise deserted corridor, crawling toward the call o
whatever was waiting in Mann's room.

Phoebe dragged herself around on the carpet until he
head was nearest the baby. Her lack of strength made he
weep. She rolled over on her belly, crying out with the pai
and managed to grab the baby by its slippery shoulders an
lift it toward her. It was blind, she saw—eyeless, and wit
little you could call a face. It struggled in her diminishin
grasp, turning its head from side to side, waving its limbs as
tried to crawl in the air. A shudder of horror at the baby an
at herself for having borne it, however she had, passe
through her, draining some of her pittance of strength. On
thought kept her going: that however dismaying the creatur
was, it still had life—a life that only she was able to protec
from the thing in Mann's room. She shrank from wonderin
what the thing was or how it came to be in the room or what
wanted with the baby: her mind shrank until it was hardl
there at all. She clutched the squirming baby to her chest an
levered herself up on one knee.

Even that effort almost made her faint away. She wa
losing blood now as well as starving. She was barely able t
hold on to the child; she would never make it to the stairs
There was only one way to keep the babies from the thing i
Mann's room, and even that would be beyond her if sh
didn't do it now. The thought sent her hobbling on her knee
toward the lift shaft, too quickly for second thoughts. She fe
before she could choose to do so, exhaustion and the weigh
of her belly taking her over the edge. At least she was dyin

272

to some purpose, she had time to think. Her fall killed her instantly and crushed the baby underneath her. Falling, she vowed that she would keep her children with her wherever she was going.

54

When Eustace's knock didn't bring an immediate response, Nick hammered on the Scraggs' front door. Someone was sitting in a chair in the front room, but that was all he could make out now that the moon was above the roof. The front door was snatched open by a small man with a clenched red face and bristling eyebrows. "What's all the row about? Who d'you think you are?"

"You know me, Mr. Scragg. And Mr. Reid here is a friend of Miss Kramer's."

The small face peered up at Nick. "You helped her cause all that fuss when we were trying to pray. I thought the police were supposed to be taking care of you."

"You didn't expect him to keep me locked up forever, surely." No point in mentioning the dogs, Nick thought—the corpse would be found soon enough. "He only wanted me and Diana kept out of the way until your meeting was over. He told me to come and fetch her."

"Did he now. I wonder why he didn't come himself."

"Don't you think he's got enough to do?" Eustace said with a laugh Nick thought sounded not at all convincing.

"He'd have a damn sight less if everyone in this town put their faith in God. I don't understand why he didn't send someone he knew we'd trust if he wanted her released."

"You're too small to be a jailer, you little runt." Before Nick could grab the headmaster by the lapels and snarl that into his face, Eustace said slyly, "Phone him if you don't believe us."

"I would if I could, that's for sure." The headmaster

frowned. "I want one thing clearly understood. If anything's happened to your friend, it's no fault of anyone in this house."

"What's happened to her?" Nick demanded. "Let me see her or by Christ, I'll hold you responsible."

"Don't you take the name of the Lord in vain here. Just you stay close to me so I can keep an eye on what you're doing," the headmaster said, a last assertion of authority, and led them down the narrow hall.

Diana was sitting in the darkening room, beside the dead hearth. She seemed to be gazing open-mouthed at a picture above the mantelpiece. A scrawny man with graying hair knelt by her, rubbing her limp hands. He scrambled aside as Nick ran to her and seized her hands, the chill of her body making him shiver. "How long has she been like this?"

"Ever since the moon came up," Mrs. Scragg said behind him, in an unpleasant tone that was meant to be meaningful.

Nick wiped Diana's mouth, and realized that her T-shirt was soaked. "Why is she wet?" he demanded.

"I threw a bit of water over her, that's all. I've cured children of this kind of nonsense so."

Nick breathed hard and tried to keep his temper. "Has a doctor seen her?"

"Never mind trying to make out we haven't taken care of her. Delbert here tried all of them."

"All the surgeries were shut," the gray-haired man mumbled.

Nick sensed that he'd learned all he could. Once Diana was safely out of the Scraggs' cottage he might be able to plan what to do next. "Give me a hand with her, Eustace," he said, and took Diana's arm in the hope of persuading her to walk. She rose to her feet at once.

Her movement was so sure and swift that he thought she'd awakened, but her eyes were looking nowhere outside themselves. Now that she was on her feet, she stood quite still. When he took her arm again, she moved with him, past the disapproving Scraggs, down the cluttered hall and out of the house.

Eustace closed the door. "Do you want to try the doctors again? That fellow might have got the wrong addresses in the dark."

They crossed the High Street to the pavement that was

moonlit, and as the light touched her face, Diana spoke in a small, halting voice. "The sky's going to fall. That's what they meant. They knew."

"What's that, love?" Nick murmured, stroking her arm through his jacket that he'd buttoned around her. She felt light, hollow, hardly there at all; it made his heart ache. She fell silent as they passed into the shadow of a terrace, and Eustace led them to a doctor's surgery between two shops.

He pushed the large brass button several times, but the bell rang unanswered. Somewhere Nick heard what must be insects, a dry sound that sounded like giggling. He led Diana after Eustace into the side streets, which grew blacker as the moon climbed over the moor. Eustace went straight to a surgery, then to another, but there was no response.

"I'm afraid that's the last. Do you want to try the hospital?"

"How far is it?"

"Forty miles or so."

"We wouldn't get there before dark," Nick said, though he yearned to be told what was wrong with her. "Maybe tomorrow, if she hasn't come round by then. I think she needs rest now, don't you?"

"Bring her back to my house if you like. That is," Eustace said awkwardly, looking away, "unless you were thinking . . . I mean, if she's got her keys on her . . ."

"Your place will be fine. It's very kind of you." Nick was glad to follow him out of the darkest streets. Moonlight still lay on the tarmac of the lane where Eustace lived. As they walked in the light, Diana's mouth began to work, but no words emerged. She was sitting in Eustace's front room when she raised her face blindly, searching. "Got to get out," she pleaded. "Got to stop it, get there before it does."

55

"I won't go if Hazel doesn't," Craig said.

Benedict squatted in front of his chair. "Look, we've been through this once. I don't want to leave the house unoccupied with several thousand pounds' worth of equipment in it. I'm not saying anyone would take advantage of the dark, but it's best to be safe."

"I thought you were. You installed your own alarm. Anyway, I didn't think people committed crimes any more in Moonwell."

"There's been no crime since Godwin came, but criminals could come from out of town if they heard about the lights."

The mention of Mann scraped at Craig's nerves, filled his mind with what he'd glimpsed in Mann's room. The appalling sight grew brighter as his mind repeated it, until he wanted to dig his knuckles into his eyes to blot out the memory. "We aren't going without Hazel," he said unevenly.

"Apart from anything else," Benedict realized, "I need someone here to take messages. There's bound to be work for me once the electricity comes back. I really think running you home is enough to ask."

"We didn't ask you in the first place," Vera retorted. "No need to pretend you don't want to get rid of us."

"Mummy, we're just worried about you," Hazel cried. "The way things are, people resent strangers who don't join in the worship."

"Yes, we saw what they did to your schoolmistress, and you stood by and let them do it, didn't you?"

"There was no reason for us to intervene," Benedict said primly. "Good heavens, her headmistress was only restraining her."

"I'm not leaving this town until you take me to see for

myself that she's all right," Vera declared, folding her arms, and Craig's nerves felt like the scrape of a nail on a blackboard. Outside the window he could see the moonlight creeping away up the moorland road. If they took the van out now, they would be following the moonlight upward until the moor sloped toward the Sheffield road, but they mustn't delay any longer. "Let's take Miss Kramer too if you like," he said, lips quivering, "but I won't go unless Hazel does."

He must sound an old fool, repeating himself like this, but perhaps then Benedict and Hazel would humor him. He had to get the women out, and they needed Benedict to drive the van; Craig's hands were shaking so much he had to sit on them. Once in the next town or, better, home in Sheffield, he could break the news that something was horribly wrong in Moonwell, though God only knew who could be sent to deal with it. "How long are we going to argue?" he said with sudden desperate cunning. "I still haven't recovered from everything that's happened, in fact I think I may be getting worse." He held up his hands to show them in the dimness, and was dismayed to realize he might not be pretending.

"Then let's get you to your doctor," Benedict said impatiently. "Only not with Hazel. We gave in to you before, asking our friends to move to the hotel, and now you aren't even staying."

"Isn't it about time someone asked me what I want to do?" Hazel said.

"I thought you understood what I was saying, dear. I need you to stay at home for the good of the business."

"I understood all right, but that doesn't mean I have to do everything you say, even in a Christian marriage." Hazel's eyes gleamed. "I want to see my parents safely home. They've been through enough without all these arguments. If I could drive I'd take them myself. And while we're out of town we can load up the van with food."

"I could do that. There's no need—"

"You just drive the van and keep quiet for a change. Are you two ready?"

"What about Miss Kramer?" Vera demanded.

"I'm not running a coach trip," Benedict growled. "I'll be driving straight up that road and stopping for nobody."

"God forgive you if anything happens to her." Vera gave

277

him a withering look. "I'm too tired to argue any more, too tired and too old. The sooner I'm out of this nightmare of a town the better."

Her inadvertent accuracy made Craig shudder. Getting out of the cottage took far too long: there were cases to carry down to the van, which had to be unloaded first; Benedict went through the cottage twice, checking locks, and then had to test the alarm as the moon began to sink. They would still have enough light to take them past whatever had stopped Craig's car, Craig told himself—enough light to guide them back to the normal world. He saw the women into the van, Hazel insisting on riding in the back so that her parents could squeeze into the passenger seat. "We're ready," Craig called, as loudly as he dared.

Benedict flung up his hands as if he were being forced to be careless, and dawdled out to the van, having shoved and shaken the front door of the cottage. When he twisted the ignition key, the engine coughed and failed. "We'll get out and push," Craig was on the point of saying as the engine rattled into activity and the van lurched toward the moors.

Craig watched the town shrink in the driving mirror, thought of all the townsfolk who didn't realize what was in their midst, thought guiltily of the teacher and her kindness. What could he do? If he tried to warn the town, they would think he was senile or mad.

The van sped out of the local speed limit and over the crest of the slope. Ahead the moors glowed white, the grass and the heather looked as brittle as fossils. "I hope we've enough petrol," Benedict said as if that were something else he'd been denied the time to check.

"You'll be able to fill up once we reach the main road." Craig willed him to drive faster, and for once Benedict seemed to agree with his feelings. The van raced into the moon-shadow and up to the next etiolated view. Remembering the sheeps' heads he'd seen on his last drive, Craig welcomed the desertion. When a jagged white object seemed to peer out of a ditch at the headlights, he looked hastily away.

Another crest brought the van into the moonlight at the edge of a deeper shadow. Craig risked glancing back, past Hazel, who smiled tentatively at him. The moon was still up, a few minutes short of the horizon. He almost wished they'd

278

gone through the woods, except that he wouldn't have been able to bear that dark.

The thought of darkness dragged at his nerves. He was remembering the end of his last drive, the cavernous dark that had stopped him. The van reached the next rise and raced down, and Craig realized that the crest directly ahead was the one beyond which he hadn't dared to go.

He hugged Vera and felt her grow tense. Perhaps she'd known where they were and had been trying to ignore it, or perhaps he'd let her know. The van sped up to the edge where the moonlit road seemed to end in the black sky, and Craig was as near to praying as he had ever been. Just let us go, he pleaded with the dark, let Benedict be able to get through. As the van reached the crest, he had to close his eyes, bracing himself for the screech of brakes, the cries of panic.

When he felt the van begin to race downhill, at first his eyes wouldn't open. Then he realized Vera had relaxed in his arms. He looked then, and saw the headlights tracing a curve of unfenced road that led to a moonlit ridge. He hadn't been able to see that ridge when he'd tried to drive out of Moonwell.

"We've done it," he murmured. Vera nestled against him to let him know she understood, Benedict gave him a sharp look. Darkness had closed over the van, but it was only the shadow of the ridge they'd scaled. Would they be able to see the main road in the distance from the next crest? They'd see it soon, they were beyond the unnatural dark. Deep in his mind, beyond the strictures of a lifetime's skepticism, Craig wondered what the dark had to do with the thing in the hotel, wondered whether outdistancing the dark meant they were beyond its reach. He was testing the idea very gingerly when the moon sank below the horizon, a minute or less before they would have reached the ridge.

Go on, he screamed inwardly at Benedict, for God's sake drive faster. Perhaps they could make it to the tinge of moonlight that lingered like mist on the ridge. Then it vanished, and all the lights of the van went out at once.

Far too long seemed to pass before Benedict trod on the brake. Craig had time to brace one hand against the dashboard so that he and Vera wouldn't be flung through the windscreen, but their lurch forward on the seat almost sprained his wrist. He felt Hazel collide with the back of the seats, crying out. "None of that, now, no hysteria," Benedict warned her. "I've enough to cope with. I don't know what I've done to make God so angry with me."

"This isn't just happening to you alone, you know," Hazel said jaggedly.

"No, but I'm responsible for all of you. Stop distracting me and let me think. What have you done with the flashlight? It isn't where it should be."

"The last I remember, you had it in the shed."

"Jesus, Mary and Joseph," Benedict breathed, and let out a sound as if he'd been kicked in the stomach. "That's what comes of you all rushing me. I suppose now I'm expected to replace the fuse without being able to see what I'm doing."

To Craig their voices sounded far away across the dark. He hugged Vera, who was trembling as much as he was trying not to, but somehow the dark had intruded between them: he seemed unable to hold her tightly enough.

"Got it," Benedict muttered. He was silent then for so long that Craig found it hard to breathe. There was a tiny click as Benedict took out the fuse from beside the steering wheel, another click as he fitted the replacement. A series of louder clicks followed, and Craig knew he was trying all the lights, which still didn't work. "Hazel," Benedict said sharply, "let's pray."

He sounded as if he blamed her. Craig closed his eyes so that the dark didn't press on them so heavily, and listened as they apologized for all their sins and promised to devote their lives to God. Listening made him hotly embarrassed; yet he was willing their prayers to work, silently urging them to ask for the lights to come on. But Benedict said "Amen" before they'd asked for anything specific, and set about changing the fuse again. The new one clicked into place, and he took a deep breath before trying the lights. They were dead.

Benedict let out a loud, harsh sigh. "Well, I don't know what else I can be expected to do. Now we're stuck out here because I wasn't allowed time to get the flashlight, because some of us had wasted so much time arguing."

"If that's meant as a dig at my parents, Benedict—"

"Shut up, woman. I'm trying to think."

"Don't you speak to her like that," Vera cried, and Craig flinched inwardly. They were all on the edge of hysteria, he most of all. If they lost control and began to squabble, they mightn't hear anything out there in the dark. The thought that they might not be alone in the dark made his legs quiver so violently he thought he was having a stroke. He forced his eyes to open to escape the sight of the thing in Mann's room, but it stayed in front of him. When Benedict spoke, Craig almost cried out, he was so on edge.

"I apologize for my lack of patience," Benedict said gruffly. "We mustn't let the situation get the better of us. I'd be grateful if you'd all keep absolutely quiet while I try and turn the van. I should be able to get us back to town so long as I go slowly enough."

Someone sucked in a breath, then thought better of speaking. Craig was trying desperately to think how he could dissuade Benedict from taking them back to Moonwell. If Benedict felt capable of driving blind, why couldn't he carry on toward the main road? But perhaps the void that had stopped Craig was waiting beyond the rise. He pulled Vera to him as Benedict set about turning the van.

Before they were over the camber, Craig's jaw was aching. The van inched down toward the far side of the road, creaking and groaning metallically, and he was afraid the engine would stall for good, they were moving so slowly. Not slowly enough, for without warning the left front wheel was over the edge of the ditch.

As the van keeled over, Benedict threw it into reverse. It screeched backward, veering wildly as he tried to prevent it from going off the far side of the road. It lurched forward as he slammed it into first gear, and then the engine stalled. He wrenched at the handbrake, halting the vehicle on a level patch of road. They'd reached the crest of the slope, but all it showed them was that they were surrounded by utter dark.

Craig sat and clutched his chest to keep his heart in. Behind him Hazel suppressed a moan as she picked herself up from the floor. "Are you all right, love?" Vera demanded, twisting round, almost out of Craig's embrace.

"Just a scraped elbow, Mummy. Hardly worth mentioning." Hazel's voice was determinedly cheerful. Craig was wondering dismally what they would all do once they'd run out of small talk to fend off the hopelessness of the situation when Benedict whispered, "God be praised, look there."

Craig strained his eyes until he felt them bulge. At first he thought he could see nothing but the effect of the dark on his vision. But no, a light was hovering above the downward slope, on a level with the windscreen and some distance ahead, for it illuminated the patch of road beneath it: he could see white spikes of grass on both sides of the lit patch. It was a will-o'-the-wisp, he told himself, and then, with a lurch of consciousness, he saw it was a bird.

It looked composed of pale light. Its wings shone brightest, blurred wings that kept it hovering. Craig couldn't see its eyes or what kind of beak it had. It was luminous with moonlight, he realized, or with the light he'd seen in the corridor at the top of the hotel. The realization clutched at his throat, held him speechless, and then he heard Benedict start the engine. "What are you doing?" he managed to croak.

The van moved forward, and the bird flew ahead, the large bright feathers of its wings coming into focus. "Following," Benedict said.

The awe in his voice dismayed Craig so much that he could hardly breathe or speak. "What do you think you're following?" he whispered.

"Can't you see?"

"It isn't what you think it is." Craig managed to organize his shivery limbs enough to grab Benedict's arm and hang on as the man tried to steer. "Don't trust it. It's a trap, it's evil if anything is. Let's just stop and wait until the moon comes up again."

Benedict pulled his arm free. "If you can't see it for what it is, I pity you. Thank God some of us have faith."

Hazel leaned over Craig's shoulder. "It's a sign from God, Daddy," she told him, almost pleading.

The van was gathering speed. Craig could just see Vera now, her face dimly outlined by the glow ahead. Her face looked old and dull, wanting to hope. The bird glided faster, the lit patch of tarmac receded. "You don't even know which way we're going, do you?" Craig shouted at Benedict. "You don't know which way the van was facing any more than I do."

"The difference between us," Benedict said with measured gentleness, "is that I have faith."

Craig felt brittle with panic. He imagined being carried helplessly onward by Benedict's faith until they reached wherever the bird that shone like the thing in Mann's room wanted them. He fumbled for the door handle. "I won't go with you. Stop the van or I'll jump."

"Don't be preposterous. Just sit quietly and trust me. Everything's under control."

Craig opened the door loudly. "Stop it right now," he almost screamed, "or I'm jumping."

He was never sure what Benedict tried to do then. The van jerked to a halt, then surged forward at once. Perhaps Benedict meant the door to slam and lock itself, but it slid all the way open and stuck. The lurch of the van hurled Craig out of his seat, out of the van into the dark.

That's all, then, he thought with a numb resignation as he fell. He hadn't even had time for a last word to Vera. Then he struck the edge of the ditch. The impact made him feel his lungs had burst, and drove a spike of agony deep into him from his ribs. One hand that seemed to be all his brain could control clutched at the edge of the ditch and dragged him onto the verge, where he lay watching the van.

At first he thought it wasn't going to stop. Then it bucked to a standstill, and the women clambered out, silhouetted against the hovering glow. "Where are you, Craig?" Vera cried. "Say you're all right, don't frighten me."

"I'm here. I'm alive." Craig raised himself on his tottering arms, and managed to sit on the edge of the ditch, squeezing his eyes shut while the pain in his ribs subsided. "But I'm not going anywhere in that van," he said through clenched teeth.

Hazel touched him gently here and there, felt him wince. "You're hurt," she said plaintively. "Let Benedict drive you. You'll be all right, I promise. You said yourself you should go to the hospital."

"That thing won't lead us to any hospital." Craig was suddenly almost in tears because of her concern for him. "Look, don't worry about me, I can walk. I'll just wait here until the moon comes up."

Vera knelt down by him. "Won't you come even for me? You can't stay out here in the dark."

"I'll be safer here than going after that thing," Craig said doggedly. "We all will."

Benedict climbed out of the van and peered back toward them. Beyond him the bird hovered, its fat body absolutely still between two fans of light. Craig saw its beak like a long sharp icicle, and was almost sure the bird had no eyes.

"Come on, old chap, don't mess us all about," Benedict called. "You're scaring the women and wasting time. Act your age, for goodness' sake."

Vera clutched her forehead as Craig withdrew stubbornly into himself. "Go on, Hazel," she said indistinctly. "I'll stay with your father. You two look after yourselves."

"We can't leave them out here, Benedict," Hazel cried.

"That's up to them, my dear. We prayed and we were given a sign, and turning our backs on that would be turning our backs on God. All I ask is that everyone make up their minds now about whether they're coming, because I'm not prepared to test God any further."

He stood gazing toward them for a few minutes, hands on hips. When they didn't answer, he turned sharply and strode back to the van. They heard his door slide shut, and then Hazel took a step away from her parents. "I can't let him go by himself when he doesn't know where he's going."

"Go with him, child. We'll keep each other safe," Vera blurted. As Hazel ran to the vehicle, her mother half rose from kneeling as if she would stop her; then she sank back beside Craig. Hazel's door slammed, and the van started at once. They watched as the vehicle sped after the shining bird, watched the bird shrink and vanish over the next ridge, and then the dark closed in.

56

Eventually Andrew's mother said she was going next door to see how the old lady was, but he thought she wanted to get away from the smell. As soon as they'd come home from praying in the square, his mother had begun to sniff suspiciously and poke about under the furniture with a broom handle. "What's died in here?" she'd demanded, glaring at her husband as if she blamed him for distracting her from finding out what was wrong with Miss Crane next door. She'd opened the windows to try to get rid of the smell and to gaze at the old lady's moonlit cottage. "She's the kind who'd get to church even if she had no legs," she'd said, but she hadn't seen the old lady in the square, nor on their way home. "I don't like it. I'm going to see what's wrong."

Andrew's father and Miss Ingham followed her out. Andrew stayed in the living room, even though the cottage made him think of the reptile house at the zoo, the dim, cold, stony place that stank of things that lived in the dark. His mother hadn't liked that place at all: she'd hurried him out before they could injure themselves or have their pockets picked or suffer something worse that she'd refused to specify. He remembered being pushed out into the daylight, the warmth of the sun on his face, but that seemed longer ago than all the days of his life.

"Go and get a ladder," his mother called, so shrilly that Andrew thought she disliked asking his father to help. The boy went to stand by Miss Ingham on the garden path. His father was loping around the old lady's cottage when a man with "Jesus" stitched on his breast pocket came looking for Miss Ingham. "The teacher you replaced has had some kind of fit. She's in a coma at the postman's house. It was her own doing, you understand, in case anyone tries to say otherwise."

His father reappeared. "Miss Crane's in there but she isn't answering. No need for a ladder," he said, and lunged at the door of her cottage.

As he passed into the moonlight that slanted across the garden path, he looked suddenly more powerful, crouching in a way that Andrew had never seen him crouch. He looked bulkier than usual, gathered together to spring. When he slammed into the door, it gave way at once.

"You stay here," Andrew's mother said, as if this wasn't fit for men to see. "Miss Crane," she called as she ventured in. Soon she fell silent, and then came out quickly, flapping her hand in front of her face. "Dead. Starved to death, it looks like," she said, and glared at Andrew for overhearing.

"I'll get a doctor if someone tells me where to go," said the man with "Jesus" on his pocket.

"I'll take you," Andrew's mother said, and looked hard at his father. "Make sure the boy stays away from her house."

Andrew wouldn't have dared go near, even though he

285

wondered what the old lady looked like now; he'd never seen anyone dead. He scurried after Miss Ingham into his house. His father stared at the old lady's cottage, licking his lips; then he came after them. In the living room, where at least the dark had the shape of the furniture, Andrew managed to speak up. "Daddy, what's a coma?"

"What?" his father growled as if he'd been interrupted. "It's like going to sleep and not being able to wake up."

"Miss Kramer's in one," Miss Ingham explained. "We should pray for her. Always pray for sinners, Andrew. They need our prayers most of all."

Andrew fell on his knees at once, clenching his eyelids to make the prayer stronger. He thought of Miss Kramer, waiting like Sleeping Beauty to be awakened. If only he could be the prince, he thought, or his father could be if that would help. Then he forgot to pray and almost gasped aloud, for he'd realized what they could do.

"Amen," Miss Ingham said, and stood up. "That poor old lady," she murmured. "I wonder if there are any more like her, starving away."

"I wouldn't be surprised," Andrew's father said thickly.

"What I ought to do is organize some people to go round the town and check."

"Go ahead if you want to," Andrew's father said in an odd, light voice. "We'll be all right on our own."

"I expect you will," Miss Ingham said, peering at him in the dimness. He's just my daddy, Andrew thought, he'll be all right if you leave him alone, you wait and see what he can do when people don't treat him like an ogre. . . . She made for the door, but glanced back. "I won't be long," she said, almost like a warning.

As soon as the garden gate clanged behind her, Andrew said, "Daddy, why don't we help Miss Kramer?"

"I'm not a doctor, son."

"I know you aren't," Andrew said, giggling at the thought, at his father's funny new voice. "But you could carry her to Mr. Mann, couldn't you? He'd make her better. People as good as him are supposed to be able to."

His father made a muffled sound. "You're a good lad, but it's no use. I don't even know where she is."

"She's at the postman's house."

286

"Is she now." His father seemed to crouch down as if he ere trying to hide in the dark, and then he rose to his full eight: for a moment it looked to Andrew as if invisible rings were hauling him up. "Well then, I'd better see what I an do," he said in that pale voice. "You stay here where it's afe. Someone'll be back before long."

"I don't want to," Andrew cried in panic.

"Can't you be left even for a few minutes? Stop that ailing, you sound like a whelp. Just you keep your trap shut nce we're outside or I'll send you back home by yourself."

Andrew didn't mind his roughness: it made his father ound more like his father. He held his father's hand tight as ey stepped into the glimmering street. Most of the light was oming from the hotel now. The idea of Mr. Mann shining ke a saint in a picture made Andrew's throat grow dry, and o did the lizardy smell that seemed to have followed them ut of the cottage. He was glad they were hurrying toward e square; they wouldn't be so close to the dark and hatever might be swarming there. Or had the light driven ose things back into the cave? Of course, that must be why od had made Mr. Mann light up.

His father halted suddenly, in sight of Mr. Mann's window, is eyes white as marbles. "Look, son, I'd rather you stayed ome. You'll only be in the way."

More than being abandoned, leaving his father alone in the ark terrified the boy. "I won't. You said I could come. I'll be uiet, I promise, only don't make me go home."

His father turned his head and looked down at him. It must e shadow that made Andrew unable to see his face properly. Iis father tightened his grip and dragged him across the quare, and Andrew kept his gaze on the blur of a face, ither than look at his father's shadow, which grew a long ead and gangling limbs as they left the hotel behind. It was is father's face, even if it seemed to be reaching forward ith eagerness to save the sleeping beauty. The dark and the eptilian smell closed around them, and the boy almost cried ut with relief when they came to the postman's lane.

"I'll knock, shall I, Daddy?" He pulled his hand free of his ather's and ran ahead, rubbing his hand on his trousers to et rid of the cold, slimy feel that was only sweat, he told imself. He dodged into the postman's garden and grabbed

287

the chilly knocker on the door. His hand was so slippery tha
he could hardly knock.

The postman looked out of the front room, then cam
quickly to the door. "What's up, Andrew? Are you on you
own?"

"I'm with my daddy. We've come to take Miss Kramer t
the hotel so Mr. Mann can make her better."

"I don't know about that, son." The postman peere
warily past Andrew. "We're going to take her to the hospit
when there's enough light."

"No need for that." Andrew's father pushed past the boy
who shivered without knowing why. "Godwin's what sh
needs," his father said.

"No it isn't," a man's voice called from inside the cottage
"Anything but. It's the last thing she'd want, Eustace."

"Thanks anyway," the postman said, and began to clos
the door. Andrew saw his father crouch. He was going t
knock the door aside, like Miss Crane's—and then the bo
realized that his father wasn't merely gathering himself, fo
he heard the seams of his father's jacket tear, no longer abl
to contain his father. "Don't, Daddy," he screamed, hardl
aware of what he was saying. "Let's go home."

Suddenly he knew that his father had wanted him to stay ;
home so that he wouldn't see what was happening now. H
was pitifully glad of the dark: at least he wouldn't be able t
see. Then he became aware that his father was glimmerin
with a maggoty sheen that clung to his tortured face and h
hands and his body where it showed through the rents in h
clothes. The door slammed, and what had been his fathe
leaped.

57

Just as the knocking at the front door began, Nick thought Diana was about to waken. She'd been lying on the postman's bed ever since Eustace had ushered him up and then withdrawn awkwardly, murmuring, "I expect you two would like to be alone, but if you need anything I'll be downstairs." He was assuming there was more to the relationship than in fact there was, Nick thought, wishing that Eustace were right, for Diana's sake: at least then he could remind her of experiences they'd shared, use them to try to recall her from wherever she was. He stroked her long black hair back from her clammy forehead and kept repeating her name. If it hadn't been for planning to drive her to the hospital at first light, he wouldn't have known what he was doing in Moonwell.

When he realized he was straining his eyes in order to make out her face, he went nervously to the window. The moon was out of sight beyond the moor, though a glassy pallor lingered in the sky. He found his way quickly back to his chair by the bed. Would it just be dark once the moon went down, or would there be worse to cope with? He made for the bathroom while he could still see dimly, then hurried back to his vigil.

He gazed at the glimmer of her face and her long legs; then he sat forward and found her hand, which was limp and cool. He was tempted to lie beside her in the gathering dark, but that seemed too much like taking advantage of her, too close to taking that risk. "I wish we'd gone to bed together while we had the chance," he murmured, and her hand closed over his.

For a moment he thought she'd heard him. Affection and desire for her blazed through him, and suddenly he wasn't shivering. He leaned forward to lift her to him. But her grip tightened, bruising his hand, and he realized she was trying to waken, her head twisting back and forth on the pillow. "Diana, you're only dreaming," he said loudly. "Wake up, I'm here, Nick Reid." Her head jerked up as if she'd heard a sound outside, her nails dug into the back of his hand, and someone slammed the knocker against the front door.

She couldn't have heard or sensed whoever was there, Nick told himself, yet he felt as if she had. He held his breath and stiffened his body to keep it still as Eustace hurried to the front door. When he heard a child's voice, he relaxed a little, until he heard what the child was saying. "Don't worry," Nick murmured, stroking Diana's hand as her head craned blindly. "I won't let anyone take you to Godwin Mann."

When a man's voice joined the child's, Nick tried to pull free of Diana's grip, but she clung to him as if he were her only chance of awakening. "No it isn't," he shouted, for the man's voice had suggested that the evangelist was what she needed. "Anything but. It's the last thing she'd want, Eustace."

Diana's other hand grabbed his. When he squinted at her face, he was just able to distinguish that her eyes were still closed, though the lids might be flickering. "Shut the door, Eustace," he murmured urgently, and a moment later the door slammed. "So much for your saviors," he said to Diana. Then something rammed the front door.

The impact made the cottage shudder. More than one of the evangelist's followers must be trying to break down the door and carry Diana away. Why was the child screaming? Nick pried Diana's hands loose from his as gently as he could. "I'm not going far," he whispered, and almost couldn't leave her, she was craning toward him so blindly and, it seemed, helplessly. The floor vibrated under his feet as the front door shook again, and he groped hastily across the room. He had just reached the top of the stairs when the front door crashed open.

Eustace must have been trying to hold it shut. He was flung backward, his shoulders thumping the wall with a sound like a side of meat thrown on a slab. He lurched forward, with pain or to block the path of the intruders. Then Nick saw him falter and retreat, almost falling, as a shape came at him through the doorway.

From where Nick stood, it looked almost like a man, except that it was shining with a faint whitish glow like decay. It darted at Eustace and seized him with its long pale hands, lifted him struggling above its head and hurled him aside, into the front room. There was the sound of furniture breaking, the thud of Eustace's body, a groan that petered out. Then the shape raised its glowing face, of which Nick could see only the bulging eyes and bared teeth, and caught sight of Nick.

As Nick stood clutching the banister at the top of the stairs, his body crippled by a loathing so intense he couldn't move, a boy appeared in the doorway. Only the glow of the shape in the hall made him visible. "Miss Kramer, watch out," he cried in a voice that sounded more like a sick old man's than a child's. "It isn't my daddy, it's a monster." Then he turned and fled sobbing into the dark, and the shape in the hall began to climb the stairs.

Nick tried to shove himself away from the banister, but he felt as if his hands had merged with the wood. He could only watch as the shape climbed toward him, its arms dangling so that it was almost on all fours, the rotten light of its face thrust forward as though probing the dark for him. The grin seemed almost to be bursting through the flesh, dragging the face into a new and inhuman shape. The eyes looked more like blobs of rot than eyes, and whatever was glaring out of them was certainly no longer human. Nick had a sudden sickened notion that perhaps they couldn't see at all. Perhaps that was why the face was poking forward, searching for the sound or smell of him.

Revulsion shuddered through him, up into his throat, and all at once he could move. He threw himself back from the stairs and stumbled across the landing to Eustace's room, trying frantically to think what was in there that he might use to defend Diana. He halted just inside the room and peered about, hardly even able to distinguish the furniture, and then he realized that Diana was no longer on the bed.

"Christ, no," he moaned. He could hear stairs creaking, closer and closer; a reptilian stench made his throat writhe. He twisted round to dodge across the landing, to look for Diana in the other rooms, but there she was beside him in the dark, just inside the doorway. It was so dark there that at first he hadn't noticed her, but now he could just see her—because of the glow that was seeping into the room, the pale glow of the thing that had reached the top of the stairs.

Diana's eyes were still closed, but now that she was on her feet she seemed calmer: because she couldn't see what was coming, he thought—God help them both. He slammed the door in its face, if it still had a face, and tried to guide Diana toward the window. She wouldn't budge. Nor could he lift her, perhaps because the horror of what he'd seen had sapped his strength. He ran to the window and dragged the sash up, only to see that it would be no use: even if he managed to lift her and jump, they would fall on the rockery or on the stone path—they would certainly be injured when the thing in the cottage came for them. He was hanging on to the sash as if it were a weapon, and then he wondered if it might provide one. He pulled off his jacket and wadded it around his fist, and punched the glass of the window as hard as he could.

The glass didn't even splinter. He stumbled back a few paces and lunged at the window, driving his fist into it. The sash jumped in its grooves, the sash weights rattled on their cords inside the frame, but the glass only vibrated. He could see it vibrating because it held a reflection of the seeping light that outlined the door. He was peering desperately about for a means to smash the glass when the room brightened. The door was opening.

He reached Diana just as it swung wide. All he could do now was drag her out of the way, place himself between her and the thing, lure it away from her by making it pursue him—but all his strength couldn't move her an inch. She stood there as calm as stone when the thing came into the room.

Before Nick could even step into its path, one long hand seized him. Fingers colder than a corpse's closed around his body, and his flesh shrank away in revulsion, seemed to wither from the touch. The stretched mouth bared its teeth, the white eyes bulged further, and then he was hurled across the room, against the wall beside the window.

Nick managed to fling up an arm between his head and the wall. The impact still wrenched his neck, hammered agony into his skull. When he tried to push himself to his feet, the room seemed almost to turn over. He could only sway in a crouch and try to regain control of his body while the long hands reached for Diana—and then she stretched out her hands toward them. "Brian Bevan," she said, as gently as if she were addressing a child.

She still had her eyes shut, Nick saw dizzily. She couldn't see the shape in front of her; Nick could scarcely bear to look at it himself now that it was reaching for her not only with its hands but, snaillike, with its eyes. But something stopped the hands a few inches short of her, perhaps her voice. "You went to him, didn't you," she murmured. "What did he promise you? That he'd chosen you to be like him? You poor thing, all he wants is to make us suffer until he's tired of that and ready to do his worst."

Perhaps the thing understood, or perhaps it was the tone of her voice it responded to, but the long hands had given up reaching for her, the grinning head drooped. Nick found the sight of its defeat almost as horrible as its touch, especially the withdrawal of the eyes into the head. "That's it, fight him, don't let him change you," Diana whispered more urgently. "You're still Brian Bevan, still Andrew's father. Where is he? Where's your son?"

The head rose at the mention of the boy's name. All at once the face looked human, except for the rotten glow and the agonized grin that thrust between the lips. Then the thing spoke in a human voice, and Nick found that worst of all. "Andrew, come back. It's me, it's your father," it pleaded, and went loping, disconcertingly fast, toward the window.

Nick grabbed the sill, hauled himself aside. The shape crashed through the window and fell in the midst of a shower of glass. Except for the glow, it looked like a man now, and perhaps that was why its leap failed. Its head struck the path with a sound so fragile that Nick's stomach writhed. As the body twitched into stillness, the glow faded.

Nick couldn't look away from where it had fallen, even when it was quite dark, and so he didn't notice at first that Diana had come to stand beside him. At least his dizziness had given way to a vicious headache, and he no longer felt in danger of collapsing. Peering at Diana, he made out that she was gazing at him, rather sadly. How long had her eyes been open? Had she seen what she was talking to? He couldn't help feeling nervous of her, unsure whether he should touch her. "Diana," he said, so low he might not have wanted an answer, "what in God's name is going on?"

"I told you, Nick, the thing Mann stirred up. Only I know all about it now."

"How do you know?"

The sharpness of his question made her face grow sadder. "Don't be afraid of me, Nick, there's enough to fear without that. I had a vision while they were keeping me prisoner. Not having eaten for so long must have helped. Maybe someone had to know, to be able to do something, but it isn't easy for me. I hardly know myself any more."

"You still seem like Diana to me," Nick said awkwardly, and managed to take her hand, which was trembling. "I'm glad you do. So what do you know? What are we up against?"

"Everything we've been afraid of since we lived in caves, maybe since before we were even human. Everything we tried to believe we weren't afraid of any longer. It's just been enjoying its revenge so far, you see, but I think it's getting tired of that now, and when it does it'll stop playing with us." Her trembling stilled as she stiffened, remembering. "I don't know if I can head it off, but I have to try."

"You can count on me—I mean, I hope you want to." When she gripped his hand to tell him so, he said, "First we have to see to Eustace. He's downstairs. That thing attacked him." Now he had to ask what she'd meant, and he knew he would have to believe her: there was no skepticism left in him, only a raw, vulnerable hollowness where it had been. "You talk about heading it off," he said reluctantly as they made their way to the stairs, "and while you were in your trance you kept saying you had to get somewhere first. Where, Diana? What have we got to prevent?"

"I should have realized sooner. I was as blind as everyone else." She sounded suddenly as unwilling to speak as he was to hear. "I just wonder how much it was able to influence events before it came into the open. It seems too much of a coincidence that there's the means for it to destroy us all and feast on our souls within easy reach, or is that just the way the world is now?" She took a breath, and then she said, "It's going for the missile base."

58

Eustace was giving the performance of his life for the best audience he'd ever had. He didn't need to be able to see them out there beyond the lit stage, he could hear their roars of laughter at everything he did. He had to struggle to keep his own face straight; a comedian shouldn't laugh at his own jokes. Now someone was calling to him from the unseen wings to make way for the next act, but Eustace wasn't about to leave the show while he was giving the audience what they wanted: he might never have another chance like this. When he opened his mouth and stepped toward the audience, they roared louder, and suddenly he saw steps leading down toward them, into the dim aisle. He stepped between the footlights, away from the voice that was calling his name.

The audience cheered him on. He could see their wide smiles in the dimness everywhere he looked. He strode along the aisle, joking about them and their glinting teeth, and they threw back their laughing heads as if that could make their smiles even wider. Would the aisle never end? He didn't care: he could keep up his performance as long as they wanted him to, as he strode over the carpet that felt soft as moss, sloping downward now. All he had to do in order to stay out here was ignore the distant voice that was calling his name. When he glanced back, the lit stage was no bigger than the patch of light beneath a streetlamp.

He'd gone too far to turn back. On either side of him, as far as he could see, pairs of hands were starting up, clapping above the heads, an oddly soft sound that reached into the deeper dark. They were urging him onward, downward, because he still had to face the most demanding audience of all. It was eager for everything he could give, and more. It was hungry for him, body and soul.

He didn't want to go down there, not when he heard its laughter. Now that it was too late, he could hear it clearly the glee of the lord of the dark, its laughter that was somehow coming from the uncountable mouths all around him. The laughter blotted out the voice that was calling his name. The audience crowded into the aisle, grinning facelessly. "Don't let me die yet," Eustace pleaded with the distant voice. "If I've got to die, don't let it be here anywhere but here." But the distant light had gone out; there was only darkness full of laughter that gnawed at him withered him. Hands seized him, dragged him into the dark.

He struggled and lashed out with his fists, and then his arms were pinned against his body. He strained his eyes desperate to see what had caught him and thrown him on his back. He jerked his head from side to side, though it felt like a bruise bigger than his skull. "Don't say I'm blind," he moaned.

"You aren't, Eustace." It was the voice that had been calling him. "It's just the dark. You're at home. We brought Diana here, remember? I'm Nick Reid."

Eustace remembered altogether too quickly and completely. The darkness seemed to rush at him. "What happened to Brian Bevan?" he whispered.

"He's dead, Eustace. Killed himself."

That wasn't all Eustace had been asking, but perhaps it was all he wanted to know. "Did he hurt Diana?" he asked sitting up on what he realized was the couch in the front room.

"No, she's fine." Nick's voice turned away then. "Is that you, Diana? We're still in here. Did you find Andrew?"

"He wouldn't answer." Diana sounded miserable as she talked her way to them. "I just hope he found his mother before it got as dark as this. I'd still be out there looking for him if I weren't afraid of being overheard."

"Why should you be?" Eustace demanded.

"Oh, Eustace, you're all right. Thank God for that anyway. You must have hit the couch when—" She went on quickly. "Just about anyone in town is liable to turn on any of us. I don't think they'll be able to pretend much longer that nothing is wrong. They're going to want scapegoats for what's happening, and that means unbelievers."

"Then we should get out of town. I've a flashlight upstairs, f it still works."

"That won't get us far, Eustace. What we need to do until t's light again is hide somewhere they won't think to look for us when they come hunting scapegoats."

"I'd like to have the flashlight, all the same." Eustace taggered to his feet, and was glad when Nick supported him. 'I'll be all right," he said after a while. "No point in us ripping up one another all over the house."

He climbed the stairs, a hand on each banister. The flashlight he kept in the bedside drawer didn't work. It had been failing when he'd had to make his rounds in a bad fog several months ago, and he could tell the batteries had leaked. Was he hearing distant laughter? He made quickly for the stairs, his skin crawling. All the way down he felt as if he were back on the sloping aisle in his dream.

"We're here, Eustace, waiting for you in the hall." Diana put her arm round both men and whispered, "I think we need to say as little as possible now and keep our voices down, okay? I don't know how much you know about what's happening, Eustace, but I guess you realize this is what Mann stirred up. As soon as it's light, we have to try and get to the missile base before it does."

"My God, you think—"

She put a hand over his mouth. "I know."

He didn't think he would be able to keep quiet for long. Talking seemed the only way to fend off the strength of the dark, the thoughts of what might be closing in unseen. There's nowhere to hide but Harry Moony hears where," he whispered, his voice catching in his throat.

"But it could be too busy elsewhere to notice us. If we don't get away nobody will. There's one place we might be safe," she said, and put her lips against his ear, then Nick's, and stopped their mouths. "The church," she whispered.

The glow from the hotel, where a crowd was murmuring, whitened the rooftops and left the street dark. As Eustace's eyes adjusted, he saw a man's body lying twisted on the garden path. The smashed head looked too large, not only because of the stain in which it lay face down. As he turned away choking, Diana murmured, "It's Brian Bevan. We can't do anything for him." All the same, she stooped to take hold

of the shoulders of the corpse, and when she glanced at
Eustace for agreement the men helped carry the corpse into
the house, to the couch. Eustace swallowed and swallowed
and tried to hold his breath until they were outside.

The lane was deserted, and so was the High Street. The
townsfolk must be clustering around the light again, but this
time they weren't giving thanks; he didn't care to wonder
what they might decide to do instead. He and Nick and Diana
tiptoed quickly along the High Street, away from the hotel,
until the road curved, leaving them in total darkness.

"It's all right," Eustace whispered. "This is what I'm here
for." But it wasn't the same in the dark: he'd forgotten how
uneven some of the paving stones were, how the curbstones
at the corners of side streets weren't quite aligned with each
other. He was leading his companions in single file, Diana's
hands about his waist as if in a blind ritual dance. His senses
grew neurotically acute; he thought he smelled stale blood as
he passed the butcher's. Once his hand, groping along the
wall, plunged into an open doorway between shops, and he
was terrified that something would touch his fingers in the
dark. After that, every door felt like the entrance to a lair.

By the time they reached the churchyard gate, he was past
feeling relieved. When he and his companions kept to the
grass so as to avoid the gravel path, the mounds on which he
had to tread felt as yielding as the aisle in his nightmare. At
last he found the heavy ring on the church door. They groped
their way into the church, away from the doors, until they
were nearly at the altar. They sat on a pew, Eustace next to
Diana, not quite touching her. That was how the night began.

59

Andrew didn't know how long he'd been at the hotel when his mother found him crouching in the darkest corner of the lobby, near the stairs. Parents of his schoolmates had kept asking him if he was all right, but he'd only wanted to hide unnoticed in the dark. He would have sneaked upstairs to hide on the next floor if the stairs hadn't been so busy with people going up to see Mr. Mann. He wanted to find somewhere nobody would find him—he didn't deserve to be with people after what he'd made happen to his father. When someone brought his mother over to him, he crouched down inside himself, because she would know something was wrong if anyone did. Most of all he was terrified that she would make him tell.

She ran to him, dragged him to his feet and shook him. "What do you mean by scaring me half to death? I was nearly going for the police until I thought of looking here. Where's your father?"

"He went to help someone," Andrew mumbled, struggling to huddle back into the corner, hide his face against the wall.

"Went where? Who does he think he is, leaving you here without telling me?"

Andrew's mind shrank back from her questions and made up one that he could answer: where was his father now? "I don't know," he whispered.

"The way he's been carrying on it's a wonder you know you've a father at all. What sort of a man is he who'd abandon you in all this dark?" She was talking for the benefit of the other parents, who nodded sympathetically, clucked their tongues. "And who's he gone off to help, I'd like to know."

Miss Kramer, Andrew wanted to scream at her. At least

the teacher wasn't alone at Mr. Gift's house, but what might his father have done to them all? He would have brought Miss Kramer to the hotel if Andrew hadn't made him turn into a monster. He'd done that by letting himself suspect his father, by not trusting him enough. Mr. Mann said you had to respect your parents, he said you must have faith, but Andrew had thought these weren't really bad sins, not if you couldn't help yourself. Now he saw how bad they were. He'd let himself doubt his father, and the demon from the cave had turned his father into something like the ones that lived down there. The first time his father had needed him, Andrew had failed him.

He'd run away from that as much as from the sight of his father. He couldn't remember what his father had looked like; the memory was a horrible dark place in his mind that he had to keep avoiding. He ought to have run out of Moonwell, because then nobody would have found him. He deserved to be caught by whatever was out there in the dark.

No, there was a reason why he'd run into the hotel. He might remember what it was if his mother stopped staring at him. At last she turned away and peered about the lobby at the crowd outlined by the glow that leaked into the hotel from overhead. "Just wait until he shows his face," she muttered. "I'll wipe the smile off it. I'll get to the bottom of his tricks once and for all."

Andrew hardly heard her, for he'd remembered: he had to see Mr. Mann. He could confess to him as he couldn't to anyone else, and once he'd confessed he would be able to ask for Mr. Mann's help. The evangelist could help his father if anyone could. But his mother would want to know where Andrew was going and why, and the thought of trying to explain made his throat clench, made him want to flee into the dark.

When she turned back to him, he made himself smaller, digging his elbows into his sides, squatting as if his bowels had got the better of him, which they almost had during his flight to the hotel. "Stand up straight, you've made enough of a show of me already," she muttered. "Just you stay here and don't you dare move. I'm going to see if your father is in the hotel. If he is I'll be having a few words with him in private."

The idea of his father mingling with the crowd made Andrew crouch down farther, terrified of so many possibilities that he wanted to wrap his arms round his head and crush his thoughts. But if his father was in the hotel, wouldn't that keep him from changing now that Mr. Mann had made it into a holy place? As soon as his mother disappeared into the crowd, Andrew managed to stand up and dodge toward the stairs.

A man with a Sacred Heart stitched on his shirt pocket stepped in front of him. "Where are you going, Sunshine?"

"Want to see Mr. Mann," Andrew whispered.

"Not just now. He's calling people up by name," the man said, pointing to the reception desk. One of Mr. Mann's ladies was listening to the switchboard and sending a helper to find whoever was called for. Andrew watched a young man climb the stairs proudly, a smile fixed on his face. He'd seen nobody come down, Andrew realized; dozens of people must be up there—soon there would be no room for him. "Don't worry, son, he hasn't forgotten about you or any of us. We'll have a prayer soon, I expect," the man with the heart said.

Andrew didn't find the prospect at all consoling, and that made him feel worse than ever: he'd sinned so badly that even prayers couldn't help him. He went back to his corner and crouched over the hardening lump of guilt and fear in his belly. He was biting his lip and rubbing his stomach when his mother came back.

"Either he's not here or he's afraid to show himself. He'll have to come sooner or later, pretending nothing's wrong, I shouldn't wonder. He'll find out this is one place you can't keep secrets," she said to herself with a bitter smile, and peered at Andrew. "For heaven's sake, child, what's wrong with you now? Haven't we all got enough to worry us without you looking like that?"

Then she sat down on her heels and took hold of him. "Don't mind me, Andrew, I didn't mean to shout. Is your tummy sore, you poor mite? Are you hungry? No wonder, with all the peculiar things you've been having to eat at home. It's far too long since you had anything to eat at all." She coaxed him to his feet. "There, there, we'll find you something. This is supposed to be a hotel."

The manager wasn't at the desk or in his office, unless he was sitting in there in total darkness. She pushed Andrew onward, gripping his shoulders tighter as she grew angrier. The ache in his belly dulled and spread through his body. If he closed his eyes it was almost like hiding; he could pretend he was somewhere else, where the sun was in the sky. He couldn't even feel his feet stumbling. If only she would let him sit down, he could stay in the sunlight for a while.

A sudden hush brought her to a stop. The lady at the switchboard was holding up a hand for silence. "Listen," she said again. "Listen to the message Godwin has for us. He says there's food in the kitchen for everyone here."

There was silence, broken by the whimpering of children, while people caught up with the idea, and then the crowd cheered, so loudly that Andrew covered his ears. He took his hands away as a man struggled to the counter and turned to the crowd, waving his arms. "Ladies and gentlemen, I'm sorry to have to disappoint you. I'm the manager, and I'm afraid there's almost no food left in the hotel."

"Hadn't you better look before you say that?" Andrew's mother said in a high, sharp voice. "There are children here who haven't eaten since I don't know when."

"I know there are, madam, and I wish there were more I could do. But I assure you I know my own hotel."

"It isn't just a hotel. It's God's house now, more than anywhere else in the town. Don't be so sure you know what's possible. If you don't look in the kitchen, we will."

"Have faith," someone shouted as the manager strode to the doors of the dining room. He flung them open and turned, arms folded, to the crowd. Andrew felt everyone grow tense, ready to rush him. "You may as well come and see for yourselves," the manager said wearily.

The crowd surged into the dining room. Andrew felt the floorboards shaking underfoot as he was borne forward. Don't let the floor give way, he prayed. The manager ought to tell them there were too many people in here, but he must know they wouldn't obey him. Andrew could only stumble toward the doors to the kitchen so as not to be tripped up.

The kitchen was deserted. Metal ranges glimmered in the faint glow that seeped in from the square; pans and knives hung in ranks in the dimness. The manager strode up and down between the ranges. "I'm sorry," he said, though his gesture at the empty kitchen seemed almost triumphant. "As you can see, there's nothing."

"Hadn't you better look in the freezer?" Andrew's mother said.

"If you insist, madam, though you realize the freezer isn't working." He stalked down the kitchen to the milky glimmer of the double doors and pulled the heavy lever that unlocked them. He stepped back as they swung open, and then he stood there, hands sinking. "Good God," he whispered.

The crowd lurched forward, and Andrew saw what the manager had seen. Beyond the metal doors, melting ice drooled down the walls; to Andrew it looked as if the metal walls were squirming. Faint light reflected from the ice outlined what was hanging in the freezer. There was a headless, limbless carcass on every hook.

The manager stepped in, his feet sloshing in melted ice, and peered closely at the nearest piece of pale meat, sniffed at it, squeezed it gingerly. "I don't know where this came from or what it is," he said. "I certainly can't be sure it's fit to eat."

"Let me take a look, sir." A broad-shouldered man pushed forward, and Andrew heard a murmur that he was the hotel chef. He examined the meat carefully, then he turned to the crowd. "I think it's all right. If Godwin says so, I'm sure it is. I'm willing to try it, at any rate."

"I want it to be clearly understood," the manager said loudly, "that I take no responsibility for this meat. I can't vouch for it, I'm sorry."

"You don't need to. Godwin's word is all we need," Mrs. Scragg shouted.

More of the cooks pushed their way through the crowd to the freezer. One tried the ranges, and looked surprised when they lit, with a pale flame that reminded Andrew of the light from Mr. Mann's window. "Could you please all go back to the lobby," the head chef called out. "We'll let you know when it's ready."

"Back to the lobby," the manager repeated. "The public shouldn't be in here at all." As the crowd trooped cheerfully after him, Andrew saw people licking their lips.

In the lobby Mrs. Scragg started a prayer. "We thank Thee, O Lord, for giving Your servant the power to perform this miracle . . ." Andrew knelt and bowed his head and said amen when everyone else did, but he felt guilty for being about to be fed when his father was out there alone in the dark.

Mrs. Scragg kept them praying and singing hymns while

the smell of cooking drifted out of the kitchen. It made the congregation sing louder, but Andrew was beginning to feel sick; the thought of the limbless shapes hanging on the hooks didn't tempt him, nor did the smell of cooking that wasn't quite like any meat he knew. Were the young people who'd been called up to Mr. Mann coming down to eat, or had they got theirs upstairs? He was praying fiercely for his father when a waitress announced the first sitting for dinner.

This was for the old folk, and for children and their parents. An old man with a drooping eyelid sat opposite Andrew and eyed the boy's plate greedily when Andrew only toyed with the slices of meat, steaming in the dimness. "Eat up, Andrew, and then you'll feel better," his mother urged, and tasted a forkful before spiking another for him. "It must be pork, it tastes like it. Don't start getting finicky over your food."

Andrew tried the mouthful and only just managed to swallow. He tried not to watch the old man, who was chewing open-mouthed as if to demonstrate how his false teeth worked; it looked like the smile Mr. Mann gave everyone gone wrong. When his mother went to get a plateful a waitress was offering, Andrew transferred his helping to the old man's plate and was rewarded with a secretive wink.

As soon as his mother finished eating, Andrew fled back to the lobby. He ought to have dodged out before, he thought, while she was busy eating and nobody was going up to Mr. Mann. How could he sneak upstairs? People came out of the dining room patting their stomachs, and the second sitting took their place. Mrs. Scragg marched out of the hotel bearing a covered plate. Andrew closed his eyes to be in the sunlight inside his head, but he felt as if he'd scarcely closed them when Mrs. Scragg came back, screeching. "There's evil on the loose out there. Our police inspector's dead, torn to bits."

In the stunned silence, people looked fearfully at each other, huddled toward the stairs and Mr. Mann. Then Andrew's mother spoke up, her voice not quite steady but growing stronger. "If there's still evil in this town, it's because there are still a few people who are against Godwin. And I know where some of them are."

seemed to Geraldine that she had been sitting by the child's
bed for days, not for hours, stroking his high forehead that
was so like Jeremy's and holding his hand since the light had
begun to fail. His hand was warm now, relaxed. If he was
asleep, she could tiptoe away to find out what Jeremy was
doing.

When the child had called them mummy and daddy,
Jeremy's face had gone blank. He'd pulled away as Geraldine
had tried to coax him to the bedside, and retreated to the hall
outside the room. She had been trying to persuade him to
stay by the bed while she went down to the kitchen when the
child had begun to call out. "Mummy, Daddy, are you there?
Please don't go away again." If Jeremy had walked away
from that, she would have wanted him to walk out of her life;
never mind who the child was, she didn't want to know
anyone who could resist that plea. But as soon as Jeremy had
heard her coming upstairs with the tray of meager food, he'd
stumbled out of the bedroom, not looking at her. A few
moments later she'd heard the door into the bookshop slam.
Presumably he was still down there, sitting in the dark
among the empty shelves. Was it just the presence of a child
in the house he couldn't cope with, having to share Geraldine
after it had been just the two of them for so long, or was it the
thought of who the child might be? Either by itself would be
enough for him to deal with, and she oughtn't to leave him to
try to adjust to them by himself. She let go of the small warm
hand. "Are you asleep?" she whispered, hoping.

The hand found hers at once. "I'm awake, Mummy. I was
just being happy. Weren't you?"

"Of course I am." But Jeremy isn't, she thought, biting her
lip. "Are you warm enough? Would you like another drink?"

"I don't want anything except to be here," the boy sa[id]
with a tremor in his voice.

"You will be as long as we are, I promise. Now would yo[u]
like to come downstairs with me, or will you wait here just [a]
few minutes?"

His other hand grabbed hers. "I don't want to get up whi[le]
it's dark. I feel safe here."

"All right, just stay here while I go and find your—" Sh[e]
couldn't quite say it, couldn't call Jeremy his father. She too[k]
a breath, and then she blurted, "What shall I call you?"

The child giggled as if she were teasing him. "You kno[w,]
Mummy."

"I just want to hear you say it," Geraldine said wi[th]
difficulty. "It might make me even happier."

"The name you and Daddy gave me. Jonathan."

Geraldine put an arm around his shoulders and hugg[ed]
him until she was able to speak. "Let me just get yo[ur]
daddy," she whispered. "I want him to hear you say that.["]

The child clung to her. "You won't let him send me awa[y,]
will you?"

"Jo—" She couldn't quite pronounce his name; it was to[o]
sudden—she felt as if her reaction hadn't yet caught up wi[th]
her. "Why should he want to do that?" she said as lightly [as]
she could.

"I feel as if he doesn't want me here, Mummy."

"He's getting used to it, that's all. He wouldn't really se[nd]
you away. Did you talk to him while I was getting yo[ur]
food?"

"He didn't want me to. He didn't even want to look [at]
me."

"Well, he was just being silly. People are like that som[e-]
times, even daddies. Let me go and talk to him and s[ee]
what's up."

The child reluctantly let go of her and sank back on t[he]
bed. She was at the door when his plea came out of the blin[d]
dark. "I really can stay, can I, Mummy? It was horrib[le]
where I was all that time before you found me. Cold and da[rk]
with things in it. I'd have to go back there if you didn't wa[nt]
me to stay."

"I promise. Let me find your daddy and he'll tell you so [as]
well." For a moment she was afraid to step out of the roo[m]

oth because he'd invoked the terror of the dark, the thing at had blocked the road through the woods, and because e feared he might be gone when she returned. She had to ring Jeremy back from wherever his brooding had taken m, she told herself, groping for the banister.

She picked her way downstairs and through the kitchen to the bookshop. The long bare room wasn't entirely dark; me light reached from the center of town, where, Geralne assumed, the hotel was running floodlights. As she epped into the room, a dark blotch against the wall oposite the lightest window leaped up, rattling a shelf. It as Jeremy. "Who's there?" he cried.

"Now who do you think it could be, Jerry?"

"I don't know," he said morosely. "Maybe I don't know aything."

"Then it doesn't make sense to stay out here by yourself, es it? What were you doing sitting in the dark?"

"Waiting for it to go away."

She wasn't sure if he meant the dark. "Jerry, we've got to lk."

"Yes, let me talk. I've been thinking long enough." He me over to her, his footsteps echoing among the shelves. That must be a young boy upstairs if you say so, whatever I ought I was seeing. But what in the name of anything that's oly are we doing kidnapping him?"

"We didn't, Jerry. He wanted to come."

"Try telling that to anyone out there. Don't you think ey've already got enough to hold against us? We can't ford to draw their attention. For Christ's sake, don't you now who that kid must be?"

"Yes," she said, trying to quiet his nervousness. "But I ant him to tell you himself."

"Tell me what?"

She sensed that he wouldn't come with her unless she aswered him. "Jerry, he's called Jonathan."

"Oh, shit." His shoulders sagged. "Look, I know what you ean, but it's just coincidence. It's fine if you want to believe nathan's alive somewhere, only don't try to tell me he's ostairs. That's a real child up there, not a fucking ghost, and ere's only one place a real child could have come from. e's one of the lot who came with Godwin Mann."

"What was he doing lying naked in the graveyard where v
wanted Jonathan to be?"

"How should I know? What does it matter? You're belie
ing what you want to believe. I thought we weren't like tl
rest of Moonwell." He went on, more gently: "Maybe he ra
away from his parents because he couldn't take all th
repressive religious shit, maybe running off naked was h
way of rebelling. I certainly wouldn't blame him. You kno
I'd help him if I could."

Geraldine felt cold and empty. "So what are you sugges
ing we should do instead?"

"We've no choice. We have to find out where he can
from and send him back, and get him to promise he won't s
he was with us."

"I don't think I want to know you any more, Jeremy."

"If that's how you feel, there's not much I can do about
But as long as we're being so honest with each other, I'
beginning to wonder if I ever really knew you at all."

Geraldine would have turned away if she hadn't still fe
guilty about leaving him alone in the dark. Surely they cou
take back what they'd said, she thought, but that wouldr
change his feelings about Jonathan. Perhaps if she cou
persuade him to listen to whatever the child had to say—ar
then the child cried, "Mummy, what's that noise?"

She was as panicky as he sounded until she realized wh
he was hearing. "Just someone singing, Jonathan. Singi
hymns."

"And you can tell he doesn't like it much," Jeren
muttered as if that proved his point.

"Why should he when we don't?" She was wonderi
whether Jonathan had shared the last eight years of their li
from wherever he was. Might he be able to prove to Jeren
who he was that way? Jeremy had turned away from he
toward the hymn. The singing was closer than she'd thoug
—it was progressing through Moonwell. She didn't reali
how close it was until someone pounded on the front doo

They heard June Bevan's voice, shrill and harsh, as t
hymn petered out. "Open up, we know you're in there. '
want a word with you."

"Well, Jeremy?" Geraldine said, almost calmly.

He straightened up and flexed his shoulders and stro

oward the door. That hadn't been what she'd had in mind.

"Say whatever you have to say, June," he called. "We can ʜear you."

"I'm not talking to a door. You just open it and look me in ʜe face."

Before Geraldine could stop him, Jeremy slammed back ʜe bolts on the door. He must be welcoming the confrontaᴛion after so much brooding in the dark, but in his eagerness ʜe seemed to have forgotten the need for concealment. She ʟosed the door that led to their living quarters and went ʠuickly across the echoing bare room to stand by him.

The Scraggs were out there with June, and several of the ɴen who'd carried out the books for burning. Two of them ʜad flashlights, which they turned on the Booths. "Well," ℳrs. Scragg demanded as the whitish beams poked at their ℉aces, "what do you mean by staying in our town?"

Jeremy laughed as if her effrontery delighted him. "We ʟon't have to mean a damn thing by living on our own ⵔroperty. If we're supposed to ask your permission, it's news ᴏ me."

"Maybe we didn't make it clear that you aren't welcome," ℶ man growled.

Jeremy stepped forward, blocking the doorway. "Want to ⵔreak another window while we're watching? I think you'd ⵔetter decide you've done enough, friend. The police might ᴛhink less of your methods than you do."

This was getting them nowhere, Geraldine thought nervᴏusly. "We don't want to stay here any more than you want ⵔs," she interrupted. "We mean to head out as soon as it's ⵏght enough. Nobody's driving while it's like this."

What did she have to do to get rid of the unwelcome party? ᴛheir faces had turned unreadable when Jeremy had menᴛioned the police. She was about to ask June, who was ⵑvoiding her eyes, if she really wanted trouble when a faint ⵏry struck her speechless. "Mummy, where are you? Is ᴏmeone there?"

"What's that?" Mrs. Scragg demanded. "Jesus, Mary and ᴊoseph, have you got a child in there?"

"Now what would we be doing with a child?" Jeremy said ⵡith an unconvincing laugh.

"I wouldn't like to imagine," June said.

Jeremy was reaching for the doorknob. Not too fast, Geraldine willed him, just let them think we've had enough of them and you're closing the door because it's still our house. . . . Then she flinched inwardly at the cry upstairs. "I'm frightened," the child's voice pleaded.

"Mother of God, there *is* a child," Mrs. Scragg almost screamed. She grabbed a flashlight and lurched through the doorway as two men shoved Jeremy aside and grabbed his arms. Geraldine backed away. All she could do now was protect Jonathan, be with him when the strangers forced their way into his room. As Jeremy's captors marched him after Mrs. Scragg, she groped her way into the farther rooms.

The intruders pursued her through the kitchen, and she heard plates smash. The sound filled her with a dull rage she had no time to deal with. As she climbed the first stairs, the flashlight beams pushed past her, reached the top before she did. She ran up to Jonathan's room, her heart pounding ever faster with the thought of the panic he must be experiencing at the commotion downstairs, the thunder of footsteps.

"It's all right, Jonathan, Mummy's here now," she said into the dark of the room, and then was shoved aside as Mrs. Scragg stalked in, probing the room with the flashlight. The beam wavered up the bed and found the small shape cowering against the headboard: Jonathan.

"You're safe now, son," Mrs. Scragg said with a roughness that presumably was meant to be reassuring. "Nobody's going to harm you any more. Who are you? How did they get you in here?"

Jonathan pressed his shoulders into the angle of the headboard and the wall as she advanced on him. "I'm Jonathan," he said in a small, unsure voice. "Jonathan Booth. I live here with my mummy and daddy."

"None of that now. Never mind what they told you to say, you just tell the truth like God wants you to. We know they've got no child of their own."

Jonathan's face crumpled. Geraldine tried to go to him but Mrs. Scragg flung her away from the bed, against the last of the men, who pinned her arms behind her back. "Don't worry, Jonathan," she said, managing to keep her voice steady. "They've made a mistake, that's all. They won't harm us. Even they wouldn't harm you."

"Shut your lying mouth or we'll shut it for you," Mrs. Scragg snarled, then sweetened her voice as she turned to Jonathan. "Just you tell the truth now. Never be afraid to tell the truth."

"You're frightening him," Geraldine said quietly, though surely his face was wavering so much only because the flashlight beam was swaying. "He's already told you the truth."

"He's frightened all right, but whose fault is that?" June cried, and slipped past Mrs. Scragg. "Let me have a look at you, poor mite. No need to be nervous of me, I've got a son of my own. You can come and meet him if you like. He's with his teacher at the hotel." When he flinched back, she turned angrily to her companions. "God knows what they've been doing to him. Something out of their filthy books, God help the poor thing."

"We've done nothing to him. If you want to hear what really happened," Jeremy said, and glared at his captors as they gripped his arms more tightly, "maybe you can let me speak."

"Jeremy," Geraldine pleaded, watching Jonathan's face draw in on itself: the child was even more afraid of what Jeremy might say than she was. He reached out one pale hand toward his father as if that might hush him, but Jeremy didn't notice. "If you're going to come clean," Mrs. Scragg said ominously, "we're listening."

"That isn't our son," Jeremy said. "We never had a child."

"No, Jeremy," Geraldine cried, and the child pressed against the wall like a trapped animal, his long hands clutching at the blankets. "That boy came looking for shelter and we let him in," Jeremy said quickly. "He said his name was Jonathan, which is what we were going to call the child we lost. We've looked after him for a few hours, but he isn't our child, even if he wants to think he is."

"Well, that seems honest enough," Mr. Scragg said, speaking for the first time, and stepped toward the bed. "Now perhaps you'll speak up for yourself," he said rather sharply to the child. But he choked on the last word, and held up his hands as if to push away from him what he was seeing.

For as long as she was able to believe it, Geraldine told herself desperately that the batteries in the flashlights were

311

failing. But it wasn't the light that was growing fainter, it was Jonathan's face. The features were fading, sinking into the head. In the shuddering glow, which Mrs. Scragg was struggling to turn away from the sight, the head made Geraldine think of a pale balloon that was deflating—think of anything that might blur the reality of what she was seeing. The eyes went last, glaring in panic, the sockets wrinkling like withered lips as they closed up. Then the face was blank except for the mouth, which might have been grinning or crying out silently. The crouching figure turned its head back and forth blindly, then it shoved itself forward with its elongated arms and leaped between Geraldine and Mrs. Scragg. It ran on all fours into the dark, down the stairs, out of the open door.

As its scuttling faded into the darkness, Geraldine felt as if it were taking her soul with it, leaving her empty and worthless and betrayed. Nothing could touch her now or make her situation worse. She hardly noticed Mrs. Scragg, who flew at her and spat in her face.

"So you're in league with the devil, are you," Mrs. Scragg said in a voice heavy with loathing. "Benedict Eddings saw you at your witchcraft in the graveyard, and still none of us realized what you were up to. We'll see if Godwin knows what to do with you," she said, and thrust her large face into Geraldine's. "And if he doesn't, there's a few of us who still remember how to deal with witches."

===== 61 =====

As soon as Diana felt herself drifting, she began to chew the inside of her cheek. It was raw by now; it stung like fire, but she didn't know how else to stay awake. She mustn't sleep, in case she did so noisily. She couldn't risk a recurrence of her vision, despite her impression that somewhere in it lay the key to what she had to do. Surely the dark would lift

312

soon—she felt as stiff as though she'd been sitting on the pew
in the lightless church for days. Once there was even a hint of
light in the sky, they would head for her car.

And then what? Did she really expect to be able to drive to
the missile base without being headed off? Even if she got
there, how did she propose to enter? What could she tell
them at the base that they would even stand still for? At least
her doubts were keeping her awake. Whatever was sent to
stop her, she told herself, she could run it down with the car.
Brian Bevan, or rather what Brian had become, had proved
to be capable of dying, after all. And the thing from the cave
must have fed on his death, on every soul who died within its
influence, however far that reached.

She drew back from the memory of Brian's face disfigured
by the grin, the eyes reaching out for her. There were ways to
keep awake that didn't make the darkness seem quite so
threatening. She hugged Nick and Eustace lightly. At least
while they were asleep, they wouldn't be tempted to talk.
Nick stirred, and she patted his side to quiet him. Eustace
gave a snore that was cut off at once as he jerked upright
from lolling. Ought they to have agreed beforehand to take
turns at staying awake? But they had no means of judging the
passage of time while it was dark, and in any case she was
afraid that sleep might lead her back into her vision. She
couldn't help fearing that her vision might make the moon
thing aware of her, and then she wondered if it already had.

Apprehension tingled through her like electricity. That was
good, she told herself—anything was that helped her not to
sleep. She tried to regain her awareness of the church around
her, beyond the muffling dark. The almost imperceptibly
faint lines to her right must be the edges of two of the
windows, touched by the glow from the square. They gave
her some sense of the dimensions of the church. The sensations of the place came back to her—the chill of the stone,
the creaking of pews, the smells of earth and mold, the way
the dark not far ahead of her was walled off, the impression
of the altar as a bulk between her and that wall. She was so
intent on grasping these details as aids to wakefulness that at
first she didn't wonder why any pew except that on which the
three of them were sitting should creak.

She turned her head unwillingly and gazed down the

church. It was darker still back there, not even the edge of a window. Perhaps it wasn't a pew, just a floorboard creaking as boards will. As for the moldering smell, that must be the smell of earth seeping in, no matter that it seemed stronger. She stared at the dark until it seemed to lurch at her, but there was no further sound. She turned away then, and Eustace stirred, mumbling.

She kneaded his shoulders to calm him. She didn't know how seriously he and Nick took the need for total silence. She could hardly blame them if they were less convinced than she even after all they'd been through; she couldn't blame them if the dark made them want to do something, anything, rather than wait interminably. Eustace was settling down again, and she suppressed a sigh of relief.

Now that she was fully awake, her fears were waking up too. The church seemed colder and more spacious, the silence somehow growing vaster, more like the silence of a cave than of a church. She hoped the increasing chill wouldn't rouse Nick or Eustace. Or was the chill coming from them rather than from the church? Their body temperatures were dropping because they were asleep, that was what she meant, not that they felt cold as reptiles, cold as things which had looked like Nick and Eustace in the glow from the square but which were reverting to their true nature in the dark. If the moon thing had been able to change Brian Bevan into something utterly inhuman, could it do the opposite? She mustn't imagine that, mustn't let the dark get into her head. All the same, she had to struggle with an urge to wake them, just enough to hear them speak. When Eustace began to mutter, the sound of his voice was so welcome that she didn't try immediately to quiet him.

Only it wasn't quite his voice. It was a voice he might have put on for one of his comedy routines, but odder. It was arguing with another voice, until Eustace's intervened, saying that they must be joking. She made to shake him gently and then she realized she must be hearing what she wanted to hear. Loud as the voices were, they didn't echo in the church.

They seemed so real that they made her draw into herself. She could almost see Eustace on a stage between two vague capering shapes, Eustace playing straight man and using everything he knew to keep up the patter, keep the act going

314

so that he wouldn't have to leave the stage and go with his fellow performers into the wings, to whatever might be waiting in the dark. You're in the church, she thought as hard as she could, massaging the back of his neck, scarcely knowing why. At last the shouting faded, and she hoped he'd sunk into dreamless sleep.

There were still voices—distant voices, singing hymns and chanting. She'd heard them earlier, ranging about the far side of Moonwell, drifting in and out of audibility. At least they made the silence less complete, especially now that they were coming closer. When she began to distinguish the chanting, she tried to hope she was being paranoid. The searchers were nearly at the church before their shouts became unmistakable.

"Eustace Gift," they were calling. "Diana Kramer." They didn't know where to look, Diana told herself fiercely, and surely that meant the moon thing didn't either. "And your friend, whatever his name is," someone else shouted. "Come out if you know what's good for you. We found Brian Bevan where you hid him."

They'd never think of looking in the church, Diana told herself. She tried to hush the two men as they moved restlessly. Stay quiet now, she thought at them, they won't come in here, they're on the pavement, they'll pass the church by. Then light spilled through the windows and found her and her companions.

The flashlight beams swayed over the wall to her left, dragging distorted shapes of windows over the rough stone, and then bobbed away along the church, wakening more thin shapes in the stained glass, turning their bunches of three heads. The searchers weren't approaching, for she hadn't heard the gate. They'd given the church a token look, and now they were heading back toward the square, singing to keep off the dark. They hadn't even wakened Nick or Eustace. A last beam of whitish light groped through the church as whoever was wielding it surveyed the churchyard, and as the light found the far end of the aisle, Diana heard wood creak.

She craned her head round, her neck trembling and aching with the effort of keeping her body still. Surely nothing had moved near the porch, surely it was just another of the noises

315

an old building makes. But as the flashlight beam angled through the last window, a dark shape rose to its feet beyond the pews.

Diana's head jerked, wrenching her neck. She forced herself to keep watching as the shape lurched forward, one hand grabbing the last pew. She saw the black cloth of the sleeve, the gleam of the collar, and dreamy relief spread through her. Who had more right than a priest to be in the church? Then she remembered that there had been only one priest in Moonwell, and as she strained her eyes, she saw that there was nothing above the stained, glimmering celluloid collar but an outrageous absence. The roving flashlight beam swung away, abandoning her in the dark.

Diana held her breath until the pounding of blood in her throat seemed about to choke her. She felt as though the dark were pressed against her head, forcing it over her shoulder. She managed to take shallow breaths, all she could bear now that she realized the moldering smell wasn't just the smell of earth. Her ears ached with the silence, with the hope that there would be nothing more to hear. Then the floorboards of the aisle began to creak slowly, closer and closer.

She made herself stay still, though her innards were trembling. She mustn't risk waking Nick and Eustace. Long before she would be able to warn them or even before they were awake enough to understand, the incomplete thing that was stumbling up the aisle might reach them. She didn't want to imagine their trying to grope their way out of its reach. Surely it wouldn't notice them if they kept absolutely still.

Or did it already know they were there? Had the moon thing sent it for them because they hadn't managed to hide after all? "'Tis tha friend come a-calling with nowt in his collar," Diana heard the blind man sing in the dark that was inside and outside her, and felt her body yearning to jump up, scream that here they were, get it over with. She mustn't panic, Father O'Connell had always been friendly with her, surely even what was left of him could mean her no harm. But in a way the idea of being shown any kind of benevolence by that thing was even worse.

The slow footsteps shuffled closer down the aisle, and then a pew creaked. The thing must be supporting itself by grabbing the ends of pews. Suppose a hand missed the end of their pew and touched Nick, or her hand on Nick's shoulder?

She pulled him against her as gently as she could, her skin crawling, her heart fluttering as he seemed about to waken. She put her hand lightly over his mouth just as the shuffling footsteps and the worst of the stench reached their pew.

Diana pressed her tongue against the roof of her mouth to keep out the smell, her head pounding. Perhaps the thing in the aisle wasn't really hesitating at their pew, but she felt as if it would never move on. Eventually it did. She heard it stumble to the altar, where it began to throw objects about; metal clinked and thumped the table. She wondered, with a sudden hysteria that threatened to make her burst into wild laughter, if it was trying to say mass. Not much chance without a head, she thought, and almost couldn't swallow the laughter on which she was choking.

She never knew how long she sat there, quieting Nick and Eustace whenever they stirred. When she began to see movement ahead of her, it was quite some time before she realized that it was anything more than an effect of the dark on her eyes. But yes, she could glimpse a vague shape stumbling back and forth along the glimmering rectangle that was the altar, and when she glanced aside, she could just see the thin crowded windows. The moon was rising.

Diana flexed her arms, which were in agony from hours of stretching, and then she put her hands over Nick's mouth and Eustace's before shaking their heads gently. "Keep your eyes shut," she murmured. "Just feel your way to the end of the pew and turn left." She was hoping they wouldn't see what was at the altar, hoping she wouldn't have to see it more clearly herself as the church grew lighter. But Nick woke suddenly, and snatched her hand away before she could stop him. "What's that?" he stammered, glaring toward the altar. "My God, where are we?"

"It won't harm us, Nick. We're going to my car now. Come on, Eustace." She gave Nick a shove toward the aisle, pulled Eustace after her as he awoke, blinking. Nick had just stepped heavily into the aisle when the remains of the priest swung round from the chaos it had made of the altar and lurched toward them.

What appalled Diana even more than the sight of it, its hands held out ready to seize whoever was there, its body stooping forward so that she could see the raw bony place where the head should have been, was how fast it moved now

317

that it was aware of them. Its lurch toward Nick had paralyzed him. She dragged him back into the pew as the blackened dead hands grabbed for him. Stepping backward, she collided with Eustace. "Side aisle," she hissed urgently over her shoulder.

The headless thing floundered toward them as they retreated along the pew. As they fell into the side aisle, Eustace almost tripping her up, what was left of Father O'Connell rushed at them along the pew, neck gaping. Nick dodged into the aisle and threw all his weight against the pew.

It was heavier than it looked. It teetered and then, just as the priest's hands with their overgrown clawlike nails lunged at him, it overbalanced, taking the priest's remains with it. As the dead thing flailed its limbs like a pinned insect, struggling to heave the weight off its back, the three of them flung two more pews on top of it, then fled toward the porch.

At first Diana didn't understand why it wasn't more of a relief to be out of the building. The streets were deserted as far as she could see, the cloudy sky was glowing. Then she realized she was afraid to see the naked face of the moon. They needed its light, but what power might it send after them? A whitish blur crept behind the clouds, seeking a way through. She had a nightmare impression of a vast grinning mask that was waiting to peer out at her with its dead eyes.

She and Nick and Eustace tiptoed as fast as they could through the side streets to her cottage. Up at the hotel she heard hymns and confused sounds, not all of them joyful. As she came in sight of her car, she became afraid that the searchers would have wrecked the engine, to trap her. When Nick and Eustace had clambered in, still speechless from the encounter at the church, the car started on her second turn of the key. She crept it through the streets and then, with a wordless prayer she couldn't even frame to herself, she sped the car onto the moor.

62

Andrew had been left at the hotel with Miss Ingham. Once his mother had gone off to look for whoever she blamed for the policeman being killed, he closed his eyes again and joined in the praying. Praying was easier than thinking; there were too many things he didn't want to think about. Those of his prayers that weren't for his father were about him, asking God not to let his parents meet out there in the dark while his father wasn't his father. The thanks for what they'd received through the miracle Mr. Mann had performed came to an end, but he stayed on his knees, swaying to keep himself balanced. "Are you asleep, Andrew?" Miss Ingham said, and he opened his eyes guiltily.

The crowded lobby was still dim. The glow that filtered into it seemed almost to be seeping out of the walls. Miss Ingham's looming face looked anxious, less so when he struggled to his feet and managed not to fall over. "Are you sure you're all right? You didn't have much to eat," she said. When he mumbled that he was, her smile filled out. "Play with your friends if you like."

His mother had told him to stay close to Miss Ingham. Besides, he didn't feel like playing, especially not when he looked at the other children, at their well-fed, glimmering faces. The dimness made them pale as the shapes he'd seen crawling up the devil's cave. Some of the older children who'd come to Moonwell were organizing games, round games where a prayer got longer as it went around the circle, Bible quizzes where you had to do a penance if you answered wrong. He felt sinful for not wanting to join in, but he was worried about too many things that made him feel more shrunken every time he thought about them. One of them got past his lips. "Who's my mummy gone to get, Miss Ingham? What'll happen to them?"

"I wouldn't like to say who it might be, Andrew. There will always be people who don't want to listen to what God has to tell us, and that means they'll hear the devil and do his talking for him." She patted his head and went on, "But as for doing anything to them, I expect they'll just be brought to Godwin."

Then they would be in the way when Andrew tried to sneak up to see him. Andrew had to get there first, while his mother wasn't here to stop him. "I think I'll play a bit now like you said," he told her, and she gave him a smile that made him feel even guiltier.

"Oh, it's Andrew," Robert said when he found a game near the stairs. "Happen this'll be too hard for you." But Andrew managed to keep the growing prayer straight in his head twice round the circle before he remembered that the longer he played, the less time he would have to reach Mr. Mann. "See, I told you," Robert said smugly when Andrew missed a phrase the third time round.

Andrew stumbled out of the circle, his face burning with self-consciousness and guilt and the fear of being noticed as he inched toward the stairs. He was sidling toward the stairs with his back to the wall as if he wasn't going anywhere really, and then he realized that was exactly how to get himself noticed. He swung round, the inside of his head turning faster than he was, and staggered forward, grabbing the end of the banister. Without warning, Miss Ingham was in his way. "Where are you going, Andrew? Your mother said you were to stay where I can see you."

Hopelessness spread through him, unstringing his limbs. "I'm tired. I want to rest," he whined.

An old woman sitting nearby in a chair and poring over a Bible while she pressed her spectacles against her eyes with one hand looked up, switching off her pencil flashlight. "If the boy wants to sleep, my bed's doing nothing. Shall I take him up? It's only on the first floor."

"I'll come with you so I can see where it is." The two women helped Andrew upstairs between them, and he realized he wouldn't have been able to climb by himself. The old woman trailed the miniature flashlight beam along the first-floor corridor, over the room numbers that gleamed like coal, and stopped at 109. When she opened the door, the room looked like a faint ghost of itself, filled with glimmering shapes that seemed about to fade into the blackness. Andrew wouldn't have cared if they did, he was all at once so exhausted. He hardly felt the old woman taking off his shoes as he crawled, eyes shut, toward the pillow. Someone kissed him lightly on the forehead, someone pulled the covers over him, and then he was asleep.

He was too exhausted to dream. When he opened his eyes, hours later, the room was brighter; the moon was up behind the clouds. He was alone in the room, perhaps on the whole floor. When he felt awake enough to push back the covers and venture into the corridor, all the voices he could hear were downstairs. He tiptoed to the stairs. Someone was sobbing wildly below him, and for a moment he was sure it was his mother. Could she have met his father out there in the dark? He mustn't go to her, not until he'd asked Mr. Mann to help them. He felt able to climb now that he'd slept. "Please," he said to anyone who might be listening, and began to climb toward the top floor of the hotel.

63

It was close to moonrise when Craig began to wonder why he felt so calm. Despite the cold—if it was still cold—he was no longer shivering. Even the dark seemed almost comforting: at least he didn't have to drive through it or find his way on foot; all it required of him was to sit on the gentle grassy slope beside the road and doze as if at the end of a picnic. Vera was nestling against him, her breaths a warm breeze against his neck. For the first time in as long as he could remember, neither of them had anything to do but sit: there was no point in even trying to plan ahead. It felt like the end, he thought dreamily, and if this was how it came, it wouldn't be so bad. Then he wondered if he was calm because he knew

they'd reached the end, knew that they would never leave the
dark.

Perhaps exposure would finish them off; perhaps it already
had. That might be why he no longer felt the cold—no
because he and Vera were keeping each other warm, but
because the sensations of his body were deserting him. Hi
growing sense of imminence was as close as he'd ever come to
a psychic intuition, and perhaps it was the only one he'd ever
needed. He wondered if everyone experienced it, at leas
everyone who was about to die a natural death.

There had been times when he'd thought he was dying
times when he'd wakened gasping in the middle of the night
when every painful beat of his racing heart had felt like the
last. He'd been afraid then—afraid because he wasn't ready
But he felt ready now. Suppose they tried to make their way
across the moor once the moon rose, what would happen
then? The last place on earth he would go was Moonwell, but
he didn't believe they had time to reach anywhere else. And
even supposing they found someone's house, say, what would
they have to look forward to? He would rather die peacefully
here with Vera than spend years turning back into an
incontinent, slobbering infant—God forbid that Vera or
anyone else should have to cope with him in that state. Better
to accept the comfortable dark.

He found he was hoping they wouldn't see moonrise
which would only make it harder for them to slip away. He
closed his eyes, perhaps to share Vera's slumber. If there was
anything beyond death, he thought it must be that your last
thoughts went on forever, or seemed to—you wouldn't know
if they came to an end because you wouldn't exist. He'd want
nothing more than this sense of peace and wordless closeness
to Vera. Then she raised her head. "Craig?" she murmured

"Yes, love," he said, willing her to go back to sleep while
they could.

"Did they get through safely, do you think?"

"Hazel and her husband?" He wondered if she'd forgotten
what Benedict had been following, the luminous bird, the
shape of Benedict's faith. "They seemed to know where they
were going."

"They had to make their choice, we couldn't make it for
them. They're young," she said as if that assured their

success. "And I don't think Benedict will find it quite so easy to have his own way in future."

He thought she was drifting back to sleep when she laid her head against his shoulder. Then she murmured, "I've been remembering."

"Have you, love?" he said, and realized that unless they shared memories now, perhaps they never would again. "What?"

"I was thinking about her first day at school. Remember how she marched through the gates and never looked back at us? And that night she told us she knew that if she looked back she wouldn't want to leave us, and she didn't want us upset."

"And that school speech day when she got the prize for being first in her class. Remember how solemn she was, saying it was all thanks to her teachers and us. And she gave us that look as if she was almost apologizing for having done so well in Religious Knowledge."

"Remember the day she brought a boyfriend home for the first time . . ."

"Yes." What had the young man's name been? He couldn't recall; perhaps the inessentials were slipping away more swiftly now. Craig had liked him—a pity she'd chosen Benedict instead. Maybe that first boyfriend had been too much like her father, which was certainly not true of Benedict; Craig hoped not, anyway. His thoughts were beginning to prod him out of his waiting calm, and he tried to sink again into the dark he was sharing with Vera. "And the first holiday we had by ourselves when she was old enough to go away with her friends," he said. "We couldn't get used to not having to say good night to her, could we? And after she got married, I kept nearly going into her room to speak to her for weeks."

"We never did go to Greece."

"No, we didn't," Craig agreed, wondering why she had suddenly grown tense. When he understood, he couldn't help opening his eyes in the dark that perhaps wasn't quite dark. He'd been trying to conceal his sense that they were near the end, for fear that it might distress her, and all the time she'd been keeping the same insight to herself—hiding it, he thought, in case the idea of losing her in nothingness dismayed him. Suddenly it did, and his eyes filled with tears. "I want to be wherever you are," he said, shocked by the aging of his voice.

"You will be. I'll make sure." She hugged him fiercely. "If there's a God, I can't believe he would separate us just because he never gave you the ability to believe in him. He couldn't be so cruel."

That might be comforting so long as he didn't examine it too closely, but he wished he hadn't opened his eyes. He couldn't recapture the warmth and peace he'd been sharing with her—he was wondering where their death would come from. Hours ago he'd told himself that nothing could happen to them if they sat still, and now he couldn't quite shake off a yearning for that certainty. The sky was beginning to pale: he could see the edge of the slope above them on the far side of the road. Soon the moonlight would come creeping down that slope. He'd wanted them just to merge softly with the dark, but it was too late for that. He wished he could close his eyes and Vera's, but he was too apprehensive now to be able to take advantage of that dark, for something pale and huge was stirring restlessly above the slope.

"Just clouds," he muttered as Vera snuggled close to him. They *were* clouds, he realized, but he didn't like the way they were shifting, almost as if the light behind them were thrusting them aside like fat, heavy curtains. It must simply be a gap in the clouds that were oozing over the slope, he told himself. Now there was a patch of clear sky above the edge, sky that flared whitely. Almost at once, far quicker than he would have liked, light spilled down the slope, fossilizing the heather, and then the forehead of an enormous skull rose over the edge.

"The moon," Craig said. Of course it was, however eagerly it seemed to be rising. It wasn't quite full, he saw. It only had one eye, which made the dead face look as if it were winking, a conspiratorial wink suggesting that it had a secret which it was about to share. The moonlight flooded down the slope toward a large rock across the road from Craig and Vera, and Craig strained his eyes to see the clouds that must be drifting across the moon, casting shadows that made the slope appear to tremble and shift alarmingly. But there were no clouds over the moon. The landscape seemed to heave like sheets on a bed from which the waking moon was rising.

324

Then the moon rose clear of the edge of the slope and leaned down at him out of the sky, grinning its crumbling grin.

Craig never knew if he recoiled or the slope beneath him moved and threw him backward, or both. He fell into the shadow that the rock on the far side of the road was casting. At first he didn't fully understand why Vera was hugging him as if nothing on earth would make her let go, and then he realized, with a shock that seemed almost to burst his heart out of his chest, that they were still falling. They couldn't be, he cried out mutely: there had been solid ground behind them in the dark. But now, in the moonlight, there was only emptiness.

He snatched wildly at the grassy edge, too late. The moonlit landscape vanished, and he and Vera fell into the dark. His nightmare had caught up with him at last, and taken her with him. The sense of nothingness beneath him flew into Craig's throat, choking him until he was actually afraid of suffocating before the impact from which his body, his whole self was shrinking. As they fell, clinging desperately to each other, their hearts beating so violently that he could no longer tell which was which, Craig willed Vera to be praying: praying that by the time they hit bottom, the two of them would be together somewhere else.

64

When the car almost left the road at a sharp bend, Diana made herself slow down. They were out of sight of Moonwell, beyond the first ridge, and surely that counted for something. She had to reach the missile base as quickly as she could, but she mustn't risk wrecking the car.

Her vision hadn't shown her exactly what would happen at the missile base. She'd seen the personnel stalking about in blind obedience, but she had to believe that the sight of their faces, the eyes turned into perfect miniatures of the moon that glowed in the sockets and shone through the surrounding flesh, was only a metaphor. Whatever happened would need the full moon, she told herself. The moon wasn't full yet, and that helped her fight off the compulsion to try to escape its one-eyed gaze. It was only the moon, she thought as hard as she could, only a moonlit night on the moor.

Of course it was worse than that, though at first she couldn't quite see how. As she drove up the next slope, her throat tightened with fear of what might lie beyond. The car faltered at the top, for she'd lifted her foot inadvertently from the gas pedal. But there seemed to be nothing to make her falter. The moor stretched around her, whitened slopes splintering into grass, shadows sketching the outlines of heather; dim trees were bunched like clumps of fog against the sky. Everything was motionless as ice, and perhaps that was the trouble: the dead light seemed to have drained the landscape of all life—she might almost have been driving across the moon. Except that she wouldn't have been able to breathe, she mocked herself, then found she couldn't breathe as easily as she would have liked, for she was too tense.

With an effortlessness that made her want to floor the pedal, the moon pursued her. Now that part of the sky was overcast, but that was no relief. A pale mass slithered behind the clouds, constantly changing shape, reaching out veinous tendrils of light wherever the clouds were thin. Whenever it reached a gap, it peered out at her, a giant, dead, incomplete face playing a game of hide-and-seek. Let it play; it wasn't really doing anything unnatural. But she couldn't help feeling that the longer she waited for whatever it or the moon thing might do to head her off, the worse it would be. Suddenly she'd had enough of brooding and silence. "Tell us a joke, Eustace," she blurted.

He glanced at her in the rear-view mirror. "I can't think of any good ones."

Nick turned in the passenger seat, which creaked metallically. "I'd settle for a bad one right now."

"Probably all I ever used to tell. I can't remember any now. I don't know where they've gone."

"I don't know what the worst joke I ever heard was," Nick said provocatively, "but it must have been in a Laurel and Hardy film."

"That's a bit harsh, isn't it? I don't think anyone else in films came close to what they achieved."

"Wouldn't touch it with a ten-foot pole, you mean. Laurel and Hardy are up before the judge for vagrancy and plead not guilty, right? 'On what grounds?' the judge says, and one of them says, 'We weren't on the ground, we were sleeping on a park bench.' And that was one of their *good* jokes."

"That would have been Laurel. Hardy wouldn't say that," Diana intervened. "I do think they knew more about how children behave than maybe anyone else in the movies . . ."

Keep talking, she willed them all, and managed not to raise her foot from the gas pedal as the car sped over the next ridge.

The sky was clearing, the moor was brightening, and the landscape was no longer entirely still. Perhaps these movements that she couldn't quite make out, movements she was always just too late to catch wherever she looked on the glowing slopes, were cast by the clouds, except that she could see their shadows plainly enough, fleeing across the moor. The car raced downhill, and she joined in the argument about Laurel and Hardy where she could, to keep off her undefined fears. Part of her mind found the spectacle of the three of them arguing about Laurel and Hardy as they drove across the dead land almost unbearably funny, but if she started laughing she might lose whatever control she had.

The road curved, and she was driving toward the moon. The last clouds drowned it, reduced it to a shapeless, sluggish pallor, crawling, growing clearer. The clouds inched back inexorably, and Diana could hardly breathe. The crumbling rim of the moon peeked around the clouds, which seemed to shrink away from it. Before she was able to brace herself, Diana was face to face with the moon.

It was dead, she told herself: dead as a hatched egg. Indeed, it resembled one, the incomplete side of the face gaping darkly. But it didn't seem quite dead enough, that one-eyed, lipless, grinning mask tilted coyly in the black sky. The thing that had given it life might be back in Moonwell, but the moon stood above the landscape like a symbol of its power, no longer simply a reflection of the sun. The colorless light spread unchecked over the moor, draining it of every hint of color, and she was almost able to see the movements

327

all around her on the slopes, a furtive swarming. She pressed the pedal as hard as she dared.

The argument was petering out, the men falling silent. She wasn't sure how much they could see of what she was seeing out there, nor did she want to ask. She wanted desperately to keep them talking, but she couldn't think of anything to say: it took all her concentration to drive along the twisting road, the blackly gleaming worm almost buried in the white landscape it squirmed through. She kept to the middle of the road, away from the ditch, the yawning dark which bordered the road and which looked far too deep now, capable of hiding far too much.

The road swung over a ridge and away from the moon, which paced the car, grinning lifelessly. Not having to confront it seemed to revive Eustace, who said "On the ground" as if he still found it funny, or wanted to.

Nick forced a laugh. "Laurel wrote that, didn't he? Wrote a lot of their gags, anyway. Took the music hall to Hollywood instead of letting it die a natural death."

"On the ground," Eustace muttered. "No, *in* the ground, Mr. Gloom. The deeper you go, the more jokes there are."

"What's that?" Nick demanded, then relaxed ostentatiously and squeezed Diana's shoulder. "Eustace is going to do one of his routines. You're sure of an appreciative audience here, Eustace."

Diana hoped he was right: she could do with some distraction from her surroundings to help her concentrate on the road, their only means of escape, if it was. She had just noticed that apart from the moon and the retreating tatters of cloud, the sky was utterly black—there were no stars above the moor. Somewhere out there was the sight of stars in a clear sky, she promised herself, and if they could reach that she was sure they had a chance. "Don't stop now, Eustace," she said.

"Down they go, Mr. Despondency. Feels like they'll never hit bottom. They'll be together all right, but they won't like what they're with. No such thing as a natural death under the moon of Moonwell."

Nick cleared his throat. "Bit close to the bone, Eustace."

"Aye, we're all close to the bone. It's part of us all, eh, Mr Gloom? He'll have it out in no time, Harry Moony will."

"Come on, Eustace." Nick glanced at Diana to see how the distorted voices were affecting her. She reached for his hand and gripped it hard, steered one-handed, glared at the road that wasn't really squirming, only meandering over the restless slopes. Surely the restlessness everywhere might just be the effect of breezes high up here on the moor. For some reason the stiff, almost inhuman voices from the back seat made her avoid looking in the rear-view mirror. "You're trying to cheer us up, take our mind off things," Nick reminded Eustace. "That's what comedy should do, at least here and now."

"Losing our audience, are we, Mr. Despondency?"

"Not a bit of it, Mr. Gloom. He's right here with us, or at any rate his face is, out there over the moor. He's sent his face to share a laugh with us."

"Look, Eustace, spare a thought for Diana, will you? After all she's been thr—" Nick's voice trailed off as he turned in his seat. He stayed like that, his body twisted, his hands gripping the leather of the seat so violently that it creaked. "My God," he whispered.

Diana had to look in the mirror then, and her hands jerked on the steering wheel, the car veered toward the ditch. She swung it back into the middle of the road, a moment's distraction from the sight in the mirror, but then she had to look again. They were still there, the two white faces flanking Eustace's. Except for their chattering mouths, they were blanker than the moon.

Eustace was huddled between them, crouched down as far as he could go, his eyes flickering from side to side as if he wanted to leap from the car. Diana was dismayed to realize that he hadn't opened his mouth for a while; his fleshless companions had been doing all the talking. Her eyes met his in the mirror, but she couldn't express all the pity and horror she felt. She could only stop the car, though she had no idea what she and Nick would be able to do to help him.

As she trod on the brake, Eustace seemed to come back to himself. His head lifted, and he blinked at the landscape. "Don't stop," he said rapidly. "I know these bastards, I can deal with them. I don't need them and they know it. I never did."

Diana's foot left the brake, hovered over the gas pedal.

The faceless heads nodded toward Eustace, open-mouthed. "Please," he said to Diana, desperation in his eyes. "Don't let them stop you. If I can't deal with them, nobody can."

"How am I going to drive," Diana said, her voice shaky with a distressing kind of laughter, "with those in the back?"

"Just don't look. Please, you too, Nick. For all our sakes."

Nick stared incredulously at him, then flung himself round in his seat and glared at the road ahead, the speeding patch of lit tarmac that seemed the only safe place to look. He was clenching his fists, and Diana didn't know how long he would be able to bear his inaction. Perhaps she should have let him drive, though she'd believed she was better prepared for whatever might happen on the journey, but it was too late to change places with him. She was sure Eustace was right that they shouldn't stop on the moor.

"Go on, then," Eustace was muttering. "Do your worst, it's all you can do. You aren't funny, you're just a joke."

"He won't be so ready to poke fun at us soon, will he, Mr. Despondency?"

"Won't have much to poke it with, Mr. Gloom. You can't joke when you haven't got a head."

"I can raise more laughs without a head than you've ever been able to raise with two," Eustace cried. "My God, look at you both. When I'm dead I won't look as pitiful as you."

He sounded close to hysteria. "I should know what I'm talking about, I've died often enough," he said, with as much of a laugh as he seemed to think that deserved. "That's what comes of thinking you two were worth inventing," he said through his teeth. Then his seatmates began to sing.

"The priest's in the well and the night's in the sun, and nobody leaves till Harry Moony is done . . ." Hearing them speak had been dreadful enough, their low misshapen voices never quite getting the cadences right, inhuman voices that had been taught to speak like people, but hearing them sing was worse. She resisted looking in the mirror for as long as she could, until they sang gleefully, "Everybody here is Harry Moony's fun," and then she risked a glance. They had their scrawny arms around Eustace's shoulders, and were swaying their blank heads back and forth, their white mouths gaping wider and wider as they sang. They were swaying Eustace in time to the song. His mouth was shaking too badly to let him speak.

"Don't let them, Eustace," Diana murmured, and grabbed Nick's arm to prevent him from turning. She forced her gaze back to the road as it began to climb. "Every body and every head," the voices chanted, and lapsed into patter. "Wait until he mixes them up for fun, her head on his body. That'll be good for a laugh."

"No," Eustace said, so coldly and clearly that Diana's heart raced. "I'll tell you what's good for a laugh—I am. I never knew how much until this very moment. Listen to this, Nick and Diana. This'll shut them up."

There was a flurry of movement in the rear-view mirror. Eustace had a hand on each slug-belly face and was pushing them away from him. The thought of touching them made Diana's hands sweat so much she almost lost her grip on the wheel. "We're listening, Eustace," she said.

Eustace swallowed audibly, then began to talk very fast. "Ladies and gentlemen and whatever you call things with big mouths and no faces, let me introduce myself. Just an ordinary fellow really, except I was born with someone else's feet and a pair of legs that came from stock, or maybe it's just that we disagree sometimes about whether I want to fall over in the street or trip over someone's dog or stand still while I'm talking to people. And oh, yes, I had a couple of heads inside mine that liked to do a bit of talking, especially when I was trying to. Or that was how it felt, anyway. So I gave them names and started letting them out so I could pretend they weren't me, that I couldn't be such a dead loss as they were, which was pretty empty-headed of me, don't you think? And that was only on stage, you understand, that was nothing to the way they carried on when there was only me to hear. Except that was me too, trying to pretend I didn't loathe humanity at large sometimes and loathe myself, the way everyone feels now and then if they'll only admit to it."

"He's trying to make out we're just part of him, Mr. Gloom."

"Wonder which part of him he thinks we look like, Mr. Despondency."

"You're even less than that, the way you are," Eustace said furiously. "No wonder I kept tripping myself over if you were cluttering up my head without an eye between you."

Diana took a breath to stop whatever was rising in her throat, but it was uncontrollable. The next moment she was laughing wildly, painfully. She wasn't sure there was anything funny to laugh at, but perhaps there was a point in the accumulation of horror when you had to laugh if you weren't to go mad. She laughed until she could barely see, had to keep wiping her eyes so as not to run the car off the road. Beside her Nick was whooping too, slapping his thighs, throwing his head back to let out his mirth, and then Eustace joined in, stamping until the car shook.

Their laughter faltered when the things next to Eustace began to laugh. "Let 'em have their fun," one said in a cruel parody of Diana's voice, and the other responded in a distortion of Nick's: "Let's leave them to it. We don't want to be around when they get to where they're going." A moment later both back doors slammed, and two shapes scuttled into the ditch.

"I wouldn't trust anything they said," Nick declared unevenly. Diana smiled at him, more gratefully than humorously, but she was wondering if the voice that wasn't his had meant the missile base or where she was driving now, under the glaring moon. Soon it would be overhead, above the long cold slopes that were growing flatter, showing her that there was nothing as far as the horizon except the domain of the moon. She couldn't even distinguish grass and heather and trees on the slopes now: the vegetation looked more like shapes of rock and stone, a lifeless crystallizing of the landscape, glowing luridly. As the car reached the crest of yet another slope, she had to force herself to look at what might lie ahead.

It was only another gradual slope, disconcertingly like the one she'd just driven up. It might have been a photograph of itself, it was so still, so robbed of perspective by the moonlight. She couldn't shake off an unnerving impression that she'd come in sight of the landscape ahead a moment after it had stopped moving, the road settling into place, the intricate unearthly efflorescence of the slopes freezing into immobility. The entire landscape seemed to threaten movement—movement so vast, or so concerted, that the thought of it almost stopped her breath.

Suddenly Eustace began to talk. Perhaps he was trying to help her through the landscape, though he wasn't doing one of his routines: he was remembering his childhood aloud—how his father had laughed at his clumsiness and told him to

332

laugh at himself, how he would hear his mother recounting his latest pratfall until he'd begun to court disasters deliberately because he thought it would amuse them. "Maybe falling down is my way of honoring their memory," he said, with a wistfulness that sustained her as far as the top of the slope.

He fell silent then, and Diana couldn't speak or even think. They had reached a plateau, a stretch of moor through which the road led flatly to the horizon, between two shallow slopes. Apart from the skeletal growths that covered the slopes, growths that looked not at all like vegetation now, the landscape was featureless and still beneath the moon. Its stillness was so full of dreadful imminence that her foot flinched from the gas pedal.

There was no point in turning back. The thought of doing so unnerved her too—she was beginning to feel that the last few slopes hadn't just been similar, they had been exactly alike. Surely it couldn't be far to the main road, and whatever she encountered on the way was meant to hinder her, which had to imply that she still had a chance. She shoved her foot down, and as the car surged forward, Nick began to talk.

She scarcely heard him. She reached for his hand, for the touch seemed worth more than talk just now, made her feel closer to him. He was chatting about the problems of being a reporter, how you could never tell the whole truth and even if you did some of your readers would think you were lying, but his voice couldn't keep back the threat of the moor. Though the white slopes were veinous with streams, no water moved in the corky trenches. Rocks rested on the edges of the trenches and among the intricate luminous growths, though perhaps not all of them were rocks: some appeared to have teeth, and holes where there had once been eyes and noses; some just had mouths. Sometimes when she came abreast of streams or ditches where they'd been perched above the edges, they were no longer to be seen.

The movements were beginning stealthily, then. Now that she was aware of them, she saw evidence everywhere— shapes that might have been rubble but that weren't there when she looked again. How long would it be before they closed in on the car? Perhaps they were waiting until the moon was directly overhead. She drove faster while the road was straight, and tried to listen to Nick's voice, offering to

333

introduce Eustace to a venue in Manchester where he could expect a sympathetic audience. Once she saw a policeman's head at the top of a slope above the road, but she resisted the temptation to stop: the helmeted head wasn't moving, didn't turn to watch the car. She still had a few minutes' driving before the moon reached its zenith, and mightn't that be enough? Or would the flat unnatural landscape never end? It had to slope down toward the main road, but showed no sign of doing so. The gas pedal was flush with the floor now; the landscape raced by; the moon seemed to brighten like a searchlight, shrinking the shadows. Whatever else was moving on the slopes, she mustn't let it make her falter. But the sight ahead of her did so, the object which, as she sped closer, she saw wasn't a large rock at all, nor was it beside the road. It was on the tarmac, and it was another vehicle.

Both Nick and Eustace sat forward, as if it was the first of the sights out there that they dared to acknowledge. Diana pressed the pedal, more gently now that they weren't alone on the road. Soon she distinguished that it was a van ahead, pointing in the direction they were following. By the time she was able to read Benedict Eddings' name on the rear doors, she had realized that it was half off the road, one wheel in the ditch.

There were two people in the front seats of the van. Their heads were very still. She slowed the car as it came alongside the van, her breath catching in her throat. The driver's window was smashed, hundreds of fragments of glass glittering in the moonlight on the tarmac. The car inched forward, and she saw the two figures in the van. They must be Benedict and Hazel Eddings, but they no longer had faces. In the moment before she managed to drag her gaze away, she saw they had been pecked to death.

She sent the car lurching onward, her hands shaking on the wheel. Neither Nick nor Eustace protested. They'd come a long way since they had at least shown Brian Bevan's corpse some respect, she realized in dismay. But the moon was still rising, brightening, and the road had begun to slope down before it climbed again. Mightn't the main road be beyond the next ridge? All she could do was drive, pray, hope, and notice nothing that might weaken her on the unearthly slopes.

But there was one sight she couldn't avoid noticing: a figure crouched beside the road ahead, just beneath the ridge. He looked as if he were staring at whatever lay beyond, but then she realized, recognizing him, that he couldn't be. He was Nathaniel Needham, and he was blind.

He didn't turn or move as the car approached. When they came abreast of him, Diana halted the car, despite all her fears. She rolled her window down and called his name. Was he too intent on whatever was beyond the ridge to spare a glance in her direction? Perhaps he was listening to sounds she couldn't hear. His face was averted just enough from the road that she wouldn't be able to see it without getting out of the car.

She called to him again, though she was nervous of attracting attention other than his, and then she opened the door. "I have to, Nick," she said when he grabbed her arm. "He's blind. We can't leave him alone out here." She left the engine running and stepped onto the tarmac. She hadn't reached the ditch that bordered the road when Nick and Eustace were beside her.

She stepped over the ditch, which was so dark it looked bottomless, and onto the moor. As her foot touched it, she was afraid that would make the vast movement she dreaded, but all was still. Needham hadn't stirred. She trod gingerly on the undergrowth that looked like a schizophrenic's carving of heather, meaninglessly intricate and luridly intense, that blackened when she trod on it and collapsed with a sluggish quelch, not like rock at all. Shuddering, she made her way to Needham.

She hadn't reached him when she realized that the old man couldn't quite see over the ridge. Indeed, he was crouching down as if he couldn't bear the sight of whatever was beyond. She mustn't keep thinking in terms of sight, she reminded herself, her mind shrinking from her sense of standing vulnerable on the unearthly moor, under the black void and the watchful moon. "Mr. Needham," she said, and touched his shoulder. Thank God, he was still warm. But when she shook him gently, he fell toward her.

She saw his face then, and clapped a hand over her mouth. Perhaps she hadn't been entirely wrong to think in terms of sight after all. Either he'd been given the power to see or he'd

335

thought the power had returned to him, for he'd jammed hi
thumbs deep into his eyes. That shock could have killed him
or it might have been the shock of what lay beyond the ridge

Two steps would take Diana high enough to see what wa
there, but a very long time seemed to pass before she wa
able to move. Nick and Eustace moved with her, but tha
made it no easier. As they gained the top, the men recoiled
almost taking her with them. Both of them cursed. Dian
found the sight beyond words. The vast movement she'
dreaded had taken place, then, and here was the result at th
end of their desperate flight. In itself the sight beneath th
smiling moon wasn't horrible, yet it withered her soul. It wa
Moonwell.

===== 65 =====

Andrew hadn't reached the second floor of the hotel when h
had to sit down on the stairs. He turned his head to look a
the flight that led straight up to the second floor. The corrido
above him was faintly luminous, but where he was sitting wa
dark. He felt safe, unlikely to be noticed. He was afraid to g
up to see Mr. Mann.

He mustn't be. He had to ask for help. He only needed t
confess how he hadn't honored his father, how he'd bee
disloyal just when his father had needed him most, and the
surely Mr. Mann would do the rest. He had to believe in M
Mann. The last time he hadn't shown enough faith, he'
caused what had happened to his father.

Mr. Mann was only like a priest, he tried to tell himsel
You were supposed to be able to say anything to priests, a
your deepest secrets—you had to, or you'd be damned. Bu
Mr. Mann was more like a saint, the way he shone and fe
them all. That must be why Andrew was afraid, worse tha
waiting outside Mr. Scragg's office or having Mrs. Scrag
single you out from the crowd in the schoolyard. You weren'

supposed to be afraid of saints, not unless you were such a sinner that you wanted to hide yourself from God. Surely Andrew wasn't that bad yet, despite what he'd done to his father and how he'd upset his mother. You couldn't hide from God, He already knew all you'd done. All you had to do was ask Him to forgive you—ask Mr. Mann, who God had sent to save them.

He could save Andrew's father if anyone could. Andrew stopped his thoughts at that before they could go round again, and stood up. His hands were prickling so much that when he grabbed the banister, it felt as if the wood were thrusting splinters in. The stairs weren't quite level, and his raw senses made him feel as if he were staggering because of it. He hung on to the banister all the way up the ten stairs to the second floor.

The empty corridor stretched away to a moonlit window at each end. At least there was nobody up here to keep him away from Mr. Mann. The boy stepped onto the carpet that felt thickened by shadow, and dodged past the lift doors to the next flight of stairs. He faltered then, staring up at the dark. Above him, Mr. Mann's floor was creaking.

There couldn't just be Mr. Mann up there, not with all that creaking. The people he'd called to his room before he'd fed everyone must still be with him, praying or holding a silent vigil, and Andrew would never be able to get close. For a moment Andrew felt cravenly relieved—but he mustn't give up now, not when he'd come so far. Surely when Mr. Mann saw him, he would take him aside, somewhere Andrew could be open with him.

Andrew hoisted himself up by the banister and tried not to think about where he was going. Count the stairs, he thought, remembering how his father had shouted at him when he couldn't count to ten; he'd let his father down that way too. Ten stairs up to the bend, like the Ten Commandments. He stepped quickly over the fourth, as if he hadn't the right to tread on it. He hadn't reached the top of the flight when he halted again. Someone was walking along Mr. Mann's corridor.

Andrew clung to the banister and listened until his ears began to pound. It didn't sound quite like someone walking. It reminded him of the sound you made when you walked your fingers up and down a table: too many limbs. Maybe it

337

was someone with a crutch who wanted Mr. Mann to work them a miracle. The sounds retreated along the corridor to Mr. Mann's room, and then there was silence except for the creaking of floorboards. Andrew grabbed the banister with both his slippery hands, and hauled himself up to the bend.

Seven stairs took him round—seven like the deadly sins, and he wondered how many he'd committed—and then he could see Mr. Mann's floor. It was the brightest in the hotel, that must be because it was holy. He could see no shadows up there, no sign of anyone, and he hoped there wouldn't be; he'd remembered that Mr. Mann wouldn't let you be alone with him to confess. He ran on tiptoe to the top of the bright stairs.

The corridor was empty. All the doors were closed except for Mr. Mann's. There was no need for moonlight up here, not with the light that streamed out of Mr. Mann's room. As soon as Andrew's eyes were used to it, he tiptoed toward the dazzling room. If anyone had stayed up here, they must be in the other rooms. Surely Mr. Mann would let them stay in there; surely he wouldn't make Andrew confess in front of them. Andrew said a silent prayer that he would be alone with Mr. Mann, and then he missed a step and caught hold of a doorknob to steady himself. At the end of the corridor a soft voice had said, "You are."

"Mr. Mann?" Surely even he couldn't hear what Andrew was thinking, unless God had told him. There was silence except for the creaking of wood and a movement in Mr. Mann's room. Again Andrew thought of fingers drumming restlessly, but the sound was far too large. "It's Andrew Bevan, Mr. Mann," he said, more loudly than he meant to. "I go to the school. I wanted to see you because—" Then his voice became a lump that filled his throat, for something had squeezed out of Mr. Mann's room.

He hadn't been so wrong about the sounds after all. It was a hand, a bright whitish hand patched with bruises like the moon made flesh, and it was as broad as the corridor. Whatever owned the hand was in Mr. Mann's room, filling the room by the sound of it, the sounds of a swollen body brushing against the walls and making the boards creak. Andrew stood there clinging to the doorknob, trying to scream with his mouth that had stiffened shut. Then the hand ose, scraping both walls of the corridor, and one enormous inger curled like a maggot. It was beckoning to him.

Andrew choked on a scream and twisted the doorknob, dragged at it, shook it frantically. The room was locked, and he couldn't let go of the doorknob. He could only watch, mindless with panic, as the hand squeezed along the corridor toward him like a flood of bruised tripe from which huge grubs were crawling. His bladder let go, urine stung his thigh, and the shame of it brought him back to himself. He flung himself away from the door, staggered backward, swung round wildly, fled as far as he could go. He didn't realize that he'd run past the stairs until he almost collided with the far end of the corridor.

He still couldn't scream, not even when he heard the hand rumble across the doors of the lift shaft, the swollen, nailless fingers groping over the walls of the corridor in which he'd trapped himself. He glanced desperately about, sobbing, and saw a door opposite him, marked Staff Only above a metal bar. He threw himself at the bar, and the door opened, so quickly that he almost fell on his knees.

The door gave onto a flight of bare stone steps leading up to a trapdoor, which must open onto the roof. Andrew arched onto the bottom step and heaved the door shut tight behind him; then he huddled shivering on the cold stone and prayed that the hand couldn't find him. But whitish light crept around the edges of the door, and there came a huge rumbling at the metal bar. Screaming at last, trapped in the dark with his own muffled echoes, Andrew scrambled up toward the roof.

66

Diana hardly knew why she went back to the car. The sight o
Moonwell seemed to render meaningless any course of actio
she might take. The hotel shone over the deserted shadow
streets like an icy beacon on which everything must converge
even the roads. The moon was directly overhead now, an
there was nowhere to hide, nowhere to go except dow
When eventually she went back to the road, it was mostly s
that she wouldn't be standing on the grotesquely overgrow
moor and to put some distance between herself and Nathan
el Needham's doubly blinded corpse.

Nick caught her arm as they reached the car. His hand fe
stiff, exaggeratedly controlled. "Shall I drive?" he said.

"Where to, Nick?"

He opened his mouth, closed it again, turned awkwardly t
Eustace. "Maybe we should all take a vote."

"If you like," Diana said, "but it won't change anythin
Whichever way we drive, we'll end up back here." Perhaps
had to be like this: surely there had been some point to h
vision other than to taunt her with the knowledge; surel
there was something she could do. "I don't want us to end u
stranded on the moor, out of gas," she said, thinking ho
absurd it seemed to appeal to reason now.

"That makes sense," Eustace said.

Nick peered at him as if he couldn't tell whether Eustac
was joking. He glanced about wildly at the transforme
moor, at their footprints blackening the parody of vegetatic
that looked as though it had never seen the sun, at th
brightness of the sky beyond the ridge, brighter even than th
unnatural blazing of the moon. He seemed to resign himsel
or brace himself. "I don't know about you, Eustace, but
don't know what the devil is going on," he said inadequatel

nd when Eustace shrugged and did his best to smile, "Since ou seem to have more idea than we have we've got to leave to you, Diana. We'll stay with you wherever you decide to o, won't we, Eustace? Maybe that way we'll end up under- :anding all this fucking craziness."

There seemed to be nothing more to say. Diana took his ice in her hands and kissed him, a lingering kiss in case it aight be their last, then she touched Eustace's shoulder to :op him averting his face and kissed him too, making him lush. They climbed into the car then, and she drove over the dge.

The sign for the speed limit glared at her from the foot of ie slope, thrusting the swollen head of its shadow at her. he numbers in the metal circle seemed meaningless as ymbols in an unknown language. Terraces the color of lackened tombs rose from their shadows to meet her. The nearthly moors rose over her, the banks of the road closed ı. As she drove into Moonwell, the moon lowered itself ıward the streets like a spider toward its prey.

As soon as she was in the town, at the end of the High :reet, she parked the car. The slam of her door resounded ırough the streets, and she gestured Nick and Eustace to ose theirs carefully. She hadn't realized how silent Moon- ell was. They ought to have walked down from the moor. She wished she hadn't parked quite so close to the church. shape was blundering about inside, beyond the stained ass, the bunched heads. It must have struggled out from :neath the pews. As soon as the men were out of the car, ıe made herself head for the square, the pitiless deathly are of the hotel.

The streets were no more reassuring than the church. Ioonlight had blinded the windows of houses and shops, and any of the terraces looked like stage sets with nothing :yond the facades. The moonlight drained everything of ıbstance, left Diana and the men no refuge from itself. 'here Diana was able to see into rooms, they looked white ith dust, abandoned for years, dead as the silence that filled .e town. It crept ominously behind her and the men, ıocking the footfalls they couldn't quite hush. Could they be one in Moonwell now, alone with the thing from the moon? 'hat could it have done with the townsfolk and Mann's followers? What about the children? That thought drove he forward, Nick and Eustace hurrying to keep up. They ha just come in sight of the hotel and the deserted glaring squar when townsfolk ambushed them from both sides of the roac

They came so fast that at first Diana didn't recognize the satisfied white faces. Her arms were pinned behind her whe Mrs. Scragg stalked in front of them. "So that's why Godwi had us wait," she sneered, "so that we could deal with all th evildoers at one go."

"I shouldn't do anything you might be sorry for," Nic warned her, gritting his teeth as the butcher jerked his arn higher behind him. "I got to a phone, and my newspap knows where we are. Reporters and photographers are o the way here right now."

"Don't waste your breath. We know you for the liar yc are," the butcher snarled in his ear. "This time the poli aren't here to stop me giving you what you deserve. Broug some dogs with you, did you, in case you met anyone wh saw through you and could stand up to you? You'll wish yc had your dogs before we've finished with you."

A cheer that had no joy in it went up from the hote Everyone had been hiding there, waiting for the ambusl They crowded out of the hotel and spread through the squar as Mrs. Scragg marched forward, as Diana and the men we forced to follow. They were nearly at the square when woman cried out and staggered through the crowd towar them.

June Bevan stumbled to a halt at the edge of the squar and crouched forward awkwardly, her fingernails reachir toward them. "Which of you killed my husband?" she said a whisper like a thin shriek.

"Mrs. Bevan," Eustace said, trying to be calm, "I'm sorr to have to tell you this, but he killed himself."

June's eyes widened, and she flew at him. She looke crippled by hatred. "Don't you blacken his name," sl screamed. "He let God into his heart. He never kille himself."

Mrs. Scragg intervened before June's nails could reach h face as his captor thrust him forward. "I don't think Mr. G would have killed your husband, whatever else he may ha got up to. If you ask me, he's protecting one of these tw

Godwin will get it out of them. We'll hear the culprit own up before they're much older."

"And when they do," the butcher muttered to June, "we'll give you a few minutes with them."

Mrs. Scragg strode away from them into the square, as if she hadn't heard or didn't want to. As the crowd parted to let her through, Diana and the men were shoved forward after her, toward the hotel. The crowd wasn't cheering now, but the silence was as cruel as the cheering had been. Wherever Diana glanced she saw faces watching her, their eyes white with moonlight and the light from Mann's room. They looked pitiless as stone, eager to see her suffer. If she stumbled or made any involuntary movement, she didn't like to think what they might do. The worst of it was that she knew them all; some she'd had in her classroom, discussing their children. The way they were now, it would be suicidal for her to remind them.

She glanced away, toward the hotel. The light from Mann's room was so dazzling that at first she thought the curtains were open. What might the thing beyond them look like now? What didn't it want the crowd to see? If only she could make it betray itself somehow—but she didn't know if they were even capable of seeing any longer; certainly none of them seemed to question the deathly light. She was staring at the window, trying nervously to make out what was moving beyond the curtains, when her captor jerked her to a standstill in front of the hotel, and she found herself face to face with Geraldine and Jeremy.

They were held captive too. Though she could see no marks of violence on them, they looked reduced almost to nothing, no light except moonlight in their eyes. But both of them attempted to speak to Diana, until Mrs. Scragg intervened. "No talking," she cried. "Don't let them even look at each other. There's no telling how their kind send messages to each other."

They were dragged apart and forced to stand in a line facing the hotel. "We'll have them kneeling to show a bit of respect," Mrs. Scragg blustered, and as the crowd rumbled in agreement, Diana and the others were hustled onto their knees. Mrs. Scragg strode along the line of them as if she were in the schoolyard, and then she turned her face up to

the hotel and called out shrilly. "We've brought them to you
Godwin, all of them that were against you and keeping evi
alive in Moonwell. Do you want to hear them confess?"

She waited, breathing heavily, hands on hips. There wa
silence from the hotel. Perhaps the curtains at the shinin
window stirred a little, but that was all. Or was there
somewhere above the square, a faint screaming? Nobody bu
Diana seemed to hear it, and when she tried to raise hersel
to listen she was forced down on her knees, with a violenc
that warned her to keep silent. Mrs. Scragg apparently hear
nothing, even though she must be listening for a response
"We'll pray for them," she said grimly to the crowd, "an
sing a hymn, and then we'll hear them confess."

She led the crowd in praying that the sinners would see th
errors of their ways and then, more ominously, that the
would repent while there was still time. As the crowd bega
to sing "Nearer My God to Thee," Diana closed her eyes, t
try to recapture her vision or at least to gain some sense o
what she could do now. Delbert was presumably among th
crowd and must have his suspicions, but what good was he
They were as unlikely to listen to him as they were to hee
her. She tried to breathe slowly and deeply, to make hersel
less aware of the uncontrollable painful jerking of he
cramped legs, but calm seemed to be out of reach. The dea
light glared through her eyelids, the hymn shrilled a warnin
in her ears. No more time, it told her, make whatever peac
you can before it's too late. Then suddenly it trailed off
leaving a few discordant voices exposed before they to
petered out, and Diana realized that everyone in the squar
was gazing up at the hotel.

She had to force herself to open her eyes, especially when
woman began to scream. Diana's vision had been terribl
enough, and so much had happened since then that she didn
know if she could cope with whatever the evangelist migh
look like now. Then she heard what the woman was scream
ing, almost incoherently, and realized that it was June. He
eyes snapped open, and she saw where everyone was gazing
not at Mann's window, but at the roof. Straddling the peak
and clinging to it with both hands, was Andrew Bevan.

The roof was dismayingly steep. In the moonlight the slate
looked like ice. Andrew was perched above the gap betwee
two dormer windows; if he let go, there would be nothing bu

344

the gutter to break his fall. He looked small and precariously clumsy and terrified out of his wits. Whatever you do, Diana willed everyone in the crowd as she tried vainly to struggle to her feet, don't do anything to make him lose his balance— and then June ran forward, screaming his name, dodging backward as she lost sight of him. "God help us, not you too," she screamed.

As she passed beyond his field of vision, Andrew leaned out desperately, searching for her. His foot skidded, and the slate it slipped onto came loose, skittered down the roof, and bounced off the gutter. People screamed as he flailed his arms to try to keep himself upright on the peak, and then he grabbed the ridge again, dragged himself up. "Mummy?" he wailed. "The demon's after me, the demon from the cave."

Diana couldn't contain herself any longer. "Andrew, it's Miss Kramer," she called as loudly and clearly as she could. "Hold on, don't let go. We'll get you down and then you can tell us all about it. Just think about holding on now. Look at your hands. Don't look down."

Above all, she thought, don't think about what drove you up there. She could hardly bear to imagine the confrontation between the boy and the thing in the hotel. She gasped, because her captor had forced her lower as June grimaced at her, her face distorted with hatred beyond words.

June stumbled backward when she saw Diana was subdued, and pointed a wavering finger at Andrew. "Just you stay there now you've got yourself up there," she wailed. "Don't you dare move. Someone's coming with a ladder to get you and bring you down to me, and then we'll see what you have to say for yourself, as if I haven't enough to bear already, God help me." Her voice was dropping as she turned to peer wildly about the square. "Who's getting the ladder? What's taking them so long? Sweet Jesus, what's he doing now?"

She meant Andrew. The gasps and suppressed cries of the crowd had drawn her gaze back to the roof. Andrew was clambering over the steep ridge, staring down at the opening through which he must have scrambled onto the roof. The opening was out of sight on the far side, but the dreadfulness of whatever was emerging was all too clear.

The hands that were gripping Diana's arms slackened, and she heaved herself painfully to her feet. Before she could call out to him or even knew what she could say, Andrew shrank back from whatever he could see on the far side of the roof. He thrust out both hands to keep it off and tried to run along the slates. One step and he missed his footing, fell on the slates so heavily that they splintered, and then he came rolling down the steep roof.

Diana thought the gutter could save him. "Catch hold," she cried, and hobbled forward to be beneath him in case he fell. Then she was aware of several things simultaneously: her legs were too stiff for her to be able to get there in time; the other captives were being held more roughly in case they tried to free themselves as she had; Andrew's grab had missed the gutter, and the small body was falling down the facade of the hotel. "Catch him," she cried, but the dozens of people who were nearer the hotel than she was seemed paralyzed. All they did as Andrew's body struck the pavement with a soft yet final thud was flinch.

June was the first to move, but not far. She let out a sound of anguish beyond words and staggered toward him, then collapsed. The crowd turned on Diana then, as if she'd caused Andrew to lose his hold on the ridge. All the same nobody seemed prepared to initiate the violence she could feel massing like a storm, and as she limped forward she thought they might even let her go to Andrew, be with him as he died, as Miss Ingham cradled his broken head. Then the children moved to block her way, moved as if they'd heard a voice nobody else could hear.

What brought her to a shuddering halt was not their concerted movement but their faces. Perhaps the dead light exaggerated their appearance, but they looked old, shrunken, cruel old faces united by hatred. They looked as if Mrs Scragg's mean spirit had invaded them, as Diana had always feared it would while she was teaching at the school. But it wasn't Mrs. Scragg who had put them in her path, it was the thing that had come to Moonwell. Why did it want to keep her away from Andrew until he died? What could she do that it was afraid of?

She saw the curtains move at the glaring window, and Mann's face peered out. It was too bright for her to be able to distinguish his expression, never mind what the body to which the face was attached might look like now. It was watching to make sure she didn't do what she was capable of—but God in heaven, what was left to her to do?

The children had surrounded Andrew and Miss Ingham. To reach the boy Diana would have to grapple with them, and some of them would be injured before she could get through. Someone grabbed her from behind to make sure she didn't try, twisted her arms again, drove a knee into her back, forced her to kneel. At that precise moment she realized that it didn't matter.

The realization felt like the core of her vision, her sharing the birth of the stars, her whole self flowering. Perhaps that had prepared her for this. The awareness was so deep in her that she couldn't frame it, only follow wherever it led. It might set even Nick and the others against her, she knew that much, but that couldn't matter now. She raised her head to the glaring face in the window and spoke in a calm, clear voice as Andrew's small body shuddered out its last breath. "You can't have him," she said, and then she began to sing.

67

There was a moment during which Diana realized that what she was about to do might be a beginning as well as an end—that she was choosing for the rest of her life without even knowing what the choice was. But she knew instinctively that it could rob the thing from the moon of Andrew, and so it was really no choice at all. More than that, unless she obeyed the instinct which that primal light had awakened in her, she wouldn't just be dooming Andrew to eternal horror, she would be betraying all that she recognized as life.

She began to sing before she knew she meant to, and didn't know what she was singing. The instinct was older than words. She had never had much of a singing voice, even when she'd led singing in the classroom, and she could barely hear herself now. Perhaps that meant the crowd wouldn't notice she was singing, or at least wouldn't find it obtrusive enough to silence. If they suspected why she was doing it, they would tear her to pieces. She was petitioning that Andrew's death would be accepted as a sacrifice.

She raised her eyes and looked past the moon. The sky seemed blacker than ever, except where it was blanched by the moon and by the glare of Moonwell. Surely it didn't matter how small her voice was; no human voice would be strong enough to reach across those distances—that kind of strength wasn't the point. All she wanted was a sign, a hint of a response to assuage the anguished yearning for the sunlight that her song had exposed in her, the yearning she'd repressed for days because there was no other way to cope with what had happened to Moonwell. Her song felt like a dying flame that was streaming up through her. Her whole body felt more and more like a wound, and the song was a cry for healing. She seemed hardly to have begun to sing before she was aware of nothing but the moon, standing unchallenged in the black sky, grinning like a mask that had been taken off and mounted on a blackness that shivered with the intensity of her yearning.

Then Mrs. Scragg's voice rasped in her ears. "What's she yowling about? What kind of witch's song is that? She'd even sing her filth over that poor dead lamb. Shut her up, shut her up!"

Diana looked away from the sky. Stinging whiteness filled her eyes, and then she saw Mrs. Scragg stalking toward her, shaking her fists. The crowd was closing in, glad of a victim for their dismay at Andrew's death, their fears, their sense of helplessness. Even the children with their pinched, aged faces were advancing toward her, without a hint of regret in their eyes, not a trace of a memory of the relationship she'd once had with them. She must be threatening the moon thing, she told herself, or it wouldn't be so anxious to silence her. The ache of her body, of her whole being, sustained her chant, drove it out of her, and she tried to keep her voice low, to buy herself a few more seconds, telling herself again that the volume of sound couldn't matter. Then a piece of wood split her forehead open.

They'd started throwing things at her, then. They were

pelting her like a witch. Blood trickled down the side of her face and soaked her collar. She wondered dully who'd thrown the piece of wood—not one of the children, she hoped, though it had come from that direction. She wondered why Mrs. Scragg looked daunted, when presumably this was what she felt Diana deserved, what she'd encouraged to happen—and then Diana realized that the woman was staring up at the hotel, at where the piece of wood had come from.

It hadn't been thrown deliberately, after all. It was a piece of the sash of Mann's window. Mann's face was pressed against the glass, flattened against it so violently that the glass was bulging outward, as if the owner of the face had no time to raise the sash or had forgotten how to do so. The next moment the window burst asunder, spraying wood and broken glass across the square and into the crowd, and the occupant of Mann's room squeezed out through the gap where the window had been.

The head and hands came first. The head looked more like a growth or a whitish mass of innards than a head, almost shapeless except for the parody of Mann's face that it thrust gargoylelike at the crowd. The hands with their disproportionately long fingers were more than twice the size of the head. They gripped the edges of the jagged hole left by the window, and then two more distorted appendages slithered into view, grasping the sill. They heaved the bloated glowing body forward, the body that hung behind them like a spider's—the gap in the wall was only just large enough for it to squeeze bonelessly through—and it came scuttling on its scrawny unequal limbs straight down the front of the hotel.

The crowd screamed and fled to the edges of the square, cowering against the walls. Parents ran forward to drag away their children, who looked suddenly bewildered, lost, more like themselves. The man who was holding Diana tried to pull her out of the thing's path, but when he realized that she was determined not to move, he let go of her and stumbled away from the hotel.

As the shadowless thing reached the foot of the wall, it seemed to lose its shape momentarily, then to gather itself together more misshapenly than ever, none of its limbs the same length now. It turned and made for Andrew, the swollen bulb of its body lurching from side to side. It poked its head snakelike at the boy's corpse, Mann's stiffly smiling face askew on the leprous head.

It couldn't quite touch Andrew, Diana saw. She had achieved that much. She raised her voice, her song lonely and desperate as the first human voice might have been on the first night of humanity. Then the bloated shape lurched around and scuttled at her.

It could tear her apart, she knew. It could wrench her head off her body. Nick and Eustace were suddenly on either side of her, but all they were doing, she thought with a distant sadness, was inviting the same fate. She looked away from the tiny eyes that glared at her out of the gaping sockets in Mann's face, she looked up at the sky to voice a last plea. Then she gasped and let the song stream out of her on the same breath, her singing more impassioned now. There was the faintest tinge of orange light on the slates of the roof.

The thing hadn't scuttled down just to claim Andrew if it could. It had been fleeing the threat of sunlight, which seemed to tinge all the unbroken windows of the top floor, or was she only seeing what she yearned to see? In any case, the sight roused her body from its resigned stupor. All at once she was dancing, oblivious to the thing that was thrusting its parody of a face toward hers. She was dancing without moving her feet, her body swaying like a flame that seemed actually to grow toward the sky, to soar with yearning. She was cupping her hands in a gesture like prayer, and for an instant she thought she felt life flutter mothlike between them. Then she opened them toward the sky, offering whatever she held, and sang passionately, no longer conscious of herself or where she was. There was nothing but the black sky. She was no longer even aware of the moon.

And then the black sky burst into flames.

It was the sun, but it was like no dawn she'd ever seen. The orange light seemed to tear the blackness apart, to flood the sky like flames on oil, turning whiter as it claimed the sky putting out the moon. So much she saw in the few instants before her eyes began to burn. "Don't look, protect your eyes," she cried as loudly as she could, and put both hands over her own. Even then the sunlight glowed through her flesh, and her skin tightened with the sudden heat. She made herself peer through her fingers and her slitted eyelids as soon as her eyes could take it, to see what the thing in the square was doing.

Daylight filled the square, and even the shadows it cast were welcome. The sun hung above the moors, a disk like blinding glass. The bloated thing was crouching low, the head with Mann's face searching the square for a refuge, the maggoty neck stretching. Diana realized where it could hide from the direct sunlight a moment before it did, and she dodged around it, ran to the steps of the hotel. "No way," she said, as it dragged itself around to face her.

The sunlight must be weakening it, and perhaps she had a touch of the power of the sun. All the same, she knew that if it tried to get past her, there wouldn't be much left of her by the time it succeeded. She could only hope the crowd would turn on it, not on her. But those of the crowd who had their eyes open seemed unable to look away from the sun. Most of the people were praying raggedly; someone was trying to start up a hymn. Only Nick ran to her, dabbing at his eyes.

The thing with Mann's face floundered at her, and she backed up the steps until she stood against the doors of the hotel, gripping the handles. The thing gathered itself, losing shape again and rearing up, a giant with spindly limbs, a loathesomely small head on a long unstable neck, Mann's face smiling still. Then it crumpled to all fours and swung round, its body smearing the hot tarmac, and scuttled unevenly out of the square.

She had to see where it was going. When she followed, Nick ran with her. As they went toward the Booths, Geraldine seemed to come back to herself: she glanced about, blinking, and tugged at Jeremy's arm. "The children," she said. "They'll hurt their eyes."

The children were hiding their faces against their parents, who were still backed against the walls of the square. Nevertheless Jeremy seemed to agree with her. "Don't look at the sun, whatever you do," he shouted. "Let's get the children into the hotel to give their eyes time to adjust."

Diana hesitated, anxious for him. Could he really expect the crowd to do his bidding so soon after he'd been one of their scapegoats? But they seemed scarcely to know who he was, and they were clearly desperate to be given some direction after all that had happened. Those who could see made gratefully for the hotel, while Geraldine and Jeremy set about helping those who were stumbling blindly. Mrs. Scragg was leaning on her husband and wailing, "Sweet Jesus, give me back my sight, there are people here who need me." As two men supported June toward the hotel while Eustace lifted Andrew's body gently, Diana and Nick ran out of the square.

The streets, the buildings, the sky looked recreated by the sun, each of them a separate miracle. The misshappen thing was no longer in sight, but Diana knew where to go. As she and Nick dodged into the nearest lane that led to the moorland path, they saw the thing crawling straight up the steep side of the moor. Its legs were withering in the sunlight, its body was shriveling as if its immense age were catching up with it. It was still able to scrabble over the rock, and by the time Nick and Diana reached the top of the path in the dazzling sunlight, it was halfway to the cave.

Nick stopped to catch his breath, and grabbed Diana's arm. "Can we kill it?" he panted.

"The sunlight will if anything can, Nick." All the same he'd made her wish she'd brought a weapon. As she ran across the charred moor, following the trail the shriveling body was leaving, she glanced about: a heavy branch might do—but the nearest tree was far too distant. The fleshless legs dragged the wobbling body over the rim of the stone bowl that surrounded the cave, and she ran faster.

She almost fell over the rock beside the path, a rock nearly the size of her torso. Nick realized as she did that it might be what they needed. They struggled to raise it, heaved it up, their arms aching with the effort, their hands already bruised and numb. Then they had it between them, and stumbled quickly up the slope to the stone bowl, the weight of the rock as much as the urgency of their task carrying them forward. Diana was praying that the moon thing hadn't yet crawled back to its lair, that it would still be within reach. She didn't realize that it had turned to wait for them until Mann's face with its shrunken eyes rose over the edge on its maggoty neck and the huge unequal hands reached for them both.

The weight of the rock carried them helplessly forward between the hands, and then she felt the rock slipping out of her and Nick's grasp. They'd failed, she thought miserably

352

After all that effort, they were going to be the last sacrifices to the moon thing, the souls it would carry back to its lair. Then the rock fell on the upturned face, which was still smiling hideously, and smashed the head.

Nick flung her aside and stumbled out of the way himself as the huge deformed hands began to flail in agony. The hands snatched at where Nick and Diana had been, reached blindly for them, then heaved and plucked at the rock. The thing was enfeebled now, but still it raised its body convulsively, trying to fling itself backward. Diana had the horrid notion that it might tear off its head under the rock, that the headless body would scuttle after them over the moor. Then it gave a last heave with all its limbs and wrenched its flattened leaking head out from beneath the rock.

There wasn't much left of its face, and nothing remotely human. The way it looked, it shouldn't be moving at all. But it tottered away down the stone bowl, waving what was left of its blinded head at them. Nick lunged at the rock for a second try, and Diana followed him, though she could see little point to it. As they grabbed the rock, the thing backed over the edge of the cave, its withered whitish body swarming with bruises. It held onto the edge with one splayed, shriveling hand; then it let go.

They shouldn't have let it reach the cave. They should have trapped it in the sunlight, but it was no use saying so now. Diana scrambled to the edge. She could see no movement down there, and there was no sound—but as she crouched at the edge and peered into the dark, something rose from the cave.

It felt like a flood of joy, of release. She couldn't perceive it more specifically than that, except that for an instant she thought of Craig and Vera, Brian Bevan, Father O'Connell . . . They were smiling peacefully, and so was the flood of other faces she glimpsed in that moment. "They're free," she murmured to herself.

At least the sunlight had achieved that much. All the same, she was distantly aware of movement, of something old and shriveled crawling as deep into the dark as it could go. She turned her mind away from that, toward the resurrected landscape, the slopes of heather and grass that looked greener than spring, the gentle dance of trees, the jagged gritstone edges gleaming beneath the eggshell sky. She took Nick's hand, and then she glanced at him to see why he felt so uncertain suddenly. He was staring about him as if he had no idea where he was. All at once she felt lonely and wistful. "Oh, Nick," she said, "I know what has to happen now."

The Following Year

ck almost missed the side road. He braked belatedly as he
ad the signpost backward in the driving mirror, and had to
it while cars raced by on both sides of the main road. He
rned the car, narrowing his eyes as the sun shone directly
o them, and swung it into the side road. The town didn't
ok far on the map, and he could do with a drink.

Limestone slopes rose on both sides of the road, casting a
lcome chill. The ferns that clothed the slopes gave way to
es that warded off the heat of the early July day. Beyond
e forest he drove up a rise from which he could see the
wn. He stopped the car to enjoy the view.

The limestone terraces of the town formed an amphithea-
for the greenest of the fields in the riverless valley, a
ying field. Above the terraces a single main road gleaming
h parked cars led to a chapel at the nearer end of the town,
hurch at the other. All this seemed overshadowed by the
nt form multicolored as the forest, the figure that stood
ne above the town, on the deserted moor.

It must have been there since midsummer. A daylight
on hung above it like a wafer of cloud left behind by the
ssy mass on the horizon. The moon's markings were as
e as the sky. Nick gazed at the floral giant for so long that
began to wonder why he was gazing; if he didn't move
on, he would be too late for a drink. He drove down
ough the fields and up to the town, and was slowing to the
al speed limit when he saw another sign beside the road.
ASE DRIVE SLOWLY—BLIND PERSON'S CROSSING, it said.

He'd forgotten that, he realized, surprised that he had. His
per had reported the events, more sensationally and
perficially than he would have liked. An American evange-
had whipped up religious hysteria in the town to such a
ch that dozens of people had gone blind from staring at the
n. The evangelist must have been overcome by the hysteria

too, for he'd wandered onto the moors and had nev
reappeared—perhaps had fallen down an open shaft. A
hadn't there been something about dogs? Yes, the town h
run out of food, and starving dogs had run wild in the stree
killing several people, including a priest whose mutilat
body had been discovered later in his church. Not the id
town for a comfortable pint and a bite of lunch, Ni
thought, but there was nowhere else within reach. He hop
the outbreak of religion hadn't closed the local pub.

Once he was past the abandoned chapel with its board
windows and fallen overgrown sign, the town seemed che
ful enough. If any of the people on the streets were blind,
couldn't tell as he drove by. He stopped at a pedestri
crossing to let a uniformed postman cross. The man glanc
incuriously at him and almost tripped over the curb. Fo
moment Nick thought he looked vaguely familiar. He dro
on, past a shop that sold climbing equipment, where
woman dressed in black despite the heat was watching t
street from the doorway, and parked outside the One-Arm
Soldier.

Several blind people sat under the low beams of the pub
bar, reaching carefully for their tankards, waving their ha
in large gestures that weren't quite precise, throwing ba
their heads to laugh with an unselfconsciousness Nick fou
somehow unexpected. He bought a pint of beer and the l
cheese roll, and was halfway through his pint before
realized there was someone in the pub besides himself a
the barman who wasn't blind.

She was sitting in a corner near the bar, a young wom
with a pale tapering face, wide greenish eyes, long black ha
As their eyes met, she smiled with an odd wistfulness.
realized she'd been watching him ever since he'd entered t
pub.

He might have gone over to her, but he felt uncomforta
with the blind people: they would be able to hear everythi
he said, however quietly. He drained his tankard and carri
it back to the bar, and was turning away when the you
woman said, "What brings you here today?"

"Just passing through." He wondered if she'd meant
emphasize "today" or if that was just her American acce

"And what brings you to the Peak?"

She spoke like a native, just "the Peak" instead of t

eaks or the Peak District. "The road to Manchester," he
id, and felt unreasonably secretive, though he didn't know
hy he should. "I'm a newspaperman. Subeditor, actually. I
as in Sheffield today for an interview."

"You aren't a reporter," she said in a tone he couldn't
ake out at all.

"Not any longer, no. How about you? You were one of the
eople who brought evangelism here, were you?"

"No, they went back where they came from," she said,
miling so sadly at his question that he experienced a twinge
guilt. "I was here before that, teaching school."

"Oh, you're a teacher."

"Assistant to the headmaster since his wife lost her sight."
e paused and added, "And I'm a watcher."

"I see what you mean," Nick said, nodding at the blind
inkers, and had an odd impression that he'd missed the
int entirely. "They must need people like you. It must have
en a dreadful shock, what happened to them."

"Almost nobody remembers what happened or what led
to it," she said with a wistfulness he found inexplicable.
They still know their way around their own town, and our
stman helps them a lot when they need guiding."

Did she want him to interview her? Was that what she was
plying, that he couldn't grasp? But his paper had covered
e story already, even supposing he'd wanted to do so. He
lt more uncomfortable than ever. He didn't have to linger,
thought angrily, and pushed himself away from the bar.
Well, goodbye," he said, and even more lamely, "Keep up
e good work."

All the way to the street door he felt she was watching him.
e didn't understand the way she had affected him, but now
felt wistful himself. He took hold of the cool latch and
ought of going back to ask if they'd met before, but the
proach seemed so laughable that he went quickly out of the
b. He'd driven out of the far side of town before he
ndered if he could really have heard her say, "Goodbye,
ck."

He stopped the car on the moor and gazed toward the
wn. Surely he'd imagined it, a fantasy of knowing her
cause he hadn't managed to. It disconcerted him to realize
w much he wished he had. He'd be passing the town again
on, but he didn't know if he would turn off the main road

when it came to the moment to choose. The one-armed gia
composed of flowers and twigs and seeds stood over the ca
that gaped amid the overgrown slopes above the town, a
for an instant he couldn't tell which of these things might
drawing him back. Time enough to tell when he returned,
he ever did. He started the car and drove across the emp
moor.